AMELIA'S GOLD

A novel of romance, ruin, resolve, and redemption
in the American Civil War

D1607543

JAMES D. SNYDER

Trade paperback ISBN No. 979-8-63174-491-2

LCCN No. 2020906014

Cataloging-in-Publication Data
  Fiction, U.S. History – Civil War
    Naval Warfare, Blockade Running
    Savannah, GA, Nassau, Bahamas
    Beaufort, NC, Portsmouth Island, NC
  Naval warfare. U.S. Marine Hospital Service

Cover and book design by Rebecca Barbier, Barbier Design, LLC.

This is a work of fiction. Names and dates of historic events are factual, but the characters in this book are fictional.

 Pharos Books
Tequesta, Florida

Author's Note

Amelia's Gold is about a young woman, but it didn't begin that way. The idea came when I was researching another book on the history of southeast Florida (see *A Light in the Wilderness* p. 368). At the time I became fascinated by how Jupiter Inlet Lighthouse, supposedly disabled and darkened during the Civil War, became a clandestine depot for Confederate sailboats loading cotton and turpentine before heading for Nassau, Bahamas to trade their raw materials for scarce weapons and uniforms. Waiting outside the inlet were bulky Union gunboats, which managed to capture over fifty Rebel boats by war's end.

Curiosity led me up the eastern seaboard, where blockade running had raged on a far larger scale in river ports like Savannah GA, Charleston SC and Wilmington NC. When the first two were sealed off by the Union navy, Wilmington became the only link between British suppliers and a railroad that led to the besieged rebel forces in Richmond, VA. When Wilmington finally fell, the supply chain withered, and the Confederacy soon capitulated.

For most of us, the Civil War musters up the names of bloody land battles like Gettysburg and Shiloh. But it was the less dramatic blockade of imports that slowly strangled the agrarian South and proved the decisive measure. And it sparked the urge to tell that story in a novel.

But novels need main characters. Who might I find to take the reader on a daring midnight blockade run? Who could help you walk midst the clamor of Nassau's waterfront or mingle at the Royal Victoria Hotel with its intriguing collage of diplomats, journalists, hucksters and "ladies of fortune?" Who could help you understand the suffering in a filthy, makeshift Civil War hospital?

Before long a young woman from Savannah began showing up in my mind. A frivolous bit player at first. But soon she had seized center stage, making the story of blockade running a mere backdrop to her own transformation.

A character in search of *character,* one might say. And so, her story became the essence of *Amelia's Gold.*

As you read, please keep in mind the relative value of money between today and the Civil War era. For example, the price of gold per ounce now borders on $1,600. In 1842 it was $20.67 and remained fixed until the onset of the Civil War spiked the price to $28. By 1864 the crumbling southern economy and debt-ridden Union had sent gold soaring to $47 per ounce. Gold worth $150,000 in 1830 would have been worth around $250,000 in 1864 and nearly $10 million by today's prices.

A word, too, about malaria and yellow fever. In 1864 both were abstractly thought to be caused by "foul air" and/or stagnant pools of water. It wasn't until the construction of the Panama Canal at the turn of the twentieth century that two types of mosquitoes were found to be the direct cause of both diseases.

This is also a good place to acknowledge others who again proved that one author doesn't a book make.

Every author needs someone who, when he erupts in white-hot anger as his computer swallows a whole chapter, is there to murmur *"There, there,"* lest his cries be like a tree crashing in an indifferent forest. My life mate, Ilse Wolff, is that pillar of patience, a solo focus group and reader of every word. So were Christine Moats and Marlyce Pedersen. Then it was Becky Barbier's turn to apply her considerable formatting and design talents.

Finally, my thanks to the many archivists, park officials, and members of historic families who were so helpful in Savannah, GA, Ocracoke, NC, Beaufort, NC and Nassau, Bahamas. I hope I've been able to tell some of your story as well.

Table of Contents

1	Savannah, December 1863	6
2	Shackleford Banks, June 1829	21
3	Beaufort and Beyond, August 1829	38
4	Savannah, January 1864	62
5	Leaving Savannah, February 8, 1864	75
6	Nassau, February 9, 1864	92
7	Nassau Life	117
8	Nassau, March-April 1864	137
9	Nassau, July 1864	149
10	August 24, 1864	169
11	Aweigh to Wilmington, August 29, 1864	190
12	Terra Firma?	216
13	Chaos	240
14	Letters from the Front	259
15	Devastation, September 28, 1864	274
16	Revival, October 1864	290
17	Resilience, November 1864	318
18	Redemption, December 1864	332
	Afterword	364

Maps/Illustrations

Map: *Savannah, Georgia Area, 1864*	6
Map: *Shackleford Banks, North Carolina*	21
Lithograph: *English-built blockade runner*	75
Maps: *New Providence Island and Nassau*	110
Lithograph: *The Royal Victoria Hotel*	116
Lithograph: *The Vendue House on Bay Street, Nassau*	137
Map: *Wilmington, NC and Fortifications*	206
Maps: *Outer Banks and Portsmouth Island, NC*	217

Chapter One
Savannah, December 1863

Early on a Sunday afternoon, Amelia Sarah Beach, twenty-four, sat stiffly in her family's upstairs drawing room massaging her fingers while gazing down warily at the square pianoforte, said to have once belonged to Johann Christian Bach. Ordinarily the drawing room was the busiest in the great house. It lay between Amelia's and sister Lucy's bedrooms and was once their indoor playhouse. Now it had become a female social center, as one could tell by the surroundings: two dressmaker's busts, a Wheeler & Wilson sewing machine, a letter-writing table, a fireplace to read and warm by, an ornate dollhouse the sisters couldn't bring themselves to evict, and a golden harp that both had given up because its strings bruised their delicate fingers.

Amelia stared out of the large lace-curtained window at Madison Square across the street. Soon a parade of fresh army recruits would halt in the public garden for a last round of marshal music and speeches about honor and glory. Then several of Savannah's finest families would cross the street, pass through the iron gate and into the Beach's reception hall to sip

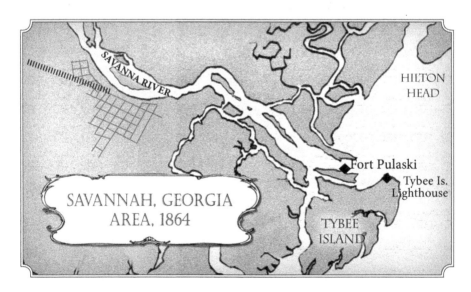

tea and punch at the first "social" of the Christmas season and breathe in the reassurance that wartime Savannah was still unscathed in at least one gracious home.

Later, a few of the families with the most promising, eligible male progeny would proceed inside to dinner, followed by parlor games and the Chopin polonaise Amelia had been ordered by her mother to "practice until perfect."

Downstairs was a noisy clatter of plates being placed on tables as Mrs. Beach clucked over her household maids. But today all was quiet in the upstairs drawing room save for the gold filigree mantle clock that ticked like a metronome and pinged punctiliously every half hour. Amelia stared out again at Madison Square, took a deep breath, and soon launched into the brisk, raucous *I'm a Good Ol' Rebel*. She had begun thumping the even louder *Dixie's Land* when the door flung open. "Is that what you're going to play tonight?" shouted seventeen-year-old Lucy, leaving the door wide open as if to hasten the noise to their mother's ears a floor below. "You're not going to catch any soldier boy tonight if you play in the cracks," she chided.

"Good. If that's what it takes to drive them off, that's what I'll do," Amelia shouted back without stopping.

"Well, at least think of *me*," said Lucy. "Both Jeremy Sloan and Marvin Branch are coming. When I made socks for them, I made red ones for Jeremy and blue ones for Marvin. Now I hear they're arguing over which color means which one I fancy more. But then I sewed on brass buttons for both of them. I saw you sewing brass buttons on a uniform. Who for?"

Amelia stopped playing and faced her sister with a glower. "Freddy Farnsworth."

Lucy shook with the giggles. With her perfect golden ringlets, she was as pretty as a wedding cake statuette, but to her older sister she was still a witless, selfish child.

"Yes, fat Freddy Farnsworth," said Amelia with mock sweetness. "Because Mother asked me to. In fact, she wouldn't stop asking until I did it."

"Well," said Lucy, tilting her head and assuming an ingratiating pose. "I mean you really can't be all that choosy, can you? Just about all the eligible men have gone off to war. It might be a year or two before they return and you might be, what, twenty-five or twenty-six? Well, I suppose you'll always be invited to play the piano at parties."

Rather than murder Lucy, Amelia changed the subject. "Do you really think there are any good ones in this batch? All the red-blooded men enlisted two years ago along with your brother Joseph. These are what's left – conscripts. Including Freddy the Flatulent."

Amelia enjoyed making Lucy draw a hand to her mouth – better when it held a fluttering fan. "Yes, Flatulent Freddy Fartsworth, I call him. He gets real nervous in my presence and when he does he breaks wind like lightning on a tin roof. I can only imagine the noise if he faced a picket line of Yankee rifles. Probably blow up his own regiment!"

"All right. What's *this*? All bickering and no music!" Sarah Chesney Beach stood in the doorway, plump, out of breath and florid-faced from climbing the steep stairway. "Now Lucy you get down there and help with the place settings. Amelia, all I've asked is that you pretty up and play us some nice music. Is that too much?"

"No, Mother. As long as I'm not playing it for Freddy Farnsworth."

"I don't see why you can't encourage him a bit. After all, he's going off to war to defend our homeland."

"Mother, the last time he thought I encouraged him, I think he tried to seduce me."

Amelia meant only to enjoy her mother's shock, but Sarah Beach turned the tables. "Oh really?" she exclaimed. "Well, perhaps you could allow him to succeed the next time. The Farnsworths own most of the railroad, you know."

With that she was off again, shutting the door with more fortissimo than befitted a society matron of Savannah.

Amelia expressed her feelings with a wild, boisterous polonaise that would have made Chopin's ears hurt. Soon she knew that she was putting off the inevitable ordeal and went to face it in the dressing room she shared with her sister. Inside, the petite Lucy stood before a long mirror while Mandy tugged on a corset covering the chemise undergarment that extended from her knees to her elbows. Rotund Mandy had been their common "upstairs girl" since childhood and part of their mother's as well.

"Child, you don't need a corset," scoffed Amelia.

"That's what I tol' her," said Mandy. "Why, you skinny as a lamp post already."

"You don't like corsets because you're afraid your eyes'll pop out," Lucy volleyed at her sister.

Amelia: "Did you ever hear of heat? I'd sweat to death with all those people and candles around the piano."

"Mama says women don't sweat," Lucy shot back. "Men sweat. Women glow. Leastways, I don't do either. Besides, you need a corset. I'll wager I could pinch enough fold in your waist to hide a clothespin."

Amelia jabbed back. "I'm going to wear a full dress with nothing on underneath. Then when I need to let hot air out I'll just pull my dress up over my head. All these layers are just Yankee fashion for women up where they probably have snow on the ground."

Lucy tossed her head so that her corkscrew curls swished back and forth. "You wear a full gown and you'll be just like Mama," she lectured. "Well, a few of us are proud that we don't have to hide our fat." The word fat came out like sizzle on a hot griddle.

"Yes, *Blessed*," Amelia replied in a syrupy voice. Her *coup de grace* was a code word sure to be understood only by Lucy. A few years back she had asked her parents why Lucy had arrived in the world nearly seven years after her older sister and ten after brother Joseph. "Why, child," her mother had said, "one day the stork just delivered us a blessed surprise." Later, when Lucy had become old enough to be annoying, Amelia could provoke tears by calling her "Storky." When the mother put her foot down on that name, Amelia switched to "Blessed," which could produce equal damage with effortless innocence.

This time Lucy simply made silent grotesque faces at her sister as Mandy finished her layering: starched petticoats stuffed with tucks and cording, a gown with broad shoulders and low-cut neckline exposing part of whatever the corset cups could push up. The gown came with the latest fashion: the gigot sleeve, which billowed wide and gathered again at the wrist. With all these components patted down in place, Mandy buckled a broad leather band around Lucy's midriff to accent her tiny waist. The piece d'resistance was a jeweled ferronnièr that Mandy fastened around her long neck.

Amelia saw another opening. "With those sleeves, you're going to knock over a whole tray of glasses," she observed.

"You're not lady enough to wear them."

"You don't have to play piano tonight. I couldn't find the keys with all that material hanging down."

Lucy, having been topped out, took a last admiring look in the petticoat sideboard – a mirror placed near the ground to make sure that a lady's ankles were properly covered – then tripped off in search of her mother's approval. Amelia, weary of the childish banter, scolded herself for not behaving more like a big sister. Then she pinched her midriff when Mandy wasn't looking and concluded that Lucy would have lost the clothespin wager. She also concluded that she didn't need a corset with cups because she had plenty on top to push in any direction she wished.

"Mandy," she said, "bring me my old green velvet gown." It had puffy shoulders but plunged straight downward with no petticoats to billow it. *Well, I'm out of style, I suppose, but then I'm not a lackey to those fashion people in New York.*

With that she threw on a cape and was off to hear war speeches in the chilly square. But as the words droned on and a military band drummed, Amelia's eyes kept returning to a tall pine in the square that was full of oval "cards" hanging from strings like Christmas ornaments. Each described the name and regiment of a Savannah youth who had gone off to war. Joseph's was there as well, and as Amelia tightened its string to keep it from fluttering away, she prayed that he might suddenly appear for a surprise Christmas visit.

Across the street, the home of William Beach beckoned, with its intricate wrought-iron porch railing festooned with a large red ribbon atop a wide pine bough. In the outer reception hall, this oasis of opulence revealed itself with the first cup of tea. Whereas most of Savannah was already thinning its tea or experimenting with substitutes, servants at the Beach home used knives to shave off pieces of pure tea from decoratively carved bricks.

From every direction, elaborate architectural touches shouted opulence: the carved wood pineapples, signifying hospitality; the drapes, puddling on the floor as if to boast that the cost of fabric was immaterial; the coal fireplace, aglow with its immunity to wartime shortages. Indeed, the mantle and hearth were made of the green gemstone malachite at a time when other households painted fireplaces a faux dark green to resemble it. And one had only to look up to see exquisitely-carved friezes wherever walls met the ceiling.

The afternoon and evening had passed without any disruptive prince charmings. The conversation was pleasant, the roast duck palatable, the polonaise passable and no bothersome approaches by soldier-suitors. She had even wished Freddy well, kissed him on the cheek and heard a squeak down below.

No, it was what happened after night had fallen and the guests had left that would make Amelia Beach's head spin and change her life forever.

Lucy had gone off with a young man for "a stroll around the block." William Beach, his wife Sarah and Amelia sat on the back veranda, all numb to further conversation and simply watching fireflies play in the moonlight when Mother Beach excused herself to visit the ladies' room.

As soon as she departed, Daddy Beach turned to his daughter and quietly asked her to leave as well and meet him in his study "in a few minutes." The only other time Amelia had been summoned to the study so solemnly was when a grammar schoolteacher had reported her for writing the words to a spelling test on her petticoat. Now she felt the same dread, and it could only mean one thing: Freddy Farnsworth was about to be foisted on her, or some other marriage already orchestrated to solidify the fortunes of two families.

Daddy Beach's "study" was as misnamed as the ladies' "drawing room" directly above it. The reason why Amelia usually practiced on the small pianoforte was that the formal living room with its grand piano was next to the study. She knew by then that if she practiced etudes or scales, the heavy walnut door would soon open and William Beach would say softly: "Can you not continue that upstairs?"

Inside the study it was dark enough to be mysterious. And the smell of old tobacco smoke, ingrained in every wall and fiber, made it seem strange and alien. At the far wall was a large mahogany desk said to have belonged to one of Georgia's first senators. Behind it a large window looking onto the garden, street and Madison Square beyond. Along the entire side of one wall were shelves stacked with forbidding leather books, although Amelia never saw her father reading one. The opposite wall was given way to a great slate fireplace. Over the mantle was a large painting of George Washington. Even though the walls of the spacious adjoining parlor were replete with paintings of her mother's Huxley family ancestors, there were none of any Beach family, nor any in Daddy's study.

Rather than a study, this small but formidable fortress was where William Beach ran Huxley and Beach Company, said to be Savannah's largest cotton brokerage, and now, by way of wartime necessity, traders in rice, turpentine, rifles, ammunition, uniforms, and whatever else would help the South win the War of Northern Aggression.

It was nearly ten when Amelia cracked open the study door and said "Daddy?" Beach, still in his formal evening frock, sat in one of two leather chairs that faced each other in front of the cold fireplace. "Come right in, Amelia," he said motioning for her to take the other seat. Since birth he'd always called her "Amie" except when admonished, and it added to her anxiety. So did his next words: "Would you like a sherry?" It was the first time he'd ever offered her one. As he poured two demitasse glasses, she couldn't help but notice that he appeared weary yet every bit as anxious as his daughter.

"I have a great deal to say to you," he said, "so much that I really don't know where to begin. So, I'll just dive into the water and start swimming. I would like for you to undertake an important mission – for our family, for our business, and for the Confederate States of America."

She felt her heart flutter. The tension broke and the tears that she vowed to avoid now cascaded down her cheeks.

Both endured a few seconds of embarrassed silence while Amelia dabbed her eyes with a handkerchief and straightened up in her chair. "You mean this isn't about having to marry Freddy Farnsworth? Or someone else?"

"Freddy?" He rolled his eyes and let out a lusty laugh. His daughter's laughter echoed with her relief. Then they both laughed together because Freddy had broken their unease. "Oh, my no," he said at last. "In fact, this might even give you reason not to marry Freddy."

"Oh, thank you," she said, taking his large rough hands in hers.

"But what I'm asking you may be more difficult than going through a wedding," he said, still holding her hand. "Let me start again by saying that the course of the war is such that I feel the need to transport certain personal and company assets to another country for safe keeping until we have peace again."

"But I don't understand why," she said, taken aback. "We won at Bull Run and practically captured Lincoln in his White House. We fought them on their own ground at Gettysburg and this fall we ran the Yankees out of Chickamauga. Why, just yesterday I read in the papers that the battleship *Alabama* sunk its 26th Union ship. Now are you saying that even Savannah isn't safe?"

William Beach had already raised his hand like a schoolboy impatient to recite. "Amelia, I read the newspapers, too," he said softly. "But I also run a large business. It's part of my job to learn about developments and interpret them before my competitors do. Much of it is figuring out the odds of success and then acting on it."

"But we did win at Chickamauga, didn't we?" Amelia asked, surprised at her audacity in doubting her father. "Didn't the Yankees lose something like sixteen thousand men at Chickamauga?"

"Yes," said her father patiently. "And we lost around eighteen thousand. Each side started with around sixty. But then they can find three replacements for every one we can muster. So, the percentage of men lost was much greater for the South. That's why we just had another conscription in Georgia. And the men filling up the ranks are mostly older and not as fit as the ones they'll replace."

Amelia leaned back, sipped her sherry and felt its warmth.

"I'm going to offer you a bigger picture to look at," said her father, filling the brief gap of silence. "Have you ever heard of Anaconda?"

"Anacon … no."

"When the war began, Lincoln and his generals decided their strategy would be to squeeze the South on three sides so they could fight the Confederate armies directly on their southern front. Just like a big anaconda snake that squeezes its prey to death. They would seal off the line between north and south then everything west of the Mississippi River. Finally they would choke off all Confederate shipping from our seaports – New Orleans all the way around Florida and on up to Charleston and Wilmington. Now you may read about these victories in the heartland, but the rest of this Anaconda plan is starting to work."

Amelia squirmed in her chair by the fireplace, her resolve beginning to fray. "But what about that battleship? It seems to be sinking Yankee ships all over."

"Maybe for now," answered Daddy, "but that ship needs coal and ammunition to keep going. And remember that sinking ten or twenty Yankee ships isn't as important in the long run as keeping thousands of infantry soldiers supplied with bullets and food.

"Now let me draw a little closer to why I asked you here tonight," he continued.

"Here in the South, as you know, we don't have many industrial factories.

In order to get arms and a thousand other manufactured goods, we import them by ship, mostly from England. To pay for them we load ships with cotton, turpentine and the like and send them across to England. Now, Amelia, so far you are largely correct when you say that we have had a rather easy time of it doing this, and it's because the North didn't have much in the way of navy ships to block or chase down boats like your *Alabama*. At first, they were seizing fishing boats and old tubs and calling them navy ships. But lately they've begun launching big powerful gunboats made specially to enforce the blockade. We're now seeing the first of them patrolling outside the rivers of both Charleston and Savannah. Things are changing, and my job – this family's very survival – depends on my ability to calculate the odds of their success."

Amelia felt like a sheltered Savannah girl again. "Are we going to lose, Daddy?" she asked, looking into his brown eyes.

"Well, maybe not, Amie," he said with a smile. It was the first time he'd reverted to her childhood name. "You see, for every problem there's an opportunity. When more of our outbound ships get captured and the cargoes confiscated, the higher the value of those that make it through to England and Europe. Just a month ago, cotton exports were going for around four hundred a bale. Now they're already fetching around seven hundred because those factories in England have orders to fill. With prices like that it becomes worthwhile to invest in special ships that are just as good at doing their job as the gunboats are at theirs."

He took his first sip of sherry and absent-mindedly added a dollop to his daughter's glass. "Over in Liverpool, England, I'm helping to finance the building of a special ship. It's no battleship like the *Alabama*. No, it's long and sleek and very lightly armed. It has a very short keel so that it can go in shallow waters where the big gunboats can't. Its motors are quiet and even the smokestacks can be lowered so the boat can sneak past the gunboats at night or in early morning fog.

"Are you following all this, Amie?"

"Oh yes," she said. In fact, questions were already beginning to fill her head. "But where is this ship going and coming? Am I going to England? How dangerous is it?"

"I'm getting to all that," her father said, raising his hand again. "But at this point I need to pledge you to secrecy, just the same as if you were a

Confederate officer going on a secret mission. That means not breathing a word to your mother, to Lucy, and especially to our coloreds."

Few slave owners in Georgia ever spoke aloud of "slaves." On farms, it was always "my field hand" or "my stable man." In urban Savannah, with mostly household slaves, the word du jour was "coloreds," which in William Beach's throat became rounded into a sound more like "culluds."

Beach tried to look his daughter over as he would a bright young officer. It should have been Joseph facing him on this night, but his only son had marched off to war and soon the women of the house would have to learn that he would not return. *But not a topic for right now.* Beach shoved the fearful subject to a back room in his head.

Amelia felt a pause was appropriate and marked it with an unladylike gulp of her sherry. It gave her courage to press on.

"You know I will, Daddy," she said, "but it would help to know more."

"And you will. Sorry, my Amie, you won't be going to Merry Old England. You'll be responsible for a shipment of gold that you will see safely to a bank in Nassau. Now then, Nassau is the capital of The Bahamas, about seven hundred miles from here. The Bahamas are an English Colony, and because England is officially neutral in the war, the Yankee gunboats can't pursue our ships in Bahamian waters. "

"How dangerous is it on the trip over?" she asked.

William Beach gave her a reassuring smile. "The chances of your ship being sunk are very small, and the reason again has to do with money. None of these gunboat captains wants to sink a blockade runner. If they do, down goes all that expensive cargo into Davy Jones' bank vault below. If they can board a captured ship, they usually release innocent passengers like yourself, then tow the ship to a government auction place. There they sell off the cargo. Honest Abe Lincoln's treasury takes about half and the rest is split among the gunboat crew. A lot of captains are already rich men, I'm told."

"And none has ever sunk?"

"None like the one you'll sail on. But if it happened, my investors in Liverpool have figured out that if a fully-loaded blockade runner makes three successful trips, it will more than pay for the ship and a tidy profit."

He thought he could feel his daughter hesitate, and he felt a tinge of shame. "Believe me," he added, " if Joseph were here, he would be having this conversation with me and going on this mission. But even so, I think you have shown yourself to be…to be… special. You have developed your own mind, I should say." He paused, again fumbling for words. "You have not succumbed to what is expected of a young woman, and I have noticed it with admiration, just as your mother has observed it with…with exasperation."

"You used to call me Spunky," she replied awkwardly. But having had a rare glimpse into her distant father's mind, and propelled by the sherry, she blurted out: "Where *is* Joseph? We used to get a letter every two weeks. Now we've heard nothing in over five. Mother and even the coloreds are walking around with long faces. You said you have all these sources of information. Have you learned something? Might he be coming home for Christmas?"

The questions were too piercing to deflect, and Joseph came rushing out from the back of his mind. "I hear only fragments, which I've been trying to piece together," he said somberly. "Just like you, all I know officially is what he wrote us: he was headed for Chickamauga after his regiment troops pulled out of Gettysburg. I think he may now be engaged in top secret work that we are not to know about."

I am lying to my own daughter and I hope she doesn't see my shame. Joseph got captured at Chickamauga and was taken to a prison called Fort Delaware, which holds over 20,000 men, and where the bastards have re-duced the rations by half because a Confederate prison had done the same to their men. I have an agent trying to buy Joseph's way out, but I don't know if I can trust him. He says they keep demanding more. Maybe he's a double agent. Or maybe Joseph will be knocking on our door on Christmas morning.

And maybe Amelia did sense something.

"Daddy," she asked, drawing nearer to him, "help me understand the Yankees. Why are they so determined to destroy us? Doesn't their cherished Constitution say that states have the right to leave if the government does them wrong?"

"To be sure," he answered, relieved to have the subject changed. "But I guess they didn't figure on so many doing it at once."

"But why do they want to come down here and destroy us…our way of life?"

"I don't have all the answers; I'm just a businessman," said William Beach. "They just want us to keep paying taxes and sending them cheap goods. "

"But if they free all the coloreds, won't those prices go up?"

"Yes, honey, but we need to talk about…."

"Oh, Daddy," she exclaimed. "I just want to do something to help. I wish I weren't a helpless woman sewing buttons on uniforms. I wish I were with Joseph!"

"Well, it seems that you are in fact about to do something just as important, my dear."

"And I do want to. How long will I be in Nassau?"

"You'll have to be there until an agent from Liverpool comes to claim his part of the gold. Maybe two weeks, but maybe longer. Communications are difficult with the blockade. It's gotten so that people in Nassau copy the same letter and put it on two or three blockade runners leaving for southern ports just to be sure one will get through."

"Will I be alone? Can I bring Mandy?" she asked.

"I don't think so," said her father. "Remember that England abolished slavery some thirty years ago. Nassau is English and just about all the people there are free coloreds. It would be very easy for any colored to walk off a boat and disappear among them."

"But Daddy, Mandy would never...."

"There are things you just don't understand." interrupted William Beach. "One of them is that I have life insurance on every colored in this house and all of them in my warehouse and docks. If any one of them should leave the country, the whole policy is null and void. Then you have the five hundred to a thousand dollars it would cost to replace each one who deserts."

Amelia paused until more questions bubbled up. She and the sherry were enjoying the first real chance in her life to "talk business" with her otherwise distant father, and the proposed "mission" was her lever to pry him open.

"Daddy, how much gold is involved here? And why gold? Don't people today just use bank drafts?"

Beach was surprised his daughter even knew what a bank draft was. "Well," he said rather obliquely, "I suppose an English shipbuilder doesn't have much faith in Confederate currency."

"But how much gold?"

There it was. He tried another sweep of the cape. "You know, my dear, that couriers on secret missions usually don't even ask to know what they're carrying so that if they're captured there's nothing to divulge."

"So there is danger." She held out her empty glass and Beach reflexively added another splash from the decanter. "Daddy, I am not shrinking at all from danger, but I do think I deserve your trust and confidence at the same time."

"Yes, you do," he said after a pause. "Before you leave, you will know all the particulars, I promise."

Or maybe all the particulars you need to know at the time. That was the way Will Beach always operated, whether dealing with family, friend or foe. The cement had already hardened around his latest plan many weeks ago. Truth was, Beach's faith in rebel currency was no greater than a Liverpool ship-builder's. He would send around $250,000 in gold ingots on the new block-ade runner. Ninety thousand would go on to the Liverpool shipbuilders to cover his half interest. The rest would stay in Nassau. Were the whole load to go to the Bank of England in London, word would leak out as news like that always does. Eyebrows would be raised in merchant circles that a big broker in Savannah had abandoned the rebel cause. Confederate currency values would plummet, including his own remaining funds at home. No. Better to stash it in a quiet Bank of England branch vault in Nassau and nearer to home if and when the war's end called for its return. That's how Will Beach schemed: always a jump ahead of conventionality. When Will put five dollars on a racehorse to win, he always hedged his bet with a dollar to show.

But he had not anticipated what came next.

"Daddy, here you've confided in me and trusted me with a top-secret mission, but you've never confided in me about how you came to Savannah or got all this gold."

"Um....I don't think you've ever asked," he said, looking out at the moon-light streaming through the window.

"Oh, I surely did when I was a curious child," she said, "but you always replied so vaguely that I thought you didn't want me to know. All I do know is that you came from Beaufort, North Carolina and came down here on the train when you were seventeen or something. Your mother died early and you have no brothers or sisters."

William Beach stretched in his chair and pulled out his pocket watch.

"Even Grandpa Huxley was vague," she bore on. "He said you started as an apprentice. But all this gold? It makes idle minds race. I once imagined you robbing a train or being a swashbuckling pirate who found a buried treasure chest. But then, you're so kind and loving and honest." She reached out to pat his hand again with a motherly smile.

I guess if I'm giving my daughter the dangerous task of shipping the gold, I can tell her how I brought it here in the first place. At least some of it.

"You weren't far off the mark with your father as pirate," he said with a smile. "I was raised....no, I just grew up because nobody raised me, on Shackleford Banks on the coast of North Carolina. Not Beaufort. My mother died of some kind of fever – maybe consumption – when I was three. My father was gone off so much on a fishing schooner that I only got to know him when he was coming or going or sitting on the front steps with a jug beside him."

In those few words, Will Beach's Savannah drawl had slackened into the Shackleford Banks slur of his youth. Sitting became *sattin* and porch became *pauch* and his sentences slowed to a crawl. "I will spare you the tedium of life on Shackelford Banks," he continued, "but a good example of it is that I didn't learn to read until I taught myself at age twelve or so. Then one day at seventeen my fortunes would change quite a bit."

It came out of his mouth as *quat ah bee-it*. Just then William Beach rose from his chair. "I do hear some clatter and voices out there on the front porch. It must be Lucy and that Robert fellow." He took out his watch again. "It's nearly eleven and that's far too late. Your mother and I need to have a talk with her."

"Oh, Daddy, but you were just going to tell me about the gold..."

To Beach it sounded like *tell m'abowthgol*. Amelia's sherry had thickened her tongue. "Honey, we'll finish the talk before you depart, I promise," he said, steering her toward the door.

She turned, her back to the door. "Just tell me: who else knows about you and the gold?"

"Well, your Grandpa Huxley, God rest his soul, and your mother and Joseph."

"And they haven't told anybody else?"

"No. When you're sitting on a lot of gold, you don't want to tell anyone else. Besides, your mother wants everyone to think I'm some sort of ar-is-to-crat."

"Then why not me?"

"You weren't old enough. Now you are. Go to bed, my brave soldier, and we'll talk again soon."

As Beach opened the study door, he saw the last of Lucy's bustle bobbing up the stairs and decided she could better be scolded by both parents in the morning. It was past his usual bedtime, too, but he had missed his evening cigar and disdained the sherry that remained half-full in its dainty glass. He lit a Virginia cheroot, poured a snifter of French cognac, and stood by the mantle pondering how many details about the trip to Nassau would be appropriate for his daughter's best interest.

Then his thoughts turned to Shackleford Banks. There was much that he'd forgotten over the past nearly thirty years: hours in Savannah negotiating with farmers, pouring over cotton price sheets, supervising the stacking of bales aboard ships.

But he could still recall almost every minute of the three days at Beaufort Inlet that would set his life on a new course.

Chapter Two

SHACKLEFORD BANKS, JULY 1829

The successful and respected William Beach was born in 1813 in the most insignificant of places and in the most pitiful of domiciles. Because the bed had but one sheet to cover the horsehair mattress, and because the mother-to-be worried that it might become too stained for further use, her issue was discharged onto a gritty kitchen floor. After a slap-dash scrub and a chop of the umbilical cord with the kitchen cleaver, the surviving infant was named Will Gaskins. There was no need for a middle name, for he would only be called Will all his life anyway.

The most insignificant of places was Diamond City, on Shackleford Banks, a strip of sand and stunted pines and wild ponies across the sound from Beaufort, a point of reference which still eluded most folks until told

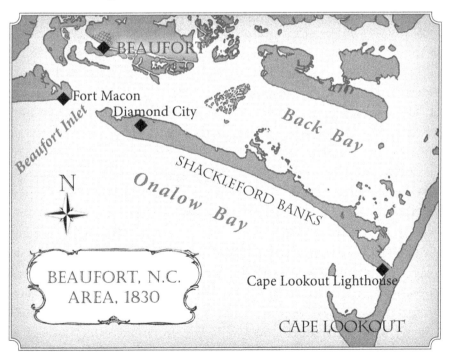

BEAUFORT, N.C. AREA, 1830

that it can be seen from the top of Cape Lookout Lighthouse in the Outer Banks of North Carolina.

No place was ever more misnamed than Diamond City, for it was neither lustrous nor a city. It was no more than a cluster of four dozen or so patchwork shacks whose driftwood walls seemed to be never sealed with enough oakum to keep stormy, salty sea winds from making themselves at home. And they say the "City's" unlikely first name came because somebody atop the Lookout Light thought the dwellings seemed to be arranged in a diamond shape.

Over on the mainland you'd probably hear Diamond City described as a "whaling town," but that could be because it was the only thing folks could think of that now and then interrupted a methodical monotony as regular as sunrise and sunset. Men spent all their days fishing, crabbing, oystering and tending a straggly gaggle of sheep. Or, just as often, they played dominoes in the shade of a gnarly live oak on the waterfront. After storms they'd go "racking" the smorgasbord of driftwood that lined the ten-mile beach for pieces to replace parts of porches and steps that got blown awry. If someone looked poorly sick-like, they might cut down a sand pine and make a coffin to be ready just in case.

When women weren't scouring the woods for berries or gutting fish or boiling potatoes, they were sewing fish nets or making and mending clothes. If a woman needed wool to, say, make a pair of socks, she'd rise early and walk out in the narrow paths where sheep had meandered and left tufts of wool sparkling with dew on prickly shrubs. She'd card it into bunches, then go home to her spinning wheel and hope to have enough to make more than one sock.

Children were breast-fed until they could eat grown-up food but were sometimes helped along the way by gobs of bread soaked in coffee. Beyond that, they were taught either to help with chores or stay out of the way. They went to the one-room schoolhouse, but their entire learning consisted of one tattered book with the name *Blue-Black Speller* barely readable on the cover. Once a child learned what was between its faded and well-thumbed pages, he knew as much as the teacher and had no further need for school.

If you needed store-bought staples, you could try your luck at Uncle Bill's Store, the only building in Diamond City that somebody didn't live in. If you needed Saturday excitement or a job that paid cash money, you could row your dory a mile or so across the sound to Beaufort. There you'd find a growing port town which shipped Carolina pine and barrel staves to Caribbean countries and imported such exotics as rum, coffee and furniture. So promising a port had the federal government deemed Beaufort that it had begun building Fort Macon, an impressive stone bastion across the inlet, to stare down any skipper who tried to elude his customs taxes.

Then, for a dash of élan, there hung over Beaufort the ghostly aura of Edward Teach, the rascally yet revered "Blackbeard." Visitors were regaled with tales of his swashbuckling just a hundred or so years before and the certainty, folks had persuaded themselves, that one or two of his pirate ships had been sunk by British gunboats in or near Beaufort Inlet. As for Diamond City, no gold and not even ghostly glory.

Now then, the recently-arrived Will Gaskins was still sucking on bread dipped in coffee and scooting around the grimy kitchen floor when he found himself with no mama to pick him up and hug him in the wooden rocking chair. Where had she gone? "Bad lungs," they told him. His father was away most of the time working on a cargo schooner bound for the Caribbean and didn't speak much anyway when he came home to their two-room shanty on the sound. The best you could say about Will was that he had all ten toes and fingers and was told he was "good looking" by a Shackleford girl when he was twelve.

By age thirteen, the most exciting event Will could remember was discovering two metal trunks, beached near Hatteras Inlet, and finding one full of soggy suspenders and the other a cornucopia of ladies' black patent leather shoes. Well, no man in Diamond City ever had to worry again about how to hold his pants up. The women, after drying and polishing their new shoes, tried gamely to prance up and down the pathway, but soon found that the high heels dug into the sand and caused too many turned ankles.

The days rolled by in monotonous torpor, but inside Will's head thoughts rolled in like unceasing breakers. Poor and ignorant as he was, he felt a powerful urge to learn new things and wonder what life might be like beyond the windy grayness of Shackleford Banks.

By age fifteen, Beaufort increasingly drew Will and his dory across the sound where a new world of discovery awaited. It had begun on a Saturday morning when he was walking the wharf and saw a man with a white beard sitting on a bench, smoking a corncob pipe and reading a large sheet of print. Just as Will passed, the man got up and walked off, leaving the sheet of paper on the bench. Will looked both ways, then pounced on it like a hen on a June bug.

When he unfolded it carefully under a shade tree, he made out laboriously, The Georgia Christian Chronicle, June 27, 1828. Painstakingly he moved his finger over the headlines and columns.

Alexander Barfield, shopkeeper from Glasgow, Scotland, found dead in the charred ruins of his shop in Savannah.

Mr. James Spottsworth, native of England, killed in Sparta Tuesday evening by a fall from his apartment on the second story of the Eagle Tavern.

Mrs. Jane Roberts died in her residence in Hancock County in her 69th year. Member of the Methodist Church 39 years. A faithful and affectionate mother, kind to her slaves, and benevolent to the poor.

Glasgow? Sparta? Methodist? Hancock County? Perhaps the man with the pipe had paid a penny for the paper at a tobacco shop and scanned its banalities in a few minutes, but to fifteen-year-old Will it was a portal to an exciting new world. He knew then that he would need money to buy more of whatever books and newspapers found their way to Beaufort, North Carolina. After pestering fishing boat captains at the Beaufort docks, he signed on with an old salt called "Westy" for five cents a day plus ten percent of whatever they could coax from the ocean.

In time, Will could afford to buy books or sometimes sneak into the small library of the Anne Street United Methodist Church and read until the setting sun dropped below the open window. His first whole book was *The Last of the Mohicans*, by James Fenimore Cooper, but the ones he liked best were of the far-off British Isles: *The Talisman* and *Woodstock* by Walter Scott. And he had stayed up all night reading *The Mummy*, about how London scientists in the year 2126 brought the mummified Egyptian pharaoh Cheops back to life.

He liked being far from Shackleford Banks.

And then one May day in Will's seventeenth year, England suddenly came to Diamond City. Tied to a tree a few feet from the rough Sound waterline and resting upside down was the grey, wind-scoured, twenty-foot dory that Will's father had left him "to earn his keep with" as he shoved off on another ocean voyage. Daddy Gaskins called it *Old Glory*. Said it reminded him of pictures of a tattered flag that he once saw a soldier carrying in a Revolutionary War poster.

Old Glory and its kin were the most common of fishing boats because one man could row them or control the lone sail from a tiller in the stern. They were simple to build, with a sharp bow for cutting through waves and a slender transom so as to avoid being swamped when pushed by big waves. And they were flat-bottomed, which meant you could glide along in shallow waters and haul them onshore whenever you could find a beach.

One sweetly warm Sunday morning Will was planning to row over to Beaufort where he would spend some time listening to the sermon outside the open window at the Anne Street church, then sneak in after they'd all left and do some reading in the stillness of its small library. At first he noticed a shadow extending from under the boat. But when Will heaved the heavy dory over, he was startled to find a young man his age on the ground.

The equally-startled stranger snapped upright to attention, blinked in the bright sunlight, then bowed with a flourish of the right hand, lacking only a lace cuff. "Good sir, I am in your debt for the shelter your fine vessel provided me," he intoned in a fine gentleman's accent that did not match his threadbare breeches and shirt of stained sailcloth.

"Allow me," the stranger said with a stretch and a yawn that unfurled into a warm smile. "I am Horatio Nelson Byron, an heir to the dukedom of Wellington. And you are...?"

"Um, Will," he mumbled, struggling to remember his last name. "Will Gaskins. What are you doing here in Diamond City?" he asked, trying not to appear unfriendly.

"Ah, Diamond City. I come across the ocean from the Misty Isles, changing ships in Bermuda to that lumber lorry that arrived yesterday. You can see it in the harbor over yonder," said the visitor with sun-bleached, curly hair, pointing to a beamy sloop at the distant town wharf. "People told me of the virtues of your fair, ah, island and I came to see if this might be the paradise I have searched the seven seas to find."

"You can probably find that out quick enough," said Will. "There ain't much here. Can I row you across to your ship?"

"Er, my thanks, but no," said the stranger. "I need to grow my land legs back. I've been at sea for months – from England to Gibraltar to Northern Africa to the shores of this young and splendid nation."

"Well, we don't get many visitors in Diamond City," said Will, not knowing what else to say.

"Well, you should, sir. Such a fine place," said the duke with the last name of Byron. He was silent for a moment, looking in all directions. "Might you know where a gent could get a bite to eat?"

"There's Uncle Bill's store over there. Mostly canned food, flour and tobacco."

He pressed the back of his hand to his forehead. "Alas, I am without funds. You see, Mr. Will," his face wreathed in sadness, "uncontrollable circumstances compelled me to travel on that ship from Bermuda as a lowly deckhand. The captain is a cruel drunkard and his first mate likes to bugger young lads. Besides, that floating rat's nest is not fit for a fellow who has sailed on a royal flagship and who has heard the roar of a twenty-seven-gun salute."

Now his face brightened again, his head cocked. "Might you have a small space for me to stay a while? I can fish. I can tie a knot. I can drive a nail, and I can teach you a hornpipe," he sing-songed with a cross-legged wobble.

Will was still trying to catch and comprehend the stream of strange words and dialect, but he was curious to know more about this short, wiry lad with the unruly, mop of sun-bleached hair. And he certainly was more entertaining than the dullards of Diamond City.

"Well," he said, "my father's been gone for weeks and I don't know when he'll be back. I guess you could sleep in his bed 'til he needs it."

"It's quite enough, and quietude suits my present circumstances. I am indeed grateful," he added with another bow lacking only a lace cuff to accompany it.

———

In the first days, the two boys talked incessantly while at chores, even continuing a conversation lying in their beds at night until one of them dozed off. Will heard eye-opening tales of soirees in English country manors, walks through the honeycombed fortress of Gibraltar, audiences before Moorish emirs and a tea with the princess Victoria, who would soon become queen of The United Kingdom, Britain and Ireland.

Then about a week after his discovery under *Old Glory*, Horatio stopped in the middle of a colorful yarn and declared, "My good fellow, this is not much fun. You're just not jolly good sport for me. You believe everything I say."

Will: "You're telling me lies?"

Horatio: "Well, not exactly all the time. You see, half of what I say is true. Your challenge is to tell which is which. But it's unfair, because you don't know anything and might be called a liar if you repeat everything to someone who does."

He looked hard at Will, who seemed to be processing everything he'd heard into lobes of fact and fiction. Then came a big smile and a slap on the thigh. "So from now on," declared Horatio, "Oy'm going to do you a favor. Everything Oy say will be the whole truth, so help me Jimmy Jennings."

"Who's that?"

"That's the name of the pot and pan Oy never knew." Horatio said it in a new way of talking he would describe as Cockney. "They say me old man was a cooper who could drain one of his barrels as fast as you could fill it. Well, one day it seems they found him floating in the Thames all bloated like one of his barrels. Me sainted mum didn't want a baby in her house, which was full of other ladies, if you know what Oy mean, but you don't. So that's when they packed little Jimmy Jennings – that's me – off to Missus Sotheby's Home for Orphans. Mostly what Oy remembers about that place was porridge in the morning, paddling in the afternoon and all manner of pestilence crawling and scratching at night.

"If there ever was a Missus Sotheby, Oy never saw her," continued Horatio. "The place was run by a crusty old bloke. Each day he'd send pairs of children – one older, one barely able to walk – out in the streets with signs that said PLEASE SUPPORT OUR ORPHAN'S HOME.

"By the time Oy was nine Oy says to meself, 'Why let this old cut purse take me money and give me wormy bread when Oy can keep all the proceeds of the day and buy meself a whole plate of bangers and mash?' So one day after a particularly fine collection of alms Oy just run off. Next day Oy used the same SUPPORT OUR ORPHANS sign to get a few coppers. Slept under bridges by the river for a week of bitter cold nights, then found a pub keeper who would let me clean up around the place after closing and then sleep on the bar counter with a wad of old towels for me pillow.

"One night, when Oy was mebbe ten, some beefy navy blokes came into the pub just around closing and began to carry off two drunks who had passed out at a table. 'Welcome to His Majesty's navy,' Oy heard one of them say as he hoisted one of the sleeping souses over his shoulder.

"So then Oy pipes up. Oy says, 'Can Oy join the navy, too?' Oy said in me best Cockney. He grabs me ear with his free hand and leads me off to this tender in the Dockyards. Oy was soon on a navy tub that had more rats than Missus Sotheby's or the pub, but in a few days Oy had me own berth and regular navy grub three times a day. Oy was a full-fledged cabin boy!"

Horatio paused as he gauged Will's reaction to this revelation. Will's first thought was of irony. *This fellow has no family. I have as much "family" as Shackleford Banks has sheep, but I feel I'm just as much an orphan.*

The other orphan continued. "When Oy left Missus Sotheby's, Oy left Jimmy Jennings, too. Left him floating in the Thames with me father's memory. Since then Oy've been free to pick the name that would best help me in whatever circumstance fate may cast me.

"Over here in America Oy use Horatio Nelson Byron because one or more of those famous names from England might draw a speck of respeck – mebbe even a lady's friendly glance."

"But all those stories......" Will was beginning to feel the fool.

"Ah, it is important for you to know what is true," said Horatio, sensing his new friend's anxiety. "Didn't have tea with Princess Vicky but did see her carriage pass by me close enough to see her inside. Did serve on a royal flagship, though Oy didn't exactly dine at the commodore's table. Oy would be amidships emptying the pisspot of some junior officer. Did in time go from cabin boy to deckhand, which took me to Gibraltar and Mediterranean ports. Didn't dine with an emir, but did see one being carried about on a litter in Tripoli."

From then on it was a new relationship between equals. Horatio offered a deckhand's colorful glimpses of a sailor's routine aboard ocean ships, perils at sea, and life in exotic harbor towns and their bazaars. In turn, he proved eager to add to his repertoire of skills whatever Will could teach, be it netting a school of menhaden, or how to shuck an oyster without cutting one's hand or learning how to recognize the difference between male and female crabs and when they molt their shells.

One thing the two shared most was the need to make enough money to escape from Diamond City and set out on another of life's adventures. For Horatio it was to reach New Orleans and "become a captain of a paddle wheeler on the great Mississippi."

For Will it was, for the moment, just to go somewhere else and see something besides the sandy, stormy spit of land that was Shackleford Banks.

Ironically, it was storm and sand – the big southeaster that blew through the Carolinas on August 15, 1829 – that would send the boys on their way. Until then they had done everything they could to save a few dollars: hauling and scraping dories on shore, painting houses, tarring roofs, to name a few.

The storm blew in on a Wednesday, and for four days the water was too roughed up for fishing. But by late Saturday afternoon the skies were clear, the wind was calm, and in Beaufort harbor the water was clear enough to see mullet and minnows all the way to the bottom. It was as if the sea were apologizing for having stirred up so much trouble.

And trouble it was. No fishing boats had gone out for four days as townspeople repaired tattered sails and shattered windows. Seafood stocks at the three markets had already been picked clean by Saturday night. On the morrow, the Sabbath, no respectable Christian man should be seen working the water.

Except for two ambitious young men. Westy, the aging sharpie skipper and Will's part-time employer, couldn't have sailed even in good weather because he was in constant pain. The gale had sent a flowerpot on his front porch flying into his collarbone.

Will and Horatio came calling that evening and presented their case. If Westy would allow them to sail out the next day on his twenty-four foot sharpie, and if the winds remained calm, they'd stay around the inlet and fish for redfish, grouper, yellow fin, sea bass and other "table fish." The chances of hauling in a good catch would be good, and the market price fetched that night might be twice what it would be once everyone else set out on Monday. And they'd give the owner a half share.

Westy puffed on his pipe, winced as he coughed, and looked the boys over. Will knew how to sail the sharpie, sure enough. Didn't know much about the friend from England, but he'd take chance and agree to the deal.

Well before any church bells pealed on Sunday morning, Will and Horatio were aboard the sailboat, bait buckets already full of pinfish, mullet and sardines. So clear and calm were the waters that it took two hours of tacking before the slackened sails finally pulled the boat past the inlet. Then they lowered the two sails and began drifting north along the coast. By early afternoon all they had to show as a return on Westy's "investment" were a half-filled box of small yellowtails.

By then Will had taken to leaning over the gunwales, peering into the water while holding the "looking glass" – a box shaped like a square megaphone that could help spot a reef or school of fish. "I see something dark," he said at last. "Drop anchor and measure how many feet when you let it out." he called.

"About twenty feet deep," said Horatio. "And Oy gave it another ten for the drift."

Soon their worries had been replaced by good cheer. Six groupers over two pounds, and an assortment of ladyfish, redfish, and sea bass, all flopping and gasping in the large fish well that was kept fresh with buckets of seawater. Westy would be pleased.

By mid-afternoon the fish box was becoming full. "We're running out of bait," Horatio called, his hands red-raw after hauling in another hand line. "We need time to get back to the wharf. Besides, Oy'd like it to be light enough to see the looks on everyone's faces when we return."

"All right," answered Will, pulling in his three lines and chucking the bait into the water. "Weigh anchor."

But he could only watch Horatio tug and twist the anchor rode with no success. Will joined in the struggle but even the two could not dislodge it.

"We cannot cut this line," Will said at last. "We will owe Westy more money than we'll get from these fish. And we can forget about using his boat again."

"Aye, mate," answered Horatio, but already he was taking off his shirt and removing his shoes. "The depth is twenty feet, we agree. Oy'm going to ride the hook line down for a look." With that he was overboard with a smart naval salute and plunging hand over hand down the anchor rode.

Ten, twenty seconds elapsed, then another ten before a white form appeared and then: a hand clinging to the anchor rode and Horatio gasping for breath, his mouth opened as wide as his eyes.

"Did you free it?" shouted Will.

"No, my captain, no!" He opened his free hand and pressed into Will's palm three slightly blackened but clearly distinguishable gold coins. "Oh Holy Mother of God, Oy think we've found something more than fish!" he exclaimed. "Our anchor is hooked on the spar of another anchor. This is no reef. It's a wreck. All around are long black cannons. Right below me were sacks of leather or cloth." He gulped for air. "When Oy lifted one up, the bottom fell out and a pocketful of coins spilled into the sand. These are just what Oy grabbed before Oy ran out of breath."

"I'm going down to see," said Will, already in a state of similar undress. He took in several deep breaths and dove in sharply so as to begin following the anchor line. In the near-darkness he saw the great anchor and the black, barnacled cannons. Lifting another cloth sack with the same results, he scooped up six coins from the sea bed and put them in his pocket. Amidst the sacks, half-buried in the sand, were several pickets or dull sword blades looking like the crooked teeth of a sea monster. He wrested one out, heavier than he had supposed, jammed it between his legs, and hand over hand, climbed the sharpie's submerged anchor rode like a sailor ascending a tall ship's rigging.

"Whoeeee!" shouted Will as he broke the surface, shaking water from his hair. "What a jolly good time, as you English say!" He passed the heavy metal blade up to Horatio, climbed over the gunwale and lay panting in the sun, his face wreathed in a broad smile. "Oh, I almost forgot," he said, digging into his pocket and handing Horatio the six coins.

For a while they just lay on the deck, warmed by the afternoon sun and thinking of what they should do next.

"We can't go back there with no anchor," Will said at last. "Old man Westy will inspect his ship – you can wager on that – and when he sees the anchor missing, that's the end of our treasure hunt."

"Aye," said Horatio, "but if we let loose that anchor we'll never find the wreck. And in a few days another storm will roll in and sand will cover it all up again."

In the end, they decided to leave the anchor rode stuck fast to the ghost ship's hook and tie the other end to a buoy to mark the location as would any fisherman his trap. They would approach Westy jauntily with no less than two dollars for his share – even if it meant cutting into theirs. They would boast of finding a grouper hole and promise him no less than two dollars again if they could take the sharpie out the next day. If Westy inspected the boat and discovered the anchor missing, they would say they left it to mark the grouper hole.

But the old man couldn't conceal his smile as he took his two dollars and agreed to the new proposition without leaving his front porch.

Over a grilled grouper dinner that night they turned over the coins and agreed that they were definitely Spanish, with all the marks of a mint in Mexico or South America. The heavy blade, shaped like a barracuda and bearing various Spanish markings, was no doubt a gold ingot. They tried to estimate its weight compared to the biggest fish they'd caught that day and reckoned it at over twenty pounds.

All this only whetted their zeal for more of the same. "Dame Fortune lifts her palms from the ocean floor to blokes like us only once in a lifetime," mused Horatio. "But quickly she will cover up her embarrassment of riches like a fine lady who discovers she's shown too much of her blubbies. We must go out tomorrow, but how much can we get diving twenty feet down into all that murk? Oy wish we had a diving bell."

"What's that?" Will asked as he stood at the sink washing dishes.

Horatio: "Picture one of them giant bells that you see ringing in a great cathedral. Nowadays they're using something like them to work underwater. You puts one or two men inside on a bench that's been welded into the bell. Then you lowers them into the water. The bell is attached to chains with weights at the end to hold it steady. Air gets trapped inside. The bell floats up just enough to let the men swim in and out. When they needs to breathe, they swims back inside and suck in some more air."

"That seems mighty dangerous," said Will.

Horatio: "Well, we had one of these aboard a frigate Oy was on. Never saw it used. Was supposed to be for caulking leaks and the like. But they says the two men inside could stay down there for up to two hours."

"How big was that bell you saw on your ship?"

Oh, mebbe ten feet tall and six across."

"Well, what if we got something smaller and lighter?"

Horatio was seated in the corner of the cabin, head in hands, as he brooded. Will finished his dishes and swung around with a clean fry pan in his hands.

"We don't need any two hours' worth of air," Will declared. "Suppose we had something light that was maybe four feet tall and three feet across. Let's suppose you lower it and water fills up the lower half before it starts floating. That would mean having an air pocket of two feet tall and three feet across. Now if that big bell of yours would keep two men under for two hours, wouldn't our little bell have enough air for five or ten minutes?"

Horatio walked outside without a word and could be seen through the window prowling about in the darkness. In a few minutes he poked his head inside the door and crooked his finger for Will to come out. He pointed to the large wooden barrel that collected rainwater from a roof gutter.

"That looks like our diving bell." he said. "It's just about the size you talked about. All we do is saw off some of it to swim under."

Their rush of exaltation was quickly replaced by chin stroking over something else. The light barrel would surely tip sideways in the current unless attached to something like the weighty metal chains that hung from the big ship's diving bell. They reckoned it would take a nail in each quarter of the inverted barrel and a rope fastened to each. At the end of each three-foot rope would be a weight so that the "diving bell" would descend evenly without teetering and upsetting the balance between air and water.

Now it was Will's turn. He walked over to a window and said, "It's right over here." He pointed to a lead sash inside the faded wood frame, conveniently forged with an eyehole that was tied to a long, heavy cord so that the window could move up and down. Also conveniently, a 5 was forged on the lead sash to mark its weight at five pounds.

Alas, Will's humble shack had but two windows that could open with sashes. The boys brooded over the need for two more five pound weights. Finally, it was Horatio who laughed and pointed at Will. "You've got one of them right under your bloomin' nose," he exclaimed. Will realized he was still holding an iron skillet, with another one hanging on the wall.

The stars were still shining over clear, calm waters just before dawn when Will and Horatio rowed *Old Glory* silently across the sound to the spot where Westy's sailboat was moored. A rooster cleared its throat and a dog barked as they crept aboard the sharpie with their fishing gear and bulky barrel.

The sun had begun to peek over the treetops when they began casting their first bait net in a secluded cove just before Beaufort Inlet gave way to open sea. Will sat in grim silence. "I dreamt last night that we searched and searched for the buoy but it had disappeared," he said at last.

"Ah, you should have dreamed *me* dream," crooned Horatio. "Oy was riding in a white carriage with a new white topper and silk suit. And as me white horse and hansom ambled down the main street of New Orleans, a fetching young lass in another carriage pulled up and handed me an invitation to tea. 'Couldn't possibly have tea with thee,' Oy replied, handing her my card. 'But you can wait in me parlor until Oy'm finished with the other ladies.'"

Horatio's exuberance was rewarded when they spotted the buoy, bobbing slowly with just a gentle current tugging it to the north. The rising sun spread an orange sheen on the waters and not a ship loomed in sight. "Make ready for the most delightful swim you ever took!" he said as he gaffed the anchor line.

"Not so fast," said Will in a stern tone. "First we fish."

Horatio spun around and cocked his head in disbelief. "What? Enough of fish! Oy say we don't need anything to do with them smelly things and their sticky scales."

"We must fish first," Will repeated. "You can't pay Westy with gold coins unless you want everyone in town jabbering. We need two dollars' worth of fish to sell. Besides, we need to give all this diving stuff a proper test."

Horatio, muttering, snatched a mullet from the bait box and slammed the lid with a bang. Nearly an hour passed in silence, broken only by the splashing surface as redfish, grouper, and ladyfish were flopping about the fish box.

Among the "stuff" they'd added the previous night was the copper carrier that Will's father used to store fireplace logs. Now attached to a long dock line, it would hoist coins and ingots instead of firewood.

Also on board was a three-minute egg timer from Will's kitchen. Three tugs on the line would tell the diver he'd been under for three minutes.

Then there was the barrel-turned-diving bell, sprawled on deck and resembling a dead octopus with its four limp rope legs and feet of window weights and skillets all askew. On top of the inverted bottom the boys had added an eye screw so that the barrel now had a twenty foot dock line attached to it.

Around ten, both boys could begin to feel the tingle of an ocean breeze on their faces. Coastal folk knew it as the "Carolina wind" and looked to it for relief on a muggy summer morning. "All right," Will said in a commanding officer's voice, "it's time to give our diving bell a try. Let 'er down about one fathom." They agreed that Horatio would make the first test dive to see if the air pocket was as large as expected. Horatio would inhale inside and expel his breath out the bottom. When the three tugs on the top line signaled the egg timer had run its three minutes, Horatio would surface.

Overboard he went. Will turned over the egg timer and began to watch every grain of sand in it slowly making its way into the funnel. Peering over the side, he could only see the blur of Horatio's legs kicking out of the barrel bottom. It seemed as though the egg timer was releasing each grain of sand like drips from a leaky faucet. When the last grains had slipped away, Will gave three tugs. The barrel wobbled in the water and Horatio's head suddenly surfaced wearing a big grin. "It works!" he shouted.

Aboard ship, Horatio was exuberant again. "The weights hang even. The barrel doesn't leak. The level of air is about what we figgered – more than two feet above the chest. Actually, Oy thinks there's much more than three minutes worth."

Next, Will took his practice turn with the barrel lowered fifteen feet. Just within reach was the wreck, with its cannons, ballast and gold treasures strewn across the bottom like fresh fruit on a grocer's table. After filling his lungs three times inside the barrel, he shot upward. "Lots of air down there," he shouted to Horatio.

"Aye, aye," answered his partner hotly, "but let's get on with it for God's sake or Oy'll jump overboard and take me chances like yesterday. It's already noon. If we keep up this bloody practicing, a squall could blow in or some bullyboys in a bigger boat will sink us and do it themselves!"

"Awright, awright," Will replied evenly. "We're both as taut as topsails on a reach. You go first, but hear me: I'll drop the bell down until I reckon it's five feet above the bottom. Then I'll sink the firewood holder – I mean the gold platter – so it sits on the bottom. Tug on the line three times when you want it raised."

Will lowered the bell down and marked fifteen feet of line. Horatio gave him a look of bravado and knifed into the water. Will lowered the gold platter until it slackened and he cleated the line. Then he waited. It was so quiet he could hear his heart pounding. A lone vessel loomed on the eastern horizon, probably a passing ocean schooner. He peered over but could only make out the watery barrel top and the black patch he had first taken for a reef.

Suddenly he saw a white form rise like a flounder on a hand line. Then it became Horatio, gasping for air as he broke water. Then a crooked smile. "Ain't yer gonna pull up the gold platter?" he yelled between gasps.

Will had forgotten it, hanging idly from the cleat. Now the "platter," a log holder just the night before, was almost too heavy to lift from the bottom but still buoyant as he pulled it slowly arm over arm. As it surfaced, it became heavier again and Will was startled to see four gold ingots garnished with several coins. He might have upended the platter had not Horatio swum over and steadied it.

Both were still breathing heavily when they leaned on all fours to study their "catch" lying on the wooden deck. Will picked up an ingot and held it over his head. "This here's more than twenty pounds," he said. "Four of 'em is over a hundred, not even counting the coins. I say we need to keep each load under a hundred...three ingots and maybe ten coins. Elseways we could spill the platter back into the water...a proper reward for being too greedy."

Horatio: "Oy says to hell with the coins. Them there gold bars is what makes a man rich!"

Will: "Now hold on. You can't go into that store in New Orleans and buy that white suit with a gold ingot. And you need them coins to git there in the first place."

From then on it was agreed: each dive would aim to fetch three bars and ten coins. They took the dive barrel down three more times that day until they had to return to the fish market and deliver old Westy his two dollars. But before they went to town, they had put the coins and bars in empty fish crates and covered them with burlap, just as they did the real fish. Then they brought Westy's sharpie to its mooring buoy, to which Will's *Old Glory* was tied for the day. After transferring the gold crates to the cuddy cabin on the dory, they left the real fish boxes on deck and rowed to the town dock. Will would climb out, take the fish to market and pacify Westy while Horatio kept an eye on the dory.

By nightfall, back in Will's shack, the exhausted boys stood with a candle looking into the windowless storage closet where they had stashed their plunder. By then, including the first day's "samples," they had piled up thirteen ingots and fifty coins.

They ate listlessly and sank into their beds, determined to start fresh after the previous sleepless night. But the same topic was on both minds. "I know it's a lot, but I wish we knew just how much they're worth," mused Will.

Horatio: "Well, since you already have twenty dollar gold pieces in this country, let's just say one of them coins is worth at least twenty."

Quickly both were up again at the kitchen table as Horatio worked a stubby pencil on paper. "So then...if one of them bars weighs over twenty pounds, how many coins could you get out of a bar? Hell, Oy dunno. Bring me one of them barracudas, will yer?"

They stared down at the narrow gray-gold slab, well over two feet long. Too tired for much arithmetic, they settled for drawing pencil lines across it to mark imaginary coins and agreed that two hundred was close enough. Horatio worked the pencil some more and announced his findings. "Two hundred times twenty dollars is four thousand for this here barracuda. Four thousand times the thirteen we got would be, lessee, fifty-two thousand. And Oy be pretty sure these 'ere bars weigh over twenty pounds. Then we got the coins."

"Damn!" they both said at once. "And there be lots more o' them biscuits down there," added Horatio.

Chapter Three
BEAUFORT AND BEYOND, AUGUST 1829

The next day's treasure hunt began in bright sunshine and the ocean behaved, with only a slight chop. The dives had become routine except that the ingots were further away from the dive barrel and some required hard tugging to wrest them free of the sunken ship's ribs. But the coins were still about as plentiful as scratching the surf for sand fleas.

It was after the last dive that the first signs of a storm appeared. But not from weather. The two had hauled up another twelve gold ingots and sixty coins. "Now we each got over fifty thousand," declared Horatio. And with that revelation, an ill wind began to sweep over him. "Now Oy'm going to have them make me a different suit for each day," he bellowed. "Maybe different carriages, too!"

"Well, maybe that's enough then," said Will. "We've pretty much caught all the fish around here anyway."

"Don't you pull that anchor!" snapped Horatio in a venomous voice. "There's more down there, and by the king's balls we're going to get it!"

Will: "Greed can ruin this whole thing. Besides, you can see that it's starting to get rougher. The weather's bound to turn."

After a tense standoff, they agreed on a compromise: they'd leave the anchor rode tethered to the buoy out one more time. If the weather was too windy or rainy the next day, they'd pull it and be gone forever.

On the sail back Horatio changed from bellicose to boisterous. "You know what, Will," he shouted from the bow, "that really must be Blackbeard's treasure except that we're the ones that get to enjoy it. Oy guess that makes us better pirates than Teach and Long John Silver and Henry Morgan all put together!"

"Don't you be talkin' pirates around these parts," Will shouted back from the stern tiller. "Everyone 'round here will show up claimin' they's Blackbeard's kith and kin, and pretty soon they'll have lawyers suing us for their rightful share."

With that Horatio gave a jaunty wave and shouted back: "When Oy were a litt'l boy and so me mother tol' me, that if Oy didn't kiss the girls, me lips would sure grow moldy." Now he burst out singing:

Oy sailed the seas for many years not knowin' what Oy was missin'.
Then Oy sets me sails afore the gales and started in a-kissin'.

Oy got meself an Oyrish gal an' her name was Flannigan.
She stole me boots, she stole me clothes, she pinched me plate an' pannikin.

Oy courted then a Frenchie gal, she took things free and an' 'aisy.
But now Oy've got an English gal an' sure she is a daisy.

Oh, King Louis was the King 'o France, afore the revolution,
But the people cut his big head orf an' spoiled his constitution.

Oh, once Oy wuz in Oyreland a-diggin turf and 'taties,
But now Oy'm on' a lemon ship an' buggerin' me maties.

Horatio was still belting out sea shanties when they pulled aside Will's moored dory and began off-loading their identical fish boxes. The town dock was quiet, and as they tied up *Old Glory*, Will lugged two crates of fish to the wholesaler across the street and returned as Horatio sat slumped in the rower's bench. "Market's down," he said. "Four Liberty ladies is all we got and Westy's going to get two of 'em. While I go see him, how about you take this dollar over to the grocery and get us some potatoes, a loaf of bread and two pounds of lard. Just keep a sharp eye on *Old Glory* here."

"Sure, Admiral," said Horatio with a smirk. *This is the last order Oy'm takin'*, he vowed.

Westy's mood had also soured. "Weather's a changin'," he said when Will asked to head out again the next day. "Swallowtails are whipped up already. Winds shiftin' to northeast. Besides I'm gettin' mighty tired of sittin' around. If you'll do the fishin' and pullin', I can steer. I don't see that being any more painful than sittin' here and listenin' to that old woman fuss at me."

The more Will insisted on one more day, the more suspicious the old man became. "What you boys doin' out there anyway?" he said with a sneer.

"You sure you ain't been out to sea? I never heard of one damn grouper hole so full of fish. How do I know you ain't runnin' rum past Fort Macon and the customs house?"

Will wouldn't have cared too much if Westy had put an end to their risky venture, but he didn't want to be out fishing with the old man because there was no telling what the moody Horatio might do if left alone back home. He stammered, his mind racing to concoct one more reason to convince Westy. "Mr. West," he said, "no way I would ever use your boat to smuggle anything. We've had good fishin', and I don't expect too much more of it in that spot. But, truth is, my friend Horatio was draggin' for scallops yesterday and darned if he didn't pull up a big old Spanish coin. We thought it was a big oyster shell, but after we knocked off the barnacles, there is was, with Spanish writin' and everything."

"Hell, they been found from here to Ocracoke," said Westy, intent on stuffing his long clay pipe. "Friend 'o mine found the same thing near ten miles north of here. It's just ol' Blackbeard's way of teasin' us all."

"Well, my friend's got it in his head to try his luck one more day. He's from England, you know, and he thinks with just one more coin he can afford passage back home."

Westy was silent, firing up his pipe while Will squirmed in discomfort.

"Show me the coin," he said at last.

"Can't. It's back at my place."

"Big coin or small?"

"Oh, big. About the same as a twenty dollar gold piece, I guess."

Westy puffed some more. "You know, you're still workin' for me. You're supposed to get half a day's catch. That there coin's 'catch,' the way I reckon."

He finally looked up at Will from his rocking chair and said: "Tell you what. You go out tomorrow morning. No two dollars this time."

Will beamed with surprise, but the old man cut him off. "The weather figgers to turn by afternoon. You finish up in time to go down to the Carolina Bank and Trust and see what they'll give you for that coin. If it's twenty dollars like you say, you can keep half. If you find another one, you've made another half. And if Blackbeard's ghost leads you right to his treasure chest, we'll all be rich and your friend can sail off to England in his own three-master."

Will was headed down the sandy street toward the town dock when he saw Horatio leave the general store and saunter towards him. "Well, you get everything?" Will asked as they untied *Old Glory*.

"Didn't have enough for taties," Horatio answered idly.

"What? I give you a Liberty and you don't have nuthin' left?" Will stuffed his hand into the gunny sack Horatio had left on deck. He came up with a tin of lard, a loaf of bread, a roll of heavy twine, a can of gray paint and a bottle of Mount Gay rum."

"Well, Oy just thought it would be nice to celebrate," said Horatio, starting to row off.

The only rum Will had ever tried made him feel like throwing up. "So now we're down to one dollar. And you just spent the other one on the most expensive rum you can buy. What was it, fifty? You coulda bought some American stuff for a quarter. Right?"

"You're thinkin' like the backwater bumpkin you'll always be," sneered Horatio.

"Lissen, Mister Duke of Wellington. If it hadn't been for this bumpkin, we wouldn't be going out tomorrow. Old Westy didn't want to give us the boat at all. My only way was to tell him you'd found a gold coin kind of by accident and thought you might find another. In any case, he wants half."

"What, half of everything?" Horatio stood up glowering, an oar raised in one hand.

"No. Calm down. Half of one coin. Or half of two at the most. Tomorrow I go to the bank and see what we can get for them. That's not so bad because we're going to need the cash anyways."

Now Horatio became the admonisher. "What? You told this old blighter? You're the one who said it would be all over town if we showed some gold!"

They bickered back and forth all the way to Shackleford Bank. Finally Will changed the subject. "What's all that twine for?" he asked.

"Oy'm goin' to be needin' it sooner than Oy thought," answered Horatio, still hot.

"Let's see, you're going to tie me up with twine and steal all the gold."

"That's close. Oy'm going to tie some bars to me when Oy walks outta here. You'll see."

"And that paint you bought?"

"You'll find out soon enough."

That night Horatio got meaner and more suspicious with each succeeding tug on the Mount Gay bottle. In what became a quick-changing kaleidoscope of demons and damnations, he was going to "even the score" with this and that captain who had treated him like scum; was going back to Liverpool, buy a fleet of ships, buy a castle in Majorca or maybe Corsica; was hearing footsteps on the path outside coming to break into their cabin and steal their treasure. Need to get out of Diamond City before ever'one pile on him and hit him on the head with a froyin' pan and then them window sashes to his legs and dump him out in the ocean for the sharks to eat. An no one we'ever know because he jumped an English ship back in Bermuda.

The last of it Will heard from his bed as he tried to cover his ears. Finally he shouted out: "No, that's too hard. We're just going to strangle you and grind you up for dog meat."

But Horatio hadn't heard. He sat slumped at the table, asleep with his chin on his chest. Will left him that way in case he'd insist he was "sleeping with one eye open."

The next morning, as the sharpie approached the anchor buoy in the distance, clouds were already building to the east and choppy waters were becoming small whitecaps as they broke on shore. It took longer to gaffe the buoy because it wiggled and bobbed. And when Will took the first dive, the barrel wanted to sway sideways. At the bottom the murky ocean floor swirled with loose sand beginning to cover even some of the cannons. Will darted straight to the old galleon's rib section, where a few ingots still stuck out from the timbers. But in three trips back and forth from the barrel, he could wrest away only two ingots before gasping for air.

The sun was now directly overhead. All morning Horatio had been sullenly silent. They'd fought wind and sea to bring up seven more ingots, but when Will shouted out, "It's time to go back," Horatio became belligerent again.

"I'm pulling up the barrel," Will said firmly.

"Then Oy'm diving for coins," Horatio said defiantly. He'd been leaning on a gunwale and suddenly took a backward summersault overboard. Soon he was popping up every twenty or thirty seconds to toss up another handful of gold pieces. By the time Will counted twenty of them strewn about the deck, he became even more impatient.

The next time Horatio's arm surfaced, he grabbed it by the wrist and shouted, "That's all, you greedy bastard. Swim down that anchor line and free us now or I'll leave you here for the sharks."

"Here, mate. Take this," were Horatio's only words. His other hand held a barnacle-encrusted metal box, about a foot square. After he had scrambled aboard, he stowed it under a bench and only glowered back when Will asked what it might be.

Horatio kept lookout on *Old Glory* as usual when Will walked down Front street to the Carolina Bank and Trust, its four Corinthian columns erected to humble all the shabby wooden storefronts on either side. Shortly after tying up, Will had picked the least encrusted coin from the day's catch and polished it as best he could with an old rag and lamp oil. But he could scarcely do as much for himself. Will looked every inch a wharf rat, and the smell of dried fish on his clothes would have made heads turn as he entered the oak-paneled lobby.

Except that it was nearly closing time and no one else was there. Inside the teller's cage an elderly man with mutton chops was peering down his spectacles as he counted bills. Will waited patiently until the man finished and looked up.

"Yes?" he said with a sniff.

"My name is Will, sir. I'm a fisherman. While we was draggin' the sea the other day, we found this," he said, sliding the coin across the marble countertop.

"I see. Old Spanish coin. We get 'em from time to time," said the teller without a trace of suspicion. He pulled out a small version of the scale used at the general store and placed some round brass weights on the side opposite the coin until the two sides balanced.

"That's about right," the teller said looking up. "You've got one and a quarter Troy ounces there."

"What's a Troy ounce?" Will asked.

"Well, don't ask me where Troy comes from, but it takes thirty-one of 'em to make a pound of gold. And the official government exchange rate for a Troy ounce is nineteen dollars and thirty-nine cents. Has been since as long as I've worked here. So the exchange rate on that coin is twenty-four dollars and twenty-three cents. The Carolina Bank can give you twenty even for it."

"I don't understand. You said it's worth...."

"Look around you, son," the old teller with a paternal smile. "How do you think we pay the upkeep on this place and pay to send that coin to the government? The difference is what you call margin."

"But it's very old," said Will. "Don't that make it worth more?"

"Maybe to a numismatic – a coin dealer. There's some in Charleston if you want to go there, but it's almost closing time here and you need to make up your mind."

Will kept his all-business expression as he turned to leave, but inside he was elated at getting twenty spendable U.S. dollars.

"Sir," he said, wheeling around and walking back to the teller's cage. "Just one more question, please. Another fisherman would like to sell me his boat. Could I get a loan to buy it with?"

"What's the price?" the old teller asked.

"Oh, around one hundred dollars."

"And your collateral? What would you put up as security?"

"Um, I don't really have all that much."

"Well, then, I don't think we could give you a loan."

The teller was closing his barred window when Will said: "But if I had this collateral – if I could show that I didn't need the loan – then I could get the loan?"

"Well, yes, if you put it that way."

"Thank you."

It was a lesson Will Gaskins would remember every day thereafter.

———

Westy had beamed when given ten dollars and Will now had eleven in his pocket. But as night fell on Diamond City, both beneficiaries of Blackbeard's bounty went about their chores in heavy silence. Horatio sat at the kitchen table, carefully chiseling off the barnacles that encrusted the small metal box that the sea had yielded up that day. Will, holding a lantern, was standing just inside the storage closet lining up the gold ingots on shelves and stacking the trove of coins. His tally came to thirty-two ingots and 122 coins. He shut the door and sat at the other end of the kitchen table with pencil and paper.

At last Will decided to interrupt the uneasy silence. "If those ingots are twenty pounds each – and I'm sure they are more than that – then we have over $130,000 between us. With the coins, maybe one-fifty."

Horatio kept chipping intently. The bottle of rum, still a quarter full, sat on a windowsill untouched. Will knew his mind was on more than chiseling.

"Got it!" Horatio exclaimed at last as the lid to the box popped open. Their eyes opened wide as out tumbled a jumble of entangled gold chains. Unlike the coins and ingots, they gleamed pure yellow gold because they'd been sealed off from the seawater. They sorted into three long, thickly braided chains, each with a locket at the end bearing the face of a saintly-looking lady.

"Aharr! Rosaries for a bishop or even a pope," Horatio bellowed in a voice befitting Blackbeard himself. "The church's treasure, fallen into the clutches o' the devil!

"They're mine you know," he added without looking up. "You'd already decided to pull up. Oy dove down with no divin' barrel, riskin' me life in them dark, dang'rous waters. Oy figger Oy'm entitled."

Something told Will to keep silent. His most pressing need now was to be rid of a pest who had changed overnight from friend to an unstable rival who might even turn treacherous.

Horatio finally broke the silence. "Awright, here's me plan," he said, with both hands still clutching the jewel box. "The next thing Oy do is paint me bars gray. Over at the store they said a packet boat leaves for Charleston tomorrow. Oy'll be there to catch it. If anyone asks about me baggage, Oy'll show them the 'lead' bars that Oy use in me profession. You see, Oy'm a highly skilled craftsman – art-tees-ee-an – a maker of stained glass windows for churches, and Oy needs a special kind of lead to seal me precious panes together. In fact, Oy am so valued that the Archbishop of Canterbury hisself gave me 'is personal rosary to see me safely on me journey."

Will almost laughed aloud as he recalled the same spontaneous imagination at work when he found the ragged refugee under his boat. He wanted to see what bluster would come next. "But how are you going to get all that gold down to the dock and into that packet ship?" he asked.

"That's why Oy bought me twine," said Horatio. "Oy lashes two bars on me back and Oy ties one to each leg inside me pants. Then Oy puts two in me satchel and walks on board."

"That's six of your sixteen," Will noted. "You'll be carryin' over a hundred pounds walkin' up that gangplank. What about the other two hundred pounds?"

Horatio paused and rubbed a hand through his curly bleached hair. "Kee-rect, guv'nor. Oy've been thinkin' about that, too. Oy need a good old travelin' trunk for everything else." He jerked his head toward the lone bedroom, where at the foot of the bed lay the steamer trunk that had once yielded up a collection of ladies' shoes. "That's what Oy need. That trunk over there would do fine."

"Yes, but it's mine, ain't it," Will said. He savored the thought that he'd wound up with the last card to play. "So it's all come down to a trunk, has it?"

In the end, Will got two of the gold chains, which were half his anyway, he reckoned. In turn, Horatio got the trunk and all but one of Will's eleven dollars so he could buy enough clothes at the general store to look more like a tradesman instead of a grubby stowaway. And Will would row him to the Beaufort wharf in *Old Glory*.

After a night when it was Will who slept with one eye open, they found themselves standing alongside the dagger-board schooner, *Agnes*, waiting for the deck hands to load the last of some pine lumber and head for Charleston.

Mostly they waited in awkward silence, with Will studying the shipping schedule posted on a wall. The only direct connections from Beaufort were to Newport News, Virginia, or Charleston and Georgetown, South Carolina. But from those ports one would have only ocean between him and places as far flung as New Orleans, Havana, Halifax and Liverpool.

"You never did say for sure where you were headed," Will ventured.

Horatio mulled the question, sweating uncomfortably in the new clothes that covered the weighty contraband lashed about his legs and torso. "Oy don't think Oy'm goin' to say," he answered at last. "You might decide to come after me." His eyes were fixed on the trunk stashed in the pile of luggage on deck.

"Not me," said Will. "I hope we never see each other again. If we do, it would probably be in jail."

They gave each other a perfunctory gentleman's bow and Will watched with curious amusement as Horatio shuffled stiffly up the gangplank, slightly bent with Blackbeard's burden.

It was over, and Will allowed himself a weary sigh of relief. It was now time to put his own plan into action.

———•———

Turns out, Will wouldn't have needed the trunk anyway. He'd already figured the odds at fifty-fifty that Horatio couldn't resist blurting out his secret in some ale house or lavishing coins on the first female to toss him a smile. If so, people would follow Horatio's trail back to Diamond City soon enough.

As soon as the ship pulled sway, Will strode to the general store and used his last dollar to buy a sharp new spade. Ordinarily he'd row across to Diamond City on the southern tip of Shackleford Banks. This time he cut east across the sound and continued up the back shore of the slender island until he could see only sand and scrub pine. Except for an occasional beach scavenger, the only living things on that stretch were sheep and wild ponies.

After beaching the flat-bottomed dory and walking into the woods with the shovel over his shoulder, Will spotted a patch of high ground and found himself in a sugar sand nook surrounded by scrub pine and thistle bushes. First he climbed a dozen feet up the tallest tree and double looped a piece of brown twine around the trunk that would be hard to spot unless one looked up for it. Then he took the shovel and dug in the afternoon heat until he had a square ditch about four feet deep.

After beaching *Old Glory* again at Diamond City, all was monotonous as ever on the pathway back to the cabin. Still too early for most boats to be back. Just the stay-behinds on a torpid June afternoon. Two women gathering dried wash from clothes lines. Dog chasing a chicken. Creaky old Robert, too old to fish anymore, disappearing behind his outhouse door. Fat old Thelma using her ample chest for a pillow as she snoozed in her front porch rocker. Flies buzzing on a pile of sheep scat. Things as usual. Nobody hardly even looking up as the richest man in these parts walks by.

Now you see me. Soon you won't.

———•———

Before long the sun was an orange ball that would sink into the sound in another hour. Will returned to his hole in the ground, *Old Glory* stacked with burlap-covered fish crates that contained all but two of his sixteen ingots and thirty of his fifty coins. He tied a rope to one of the heavy fish boxes, located the twine in the pine, and, like a muleteer, dragged the crate to the hole. The new shovel stood like a sentry in the adjacent dirt pile where he'd jabbed it.

The last thin layer of orange sky lined the horizon before Will had wrestled all of the crates into place. Then he swatted mosquitoes as he carefully covered up his treasure trove and swished away his tracks from the shore with a dead pine branch.

All during July Will went to sea with the recovering Westy, humbly thanking the old man for giving him such a fine job. But each day he would stop by the Beaufort town dock and memorize the shipping schedule and fares. By August, when Westy declared that fishing had "pretty much dried up" and he needed to keel haul his boat, he seemed relieved when Will announced that he "might take some time" to go visit a distant aunt. By then Will had saved enough for a fare to Charleston and a new pair of work shoes.

Then one morning he was gone. And just the way he'd planned, a poor work boy on a steamer-sailor to Charleston with a canvas satchel containing one shirt, some store-bought underwear and towel that wrapped two Spanish ingots worth more, he reckoned, than the boat swaying beneath his feet. And for survival money, twenty gold pieces were stuffed in his pockets, in his shoes and inside the crown of his wide-brimmed straw hat.

In Charleston, Will would learn a trade, then buy a business, then become a true gentleman with a fine home and family. That was the hazy vision in his mind, but his confidence began to buckle as soon as the ship disgorged its herd of passengers onto a wharf ten times the size of Beaufort's. Suddenly he was in the midst of thirty thousand souls who lived in the most important, sophisticated city on the southeastern seaboard.

Will found himself flushed onto King Street, where he shuffled along with his neck careening at the thicket of warehouses, taverns, livery stables and slave markets. He felt himself a stray dog on a street full of fast-moving carts, horses, carriages and people striding by as if he didn't exist. *Even slaves have people who would search for them if they disappeared.*

One storefront was suddenly compelling:

PHILIP H. KEGMAN
GOLD & SILVER
Bought and Sold
No. 225 King Street

Will entered with Spanish coin in hand, expecting the same routine transaction as the bank in Beaufort.

"Hmm, where did you get this?" said Philip H. Kegman himself from behind a counter displaying an array of rare coins.

"I won it in a bet with a friend," said Will according to plan.

Mr. Kegman, who never introduced himself, studied the doubloon with an eyepiece, then weighed it on the same type of scale Will had seen in Beaufort.

"Well, I suppose I could give you seventeen dollars for it," he said at last.

"Sir, I know it's worth twenty at least."

"Young fellow, I'm a coin dealer," he said sternly. "One must calculate a certain actuarial risk for the possibility that a, uh, your friend might have come upon the coin by nefarious means. And if you'll forgive me, I'm not acquainted with you either. You're from Charleston?"

"Um, no."

"Well there you have it." In the end Will took seventeen dollars in assorted U.S. coins and made straightaway up the street. It was now late afternoon and he hadn't yet searched for lodgings, but he had decided that to make proper acquaintances in such a large, prosperous city one could no longer look like a country clod from Diamond City.

Just up the street, Will read a sign in a storefront:

OFFERING A SPLENDID ASSORTMENT OF GOODS FOR GENTLEMEN.
Summer wear direct from New York
Cashmeres, Vigona tweeds, satin, worsted
Silk & cotton gloves & mitts from 12 cents to 50 cents.
Brown and bleached shirtings
Men's kip brogans, 75, 87 and $1.

FOULK AND JUDD
262 King Street.

Judging from the fine suits and top hats in the window, Foulk & Judd was clearly a gentlemen's shoppe as advertised. When Will ventured across the threshold, a smartly-dressed attendant looked up briefly from arranging cravats on a shelf and looked away.

Will approached him and unfurled seven Liberties in his palm. "Good sir, I have saved this money to buy a fine suit and would surely appreciate your help. You see, I'm courting and hope to be married."

The icy salesman's face melted into broad smiles. "And I shall endeavor to render my best assistance," he beamed. Indeed, when Will stood at a full-length mirror forty minutes later, he didn't recognize the ragtag wharf rat from Diamond City. From his crown down he now sported a black silk topper, a beige silk shirt, silk pongee scarf, and a blue velvet vest, all bound up in a burgundy frock coat of English wool trimmed with velvet and lined with silk. Below he wore machine-knitted silk pantaloons. He could not abide by the last fashion requirement – narrow, thin-soled gentlemen's shoes of calf's leather – but his pantaloons, when tucked inside his new boots from Beaufort implied that he might have come from riding about his plantation.

Will barely muffled a laugh when he gazed up and down the mirror, but the salesman assured him that his "lady" would surely succumb to the charms of so finely attired a beau.

"I'm in need of lodging for the night until I'm situated," Will added upon leaving. "Can you recommend something?"

"Indeed. A gentleman of your station would enjoy the Plantation House two blocks up. Fine dining as well."

As the newly-christened gentleman advanced up King Street, two equally attired older men nodded his way respectfully and he enjoyed returning the salute. His self-esteem now in full bloom, Will couldn't resist entering the shop of a second rare coin dealer on King Street.

"A family heirloom, I presume," said the dealer after they exchanged bows and greetings.

"You guessed correctly," said Will with a crooked smile. With no further questions, he emerged with twenty two dollars, which he considered a profit on his investment in Foulk & Judd's "Splendid Assortment of Goods for Gentlemen."

In fact, Will Gaston was now feeling refreshingly jaunty – even when the desk clerk at the Plantation House said that his room would cost three dollars. He was so enamored with his new demeanor that he decided to treat himself to a fine meal in the dining room just off the lobby. Everything there was a first experience. The Diamond City lad had never leaned upon a linen tablecloth, had never been fussed over by a uniformed waiter, had never seen so many spoons and forks on one setting and had never ordered a tankard of ale until he decided that it was high time to do so.

Because most everything on the menu was in French or fancy English, Will ordered all-too-familiar fried oysters, trying to forget that oysters brought a penny a pound in Beaufort. He had just taken his first timid sip of Irish ale when a man wearing a plain brown cloak stood over his table with an outstretched hand. "Good evening, sir," he said effusively. "Mind if I join you at your table? It gets lonely traveling alone and I thought you might be in a similar way." With that he pulled out a chair and sat down, crooking his finger for the waiter.

"The name is Geoffrey and I'm here on a trip from Savannah. And you, sir?"

"Name's Will, from up around Beaufort, North Carolina."

"What do you do there? On a holiday? Staying here long?"

These and other questions continued to come faster than Will could assemble answers – almost too penetrating for a fellow just trying to pass the time of day. Besides, the beefy, red-faced, supposed gentleman opposite him looked more like a salesman or store clerk with his deerskin cloak and cotton pantaloons. Thus, a cautious Will offered only that his family owned a fleet of fishing boats. Then he decided that the time could better be passed interrogating the other fellow.

"Tell me about Savannah," he said. "I've always wanted to visit there." He knew nothing about Savannah.

"Well, it's a lot smaller than this. Maybe seven thousand people, growing just as much as Charleston. Of course there's been a lot of catching up to do after the fire."

"How much catching up?" Will asked, trying not to reveal his ignorance about a fire.

"I suppose it's been ten years now," his new companion said, buttering a piece of Will's table bread. "Over four hundred buildings destroyed. Two-thirds of all the people left homeless. But in a way it's been like one of those scrub fires. The dry brush gets burned out and new growth comes in. Same with Savannah. It needed people to rebuild and pretty soon it was getting boatloads of Irish and German carpenters, Jewish bankers, all people trying to make a fresh start in a new country."

"And what do you do there?" Will asked.

Geoffrey chewed on more buttered bread. "Did you know we're going to build a railroad to Savannah? They say you'll see a lot more cotton headed to the port there instead of Charleston."

"But what do you do there?"

Will never got an answer. They traded other banalities through dinner until Geoffrey excused himself and walked into the hotel lobby. He never returned, and when the bill of fare arrived, Will paid it while the waiter hovered above him, no doubt fearful that this young man would also bolt.

Will arose and walked into the lobby, about to head to his room when two large men in leather easy chairs suddenly rose from reading newspapers and crowded him so tightly that he could smell their tobacco-stained clothes. One said in hushed tones: "We are from the Charleston City Guard office and ask that you come with us for a visit. If you don't, things could get ugly."

As Will jostled along in a hansom cab seated between his two captors, the sun had long set and the only illumination on a moonless night came from the flickering lamp lights. In a few blocks they dismounted in front of a dingy stone building. Two torches burned dimly on either side of an open door and above it was a hand-lettered sign, Charleston City Guard.

In better days the building might have been a store or tavern. The two men pointed Will to a door to the left, then sprawled on a shabby settee in what served as a lobby. Will found himself in what might once have been a stone-walled storeroom, only in this case containing a brown pine desk stained by the rings of many coffee mugs. Behind the desk was a squat, bearded man, his forehead beaded with sweat in the airless heat.

Will still hadn't had time to collect himself, to devise a plan for a kidnapping. "Who are you?" he asked, trying to mask his fright with indignation.

"You are a guest of the City Guard, until recently known as the City Watch," and it is our job to keep peace and order and to prevent crime in this city," said the squat man as if he were born to play such a scene. "This is why we have brought you here. Tell us about your Spanish gold."

Will froze with fear. "Spanish gold?"

The bearded man slapped a gold coin on the desktop and stared silently. "Why? Is it a crime to own a gold coin?"

"It may be. Several coins just like this turned up around town a month or so ago. Were you here then? Are you in the smuggling business? Today you told a dealer you won it from a friend on a bet. From whom? We need to confirm it with this friend."

"It was back in Beaufort where I'm from," stammered Will. "Does a gold dealer work for your Charleston City Guard?"

"No, but we stay in close touch. They come in contact with many people like you." With that he produced a second coin. "Now you go to a second dealer and say your coin is a 'family heirloom.' I'd say you are fast sinking into quicksand here."

Will's mind raced lest his new life be over before it began. He forced himself to become calmer, less combative. "Wa'll, sir," he drawled, "you see over in Beaufort we've had two, three big treasure ships sink offshore over the centuries. One o' them was Blackbeard the pirate's. So, you see, coins like this wash up on the beach all the time. One of my friends has three, and that's who I got that coin from. Won it on a bet when we were racing our sharpies one Sunday afternoon."

Will felt he'd begun to turn the tide in his favor. Just then his heart sank as the brown-suited Geoffrey suddenly reappeared in the stuffy interrogation room. Without looking at Will, he held up Will's straw hat proudly. "Well, Capt'n, I made a search of the room," he proclaimed. "See this here hat? Here's what I found in the band." He plucked four gold coins from inside the broad hatband and spilled them on the table.

The bearded captain simply stared across at Will. "More bets?" he said. "Stand up, my good fellow, while we search some more. Now empty your pockets. And your fancy vest pockets, too."

Again, Will felt both relief and fear. The two ingots had eluded Geoffrey in his room search. These and the waist pouch with a dozen more coins Will had stashed atop a sturdy cornice valance above the tall drapes in his hotel room. He still had hope.

And his indignation was rising again. "Sir, please tell me why it's a crime to own some gold coins," he nearly shouted. "I've done no crime. I'll wager that many merchants have gold saved up all over this town. Is it only visitors you rob?"

The bearded one rose and left with beefy Geoffrey, who continued to look away from his glare.

"And visitors you also steal food from at the dinner table?" Will shouted after them.

He waited alone in his hard wooden chair. The only sounds came from Geoffrey and the bearded captain in hushed debate and an occasional ping as one of the two loungers hacked and hit the spittoon near his feet.

The captain re-appeared and sat solemnly at his sordid desk. "The Guard has decided that you can be released on three conditions," he announced. "The first is that you leave behind these six Spanish gold pieces as evidence in the case under investigation."

He looked at Will for a sign of resistance. He got none.

"The second is that you attempt to exchange no more such coins. And the third is that you depart Charleston, South Carolina within twenty four hours."

"Where should I go?" Will asked lamely.

"Anywhere you wish besides Charleston, South Carolina."

Will knew he'd been swindled and robbed just as surely as Blackbeard would loot a ship and send its captain off on a longboat as a gesture of "mercy."

At the very least he could become an irritation. "Do you have some papers you want me to sign?" he asked.

"No. No papers."

"Well then, I would appreciate your giving me a receipt that says my six Spanish gold pieces are being held for an investigation."

The captain grunted, then disappeared for another two minutes. He returned with a small folded white sheet. "Here you are. Now you better start walkin.'"

"Oh no," Will answered. "I'm going to wait under the street light outside your building until I find a carriage to my hotel. You never know what criminals are out there in the territory of the Charleston City Guard."

Later, as the cab wobbled over the cobblestones, Will remembered the folded slip of paper he'd stuffed into his pocket. It had no name, no date, only the following in scrawled pencil:

Recvd six Sp g p on this nite.

The clerk who checked Will out of The Plantation House the next morning seemed puzzled. "We registered you last night?" he asked. The youth standing before him wore a broad straw hat and plain cotton shirt. He held a large sailcloth satchel in one hand and an expensive silk top hat in the other.

Will headed straight for South Wharf, twirling the topper rhythmically around his wrist as he whistled in the clear morning air. Along the way he encountered an old slave sweeping the stoop of a row house. "Here, my good fellow," he said merrily. "Wear this and you'll look like a million dollars!"

The old man held up both hands. "Oh, nawsuh," he said backing up. "Thankee suh, but my massa gwine gimme a whuppin' he see me in dat."

I already got a whuppin' in that hat, Will thought.

Next he saw two schoolboys approaching with books in hand. "Here, this is for you," he said to the nearest one and plopped the hat over his ears before he could react. As Will quickened his pace, he looked back over his shoulder and saw both boys already having a tug of war.

Soon he was at Smith's Wharf, the port for mostly short hauls. He scanned the daily *Ship News*, which was posted on the door of a warehouse. A dozen ships would leave that day. Will was determined to pick the one with the destination closest to Shackleford Banks, which he hoped to revisit soon enough. Only one sailing filled the bill: the two-master sloop *Montgomery*, departing for Savannah, Georgia on what was posted as an eight-hour journey.

After five hours of open sea, the ship passed the venerable Tybee Island Light Station and entered the South Channel of the Savannah River with sixteen miles still between it and the city. At first Tybee Island looked like a copy of Shackleford Banks, a low-lying, windswept scrubland. But soon the riverbanks became covered with pine and cypress. Here and there were wooden boats of oystermen and crabbers. In five or so miles the landscape was broken by small farms growing rice, indigo, and corn. Then, a corn mill, a sawmill and a passing paddlewheeler stacked with lumber. All were invariably with decks and docks occupied by black men in varying states of lifting and lading.

Before Will got his first glimpse of Savannah, he saw wisps of black smoke rising above the tree line and drifting gently towards them. "I hope that's not another fire of 1820," he said aloud, remembering the blaze that had destroyed two-thirds of the city.

"No, but could've been," said a deckhand about the same age. "That one you're lookin' at over there happened about a week ago. Steamboat named the *Thomas Jefferson* got too hot and blew up right at the wharf. Bunch of cotton bales were stacked on the wharf and it spread from there. Two or three big warehouses got burned out. Would've taken the Cotton Exchange building right along with it, but thank the Lord, they learned a few lessons from the Big Fire. Savannah got itself a volunteer fire brigade and they snapped themselves into place right quick. That smoke over there is just what's still burnin' itself out. Steamboat's still on the bottom."

Will saw for himself soon enough as the schooner glided past the large, stone Cotton Exchange building, the steamboat's smokestacks sticking out of the water like tombstones of the dead crew below. He'd already concluded that Savannah was about one-fourth the size of Charleston, but as he allowed himself a leisurely stroll down Bay Street and over to Oglethorpe Street, he liked what he saw. Buildings were newer than in Charleston and the Big Fire had no doubt allowed the city fathers to clear away tired, blighted areas and replace them with pretty squares of dogwoods, tall oaks, benches and bandstands.

A fancy hotel was no longer in Will's plan. He returned to Bay Street where the wharfs petered out and soon found himself walking up the porch of a red brick house with a ROOM TO LET sign in the window. The proprietress, a plump widow who introduced herself only as Mrs. Talley, charged four dollars a week for a second story room overlooking the alley and outhouse. But it included breakfast and dinner except on Sundays, when Mrs. Talley prayed in church, sang in church and went to the Sunday church supper. Compared to the three dollars charged by The Plantation House for one night, it was just the place for a lad from Shackleford Banks.

But best of all, the common meal table was a place where Will could ask questions about Savannah and launch a new stratagem. His tablemates were three, all in the middle of their bacon, eggs and fried oysters when Will sat down to his first breakfast on a Tuesday morning. They quickly introduced themselves as Tom, Silas and Murphy, then continued chewing in silence. Will had nearly concluded that each had said all there was to say to one another long ago when Tom piped up and said "Will. Well, Will *what*?"

An embarrassing question. Actually, when Will had been sailing by Tybee Island the day before, he'd thought about celebrating his new life with a new name and wondered if Horatio had picked a new one as well. At first he was inclined to pilfer the name Teach in subtle respect to his likely benefactor, Blackbeard the buccaneer. But that was asking for trouble. He'd mused about Beach to remind him of where he'd stowed the gold. So when the question came:

"Beach," he answered. "William Beach." *The die is cast.*

At that they began to pump Will like a well handle as he tried to accommodate Mrs. Talley's generous breakfast. He answered patiently that he was from "the North Carolina seacoast," owned a small fishing fleet with his father and was in Savannah to scout for a new fishing boat. Or maybe they'd start an altogether new business, he added. "What, in your opinion, is the best type of business in Savannah?"

The question ignited a spirited discussion. Tom, it was quickly revealed, was Tom Trowbridge, an eager-to-please young man from London who called on stores in the American South to sell them British-made ladies' apparel. Twenty years older than Will was Silas Wentworth, a taciturn New Englander who worked for the new railroad abuilding on Savannah's outskirts. His job was to "obtain men and materials," he said vaguely.

The oldest by yet another ten years was Murphy, who no one called by his first name of Jehoshaphat. Murphy, a gray-faced clerk at the South Wharf shipping office, seemed to have lodged with Mrs. Talley for many years as others came and went.

"Everyone today would say cotton," ventured Tom the traveling salesman. "But for how long is anyone's guess. The new Tariff Act might just send blokes like me packing for home again. I don't know what's gotten into your Congress. They exempt American textile manufacturers from all duties and then put a sixty-two per cent tariff on just about everything English."

"Perhaps our Congress still remembers fifty years ago when a certain kingdom taxed their colonies on everything arriving from the mother country," said Silas the railroad man while reaching for the rack of toast.

Will thought of ways to disguise his ignorance. "Well," he said, "when you're in the fishing business you're only concerned with getting your catch to market before it spoils. Why is this tariff act so important?"

"Because it hurts Savannah and the whole South," responded Tom. "Congress may think it's protecting northern manufacturers from cheap British imports, but if companies like mine can't sell their goods, then they can't afford to buy cotton from the plantations around here. And then the plantations can't afford to buy machinery and all the other things they don't make here. It's a vicious cycle and that's why it's called the Tariff of Abominations."

"So," added Tom, "if you're looking for a ship to buy, I'd boldly urge you to forego fishing and buy a steamer that will ship cotton to other places in Europe besides England."

"Piffle," mumbled Silas the railroad man, smearing jam on his toast. "You're missing the big picture. Soon Savannah will have a railroad. The railroad will have links to all of Georgia and then to the entire north. Cotton will ship faster and cheaper. But so will rice, silk, corn and other crops that aren't even grown yet. You'll be able to have textile plants here in the south and ship clothing north. You'll see."

Now it was Murphy, the shipping clerk who spoke up. "I cannot speculate on the effects of a railroad," he said, "but if you're asking what makes money, it's factoring, my boy. Buying, selling, lending, taking a commission on everything that moves, be it British or American. It doesn't matter if it's cotton or rice or gum balls, it's the middleman who always takes his cut no matter where the goods are coming or going."

With that, Murphy, his short sermon concluded, struck a match to a cigar, leaned back, and exhaled a cloud that hung over the breakfast table.

"Which is the biggest company at this factoring?" Will asked.

Murphy: "That would probably be Savannah Cotton Merchants. They might even get bigger after the fire."

Will: "Why?"

Murphy: "Well, it's near wiped out their competition."

Will: "Which ones?"

Murphy: "Well, the one I feel sorry for is Huxley, Charles Huxley. His warehouse was closest to that steamer and it was his bales caught the blast when the steamboat exploded. Now his warehouse is pretty near gutted. I think he's rented a little office at the Cotton Exchange. But what he's goin' to do with all those colored he had working the docks, I don't know. Gotta feed 'em, you know. Must be fifteen."

"Sixteen, to be exact," piped up Silas the railroader. "Part of my job is to get work gangs to lay track. I've already talked to Huxley about contracting out all of his coloreds for as long as it takes. We're still working out details."

"What kind of man is he?" asked Will.

"Kind of man?" Silas scratched his Yankee lantern jaw. "Oh, right proper and courtly enough, but seems sort of quiet, like lost in thought. 'Course he's got a lot to think about."

After breakfast the roomers went their separate ways and Will sat silently in Mrs. Talley's front porch rocker. By ten he had formed his plan. Soon he was in the busy Cotton Exchange mingling among the clusters of men shouting numbers and holding up fingers. Darting in and out among them were boys, most younger than Will, who appeared to be delivering messages from one trader to another.

Pointed out amidst the hubbub was Charles W. Huxley, attired in an informal buff linen suit, but still exuding elegance with a black silk vest and top hat. Short of stature and a trifle stout, his close-cropped gray beard and blue eyes painted him as a man not to let setbacks erode his kind and courtly disposition..

That day and the next, Will, the distant observer, had established Mr. Huxley's daily pattern: a walk from his handsome front porch, a stroll through one of the squares on Oglethorpe to the Cotton Exchange, a busy two hours of trading, lunch (preceded by just one whiskey) at an eatery frequented by other merchants, a walk along the docks to stand and brood inside the charred walls of his warehouse, back at his small office at the Exchange for tidying up and bookwork, and a stroll home across another of Savannah's twenty public squares.

Four o'clock was quiet time, Will deduced.

Charles W. Huxley sat at his temporary roll-top desk, face to the wall, fixed on a long sheet of paper with rows of fine print. He heard feet shuffle and looked up to see a youth of not yet twenty standing erect, dressed in tradesman's colorless cotton. In one hand was a satchel, apparently heavy.

The lad cleared his throat. "Excuse me, Mr. Huxley, but I would like – hope to – have you take me into your firm."

Huxley was annoyed but aimed to be pleasant long enough to turn the lad on his heels and exit. "I have no warehouse work," he said evenly. "In fact, I have no warehouse at all. If you're looking for work as a runner..."

"No," interrupted the youth. "My name is William Beach and I would like to invest in your business."

"Young fellow, who sent you here?" said Huxley, warily. Could someone be playing a cruel practical joke?

Will: "Sir, I have come into some money. I am aware of the fire and your misfortune. I am prepared to invest it in your business in exchange for your teaching me how to become a cotton factor, a merchant like yourself."

Huxley began to rise from his seat, but the youth's next words sat him down again. "You see, when fishing near my home in North Carolina, I discovered a Spanish treasure." He reached into his pocket and produced two Spanish gold pieces and placed them on Huxley's desk. "I can't better my station by buying more fish pots and nets."

Huxley seemed to admire the coins without touching them but said: "I can't teach you a lifetime's lessons for two coins. And my situation is beyond two coins."

"Well, thank you sir," said the youth. "But, you see, there's more to it than two coins." He put the satchel on the ground and lifted out a gold ingot. "This bar weighs over twenty pounds," he said to the open-mouthed Huxley. "When I was in North Carolina I was told that gold was worth $19.37 a Troy ounce. I don't know anything about Troy ounces, which is why I have come to a man of your experience."

Huxley rose, still outwardly impassive. He lifted up the ingot and walked to a table with a larger scale used to weigh cotton samples. "See here? This reads twenty-four pounds, ten ounces," Huxley said. He strode back to his desk and added quickly on paper. "I don't trade in gold, but this bar, which is called bullion, should be worth about $14,400 if I walked it into the U.S. Treasury Department and asked to trade it for dollars."

Horatio and I had been short by half with our clumsy arithmetic. "Sir, you do numbers so quickly," Will said. "I'm just a poor fisher boy who would like to learn a skill like that."

Huxley watched wide-eyed as the young man lifted his shirt, revealing his bare chest with a bow of Horatio's twine tied around his ribs. Will held one hand behind his back, unloosed the twine bow, and showed Huxley another gold ingot.

"Mr. Huxley," he said with a smile, "I have fourteen more of these hidden in a secret place in North Carolina. Can you please figger up the value for me?"

Huxley, stunned and stupefied, pivoted back to his pen and paper. "I come up with just over $230,000," he said.

They both sat in silence while Huxley tried to decide whether the youth in front of him was a poor fisher boy or a guardian angel in disguise.

"Oh yes, I'll teach you," Huxley said at last. "And one day when you've learned it all, your name will be on the best and biggest warehouse in Savannah."

Within a few days, Will, Huxley and the latter's long-time manservant journeyed to Beaufort, checked into a hotel as gentlemen, snuck out before dawn in fisherman's cotton, rowed to Shackleford Bank, found the fish boxes exactly where Will had buried them, placed them in a fancy steamer trunk and sailed back to Savannah.

Huxley deposited the gold with Savannah's largest bank with one condition: that his firm could borrow up to the value of the gold collateral. And so, for over thirty years, Huxley and Co. rebuilt a warehouse and bought two trading ships with other people's money without ever touching his gold. And shortly after the name Huxley and Beach had been engraved over the new warehouse entrance, Will would be inveigled to rescue his senior partner's endomorphic eldest daughter from a future of certain spinsterhood.

But by then, Will Beach had come to understand the term *quid pro quo*.

Chapter Four
SAVANNAH, JANUARY 1864

My homespun dress is plain, I know
My hat's palmetto, too.

But then it shows what Southern girls
For Southern rights will do.

We send the bravest of our land
To battle with the foe.

And we'll lend a helping hand,
We love the South, you know.

[Refrain]
Hurrah! Hurrah!
For the sunny South, so dear.
Three cheers for the homespun dress
That Southern ladies wear. [Repeat]

As the defiant resistance of 1863 gave way to a winter of shambles on the front lines and shortages at home, *The Homemade Dress* became the day's most popular ballad because it symbolized the spirit of coping, yet hoping, that filled Savannah. But within the Beach household, any expressions of optimism were but passing flickers of sunlight among the gray clouds that loomed over William Beach.

Often he picked at his dinner while seemingly lost in thought. But all knew that chief among his worries was the delayed arrival of the new blockade runner in which he was heavily invested. The first disappointing letter had announced that the ship had been delayed a month in sailing from the shipyard in Liverpool. A second letter, delivered by another blockade runner from Nassau, stated all too briefly that the ship had snapped a mast crossing the Atlantic in a winter gale. Repairs were underway in Nassau, but sailing couldn't commence in any case until the port could replace the piles of anthracite coal that the storm had blown into the Bahamas channel. Meanwhile, word had circulated on the Savannah docks that the Yankees had added a third gunboat to the blockading fleet that prowled around the mouth of the Savannah River. Beach speculated that it would probably mean further delays until the ship could sneak past its foes on a new moon. Amelia had given up on asking when their next "talk" would take place because the answer was always "Not yet, but always be ready to leave on short notice."

To Amelia, "being ready" included knowing more about the War if Northern Aggression, so when Daddy Beach was away she would slip into his study and pour over the newspapers from the stack on his desk corner. Front page news centered on the recent Impressment Act of the Confederate Congress giving the secretary of war the right to seize private property anytime, anywhere, for military needs. Other articles reported debates in Congress over a bill to outlaw "speculation." Editorials warned against the evils of hoarding, citing egregious examples, to wit: the hardware store owner who, learning that his town was in the Yankee warpath, bought up all the plate glass for miles around. Sure enough, when the aftershock of artillery shelling shattered windows throughout the town, he cleaned up by selling his hoard at three times the usual rate.

Advertisements also provided useful barometers of the times. Because inflation was soaring, merchants were turning to barter. Thus, one could track the value of everyday necessities through ads in the *Savannah Republican*. A salt supplier, for example, offered four bushels of salt for five bushels of corn or peas; one bushel for five pounds of lard; two bushels for seven pounds of sugar; two bushels for one pair of shoes.

Supply scarcities were even hurting newspapers themselves. Those on William Beach's desk were slimmer and smaller, and their ink was quick to stain the hands. The reason, Amelia learned from an editorial, "We Appeal to our Readers," was that, while the South had several paper factories, the owners couldn't obtain the necessary rags, chemicals, machines and type to maintain production. Unless readers donated more rags in the name of a free press, the editorial warned, newspapers would be forced to print on such experimental materials as straw, pulverized corn husks and sunflower stalks.

Meanwhile, the demands on a Southern woman were never greater. Routine supplies that once attracted scant attention now became bedeviling. Coffee became the coin of the realm: something to barter and hoard in each household regardless of editorials preaching selfless patriotism. Knitting needles and corset stays were now fashioned from wood instead of whalebone. Increasingly, women went into their gardens or into the woods to get dyes for their homespun clothes – indigo for purple, cocklebur leaves for yellow and myrtle bush for Confederate gray. And during all the consternation, properly patriotic women were expected to be seen knitting socks for soldiers, sending food and meeting troop trains with coffee and snacks.

William Beach was not always silent and sullen at family meals. Every so often he would feel a need to take the pulse of female gossip and opinion as part of deciding what goods to order and ship. For instance, during an idle chat with a fellow trader on the Cotton Exchange he had mentioned how the ladies in his family were complaining about the lack of whalebone stays for corsets and hoop skirts. The friend happened to be leaving on a ship for Scotland the next day. When he arrived at Glasgow, the friend startled a local manufacturer by ordering a thousand whalebone stays. He was equally surprised when he sold all of them quickly back home for a profit of a thousand per cent.

One evening in January Daddy Beach looked up from his dessert of cherries jubilee with an engaging smile. "Let me ask you about shortages," he said. "As you have seen, we have none in this house. We've just enjoyed a pork roll, a fine Madeira, and now we're about to have our coffee as usual. But I daresay we are hardly typical because we can afford what the blockade runners bring in. What are you hearing in the shops around town?"

With that his wife and two daughters chirped in with pent-up complaints, almost as if the questioner possessed the power to redress them.

Mother Beach: "Oh, the destitution of manners in shops is appalling! Why, just yesterday I stood at the counter of a yard stick salesman when a woman came in and meekly asked for a skein of silk. The man actually sneered at her saying that he would only sell the entire bolt for a hundred dollars."

Amelia: "It's true. Last week I was with my friend Dorothy and her mother in Johnston's Mercantile and I heard the proprietor tell them that the price of all piece goods is going to go sky high and that they should buy a year's supply now if they could."

Mother Beach: "You know my friend Mrs. Beasley down the street. Her sister has a big plantation out on Macon Road. She visited out there a couple of weeks ago and told me they had brought in an astonishing amount of goods by the wagonload. She said the lawn looked like a wharf with a ship about to be loaded. I remember her saying she counted thirty barrels of dried fish, three hogsheads of molasses and all sorts of containers of sugar and coffee."

Lucy: "My friend Jocelyn… her mother has a friend down in Louisiana who had a bonnet she paid five hundred dollars for. She traded it for five turkeys."

"Well, anyone who paid five hundred for a bonnet deserves to be plucked like a turkey," interrupted Daddy Beach. "Inflation hasn't reached a hundred dollars a turkey – yet."

The conversation was veering off the path he'd intended. "I daresay some of these stories tend to smother the truth under layers of exaggeration that get piled on top with each re-telling," he mused while stirring sugar into his coffee. "What about specific goods? Which shortages are most acute?"

The question ignited another flurry of competing claims – coffee, flour, sugar, corset stays – until Mother Beach out-shouted her daughters by declaring: "Shoes!"

"Shoes?" said Lucy in a mocking tone. "Why, I have twenty, thirty pair."

"Of course you do, precious," answered her mother. "But your father asked about shortages among ordinary people. I hear of some folks folding up newspapers and using them for soles. I hear cobblers are now using mule hides for leather soles – even goat, sheep and dog skins. I hear tell that you 'd better not leave your horse tethered outside a store anymore because the saddle might be gone when you come out. Will, what happened to the Southern factories that used to make shoes?"

"The buildings are still there," he answered. "I know of one upstate that has just started to turn out shoes with leather uppers and wooden soles. But the rest of them can't get materials such as tacks and the chemicals that go into the tanning of hides."

"You know what I'm really concerned about?" his wife said. She glanced towards the end of the dining room where a gray-haired colored man stood quietly with a towel over one arm. "Andrew, that will be all for now, thank you," she said with a flick of the wrist.

"What worries me is shoes for the coloreds," she continued in hushed tones. "We can wear old ones until the war's done with, but they have one, two pair at the most. You don't want your coloreds walking around barefoot, do you, Will? And what about your warehouse boys? You don't want people to start whispering that the Beaches are in straits."

Sarah Beach had begun to seize the family podium as she often did after her third glass of wine. "I fear we're becoming a nation of Robinson Crusoes," she lamented. "Why can't these blockade runners bring in the little things that make life livable?"

"You've already answered your own question," said her husband. "Most of the cargoes are strictly for military – guns, uniforms and the like. When you speak of 'little things' for common homes, you must understand that the incentive for ship owners taking all those risks is to sell high-profit goods like liquor and medicines. Now quinine is a 'little item,' but it's so desperately needed for malaria that it's fetching almost as much per ounce as silver."

But Will Beach had said much of that before. Where he really wanted the conversation to lead was to the subject of shortages and appearances. "While we're on the subject of war shortages, there is something I would like to emphasize to all three of you," he said with careful deliberation. "At this very critical time, when public sensitivity is very high, the Beach family must be seen as supporting the war effort by not shopping excessively or hoarding.

"Or profiteering," he added. *How ironic that I am preaching this at a time when inflation is pushing up my trading profits higher than ever. But all the more reason to restrain appearances.*

Amelia made a stab at displaying her new interest in current events. "Recently I read an editorial in the *Republican* saying that the blockade is probably all for the best – perhaps God's way of teaching the extravagant lessons they need to learn," she said.

"That's the kind of thing I'm getting at," said Daddy Beach.

Mother Beach again: "I don't see how looking our best is any less patriotic. Indeed, I believe it tells the Yankee that we are proud – defiant – and that this cruel blockade is an exercise in futility. In the Old Testament," she said after another sip of Madeira, "there was a battle where the Canaanites surrounded a Jewish fortress. After a few weeks, the Jews were nearly out of water. But in an act of defiance, they washed their clothes with what was left. Then they hung the wet clothes from the ramparts so the Canaanites would believe they had plenty of water and give up the siege."

Lucy: "There's a beautiful yellow bonnet in the window at Johnston's. If we are so prosperous – well provisioned – why can't you buy it for me?"

Beach: "Because I forbid it. And your Jews were stupid."

At noon on January 16, 1864, Amelia returned home hungry after a tiring all-morning class at church on how to use looms to make sweaters for soldiers. As she entered the front hallway, she stopped, startled to hear her mother's loud voice from inside the adjoining study. The voice would rise, then subside, like gusts of wind in a storm. Then would come the muffled steady tones of her father. It was unusual enough that Daddy Beach was home at noon.

Amelia went to the dining room and sat fidgeting at a table set for three. Lucy was gone for riding lesson. Andrew stood nearby, also enduring the silence. When the old servant raised his palms upward with a quizzical look, Amelia excused herself, walked to the study door, and knocked softly.

The door opened slowly. Her father, a grave expression on his face, seemed to be blocking her entry. Amelia glimpsed her mother, seated at one of the fireplace chairs, dabbing a handkerchief at her puffy face.

"Andrew wants to know if you'll both be having lunch," Amelia said timidly.

"We'll be along in a moment," her father answered.

"No, let her in," said Sarah Beach, looking up and revealing reddened eyes. "I want her to hear this." She jerked her head towards her husband.

William Beach admitted his daughter with a shrug, walked to his desk, picked up two envelopes, then stood erect at the fireplace mantle as if trying to assemble his thoughts. "The first one here is from the War Department," he said, holding up a single sheet of paper. "It informs Mr. and Mrs. Beach that their son Joseph is a prisoner in the Union detention facility at Fort Delaware, Delaware City, Delaware. It promises to 'make every effort to secure his release', whatever that may mean. And that's really all there is to the letter."

The shock left Amelia's brain numb. Her first thought was trivial. *Would*

Joseph receive a warm sweater if I sent it there?

"There's nothing we can do," wailed Sarah Beach, beginning to sob again. "My boy...I'll never see him again."

"Sarah!" He cut her off. "He's not *dead*. It might even be a good thing in the long run. If he'd gone off to some other battle, he might have been killed or wounded."

"And now you take my second child!" his wife shot back in anger.

"What's *that* about?" Amelia stared at her father, who was clearly uncomfortable.

"A second letter arrived today on the *Rover* by way of Nassau," he said. "It's from the captain of the *Sea Breeze*, which is what we named our new ship. He said that repairs have been completed and that he hoped to sail for Savannah on the fifth of February. If so, it would put him here on the night of the seventh, which would coincide with the new moon. I have told your mother about your plans to sail for Nassau..."

"Which I heard about only this morning," Sarah Beach hissed through clenched teeth.

"I told her of the importance of having a family member accompany the gold to cover our investment..."

"Gold!" She spat the word out like a piece of wormy fruit. "You're trading my daughter's life for gold?"

"It's not forever, damn it. She'll be back in..."

"Don't raise your voice to *me*," his wife interrupted in a louder voice. "You're showing that your buying and selling comes before your family."

William Beach returned the fire. "Did it ever occur to you, woman, that it is gold that might deliver your son – my son, too, I might add – from his prison?"

He looked sideways at Amelia, still standing, whose open mouth showed that she had never heard her genteel parents in bitter combat. "I told her that I would gladly go myself were it not for another situation that has arisen. It's very complicated and my wife doesn't have the patience to listen, so I'll try to explain to you, Amelia. You see, some officials from the War Department are coming to see me in a few days and I must be here to meet them. They want me to represent them..."

"I don't want to hear about it again," Sarah Beach scowled with a vigorous wave of her hands. "If you let her go, I will consider her missing in war just like Joseph. And I'll not speak to you until her return – or ever again if she doesn't. And you, Amelia, put too cheap a price on your life."

As his wife began to open the door, William Beach put his large hand firmly on her forearm. "Now I'll be the one to make threats," he said with burning eyes. "You will be as silent as a Benedictine nun, because your speaking to anyone – *anyone* – about this matter could be treasonous in the eyes of the War Department and ruinous to your family."

When Amelia and her father finally sat down to lunch they were told by Andrew that Mrs. Beach was taking her meal in her sitting room. They took their beef consommé, finger sandwiches and iced tea in silence. Amelia's mind wandered off to Joseph again. She knew of only one photograph of him as a grown-up – one that sat atop the grand piano showing a smiling soldier resplendent in his officer's uniform. *Is this all he has to wear right now – after so many months? Could Daddy actually buy his freedom?* She started to speak, but her father put his finger to his lips after a glance at Andrew standing like a statue beside the kitchen door.

"You never know," he whispered.

Amelia and her father emerged from the dining room just as a clerk from his warehouse office was climbing the porch steps with a leather satchel in one hand. Beach motioned her into his study, and she could see him out the large window signing several papers and then dismissing his assistant.

Back in the study, Beach pulled one of the fireside chairs to his desk and seated Amelia before facing her across the desk. Suddenly she felt more like a buyer or seller than a daughter. Daddy Beach was still tense but tried to smile. "I know it's been a while since I promised you a second talk," he began, "but now I feel in a rush to do so. And I regret that it comes so soon after that bit of ugliness, but the correspondence you just saw me receive was evidence that we both need to be ready for that trip."

"I'm sorry that you two are at odds. I'll try to talk to Mother," Amelia said, hoping to put her father at ease.

"I'm going to start by asking you the same question I did before Christmas," he said, "but first I want to lay out some additional facts. I want to explain to you the situation that your mother said she didn't want to hear any more about. The War Department has convinced itself that when it announces a requisition – an intent to buy goods such as blankets and rifles

– suppliers jack up the price. They think the government has a bottomless treasure chest, which, of course, it isn't.

"Anyway, Amie, I think the government's concerns are justified. The same thing happens with regard to goods arriving on the blockade runners. And as shortages become more acute, the blockade runners bring in an ever-greater portion of all items the War Department buys."

He paused. "Are you getting this, Amie? Your mother doesn't seem to."

She nodded. "I'm smarter than you think, Daddy."

"Good," he said. "The War Department has contacted Huxley and Beach because it thinks we are perhaps the largest broker in Savannah and – so it thinks – don't own ships and don't actually take possession of goods before we re-sell them. But the reality is that we now do own a ship – this *Sea Breeze* – and will indeed own the goods it brings in.

"So you see," he said, watching her face for signs of understanding, "the visitors from the War Department are coming to ask me to buy secretly for their own account and resell to them at a modest commission. Well now, if that happened, I would be in the unhappy position of risking all to buy this expensive ship and these goods, then selling them to the government for a very low commission – one that could not possibly cover the cost of building the ship and risking so much to run the blockade."

Amelia nodded again. "So, maybe you'd make five per cent as their agent when you could make a much bigger profit selling your own goods."

"Yes, you've got it." *It's more like five per cent versus a thousand per cent. Good God, am I really exploiting my own daughter for profit? But the other investors are at risk, too, and I've given them my word of honor.*

"Compounding the dilemma is this," he added. "If the government knew of my ownership in the ship, it could well be confiscated under the impressment laws. So I must be on hand when they arrive to refuse their secret brokerage proposal. It would be equally well if the ship were not sitting there at port to put thoughts into their heads."

Amelia wished she could alleviate her father's discomfort by embracing him and swearing to do anything he asked. But she said only: "Are you going to ask me the question?"

"Not yet," he answered. "If this meeting involved a business contract, I would be performing what is called 'due diligence.' It means that I am legally bound to inform the other party of all liabilities and risks before entering into the agreement. I am telling you all I can because you are my daughter, because I trust you and… because I have no one else with whom to share my confidence. A man usually has his wife, but with mine it seems not to be – nor has it really ever been. One cannot share a confidence with someone who has no desire to receive it."

Amelia glanced at the sherry in its decanter and wished he would suggest some. She had already felt her chest tighten because she knew there was more to come.

Daddy Beach paused to light a cigar – he usually asked the ladies' permission, which was never refused – and stood at the window behind his desk as if to keep the smoke at a distance. He gazed out, a sign that he was organizing his thoughts, then turned and looked directly into his daughter's eyes.

"I believe that things are quickly coming apart for the Confederacy," he said in a low voice. "Remember last summer when you were so enthusiastic about Chancellorsville? Then in the fall when the newspapers said we won at Chickamauga? But in both cases we lost more men. And maybe you hadn't noticed something else…"

"What?"

"Our so-called 'victory' at Chancellorsville was on Virginia soil. Our 'victory' at Chickamauga came in northern Georgia. How long before we're 'beating' the Yankees in South Georgia? And now they have a general named Grant who is said to be more aggressive and ruthless than all the others. You see, Amie, unlike the newspaper people, I don't view a war strictly as soldiers versus soldiers. I see it as troops being able to have enough bullets, canned beef, blankets and the like. We're running short of everything, and the government's effort to correct it is creating even more chaos."

Amelia, groping for some way to assert competence: "Did you know that since last summer I've been sneaking into this study in the mornings to read your newspapers after you've gone to work?"

"I wish your mother might have, too."

"A few days ago there was an editorial about shortages. It was urging farmers to plant less cotton and more food crops."

"Well, there you have it," said William Beach. "What these people don't seem to think about is that cotton is just about the only export that yields enough money to buy food and the other necessities of life. The editor wants more food production, but that requires farm machinery, which in turn requires iron and steel, most of which is already requisitioned for cannons and ironclads. The more government tries to manipulate supply and demand, the more confusion it creates. Last summer the War Department used the new impressment law to confiscate forty thousand bushels of corn to feed troops in Tennessee. Two months later someone found the same forty thousand bushels rotting away in some warehouse in Alabama, probably because some fool quartermaster clerk filled out the wrong forms."

Beach had been quiet around the Exchange floor because he feared censure from his peers. Now he had an audience of one for his inner convictions. "Everywhere you turn, the War Department is trying to plug a leaky levee," he declared, abandoning his muffled tones. "It decides that it has the right to take 'materials' for troops, but now we have soldiers selling their supplies to civilians, knowing that they can get more from their quartermaster whenever they please. And this week they issued an order forbidding the use of corn for distilling. Do they really think people will forego spirits? Or might people just use potatoes instead and reduce the army's potato supply?

"Well, I won't prattle on much more," he said with a heavy voice. "I have always been a man who favors order and organization. Looking ahead, I see no way to bring any sense to this chaos. I also see the War Department growing more desperate and expanding the impressment laws to seize more property. Our ship? Our business? Our home? In any case, Amie, I have decided to send on the *Sea Breeze* – that's our ship – both the gold I already mentioned and most of our own family fortune."

He paused and stared at Amelia, as a doctor would a patient, for symptoms of shock or distress. Amelia pictured herself sitting atop large canvas sacks of coins and bills.

As if reading her mind, her father continued: "It's not so complex as you might imagine. The entire shipment will consist of twelve ingots of gold, each weighing from twenty to twenty-seven pounds. Four will be claimed in short order by the shipbuilder's agent. Eight will be stored at the Royal Bank of Nassau until such time as sufficient order has been restored in America to reclaim it."

Amelia squirmed in her chair as she tried to envision twelve slabs of pure gold. "Why can't it be paid in a bank draft?"

"Because the shipbuilders don't want Confederate dollars. Their value is fading so rapidly that the price today in CSA money could be worth much less by the time it reaches England a few weeks hence."

"How much is all that gold worth?" she blurted out without thinking.

At their first meeting her father had let the same question drift off. Now he paused thoughtfully. "It's difficult to be precise," he answered, "again because the Confederate dollar is subject to such rapid inflation. Sorry to say, but the only reliable way to gauge the value is by what the Union treasury pays for gold. When I found the gold as a lad, the price was $19.46 an ounce. It's now something like forty-six in New York."

This time Amelia pressed on. "Then what would twelve of these bars be worth in New York?"

"I did some calculations yesterday," he answered. "Just over $400,000 in Union dollars, I reckoned. That would be in excess of three million Confederate, but that could change before sundown."

"Now are you ready to ask me?"

"Not quite yet," said her father. "Not only are the stakes higher than when we last talked, there is also a greater need for secrecy. You must understand, Amie: if the Southern press learns that Will Beach, maybe the biggest merchant in the biggest city in Georgia, is removing personal gold to England, he and his whole family could be branded as traitors. When bankers in Savannah come upon this information, it could create financial panic and fuel more inflation in the process. And when bankers in England hear this news, it could weaken their desire to support the Confederate cause."

"Daddy, isn't England neutral?" she asked.

"The queen proclaims it so," he said, "but all England seems to look the other way. Too many of its merchants are making fortunes selling to the rebels and people like me."

With that he leaned back in his desk chair and exhaled a cloud of cigar smoke. "Now I have discharged all the information I can possibly deem relevant to your decision," he said. "And I repeat that I am willing to make this voyage myself, even though it might have consequences with regard to those visitors from the War Department. I await your answer."

"Oh, Daddy," she said with tears welling in her eyes, "there was never any hesitation on my part, especially if I can personally do something to save what you've worked so hard for and help free Joseph from that terrible place. I only wish I could have Mother's blessing. May I talk to her and try to soften her heart?"

"You may try – as will I," said her father. "But in no case can you tell Lucy. If you do, both Jefferson Davis and Abraham Lincoln will know everything before the ship even docks."

———

Sarah beach's heart did not soften, nor would she speak to her husband and oldest daughter.

In the meantime, William Beach distilled everything that had transpired that day with Amelia to a concise strategy. He personally would retrieve twelve gold ingots from the First Bank of Savannah. Although vice chairman of the board, he would do no less than what Horatio had done over thirty years before. Each day for three days he would visit the vault and strap four ingots beneath his trouser legs and walk out unchallenged. All would then be painted the grayish color of lead. At the same time, twelve specially-cast and gold-painted bars of lead would be replaced by the same method.

Next, Amelia would pack liberally in several small sea trunks so as to spread the weight of the ingots. Should a porter or deckhand complain of their unusual weight, she would be prepared to jest that "a woman can never be too prepared for all the demands of her social life."

Finally, Amelia would not tell the ship captain, crew or anyone else about the gold except for the managing director of the Royal Bank of Nassau and the agent of Wainright Shipbuilders Ltd. of Liverpool, Great Britain.

Chapter Five

Leaving Savannah, February 8, 1864

On this sunny Monday morning, it was eerily quiet upstairs at the Beach household. Lucy was off riding at a friend's plantation home, having begged her parents for days for permission to go, then being astonished when her father actually suggested it. Mother Beach was in the pantry counting her jars of fruit and vegetable preserves and wondering how to get more to last the winter. Amelia, alone in her bedroom, had begun selecting some dusty travel trunks and suitcases from the family attic for a trip she knew to be close at hand.

Suddenly she heard a low hoarse voice calling up the grand staircase. "Amie, are you up there?"

When she appeared at the top of the stairs, her father beckoned below with a silent crook of the finger. "The ship's arrived," he said in low tones and a broad smile that she hadn't seen in weeks. "Came in about 3 am this morning and they're already unloading. Would you like to pay it a visit?" With eyes wide, she gave several vigorous nods that revealed her excitement. "Hurry – and no fancy clothes," he called upstairs. "Remember, you're going to a wharf full of dirty cargo."

English-built blockade runner

In barely two minutes Amelia was tripping downstairs and onto the front porch, surprised to see a one-horse hansom cab waiting in front. "It's supposed to reach seventy degrees today," he said, "so I thought I'd treat us to a ride so we can enjoy the day and arrive in style," Daddy Beach said when they were clopping along the cobblestones. "The ship is already the main event of the day. People walking around and gawking. But remember, you're just the owner's daughter, out to gawk like everyone else. None of my people know you'll be on that ship."

As the carriage made its way down River Street, Amelia could see the tall gray bow of a large ship docked at the Huxley and Beach wharf, and as they drew near she was astonished at its length. A tall mast fore and aft. Two tall smokestacks in between a large paddle wheel on each side. Stacks of boxes peering over the gunwales. The British Union Jack at rest on a stern pole.

Once alighted, Amelia found herself standing amidst crates and boxes being unloaded down a wide, steep gangplank. Shirtless, sweating black men pushing carts, swinging crates from an overhead hoist aboard ship and stacking boxes on the wharf.   White men shouting and pointing. Amelia and her father standing motionless and ignored among crates stacked above eye level:

- Cases of 12 lb. James Shot. Reed-Parrott, 10 lb. Shot. Hotchkiss 3 in. Shot.
- Boxes: Boots, Common. Steel Shank. Leather Cav. Artillery Boots. Pegged Leather Brogans. M1851 Artillery Driver Boots.
- Stacks of Caissons with wheels piled in separate stacks: Napoleon 12 lb. Cason guns. 3-inch ordnance rifles, Parrott 10 lb. rifles.

"You see, when assembled," her father explained, "each of those caissons comes with five guns of various sizes and purposes."

Amelia and her father swung around at the sound of a clipped British accent to see a tall, sandy-haired man of about thirty. He was beardless, which made him seem boyish.

"Ah, Captain Timmons," exclaimed William Beach offering his hand. "I was keeping an eye out for you. Reckoned you must be up on the bridge barking out orders."

"Actually, I was trying to lie low," said the captain with a laugh. "Your men seem to know what goes where." With a smile and a bow, he turned to Amelia, who felt flushed and tingly beneath his gaze. "Ah, you must be Amelia, the passenger who will favor a ship of wharf rats with a lady's charming presence and keep us all gallant.

"I'm sure you must be confused by all this bounty from the sea," he added. "You happen to be standing amidst all the military supplies, which will soon be carted off by various quartermaster people. Then beyond in that sector we have civilian goods, which will be picked up by individual merchants as arranged by your father."

Actually, what confused Amelia more was that the so-called captain was not dressed like one. He wore civilian britches tucked into black boots, and his dark blue cotton shirt was topped by a broad-brimmed straw hat.

Amelia decided to show her pluck. "Well, I expected to meet Captain Horatio Nelson with braided cap and medals on his chest and gilt-edged sword at his side," she teased.

"That would be like a fox coming out of his hole and waving its arms at the hounds," he bantered back. "I am but a private citizen from The Misty Isles offering his navigational skills to escort goods to various ports. If I should ever encounter someone perceived as your foe, I would not like him to confuse me with General Robert E. Lee."

Then he changed the subject. "Miss Beach, it would be my privilege to escort you about the ship right now, but I'm afraid we could be run over by a pushcart or smacked silly by that swinging hoist up there. But I can tell you that the *Sea Breeze* is a sleek beauty, and coming across from Nassau we were doing sixteen knots at one point."

"And how fast are your adversaries?"

"It depends on how heavy they are. Most of the ones that aren't too loaded down with cannons will do eight or nine. So, the trick is to be quicker – like the fox. And there are certain special features that help us in that endeavor. This ship is 196 feet long, but its draft – the part below water – is only ten feet, which helps make it go faster. See those smokestacks? They can be lowered to deck level so as to reduce visibility and wind resistance. And those big paddle wheels.... if you've been on a steamer before, you know they can be noisy when they slap the water. Thus, we have specially-made canvas covers that can be put over them to muffle the sound."

"Very interesting," she said. "Why did you name it the *Sea Breeze*?"

"I didn't," said the captain, "but I don't think your father and the ship-builder wanted to call it the *Jefferson Davis*."

"That's correct," broke in William Beach, who had been enjoying the repartee. "My partners – and I agree – wanted something that would sound more like a private English racing yacht, a pleasure boat out on a holiday romp."

"One thing more," said the captain. "A fox need not be chased in the first place if he can't be seen. "The misty gray color makes the ship all but invisible in ocean fog. Fog is our friend."

Said Beach: "I think we'll end our visit now because we know how busy you must be, Captain. But may I ask that you take a little respite from that work and join us for dinner – say, at six-thirty?"

"I am honored," answered the captain with another short bend. "I will say, sir, that I haven't had much sleep since our arrival, so if I might slip away to my bed early I would be appreciative. If we finish lading by tomorrow afternoon, we'll sail at dark, as I mentioned earlier. We were absolutely moonless last night and we'll have but a tiny sliver on the morrow."

Amelia was silent on the carriage ride home, then turned to her father. "That certainly will be a short stay for him," she said at last. "I'd been thinking we might show him the sights of Savannah."

"Well, the faster he returns, the more money he'll make," Beach answered." You see, most of the men who captain blockade runners are regular English navy officers. The navy doesn't pay very well, so officers with navigation skills take leaves of absence and go on half-pay so they can pile up the kind of money they may never see again. Mr. Timmons, our captain, will make about four thousand dollars for each successful run plus the right to sell four bales of cotton for his own account. The rewards go right down the line to the least of the deckhands."

Amelia seemed lost in thought as they passed by the leafy squares along York Street. "Of course, it works the other way," her father added. "If a ship is taken by one of the blockaders, it's sent to auction and the capturing crews divvy up big bonuses. And when the ship is sold at auction, sometimes the winning bidder is the original owner."

"That's the way the game is played," he added with a sheepish shrug.

Captain Charles Timmons arrived for dinner wearing a formal evening frock and an English captain's cap, which, he said, "is just for you, Miss Amelia, on this special occasion." Again, he apologized if he should appear "groggy" from lack of sleep. William Beach apologized in turn for the absence of daughter Lucy and the fact that Mrs. Beach was "not well of late" and upstairs in her room.

After a stroll through the gardens and a brief tour of the downstairs, the three headed for the formal dining room. Just as old Andrew had begun to serve a bisque of shrimp, in walked a grim Sarah Beach stating that "my infirmities are outweighed by my desire to meet the man who will be escorting my daughter to Nassau."

After introductions and being seated, Mrs. Beach waved off the bisque, and, as the others started on theirs, she started in on Captain Timmons. "How long have you been a navy captain?" She began.

"Actually, I'm not a captain in Her Majesty's Navy," he replied. "I am a commander and navigation officer, but I've been at sea now for ten years this January."

"He comes highly recommended," chimed in William Beach in an effort to relieve the young man's discomfit.

She appeared to ignore her husband, staring only at the captain as he accepted a glass of red wine. "And where is your home when you aren't at sea?"

"My ancestral home is in Cornwall, high on a bluff overlooking the sea," he said with a theatric wave. "Quite a different terrain than you have in Savannah. I suppose it was that view from the cliffs that called me to the sea in the first place. You'd think that when I go home I'd be eager to see nothing but terra firma, but I guess I need to be reminded that it's still there and providing me with a profession."

Timmons searched Mrs. Beach's round face for a hint of humor or empathy. He found neither.

"How do you find The Bahamas?" she said, taking a different tack.

"Oh, fascinating in all respects, Mrs. Beach. It can be quite hot and sunny, of course, which is why I wear that straw hat while on duty. I see your daughter is fair, with a freckle or two, so I would recommend the same for her. But I must say there always seems to be a refreshing breeze in the air in the islands, almost as if one is still sailing at sea."

"But what about society?" she continued as Andrew arrived with plates of roast beef and potatoes. "Are there families there, like ours, if you will?"

"Well, I'm sure there are few anywhere of your great distinction," said Timmons in his most ingratiating mien, "but if you mean are there friends to be gained and social events to attend, why they positively abound in Nassau. You see, the War Between the States has turned the sleepy little island of New Providence into a beehive of international activity. If you go back twenty years or so, the entire black population were slaves. Since England outlawed slavery, they've become more assertive, more energetic, if you will."

Amelia glanced up at Andrew, still a stony statue in the corner, because such talk was never heard in the Beach dining room.

"To that burst of energy, you now have the bustle and confusion associated with the official neutrality of Great Britain," Timmons continued between bites of beef and sips of wine. "You have commercial agents from many countries, ambassadors and counsels, newspapermen, spies, crews from blockade runners like ours and crews from blockaders who spend most of their time off the island trying to catch us. But on that neutral island hostilities are forbidden and everyone who is anyone seems to gather for soirées at the Royal Victoria Hotel almost every night. Three years ago, there was no Royal Victoria. Now it's among the finest spas in the world. And the wealth that is centered there has spilled out to common sailors and shopkeepers, even to the men who work the docks and the women who sell straw hats in the market. Am I talking too much, Mrs. Beach?"

Her grim stare remained fixed on the captain. "Where will my daughter stay...at this Royal Victoria?"

"Yes," interjected her husband. "I have already sent correspondence ahead of her and she will have a letter of introduction."

"How will she sort through all these strange people," Sarah Beach forged on as if not hearing her husband. "How would she know who might want to compromise her virtue? She can't expect to have letters of introduction for every..."

"I am not a child, mother," Amelia broke in at last.

"I doubt that the dangers are as great as have been imagined," said Timmons, fumbling for words of reassurance.

With that Mrs. Beach rose and announced: "I'm afraid my few bites of dinner have not been well-received by my delicate stomach. It has been interesting and illuminating to meet you, Captain, or *Commander* Timmons, but I am compelled to retire for now. Andrew, please send a cup of hot tea to my room."

When she had departed, Amelia decided to explore a subject that had escaped mention. "Well, captain, what *are* the dangers?" she inquired as if taking over from her mother. "After all, we are about to sail past three Yankee gunboats. It can't all be a holiday romp."

Timmons glanced at William Beach for a sign of guidance, found none, and decided to steer a middle course. "Miss Amelia, let us discuss danger in terms of blockade running in general," he offered. "Shoals, for example. All of southeastern America is flat and the rivers build up silt. Storms constantly shift silt and sand around, altering the depths of rivers. Hence, ships on both sides can suddenly strike bottom. And you may have to wait until the next high tide to free yourself. That is when you pray that a hostile force doesn't discover you."

"That's the biggest danger?" she bored in.

"One of the biggest. There's yellow fever. You never know when some deckhand will come down with it. And if it spreads, your ship can be quarantined before it reaches port. You may pass by one of them tomorrow night.

"Then there's the coal supply. Ships like ours need anthracite coal because it burns better and produces less smoke for other ships to see. But it's more expensive than what they call soft – bituminous – coal, which is cheaper and more plentiful. When you use soft coal, your danger increases."

"Yes, but you haven't mentioned the three blockaders with all those cannons," she said impatiently.

Timmons looked sideways at Beach with a disguised wink. "Miss Amelia," he said with exaggerated gravity, "I would say that your greatest danger would be a dress like the very lovely gingham gown you are wearing now. In such flowing attire, you could scarcely climb from one deck to another without catching something on a railing. A wide skirt could get caught in a paddle wheel or even start a fire if you backed into the galley stove."

"Well, what then? Should I dress like one of your sailors?"

He thought a moment. "Do you have jodhpurs here in Savannah? When the British first came to India, we admired the puffy trousers that the local army people wore with tall boots. Recently English officers in India have adopted something similar, and some ladies back home have begun wearing their own version of jodhpurs for riding horseback. It's much safer than getting your riding habit tangled in a saddle horn, and it would also work well on a ship. But I regret that I can suggest no more, and I have probably worn out my welcome with too much talking. I really must be getting back to make sure my men have not succumbed to the temptations of the Savannah waterfront."

As Amelia walked Captain Timmons – he now insisted on Charles – onto the front porch overlooking Madison Square, she felt secure on his arm and calmed by his constant good nature in the face of the dining table inquisition.

As if their thoughts converged, he said quietly: "I hope I didn't do or say something to offend your mother."

"Be not concerned," she answered. "Did you notice that she didn't say a word directly to me or my father?" And then she explained about Joseph and her mother's acute fears for her daughter.

"Thanks for your confidence and candor," answered Charles. "But I don't want to leave you sleeping on a bed of worry. Let me just say that when you enter the Bahamas Channel, you will experience a rare thrill: the bluest of waters and the most caressing of breezes. And I will try to arrange for dolphins to be jumping and cavorting all around you."

———

The next morning saw Amelia flitting between her bedroom, Joseph's vacant room and the sewing machine in the sitting room, with Mandy trailing behind and trying not to stumble over the four trunks and suitcases that lay on the floor with open lids.

"Why don't you just put all that in one steamer trunk," groused the plump maid with hands on hips.

"Because I like to have one for teas, one for dinner, one for traveling – one for each occasion," answered Amelia cheerfully without looking up from her sewing machine.

"Well, what you doin' with Joseph's pants?"

"Shortnin' 'em," Amelia muttered in colored talk.

"Well, I know *that*."

"Going to use them for riding. I'll get Joseph some new ones when he gets back."

Shortly after noon they heard men's voices below and looked out to see William Beach standing in the entrance hall with two large black men whom Amelia recognized from the warehouse. "Mandy," he called up, "I'd like you to go to the kitchen and fix a nice lunch for these boys."

When she disappeared down the rear servant stairway, the two men bent over a suitcase-sized metal box and began struggling upstairs with it. Within five minutes they had brought another and were gone off to their meal. Amelia found herself staring down at two square crates each with black stenciling: *London Armory Corp. Colt 1851 Revolver (24).* And each was padlocked.

Then more footsteps on the stairs and her father re-appeared. "Well, what have we here," he said in mock surprise as he closed the door behind him.

"It looks as if I'm to be well-armed," she said.

Beach bent down with a key, unsnapped the first lock and raised the lid. Facing them was a layer of plain gray cloth. Then her father began rolling up the cloth, exposing seven gold ingots as one would unravel a household's best cutlery. They looked like roughly forged swords before sharpening. Amelia guessed them to be from two to two-and-a-half feet long each. They bore many markings, the most common ones being the Roman letters XXII.

"None of them weigh the same," her father said. "They range from twenty-two to twenty-seven pounds."

"What do all those markings mean?" she asked, rubbing her hand over one of the ingots.

"I think it indicates the mine they came from in Mexico," he said, "but truth to tell I don't know any more about them. I've always kept them hidden and no expert has ever seen them. But I have had small pieces assayed and know they are 24-karat gold. Now be sure to wrap each one in cloth and spread them about your trunks and suitcases. The odds are great that no blockading captain would search a lady's personal effects."

"There are fourteen here," she said. "You said there would be twelve."

"I like the questions you ask," Daddy Beach replied. "I think you're developing a good facility for business. The answer is that since we first discussed this subject, the reliability of the government to pay its obligations has diminished."

That's true, but there's more here that would be treasonous to whisper about. English and French suppliers are now demanding payments from the Confederacy in gold, and what we have in the bank here could well be confiscated by Richmond itself before long. Besides, the day may soon come when Huxley and Beach will be forced to demand payment in gold as well.

At precisely six o'clock, William Beach and the two negroes had returned, except that this time they came to the servant's entrance on a side street and in a large two-horse wagon. As the two men came and went with her trunks, Amelia's excited anticipation had given way to worry and melancholia. Sarah Beach had gone off to "tea with friends" at four and had not returned. Would Amelia be denied her mother's blessing? Yet, her mother's heart would scarcely soften if she saw her daughter's travel attire. Taking the captain's advice to heart, Amelia was dressed in Joseph's beige saddle pants, a man's brown merchant shirt and a broad-brimmed straw hat that was once ringed with flowers for Sunday morning services.

"What do you think?" she said with a curtsy to Daddy Beach on his wagon perch.

"Well, just promise me that if any blockading crews board your ship, you will have changed back into lace and silk." And that was all he said about the matter.

How starkly different the scene when they pulled beside the *Sea Breeze*. The curiosity seekers had melted away and streetlamps now offered more light than the fading sun. The sleek, glamorous "racing yacht" was now sitting low in the water, groaning and creaking under the weight of eight hundred cotton bales packed from bow to stern. The sharply-inclined gangplank of the afternoon had leveled off to an easy climb of a few feet. Ugly barrels of turpentine were jammed into every other available space. Only a few odd boxes – fresh food supplies – remained on the wharf, and Amelia's luggage was soon piled alongside.

She soon spotted Captain Timmons – Charles just the night before – on the bridge, shouting orders to a sailor while signing some papers for another. Gone, along with his gracious aplomb at dinner, were the formal jacket and captain's cap, replaced now by the same straw hat and country-boy garb she had met on their first encounter.

A quick wave from William Beach got the captain's attention and he immediately strode across the gangplank with an extended hand and engaging smile. He did a theatrical double-take at seeing Amelia and said: "Mr. Beach, you said you'd be bringing your daughter. You didn't mention a son."

"Mr. Timmons, I've taken your advice and am now ready to climb the riggin' with the best of them," she replied.

"Well now," said the captain as the last of the crates and luggage went aboard, "now that the passenger has adopted the official uniform, let us discuss the passenger's quarters. As you no doubt know, this sort of ship was built without amenities worthy of a lady of your station. Since your comforts require the utmost in space, I have arranged for you to occupy the captain's quarters, which are still pitifully inadequate."

"Oh my," she replied, fluttering an imaginary fan. "This is gallantry unsurpassed. But where will *you* be housed?"

"I will occupy the first officer's quarters. Be not concerned. None of us gets much sleep during these runs. We old tars are used to sleeping in short stretches and the two of us can trade on and off. Besides, the presence of a lady will keep the crew on their best behavior."

With that, Timmons was off on another duty and the two Beaches were left alone standing at the base of the gangplank. For several awkward moments they were as still as the evening air.

"Well, then," said William Beach, clearing his throat. "There are some things I need to give you. Here are the letters of introduction to the Royal Bank of London and to the Royal Victoria manager. And there is one thing more."

Daddy Beach took a small box from his evening coat. He opened it only slightly in the lamplight, revealing a glittering gold chain with a locket. Inside it was a cameo of the Virgin Mary that looked very old. "This is perhaps the most valuable thing I discovered as a lad," he said looking into her eyes. "I want you to have it and carry it at all times. It can be your source of security and a reminder of my love. I have a second one like it which I will carry with me always until you are safely home."

In the flickering lamp light, she could see tears betraying the faith and emotions of a man who had seldom shown them. They embraced. He began to walk away.

Amelia had not experienced such a moment and didn't want it to end. "Daddy," she called in a child's voice. "I feel so alone."

He turned back towards her and took her hands in his. "So was I – many times – when I was young," he said. "The best advice I can give you is this: You can and will become what you think you are. If you think as a person of courage and strength, you will become that person."

Then he walked into the dusk and disappeared into the last glow of the setting sun.

Amelia took a brief tour of the ship, squeezing herself along the narrow aisles between cotton bales and turpentine barrels. Not knowing what else to do with herself, she headed for her new quarters, only to find the captain inside gathering some papers from a desk. "I hope I won't have to bother you often," he said without looking up. "I may need some charts and clothing from time to time, but I think I've got all I need for now. And you, it seems, have everything you need," he added with a glance at all the luggage piled up on one wall.

"When do we sail?"

"In less than an hour, as soon as it's black out there."

"Is there anything I'm supposed to do?"

"The most important thing would be to become invisible," he said. "The next two or three hours will be very crucial to our success. Each crew member has his own station and responsibilities."

Sensing disappointment on her part, he added: "Would you truly like to see the show from the best perch? Then come with me."

He led her outside to the bow, where the cotton bales were piled highest. Then without a word he put his strong arms around her thighs and hoisted her atop the cotton bales.

"You'll like the view," he said.

"It's already glorious," she answered.

At first it was the vibration and hum of the boilers firing, the first belches of black smoke, then wharf men tossing mooring lines to crewmen as the huge paddle wheels began to churn.

Soon they were leaving the city lights. The river Amelia had occasionally toured by day became a murky unknown, its shores marked only by the dim glow of stoves and lanterns of houses along the way.

After another half-hour of blackness, she heard men calling out as they tested the river depth with hawser cables and kedges. Then they bumped gently against the stern of another ship flying the British flag. "She ran aground last night," the captain called out from the open window in his pilot house. "Just stopping to pick up their mail."

Then more miles of blackness. The moon rose, offering only a sliver of light.

Suddenly three short bells rang out and men began to emerge from be-low-decks. Captain Timmons appeared below Amelia, motioning for her to alight by the same way she had reached her perch. "We're approaching the inlet and Tybee Island, where the biggest gunboat is moored – or was when we came in," he said in hushed tones. "You can watch from inside the pilot house if you'll promise to be a mouse in a corner."

As Amelia stood against a wall, two men entered the pilot house and only paused long enough to nod in her direction as Timmons made quick introductions. "This is Edgar, our quartermaster, who doubles as the steadiest helmsman in the northern hemisphere during times like this," he said of a stout, bearded man in his forties.

Timmons then turned to a wiry, nearly bald man who looked too old to be in anyone's navy. "And here we have Seaman Jimmy, who brings a unique talent to this enterprise. When aided by a dollop or two of gin – which I keep under lock and key – he can spot other ships at sea quicker than any of us. And very often, he can smell their smoke – and even iden-tify their type of coal – while all we smell is salt air. Tonight the breeze is from the north, which should help him."

Jimmy gave a wave and was quickly outside and stop the crossbar in front of the wheelhouse, scanning the river with a brass spyglass. At that point, the captain ordered a well-practiced drill. The stacks were cranked down to the level of the bulwark. The two wooden masts were collapsed atop the bales on deck. Heavy tarps were thrown over the two paddle wheel housings to muffle their sound. Another tarp covered the fire room hatch. The only lights remaining were the shaded compass light and the dimmed oil lamp on the chart table in the pilot house. "From now on," Timmons whispered in Amelia's direction, "the penalty for exposing any light or making a noise that can be heard by another ship is death without trial. *Death.*"

His charming banter had come to an end. For the next fifteen minutes the only sound Amelia heard was the rhymical slap, slap, slap on the water by the paddle-floats.

Without turning around, Jimmy held up a hand. "Better ease off for now, Captain," he whispered. "Oy smells stack smoke. Probably the *Seneca*, tethered between Tybee and the sea like last time."

Timmons thought a few seconds, then muttered an order down the engine room tube. He'd needed a moment to weigh the consequences, because shutting down the boilers too quickly could cause the stacks to belch, giving away a ship's position immediately.

"Steamer on port bow," Jimmy whispered. Amelia could see nothing. "Aye, the *Seneca*," he added. Within seconds a black form could be seen in the distance.

"Execute our plan, "the captain whispered in the helmsman's ear. "Port two points and steady."

Amelia gave a start. Their unarmed ship was headed right toward a blockader loaded with guns!

Timmons eased over to her side. "I should have told you," he whispered. "We know that when the *Seneca* is moored at sea, she leaves a safety radius of two hundred yards so as not to fire on her sister ships in the dark. We're going to slip by inside that circle."

They crept on. Soon the black form of the *Seneca* had disappeared off the port side. Everyone had begun to breathe easier. A few twinkling lights to starboard indicated Tybee Island and their gateway to the open sea. Then ...

"Cruiser to starboard!" Jimmy nearly shouted. It was headed north across their path. "We need to get past it before it can turn," said Timmons, standing beside his helmsman. "Full steam!"

Stealth was soon forgotten, because in the next few seconds a rocket lit up the sky above them. At this point the *Sea Breeze* was but a bulky giant bale of cotton that tended to roll in the waves. For a few terrifying seconds, the rocket's glare illuminated a cluster of men moving about a large cannon on the bow of the cruiser.

"Come, come, Edgar," the captain said as if a Cambridge coxswain. "We can still get twelve knots out of this freighter. I'm betting that cruiser can't do nine."

Suddenly a bright fiery burst came from the blockader and Amelia's heart jumped in her throat as two geysers erupted several yards behind the stern. Then another boom and a cannon ball went skipping alongside the *Sea Breeze* like a flat stone flung from the beach.

"Those aren't our big concern," the captain shouted in her direction with his eyes on the pursuing vessel, now a half-mile astern. "Our engine room is below water. We have four water-tight compartments to keep us afloat. What you can worry about is that a direct hit could cause sparks and light up the cotton or turpentine."

"We're gaining," the helmsman cried out as the ship charged into the open Atlantic. "Twelve knots." The captain poured himself a coffee and looked at her with a broad smile intended to calm her fluttering heart.

The blockader fell farther behind until its form faded from view. At that moment Timmons ordered a radical ninety-degree swerve to port that took them well north of the well-traveled path to Nassau. Then he ordered all engines to stop. As the *Sea Breeze* rocked gently in silence, the Yankee gunboat loomed again in the misty distance, still headed on the course to Nassau and still firing into the empty sea ahead.

It was just past midnight. After the stacks were raised, the masts hoisted, the sails unfurled and the engines re-started with a loud blast of black smoke, the captain unlocked a cabinet in the wheelhouse and declared: "Champagne for everyone!" Suddenly salts of all colors and ages were clinking seconds and thirds.

And Amelia Beach was merrily among them. The first glass she regarded as medicinal, having toasted with small flutes of champagne at weddings, but reasoning that something therapeutic was now required to calm the tightness in her chest that remained from sneaking under the nose of a powerful gunboat. The second glass came from a need for courage to emerge from the shadows of the pilot house and make gay conversation with strange men. The third one came because Amelia Beach was now the center of attention – witty and a font of hilariously entertaining remarks.

She was especially drawn to the equally entertaining Jimmy, who tried to teach her a hornpipe to the tune of a deckhand with a squeak box. When it was over she drew him aside and said, "I simply have to know. How did you acquire this talent for spotting ships?"

"Well, you see, milady, whenever we be runnin' the gauntlet, as we calls it, the cap'n asks for someone to climb up in the crossbeam to look for other ships. If he spots one he gets a dollar."

"That sounds easy enough," she said.

"But there's more to it, y'see. If someone on deck spots a ship before the man up in the crossbeam, he gets fined five dollars. Now, too many blokes got fined more than they made, and Oy'm the only one left what does it and still makes money."

"And what about this ability to tell a ship by its smell?"

"That's a secret, but Oy'll tell you if you'll ask Cap'n for a little gin in me bubbly," he said with a wink. Amelia disappeared inside the pilot house and returned with a full cup of champagne for herself and a "special" one for Jimmy.

"Most 'o these blokes growed up in places where everbuddy burns the same stuff to keep warm. But Oy've been everywhere from London to Liverpool. You get so you can walk below the chimneys on a cold night and tell who's burnin' peat, who's usin' wood, who's usin' soft coal or mebbe soft coal mixed with slate. Out here is easier because the runners – that's us – burns anthracite. The blockaders use soft because they don't care so much about speed or it's all their navy can afford. Blockader smoke is foul – sooty like. Our stuff almost smells sweet.

"But don't tell Cap'n er Oy'll lose me gin ration."

"You may be English," she said, "but you talk funny English."

"W'all, ma'm, no disrespeck, but y'all tawk funny Southern English," he answered. They laughed merrily while holding each other up on the swaying deck.

Amelia had emptied her fourth glass of champagne and was remarking that the deck seemed a bit more "wobbly" when she felt a firm hand on her arm. "Miss Beach," said the captain looking down with a paternal smile, "it's been a very long day for you and tomorrow will be a busy one as well. Let's get you below deck and make sure you know where to find your quarters."

"It's even more wobbly down here," she said woozily as he guided her to the captain's quarters.

"Here's a wash basin," he said when they were inside. "Use it if you have to. Over there is the head. Have you used a head on ship before?"

"When can I call you Charles again?"

"When I'm not on duty."

"Are you on duty now?"

"Yes."

She was sitting on the edge of the bed as Timmons stood beside. "I've never been in a man's bed before," she mumbled.

Carefully he swung her feet – high-buttoned shoes and all – up on the bed and unfurled a blanket to cover her.

"Why were all those men looking at me?" she said with eyes closed.

Because they'd never seen a woman in men's clothes, and because they are males, like me, who have been to sea for weeks and were imagining what is under those clothes.

"Because you are very attractive and charming," he said. But the words fell on ears that were deaf to the world. And he would tease her on the morrow as to how loudly she snored.

Chapter Six

NASSAU, FEBRUARY 9, 1864

Amelia Beach was swaying lazily on her back-porch swing in Savannah until she opened her eyes abruptly and realized she'd been dreaming. She was still in her saddle pants and shirt, lying on her back on a thin mattress in a swaying room full of heavy oak furniture and manly accoutrements – a barometer on one wall and a clock on the other that told her eleven a.m. Her mouth so dry she could barely swallow and her stomach grumbled impatiently, but she lay back to absorb the moment: the steady rocking, the rhythmic slap of the paddle wheels, and a loosely-latched closet door that clicked and clacked with each roll of the ship.

But reverie was no match for hunger and thirst. After some daubs from the wash basin, a few tugs on her hairbrush and a quick look in the captain's mirror, she was soon rapping at the door of the pilot house, causing three men to look up from a chart. "Ah, the life of the party has returned," said Captain Timmons, waving her across the trestle. "We had a lovely pod of dolphins show up to perform just an hour ago, but we had to tell them to come back later because there was no audience."

"I suppose I missed breakfast, too."

"Yes, by a mile. But come aft with me to the galley and we'll try to beg Saint Matthew for a scrap or two."

"*Saint* Matthew?"

"Yes, captains have great power aboard ship, so I canonized him for his splendid culinary skills. Some of his finest stews have been inspired by one pot spilling into another while trying to cook on a raging sea."

As [1]they entered the mess room, Amelia was surprised to see a small, bearded black man in a stained undershirt peeling potatoes as he sat at the end of the long crew table. An image of the Beach kitchen servants in starched white cottons flashed through her mind.

"Saint Matthew, you haven't yet met our distinguished passenger," said Timmons. "This is Miss Amelia Beach, whose father owns the deck we stand on and the stove you cook on."

Matthew wiped his hands on a towel, stood and offered a hand. "My pleasure," he said. "Hope I can do awright for you." She grasped the outstretched hand timidly, as if she'd been dared to pet a snake.

"Miss Beach was unable to partake of your unsurpassable sausage, eggs and black pudding this morning," said Timmons in his most ingratiating manner. "Might I beseech you to find her a scrap or two that she might gnaw on to avoid starvation?"

"Well, you missed the sausage and eggs part, but I still got some porridge on the stove if you can't wait for lunch," he said in a lilting voice that she would come to know as uniquely Bahamian. "Got some coffee, too. Take a mug over there and pour yourself some."

Timmons was outside, staring over the railing, when Amelia emerged from her porridge fortification and joined him. "We've got another two days to go," he said, "but I never tire of staring at the cobalt blue water. It's well over a mile deep here. Tongue of the Ocean, they call it."

Then he changed the subject. "I sensed your discomfort with Saint Matthew," he said quietly.

"Really? Why, no! My goodness, did I seem….?" She shrugged. "Well, I suppose I was, er, put off. In my land, servants bow or curtsey when introduced. And I'm not used to serving my own coffee."

"You do know he's not a slave?"

"Yes, I suppose. Or I should."

"The Bahamas outlawed slavery nearly thirty years ago," said Timmons softly, still staring into the bright sunshine and deep blue sea. "Saint Matthew thinks of himself as a free man. He might have to obey orders on ship, but not once we get on land."

"Yes, I know," she said like a child who had just brought home a failing report card. "I'll try my best to do as the Romans do when we reach Rome."

Timmons started to walk off, then turned around. "I know I make a big fuss over Saint Matthew, but I think you should meet some people who are even more valuable."

He pushed on Amelia's elbow and led her amidships and inside the cabin. "Down here," he said, pointing to steep stairs leading to a barely lit landing below. It was already several degrees warmer, and Amelia was again thankful she'd traveled in saddle pants and shirt.

"Now where?" she asked at reaching the landing. He twisted a heavy handle on a large oval steel door, admitting a blast of intense heat and a straight ladder leading below. "Just one more level," said Timmons. "We won't be long."

Her hands were already grimy with soot from the ladder when they stepped into a large metal room manned by three shirtless black men, all holding shovels and fixed in place by the sudden intrusion. "Just giving the lady a tour," shouted the captain over the din. "Telling her about the fine work you do."

They waved self-consciously. Each was covered with glistening soot and sweat.

The blast of heat had come from a roaring fire inside the coal furnace. On either side was a bin of coal. Two of the men went back to their rhythm of shoveling from the bin and flinging coal into the hot furnace, with the third scooping up pieces that fell along the way.

"We have six men like this in all," Timmons continued. "They rotate a few hours on and off. These chaps have the most important duty because at sea on full steam the boiler needs a steady feeding. One can't afford to get tired, and both bins have to be kept evenly weighted so that we don't list and make all that cotton tumble.

"But their most important job is to prevent fires and put them out if one should happen. If we have a coal bunker fire down here and we're carrying munitions, we can light up the ocean from here to Charleston."

Amelia could only nod her head. Her lungs felt on fire and she felt woozy. "Let's go up," she implored.

Out on the breezy deck again, Amelia leaned over the bulwark, gulping in sea air and dabbing a kerchief at her forehead, but determined not to show a soft side to the man who now gazed down at her. "Was that my rite of passage?" she asked at last.

He fell silent for a moment, then said: "I only wanted to make sure your inspection of the ship was complete – to show what it requires below to provide comfort to those above. And I suppose I wanted to show you as well that despite their hardship, those stevedores are free men as well. Their shares are as much as the cook's."

Just after lunch on February 10, Amelia stood at the port railing, ahead of the smokestacks and their sooty spray, thinking how wonderfully prescient the shipbuilders were when they named their new vessel the *Sea Breeze*.

Jimmy, the eagle-eyed deckhand, was perched in his lookout atop the crossbeam in front of the pilot house. "Didjer notice that the water's now different?" he called down.

Indeed, the color was no longer deep cobalt blue. It was now a peacock blue-green. "You're so right, Jimmy," she called up.

"That's because we've crossed into the Great Bahama Bank. The deep stuff was mebbe one – two miles deep. Now we're in a hundred feet or so and heading towards thirty. The Great Bahama Bank is like a big tabletop of limestone underneath. So here we'll get reefs and fish – and gunboats on the prowl when we get closer to Nassau." Then: "Look! Look to starboard! Them's flyin' fish, puttin' on a show just for you!"

Sure enough, a stream of a dozen or more small fish with gossamer-like "wings" on their sides were actually flying in the air as if trying to race the ship and leap over its wake. "Amazing!" she called up to Jimmy. "What makes them fly?"

"Some says they just likes to fly," he shouted. "But Oy thinks they thinks they're being chased by a giant fish. That's us."

The conversation brought Charles Timmons out of the pilot house. "Speaking of fish," he said, "maybe it's time for Saint Matthew to give us a shark show."

Amelia had already seen enough dolphin cavorting so as to hardly notice them anymore. She'd even learned that "dolphins" are really *porpoises* and that dolphins are blue-green fish that make for the best eating in these waters. But *sharks*! "Oh yes captain, let's have a shark show," she exclaimed.

In a few minutes Amelia and Timmons were standing above the stern with a few idle crewmen while Matthew the cook hovered with a large pail of fish bones and other leftovers from lunch. "First, we find a nice patch of Sargasso weed," he said. "Some call it sea holly."

"What should I look for?"

"It's a brown or gold layer of weed that's all over," said Matthew, his bucket swaying over the rampart. "You don't have to look very hard for it. It has little yellow berries, and bugs lie on it like a big blanket. Then you get big fish like dolphins who come up to eat whatever's floating along with the Sargasso. Then comes the show – you'll see."

In another ten minutes the ship was nearly upon a fifty-foot-wide blanket of Sargasso when the pilot called out, "Leave it clear! We're not going to foul the paddle wheels just for a fish show."

Soon they found a smaller, golden brown patch. As they idled towards it, Matthew pointed to swirls and bubbles. "There's some under there," he shouted and dumped the contents of one bucket overboard.

Within a minute the water and seaweed were churning and swirling. "See," said Matthew, "we got catfish and sheepshead. That big green one in the middle is a bull dolphin. And look just ahead." A fin made a vee in the water. "A hammerhead shark is comin' to see what the commotion is about. And there's a lemon shark just behind him." For several minutes, they watched the black forms of sharks, seven to ten feet long, gliding back and forth beneath the stern railing.

"Hog Island Light!" Jimmy cried out from his perch above the pilot house. Amelia squinted and in the far distance glimpsed the fifty-year-old lighthouse that marked the westernmost tip of the narrow strip of sand and scrub that created a protected channel for ships entering Nassau. "Ship ahoy," cried Jimmy with spyglass affixed to one eye.

The captain was out of the pilot house, staring up. "Look like the *New Jersey*?"

"Too far to tell, but wouldn't be surprised."

"Well, I think it's *Jersey's* turn to be on patrol."

Amelia heard the exchange but felt the two were having a conversation meant to exclude her. She wouldn't give them the satisfaction of a question.

In a few minutes, a large beamy ship loomed closer. Amelia could make out a large cannon on the bow, smaller guns protruding from the port side. Standing straight out from the stern was the striped and starred flag that she grew up pledging allegiance to in school. The ship was gaining slowly. Amelia held her silence, but her eyes widened as the Yankee ship closed to within a half mile. Her jaw dropped as two cannons discharged loud shots in puffs of white smoke. The shots splashed down several yards behind the *Sea Breeze*.

Even I could have hit our ship broadside from that distance, Amelia thought.

"All right, run up two," shouted the captain to a sailor standing below the aft mast. Immediately two small white square flags ran up the halyard.

"Now up you go," Timmons yelled to three deck hands. They scrambled atop the cotton bales stacked furthest astern. As they grunted and pushed at the bulky five hundred pound bundles, the captain yelled again: "Now roll two!" And in seconds, two bales tumbled into the sea.

A signal flashed from the Yankee blockader and Timmons hollered "All steam ahead" down the pipe to the engine room. The *Sea Breeze* gave a belch of black smoke and began to slice through the gentle sea. It was quite unnecessary because the *New Jersey* had gone dead in the water and its crewmen were now trying to lift the bounding bales with grappling hooks.

"The trick is to snare them before they get too soggy to lift." Captain Timmons had snuck up behind her and was clearly enjoying Amelia's confusion.

"What was that...." she started to say, but he interrupted. "That probably does warrant an explanation. Hmm, where to start?" he said with some strokes of his clean-shaven chin. "It's all part of what we might call 'the system.' You see, it's like a game of fox and hounds. But just as the hounds are about to close in, the fox drops them a nice beefsteak and they all stop to enjoy it."

She put on her best scowl.

"Well, I'll try again," he said. "You see, the Yankee crews aren't paid much and are jealous of us Brits getting rich when they get left out. They've been sent out here to catch us, but their ships are too slow and the government in Nassau forbids them from buying ammunition to replace whatever they use. And how are they going to get enough coal for the trip home after all this patrolling around the Bahamas? So, Miss Amelia, they challenge us like snarling guard dogs. Then they fire a few shots and write in their logs that they pursued their quarry in a sea battle to rival Trafalgar and Cadiz. We drop them a little offering of a bale or two and no one gets hurt or sunk."

"All that for two bales of cotton?" she said.

"Ah, but let's do a little arithmetic," he said. "Before your little war broke out, Europeans were paying thirty cents a pound for American cotton. When we unload on the docks today, some wool merchant from Leeds or Lancaster will offer nearly two dollars U.S. per pound or so. Each bale of your Georgia's finest weighs around five hundred pounds, so one of those bobbing bales out there is worth nearly a thousand dollars."

"Even so, how can that be worth all the time and expense involved?" said Amelia.

"Righto, as far as you go," answered Timmons. "But consider that on an average day four or five blockade runners may arrive in Nassau harbor. The smaller ones may not drop two bales, but if a boat like the *New Jersey* gaffs five bales a day, that's real money and maybe as much as our own crew will earn.

"So, you see, it's a rather symmetrical system," he said with hands cupped around an imaginary globe. "Fair to all, and no one gets sunk or runs out of fuel." He was beaming at his own eloquence. "And now I have work to do and you have, perhaps, a change of clothes back into a fine lady's raiment to dazzle all of Nassau.

"And once we're ashore I hope to become 'Charles' again."

Metamorphosing into a well-attired lady was easier said than done as Amelia stood at the captain's wash basin dabbing at her face while trying not to splash sloshing soapy water on her chemise and bloomers. Yet, she had come to feel quite at home in this man's surroundings. Freddy Farnsworth's bedroom probably had a closet full of foppish costumes. Here was a real man who seemed secure in having but three pairs of trousers hanging in his closet along with just two formal coats and a uniform jacket bearing ribbons of actual bravery and accomplishment.

Amelia turned to the small dresser beside the wash basin and picked up the mug and shaving brush that lay on top. She opened the top drawer and peered in at a pipe, a pouch of tobacco and a revolver. In the rear was a small velvet-covered jewel case. She was about to open it when,

Stop! Enough snooping!

Above the dresser was a large hickory-framed oval mirror that jutted out from the wall. *Here is the captain's mirror, staring at me in my underwear. It feels strange – and sensual.*

Well, what do you see, mirror? I think you see a slender face. Average brown hair, but a dash of gold when the late afternoon sun shimmers through the port hole. Eye tooth hanging too low like a mad dog's fang. Quick to smile even though Mother says don't smile broadly because you look toothy. Also quick to frown, with Mother warning that frowning makes your eyebrows scrunch together. Slender neck. Enough flesh below to wear a low-cut dress and cause a man lean over to see more. Well-shaped legs, although no man has ever seen them.

And what of all this? Daddy says always have a plan. Daddy says you can become what you think you are. But what should I think to become? All I know is that I'm not meant to become another mammy to a gaggle of Lucy toddlers in little blue velvet suits with lace cuffs. I know I'm not meant to play the piano in the parlor while Mother's club friends chatter all about. And maybe I'm not even meant to knit blankets for an army fighting for a tarnished cause. Isn't it a bit too early to call a twenty-four-year-old woman a "spinster?"

In the deck house the captain and his pilot were too embroiled in a discussion about finding suitable dockage to pay much heed to the lady passenger who entered wearing a blue calico gown. And so, Amelia resumed her position as mouse-in-the-corner and feasted her eyes on a dazzling scene of blue sea, white sands and colorful blooms. The *Sea Breeze* was just passing the venerable lighthouse at the tip of Hog Island. On the north side of the slender barrier island lay an almost pristine stretch of broad sandy beach, broken only by a few bleached wood huts and poles with drying fish nets.

Once leaving the lighthouse to port, the ship glided into a wide channel. Along the inner side of Hog Island was a large coal yard surrounded by hardscrabble shacks that resembled the jumble of slave quarters on a large Georgia plantation. Across the channel to the south was a stark contrast: a harbor beehive of ships in various stages of unloading and loading. Amelia counted twenty, ranging from sleek new English blockade runners to small sloops from Florida that had been coastal fishing boats until lured by the profits that could be gained from cramming a few bales of cotton onto their narrow decks.

Now the *Sea Breeze* was fifty feet from the wharf, the pilot trying to find a spot roomy enough to accommodate a nearly two hundred-foot paddle wheeler. When every space seemed taken, Timmons shouted up to Jimmy, still perched on the crossbeam. "Lower the tender and row Mr. Stone in there. Mr. Stone, here's a ten-pound note. Do what you can to rent us a crane. And Jimmy," he called to the deckhand, "a thimble of gin if you'll run up to the Royal Vic and get them to bring down a carriage for our Miss Beach."

After the *Sea Breeze* finally eased into a spot near the end of the wharf, Timmons turned to Amelia. "I'm going to be very busy for a while," he said. "The customs agent will be coming to inspect the manifest, which is good because I must verify the cargo in order to give the crew their shares. Then the place will be bedlam because the commercial agents will arrive to start bidding on the cargo."

"Should I be on hand?" She asked. "I mean on hand as the representative of Huxley and Beach."

"I don't think so," he said. "It's *my* head that'll roll if we get less than fair price. Besides, once that's done I'll have to get coal. But my most important duty is to see that you make the right friends and not the wrong ones. So, I'll meet you in the lobby of the Royal Vic at seven. Yes?"

———

By the time the gangplank had been wheeled into place, Amelia had spotted Jimmy the sailor atop a two-horse carriage with a smartly-attired Bahamian driver wearing a top hat. After the two had strapped her two trunks and four suitcases into a pile on the rear, the driver's finery was drenched with sweat. Jimmy then scurried up the gangplank to get his reward. Amelia's carriage plodded down the waterfront Bay Street, past a jumble of open rum shops, fruit stands, straw markets, fishmongers, sponge piles and crowds just milling about with no apparent purpose except to exhibit a loud, gay abandon that made the only white woman in sight shudder. *But will I show fright? I shall not, because I am a person who does not show fright.*

After a few blocks, the driver got off and tightened the straps around the luggage. They had come to the intersection of Bay and East streets. Looking up a long incline, Amelia could see the spires of two impressive churches to the right and, to the left, the columned Assembly building, English to its foundation except for the pink covering its limestone walls. On the hilltop beyond loomed The Royal Victoria Hotel, the island's largest, grandest structure. On the opposite side of the coral street, jutting out like a frigate's bow, stood Fort Fincastle, with cannons peering out from somber gray walls to defy anyone who might threaten this outpost of the British Empire. And leading up to the fort was a steep set of stone steps that Amelia would come to know as the "Queen's Staircase." She would also learn that in 1792 it had taken some six hundred slaves over sixteen years to carve the staircase out of the coral rock, all so that the citizenry in the town at sea level could escape to the fort above in the event of a pirate attack.

The driver was clearly worried about having two tired horses and much more luggage than expected for a single woman. But after a deep breath, all he said was "Well, here we go" as he snapped the reins on the horses' rumps. As the carriage lurched forward, the luggage slid against its straps and Amelia felt a jolt of panic. *The baggage is going to tumble down and spill all down the hill. Crowds will rush in and swarm over the gold and tear me to pieces looking for more of it. Stop! I won't allow such thoughts!*

But the team kept clopping upward, the driver sympathetically allowing stops along the way. After four blocks only the Royal Vic stood ahead and Amelia could see why it was Nassau's proudest treasure. In contrast to the stark, stone Fort Fincastle across the road, the hotel loosely resembled a thousand-foot-long paddle wheel steamer. A large portico in the center might have been designed to mimic an outsized paddle housing. Long piazzas adjoining each of the three floors above might have been promenade decks on a passenger ship. Two rooftop cupolas resembled smokestacks. But why not? The hotel had been built to cater to passengers of the Cunard steamship line.

As the carriage approached the walled gate, another gaggle of straw hat, trinket and fruit sellers awaited to descend on any guest who ventured in or out. But after the carriage had inched its way through the portal, Amelia found herself in a quiet oasis of royal palms, hibiscus bushes, and bougainvillea trees festooned with red, yellow and peach-colored blossoms. A gentle breeze swept through the hillside grounds, and as the carriage approached the front portico, she could look back on the harbor below and the turquoise sea beyond.

Two well-dressed black men were standing on the portico steps. One seemed to give orders to the other, who quickly joined the driver in piling the luggage on a flat cart and disappearing into the hotel lobby. As the remaining servant stepped forward, Amelia realized he was lighter-skinned and carried himself with an aristocrat's air. Almost bald, and perhaps approaching her father's age, he was clad in a white shirt, black cravat, formal waistcoat and striped trousers. He offered his hand to help her down from the carriage and said in a crisp French accent, "Welcome to the Royal Victoria. We hope your stay will be magnifique."

She took his hand but said nothing. *The chief butler? The owner? Do I give him my letter of intro....?*

Quick to sense her unease, he quickly relieved it. "I am Felix DuBois, the managing director of this humble auberge," he said with an officious bow.

"Delighted," she said, suspecting that he enjoyed her confusion as much as the captain. "May I present a letter of introduction?"

"Merci, but it's really not needed, Miss Beach," he replied. "Your father has already introduced you in a most eloquent way. We hope to reward his confidence in us through our hospitality to his daughter. May I show you to your room?"

Mister – *monsieur?* – DuBois walked erectly through the main lobby, pausing to nod politely at guests along the way until they entered the main wing of rooms. He unlocked the key to one door and ushered her inside with a bow. "I trust this will be *adequat?*"

Amelia's eyes swept over a room that seemed like an extension of a tropical garden. Instead of the dark oak floors of the only home she knew, the flooring was of wide terra cotta squares, broken by oriental throw rugs. A vase of fresh-cut hibiscus and bird of paradise stood on a marble table next to the French doors that led to a balcony overlooking a garden and the distant blue sea beyond.

"I hope you and your, ah, companions will be comfortable," DuBois said with a bemused nod at the luggage stacked along one wall. As the door closed behind him, her eyes turned to the white bed with blue satin cover and soft pillows. "Yes, I can be comfortable here," she said aloud, "even if I have to stay a month." And she sunk into the featherbed for a few minutes of lazy luxury. She might have dozed off altogether were it not for hearing a rustling or swishing in the wall between her room and the hotel hallway. A rat gnawing. A trapped bird ring to escape. Or maybe someone spying through a peephole to see if the new guest had something worth stealing?

The gold! Amelia snapped upright as if a sentry caught napping by a commandant. With racing heart she unpacked the ingots from all six pieces of luggage. *All fourteen intact – a victory of sorts.* She placed all fourteen in the biggest trunk, padlocked it again and stacked all the other suitcases on top like a wedding cake.

Next, Amelia decided to reward herself by exploring her surroundings. The Royal Vic was sultry and somnolent in the late afternoon. Her heels were the only noise on the terra cotta lobby floor as she admired large urns of native flora. Colorful Spanish tiles popped up in the flooring and on walls, almost as art pieces in themselves. On one table was a collection of decorative fans, ranging from elaborate Chinese folding fans to paddle fans painted with tropical scenes.

The only voices to be heard were those of servants on the outdoor piazza as they hung Chinese lanterns and set tables for some later event.

Amelia had begun to amble back to her room when she encountered the French mulatto walking head down as he scribbled on a sheet of paper. "Hello, again, Mister DuBois," she called out.

"Ah, Mademoiselle Beach," he answered. "May I be of service to you?"

"I was curious as to all the activity outside on the veranda."

"Tonight is the governor's reception," he replied. "It takes place once a month. The governor will appear and give us some good news about the Assembly or perhaps read a proclamation from the queen. He will also welcome some visiting dignitaries, including the captains of ships that have enriched our customs collections of late. Won't you please attend?"

"Since I will be meeting the captain of my father's ship, I expect to be there," she answered. "In the meantime, Mister DuBois, perhaps you can solve a little mystery for me. My room is exquisitely lovely except for a swishing or fluttering sound I hear between my outer wall and the hallway. Do you have gremlins in the woodwork? Ghosts of pirates?"

"Ah," he said with a raised index finger, "you may think them gremlins or hobgoblins, but I know them to be your housekeepers. That rustling sound you hear is no doubt made by maids going back and forth in an inner corridor as they bring things like towels and toiletries to our guest rooms. In your room is a door that may seem to be a closet. But it is in fact a locked door to the inner corridor that can be opened by a housekeeper. They always knock, of course."

"I don't understand," she retorted. "It seems like a needless expense,"

"Well, I am surprised that a lady from a slaveholding state would not understand," he answered in a tone more pedantic than she had been addressed by a man of color. "In the older plantation homes of the Caribbean the owner's family did not wish to see slaves parading about their family corridors, so they built separate ones so the slaves could be heard and not seen. Thus, in that style we built the Royal Victoria. Is it not so in your Georgia?"

She could sense the preamble to abolition lecture, but she let him continue. "Miss Beach," he added, "is it possible that you are uncomfortable in my presence and that this because all of the dark-skinned people you encounter are slaves?"

"No, well maybe yes," she stammered. Then stiffly: "You aren't the first to remind me that Nassau is a different society than our South. But who is patronizing whom here?"

"Not patronizing, mademoiselle, just having a get-acquainted conversation that I often have with visitors from the Southern U.S. Understanding that Bahamians are not slaves is important to the happiness and success of your stay at the Royal Victoria. And in the interest of that happiness, would you do a Frenchman the honor of pouring an English tea for an American lady?"

She met his ingratiating smile with one of her own. "I'd be delighted, but you really must if tell me how a Frenchman came to an English isle," knowing that it would be the first time she sat down with a man of color. *No, stupid. The second time after yesterday when you sat with Saint Matthew the cook.*

"I'm delighted to show you our Orangery," DuBois said. He led Amelia to a tearoom adjoining the main portico. It was a large, sun-filled room of white walls and tablecloths, cheerfully accented by wall murals of orange and lemon trees in bloom.

They were nearly alone as a waitress in black dress and white lace apron brought them sterling silver pots of tea, water and hot milk. "No, I am indeed not Bahamian," he began while passing her a china sugar bowl. "When you dip your teaspoon in this bowl, you will know why I am here before you now."

"Are you giving me a riddle?"

"I am referring to sugar," Miss Beach. My family's roots are in Paris, but they owned a sugar plantation in French Guinea well before I arrived on the scene. My father, it seems, was restless like most young males and decided that he would escape winter and the humdrum of Paris by journeying across the sea to become overseer of our plantation. Well, after a year or two Paris began to seem just a bit more exciting again than watching sugar cane grow, and Father soon departed. But he had become, let us say, quite attached to a certain Guinean housekeeper. One would call her a chambermaid in old Europe, and I am the result of that liaison."

"And she stayed behind?" said Amelia.

"Yes, of course. She remained behind. And I stayed behind for the most part except for visits to Paris now and then as a boy. Later I think Papa thought he could save money by grooming me to be the plantation overseer. So I studied at the Sorbonne so that I could speak to the cane cutters in Latin, I suppose."

DuBois grinned at his own joke and leaned back.

"But there must be more to the story," she said. "After all, here you *are*."

"And here *you* are," he replied. "Life leads us – sometimes lures us – down unplanned pathways. I suppose that you, Mademoiselle Beach, probably never expected to be visiting Nassau today were it not for some unexpected development. May I guess it to be your war?"

"A good guess," she said. "My father had need to supervise the sale of the cargo on the ship I arrived on and then to meet with an agent of the English company that built it. My older brother would have been the one to make this trip and I would be back home whipping my slaves (*touché, monsieur*), except that my brother was captured in battle and is now a prisoner in some horrible Yankee camp." *And that is all you're getting from me, Mr. DuBois.* "But please tell me about your unexpected pathway."

"Well, I shan't say that I ever felt managing a sugar plantation my life's calling, but I was quite good at it," he said. "We even prospered until external forces intervened. Cuba began expanding its sugar production, as did Martinique. They were closer to markets in Europe and America than Guinea. And they always could undercut our prices."

"And then? I expect a happy outcome," she said with an encouraging smile.

"You might call it that. I had an opportunity to sell the estate. And then, as I was on a leisurely trip through the Caribbean and Bahamas, quite expecting to return to France, fate guided me to Nassau and another opportunity. I was invited to invest in a new resort hotel and become its managing director as well. So that is how I came to the Royal Victoria. You know, Miss Beach, managing a large estate with many workers is actually quite similar to managing The Royal Victoria."

Looking out of the tall window onto the front portico, they could see the same two-horse carriage plodding up the driveway with new guests. "Along the way," he said standing up, "I have discovered that I derive great pleasure in accommodating guests like you, dear lady, and the ones I must now go and greet.

"But not as a slave," he added with a departing bow.

———

Amelia returned to her room and wrote a letter to her father describing all that had transpired with business-like efficiency. Then she turned to her wardrobe, now neatly arranged in drawers and closets.

At five minutes of seven Amelia poked her head out the door and quickly realized that the afternoon's quiet had given way to a promenade of couples leaving wisps of perfume, cigar smoke and gay conversation as they strolled by. After grabbing a flowery silk wrap from atop the bed, she was out the door and headed for the lobby. She quickly spotted Charles, dressed in black frock coat and beige trousers, leaning against a post with arms folded and staring out at the portico with its arriving guests. Easily the best – looking man in the crowd, she mused with inexplicable satisfaction.

It is now my turn to play the joke. Amelia sashayed past him so that her wide skirt brushed by his legs. "Oh, please pardon," he said, still staring ahead.

"Ahem!" She said, wheeling about.

"Miss Amelia Beach!"

"Charles Timmons, plain citizen!"

"You have put moths and butterflies to shame by becoming a princess," he exclaimed. Indeed, she had donned her best ballroom dress, a low-cut satin gown of gold and emerald green. Adorning her neck was her double-stranded gold necklace with its small locket. White pigskin gloves covered her arms to the elbows.

With her arm in his, they walked to the end of the covered veranda and stood at the stone balustrade overlooking the twinkling lamp lights of Nassau below, the setting sun to their left, and a stately columned building that Charles cited as the governor's mansion.

"How much time do you have to squire me about?" she asked.

"Just these next two nights for now," he said. "There seems to be great urgency in getting to Wilmington."

"Wilmington? North Carolina? But I thought Savannah. I have a letter to give you for my father."

"I'm so sorry," he replied. "Savannah, as you experienced, has simply become too risky for an unarmed and expensive ship like the *Sea Breeze*. Besides, once they unload a cargo there it has too far to travel to reach the troops. You see, a rail line runs from the center of Wilmington almost directly north to Richmond, and I'm sure the capital city's defense gets priority. Wilmington is safer as well. Once you can sneak by the blockaders, they won't dare chase you up the Cape Fear River because there are several Confederate forts along the way that can blow them out of the water."

Just then a small orchestra struck up a waltz. "Well, Amelia," he said, "let's go to the party and see if we can find you some new friends."

"Of course," she said, but all she had really heard was that it was the first time Charles had called her *Amelia.*

Suddenly the floor filled with a collection of mostly bearded, round-bellied, middle-aged men twirling women who were mostly younger and more attractive than their partners appeared to deserve. "Where do all these good-looking ladies come from?" She wondered aloud. "I saw none during my ride up here and scarcely any at the hotel this afternoon."

"Let me see," said Charles surveying the crowd. "Some are wives of Assembly members. Some are wives of government clerks being taken out on their birthdays and so forth. And some are what one might be called 'soldiers of fortune.' You know what I mean, of course."

"Of course," she answered, "but aren't they confined to their houses of ill-repute?"

"Most are, I suppose, but perhaps the most beautiful and proficient at their calling would rather flock to the money rather than sitting in a window and hoping it will come to them. Bees to honey, you know."

"Well, then, where do these ladies take their prey to work their wiles?"

"Oh, the most successful have rooms right here at the Royal Vic."

Amelia raised her gloved hands in mock horror. "That would never be allowed in a Savannah hotel," she declared with eyelashes fluttering.

"Perhaps you can think of it in another way," he said, rather enjoying her angst. "The men are all here, trading information, making money. The women would simply like to get in on it. The *act* you alluded to is just a part of it. They're probably here more in hopes of overhearing a profitable scheme in the making or perhaps of snaring a gentleman who will lead them away from the devil's clutches and give them a lifetime of respectability, perhaps as your neighbor in Savannah."

"But I'm serious," said Amelia. "How does a sincere and virtuous lady distinguish herself from all these soldiers of fortune swirling all about her? My mother's concern, you'll recall."

"Ah well," said Charles. He paused for a chin stroking, which he seemed to resort to whenever baffled. "Avoid wearing red," he said at last. "*They* seem to like it…to stand out in the crowd, I suppose."

"Does that include the lady over in the red gloves?"

"Um, no. She's a vicar's wife."

"Well then?"

Chin-stroking again. "Try to associate only with older women. Yes, *there's* good advice."

Then, with a flourish of bravado: "A lady of your superior upbringing simply stands out. She just *does*. It's a matter of experience, like recognizing a sloop from a schooner."

Now Amelia would toy with Charles. "Ah, then you have experience in identifying these soldiers of fortune."

"Miss Beach, I can assure you that you are the only woman ever to occupy my quarters." He said it so deliberately loudly that a few heads turned their way, and they walked laughing to the buffet table. Soon Amelia was proclaiming herself "in love with" conch fritters, fried calamari and cheese-stuffed clams after tasting each for the first time.

"And now I would guess you are thirsty," said Charles. "We'll need to find something that will guide you smoothly through the evening…."

"Without falling on my face," she interjected.

"Your words, my lady," answered Charles, approaching a table laden with bottles of all sizes and labels. "Let me see. Rye whiskey? No. Gin? Absolutely no. Merlot? Too heavy for milady. Ah, please try this light French Chablis."

He poured a partial glass and she took an un-lady-like swallow, followed by an exaggerated lip smacking. "You're in trouble again," she said. "This is even better than last night's champagne."

Just then the orchestra abruptly ceased the waltz and struck up *The Queen's March*. All rose and stood at attention as a tall man with slicked-down gray hair and mutton chops stood rather self-consciously at the entrance. He remained aristocratically erect, with hands folded in front of him until the march ended with a clash of cymbals, then strode across the floor to the podium.

"Ambrose Lord Fairchild," whispered Charles. "Our Majesty's Governor of The Bahamas. Master of all he surveys – except his own estates in Yorkshire, which have fallen into disrepair, I've been told."

Polite applause subsided quickly as the governor stood at the podium with a benevolent smile and raised his wrist ever so slightly. "My good friends, I welcome you here as I try to each month, whether or not I bring news to warrant your attention," he said in a wispy tone that made people lean their heads in to listen. "Well, you know I love a good party in any case," he added to a few titters. "However, tonight I do have some glad tidings I believe worth sharing. The Customs Office has just given me a report tallying up our exports for the year 1863. I am happy to say that exports, for the first time, exceeded five million pounds sterling. No less than 512 steamers and 186 sailing vessels came to our friendly port. I said friendly, but neutral," he added with mock severity while wagging a finger.

"I know that the captains of some recently arriving vessels are here with us tonight, and I shall be pleased to greet them now, as well as all old friends and visitors new to Nassau," he intoned.

With that, a receiving line began to form about the governor and Charles nudged Amelia. "Come, let's meet him before the line gets too long," he said.

"Do you know him?" she asked.

"Only met him once – in the same line – and only as a civilian like tonight. One doesn't want to flaunt military insubordination in his face. Last year the prime minister issued an edict saying that any ship identified as a 'belligerent' – meaning the two sides in your war – was to be denied entry except in case of 'extreme distress.'

"What might *that* mean?"

"Well, now, you've got the crux of it," said Timmons. "The PM described 'extreme distress' as fire, de-masting or serious leaking. Alas, he did not further define 'serious leaking.' Thus, the customs people have since been happy to agree that we are 'leaking,' or whatever else it takes to let us dock and feed their economic needs. And that includes the governor, I'm sure. But one doesn't wish to rub his nose in it by coming to his levee wearing battle ribbons."

"He looks mild enough to me," Amelia said as they advanced another step down the line.

"Actually, he is given great credit for the island's sudden prosperity," answered Charles. "Almost as soon as he arrived five years ago he persuaded the Cunard line to make a mail stop here once a month. Then he sold the Assembly on the idea that Nassau could become a winter paradise for New Yorkers and Londoners. Soon thereafter they had pried loose one hundred thirty thousand pounds to build the Royal Victoria.

"But then he was plain lucky," added Charles in a lower voice as they drew near the governor. "The war came along just when the hotel was finished. Who knows how it would have done without all this blockade running. But give him credit. Bay Street was paved last year and the first streetlamps went up just before I arrived."

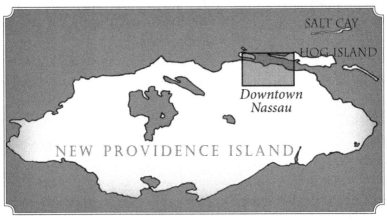

NEW PROVIDENCE
ISLAND, 1864

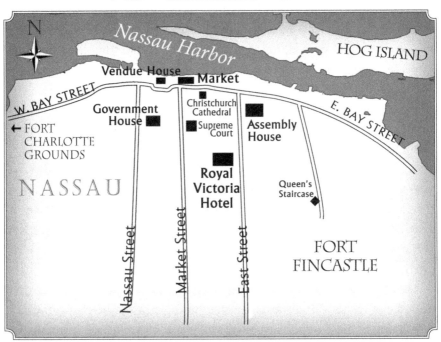

"Well, well, who have we here?" The great man reached out with both hands and Amelia's right forearm was swallowed up in their grasp.

"I'm sure you don't mean *me*," quipped Charles as the tall man's eyes remained affixed to Amelia's. "Sir, I am Charles Timmons, captain of the merchant ship *Sea Breeze,* lately here from Liverpool, and I am pleased to present to you Miss Amelia Beach. Her family owns the *Sea Breeze* and the very large trading firm of Huxley and Beach in Savannah, Georgia. Perhaps you've noticed all those bales of cotton on the docks with the big HB labels on them."

"Oh, to be sure, to be sure," the governor intoned with eyes still on Amelia. "Well, you must certainly pay us a visit at Government House and sign my book. "Staying here at the Royal Vic?"

She began to answer when the governor's hands freed her arm and reached out for the next supplicant's wife.

"I would doubt that he goes down to the docks often enough to see any HB bales," said Charles on the way back to the bar table. "I don't think he really wants to know who'll be hauling all those guns and bullets."

Amelia accepted another Chablis. "What is this 'signing my book' all about?" she asked.

"Just an old quaint English custom," he said. "He's referring to a guest book in his reception hall that distinguished visitors are presumably pleased to sign. Perhaps the governor invites the prettiest ones to tea," he added with a wink.

"Perhaps I'll just leave him an arm," she winked back.

As the reception line petered out and the orchestra began a zesty meringue, Amelia and Charles shook their heads in silent dissent and retreated to the back of the room. Formality around the room was quickly being eclipsed by merriment. "So many people to meet," Amelia said aimlessly.

"Buzzing all about you are diplomats, navy officers, newspaper people, brokers, shippers, stage actors, and those 'soldiers of fortune' we discussed earlier," said Charles.

"Are any of them illustrious personages worthy of the governor's guest book?" Amelia asked.

Charles scanned the room with a chin stroking she had already seen often. "Ah, the Victoria Cross," he exclaimed. "There's Captain Hewitt, who won the VC at Kamchatka, a battle off the Russian coast."

The man was thin and frail. "I think he signed the guest book many years ago," she opined.

"Righto. That decent-looking chap waltzing by with the lady in red – actually not a lady – was captain of the queen's yacht until six months ago. Created quite a stir when he announced that he had contracted consumption and wished to come to The Bahamas for his health. I think the aroma of money has improved it considerably.

"Diplomats, diplomats." Charles scanned the room again. "There, we have the French consul in serious discussion with the consul from Germany. I do know that the French one earns many times his government pay by shipping champagne to thirsty Southerners – perhaps some to the Beach wine cellar. Now the German consul I know not. I can't imagine why he's here except to have a merry time in a post he would have abhorred three years ago.

"Remember, I'm also here to help you avoid certain people," Charles added. "For instance, Frank Tortelli, that pumpkin by the bar. He's a correspondent for the *Illustrated London Times*. He writes most of what England knows about your war. If he can unearth a teaspoon of dirt, he'll make it into a mountain of misinformation. You see his big bushy mustache? They say it hides the teeth of a rodent.

"And over there is one who might be even worse for you," said Charles, pointing to a short waist coated middle-aged man clearly engaged in serious conversation. "Behold, I present to you – but only from afar – John Flemming, the United States consul to The Bahamas and potentially your biggest annoyance. Despite his lofty title, he is a glorified spy who snoops about the docks in hopes of learning what people like me are shipping to people like your father. In fact, he employs several assistant snoops in the same endeavor."

"Oh dear," said Amelia feigning a swoon. "Is there anyone I *should* meet? How about someone from the Royal Bank of London?"

"I would wager on it." Charles scanned the veranda again. "Managing director. Geoffrey Peters and wife. Permanent fixtures at these things. Probably drums up most of his business at the Royal Vic. Yes, I see the two of them over there by the bar table, he with the pencil mustache and gin glass in hand."

Dodging dancers as they moved, Charles continued his pre-introduction. "He's more wooden than a coffin. Pursed lips with hardly any air moving through them. But the wife is a jolly good sport. Beatrice. She seems to know everybody here.

"Ah, Geoffrey and Beatrice," announced Charles, cleaving their conversation to the apparent relief of both. "Captain Charles Timmons here, as you may recall. I have someone here who would like to meet you."

After a lavish description of Huxley and Beach by Timmons, Amelia announced that she had a "deposit" she should like to discuss with Peters on the morrow. "Very well," he uttered almost inaudibly. "Would ten am be convenient?"

Charles and Amelia excused themselves just as the orchestra began one of the new Strauss waltzes. "Well, I suppose it's now or never," he said. "I get around quite well on a pitching deck, but my feet seem to fail me on a dance floor."

"Well then, I think we're even in the bargain," replied Amelia. "You see, my terra firma is still swaying back and forth after three days at sea." But they managed by holding tight to each other, and for a few blissful moments all thoughts of banks and ships and Huxley and Beach were swept aside by the music, the array of stars above, and the man who held her by the waist.

But when the music stopped, the first image in her mind was of gold.

"Charles," she said, "you do know the main difference between a prince and princess?"

"I would like to think so."

"But I think not. When a prince needs relief, it can be achieved quickly with the help of a chamber pot or large tree. But a princess must first, shall we say, be disassembled by a covey of ladies-in-waiting. As you see, I have none. So, Charles, I will repair briefly to my room and reappear momentarily."

Back in her room, Amelia looked for any sign that her stack of suitcases had in any way been disturbed. Then, not even trusting rational judgment, she flung the empty suitcases to the ground and unlocked the bottom trunk. All fourteen of Blackbeard's babies, as she had come to call them, were sleeping peacefully.

How stupid. How irrational, she thought. *But it shows how vulnerable I feel about carrying out this task. Tomorrow I will be relieved beyond measure when all this gold is safe in a bank vault.*

Amelia returned to the hotel veranda to find Charles in a merry discussion with a handsome man of similar age. "Ah, Amelia Beach, I would like you to meet my friend John Brogan, and a fine dancer he is. If you'll join him in this waltz they've just started, he'll show you."

Suddenly Amelia found herself being swept along gracefully by a slender, black-haired young man with an engaging smile. "Charles has told me all about you," he said. "Now how about taking a guess about me?"

"Well, I shall guess that you are not from England nor our South," she answered. "But perhaps you owe me a hint. What were you and Captain Timmons talking about when I walked up?"

"All right, a hint. I was saying to Charles that he owes me some more bales."

"Oh, you're a cotton broker."

"No, indeed."

"A banker."

"No again." With a mischievous grin, he announced: "I am the captain of the *New Jersey,* the ship that was firing at you earlier today."

Amelia froze in place, nearly toppling another dance couple, and gave the fellow a stare of icy ire.

"I'm sorry if this has upset you," he said, taken aback.

"My brother Joseph is in one of your damned prisons," she said. "We can't even get word about him."

John Brogan made a sad face. "My brother died at Gettysburg," he said.

The two stood still amidst couples swirling all about them. Finally, he spoke softly: "Look all around this room and you will see Union officers – damned Yankees. We arrive by tender from our various sea patrols and hope for a little merriment in the midst of a stupid war we didn't start and don't have any say in ending. Let us just hope that the people you see enjoying themselves together might prove to be an example of how we can all get along again one day."

"Yes, let us hope so," she said stiffly. With that he walked her back to Timmons and departed with a hasty bow.

Charles and Amelia were left with more awkward silence. "It looks as if the two of us played a bad joke on you," he said at last. "Let's leave the scene of battle and go to the most peaceful place in Nassau." They left the veranda, walked out the entry portico and across the carriage road to a banyan tree that was as wide as a Bahamian cottage.

"Come, let's climb a tree like when we were children," he said taking her by the hand. Wooden steps led them up to a platform built around the broad trunk where they could sit on wicker chairs and look down on the harbor below and the sea beyond. The smell of night-blooming jasmine enveloped them and the stars of the Milky Way seemed as if they could be touched by just reaching out.

They sat in silence, and after several minutes Amelia's hurt had surrendered to the soothing breeze and jasmine. But Charles – perhaps his "bad joke" had broken the spell of magic – had clearly ceased exuding charm or romance. When he walked her to her room, she and the wine were expecting perhaps a kiss – at least something that would improve on Freddy Farnsworth – but he lingered awkwardly.

"Still on duty?" she asked.

"Yes, still on duty."

She looked up into his eyes. "Charles, is my father paying you to be a governess?" she asked.

"No, of course not," he said. "But I surmise that without proper attention to your safety, I might never sail the *Sea Breeze* again, nor collect my share. But you are intriguing all on your own, Miss Beach."

"Perhaps you can tell me what intrigues you."

"Well," he said, "I find that you have a tough hide, yet a thin skin."

With that, he gently pulled off her glove, took her hand and kissed it with a lingering tenderness that sent chills up her arm.

"Yes, this hand is very soft," he said offhandedly. "Very intriguing altogether, I should say."

The Royal Victoria Hotel, Nassau, Bahamas

Chapter Seven
NASSAU LIFE

The next morning Amelia treated herself to fresh orange juice, biscuits and jam in her room. She emerged dressed casually as one would go marketing in Savannah, her only accompaniment a large parasol that she held in both hands. In the nearly empty lobby, the only hangover from the previous night's festivities was a tinge of cigar smoke. It was as if all the guests were waiting for the ten o'clock ocean breeze to stir them from their rooms.

"To the Royal Bank of London," she told the driver. "Four blocks down to Bay street and left for a few more."

"Know it well," he said. "Looks like you're not going to need that umbrella. Not a cloud in the sky."

Clattering down the unpaved limestone, it seemed that the Royal Victoria had set the pace for all Nassau. Women with bandana head wraps idly switch-brooming walkways. Others ambling towards the market with empty jugs and baskets on their heads. Dogs already snoozing under shady stoops. Two old men staring across a chessboard outside an empty bar.

As the carriage turned onto Bay Street, the life juices of Nassau were beginning to flow. Women arranging piles of straw hats under a tattered tent. Shopkeepers propping open metal shutters that revealed hanging banana bunches and rows of pineapples. A one-horse wagon straining to pull a large cart with a teetering pile of sponges. Flies also stirring and deciding whether to breakfast on melon or meat.

A few blocks down Bay Street the carriage stopped. "This is it," the driver announced.

"It? What?"

"The Royal Bank of London, milady."

'But I don't see…"

"Right over there." The driver pointed to a row of shotgun stores and warehouses. At the end of the block was a two-story yellow storefront with, sure enough, a hanging *Royal Bank of London* sign that might have been more apropos for a boarding house or saloon.

Amelia stepped down and stood staring at the building while paying the driver. "I suppose I expected something with Grecian columns like the Assembly building," she said.

Still clutching the folded parasol, she pushed an imposing gray door with an ENTER sign above the latch. Inside to her left were two teller's cages, occupied at the moment by one elderly clerk busy counting some bills. To her right, a standup counter with various deposit slips, and above, a large wall calendar showing a buxom woman on a bicycle and the month still fixed on JANUARY. The rear of the building consisted of two desks behind a low wooden balustrade. Hunched over one of them was the man Amelia had met the night before, apparently so transfixed by a sheet of paper in his grasp that he had not noticed perhaps the first customer to enter his establishment that morning.

While Amelia scanned the room for signs of a vault and a guard, Geoffrey Peters, he of pencil-thin mustache, sagging pince-nez on a slender nose, and wispy Van Dyke on a weak chin, rose and opened the rail gate for her to enter his sanctuary. When she declined his offer of tea, she wondered how he could bear to be further warmed while already encased in a shirt, velvet vest and heavy morning coat.

Amelia presented her letter of introduction. As banker Peters mused over it, he looked up and said, "This mentions a 'deposit, pending transfer of some portion to Wainright Ship Builders in Liverpool and the remainder subject to later instructions.'

"I'm unclear," he said stiffly. "What is the nature of this deposit?"

"Its nature is gold," she said with starch to match, "to be held in your safe deposit vault pending the conditions just described."

"Gold?" He seemed uncomprehending.

"Spanish gold," she said. "Am I correct that your Assembly has made Spanish gold legal tender in The Bahamas?"

"Yes. In what form is yours?"

Amelia's parasol had remained in her lap during the conversation. Now she unwound the parasol and pulled out an ingot that she had wrapped inside. "In the form of several gold ingots like this," she said, sliding it across Peters' desk.

He recoiled as if being handed a live hand grenade. "Oh, my," he said.

Amelia's irritation was rising as fast as the room temperature. "Sir, aren't bankers supposed to welcome valuable deposits?" she said crisply. "It was not exactly earned in a poker game. It comes from the honest toil of one of the most respectable mercantile companies in the Confederate States of America."

Peters' chin snapped upward in indignation. "Young lady," he snorted, "there are things here you may not understand. Only a few weeks ago the prime minister sent orders that all British banks must adhere to our strict neutrality in this war of yours or face serious consequences. Even more recently, the chancellor of the exchequer issued regulations forbidding banks from trafficking or financing trade from one adversary to another."

Amelia felt herself suddenly flailing about in heavy seas and sinking under the weight of her burden. She was totally unprepared for such a response, but something told her to be calm and charming. "Now, Mister Peters," she said constructing a stony smile, "suppose that the master of an English fishing vessel asked you for help in financing a larger ship. Would you not be favorably inclined to support him? Yes? Well, of course! Now then, most of my proposed deposit is intended as payment to a company in your native England for a merchant ship that will help bring further glory to the British Empire."

He fell silent, moving his head back and forth as if weighing pros and cons.

Then: "I applaud your good intentions, Miss, but the most the Royal Bank of London can do is to ask the Office of Exchequer to rule on whether it is permissible to store gold for a Confederate party. But before that can occur, the bank must write to your Huxley and Beach asking them to furnish proof that the gold came from trade that was non-combative."

Amelia was now ready to settle for a life buoy. "All right, but will you store this gold for me in the meantime?" she asked.

Peters: "I suppose we could, but I cannot issue you a receipt for it. You see, that would be tantamount to disobeying or ignoring the exchequer's ruling on the matter before we receive it."

Businesswoman Beach, opening her purse and drawing out two Spanish gold pieces: "May I assume this will cover the fee until we receive word?"

Peters: "It depends on the size and volume of the deposit."

Beach: "Very well. It will consist of two steamer trunks."

Peters: "Steamer trunks?"

Beach: "Yes. Two ordinary trunks of average size. Since the bank – and all England, it seems – are so skittish as to the nature of this deposit, let us simply treat it for now as two locked trunks that could contain my dowry or my grandmother's sentimental heirlooms. Would these coins then cover storage for now?"

Peters: "Um, well yes. May I inquire as to where these, ah, heirlooms are presently stored?"

Beach: "On a ship."

Peters, with pursed lips: "Well, I daresay that this ship probably didn't issue you any receipts or guarantees, either. Ships are not exactly safe depositories."

Beach: "That is why I am here. Now may I please visit your place of safe deposit?"

After slowly opening his desk drawer as if it also contained precious heirlooms, Peters lifted a metal loop with a single large key hanging from it. He rose and opened what appeared to be a nearby closet door, revealing a second door of solid steel with a round cylinder in the middle. Amelia had never seen a bank vault, but she couldn't resist vexing her tormenter.

"That lock looks rather old," she observed as he inserted the large key.

"Madame," he said with equal annoyance, "you may be confusing this Chubb lock with the old four-level tumblers of the eighteen twenties. This is a six-tumbler lock, invented five years ago just before this branch was opened."

The door swung open, revealing a narrow but deep room lined with boxes resembling those she had seen in post offices. "Lined with steel-reinforced concrete all around," Peters added.

"Well, hardly like the ones we're used to in Savannah, but if it's the best Nassau has to offer, it will do," she replied. *Enough of this haughtiness. It's a dozen times safer than a hotel room with secret corridors.*

No sooner had Amelia emerged from the inner sanctum when the bank front door opened and in swept – Bridgett? Bertie? Bernice? – the banker's wife she had met so briefly the night before. "Miss Amelia Beach! I'm so happy that you haven't left yet," she gushed. "Do you remember Beatrice among all the people so eager to meet you last night?"

Beatrice Peters was such a burst of sunshine and fresh air in the stale, stuffy bank office that Amelia felt drawn into her aura at once. Plump but pleasantly apportioned, she might have been a mother goose spreading her wings to gather her goslings.

"I was thinking last night that here you are, a single young thing, probably abandoned as your captain goes about his ship business by day," she exuded. "Suppose you let me show you the wonders of Nassau. It's not New York or London, but we have gardens and churches and history that no one else has. Did you know that we were a pirate refuge for a couple of centuries? Oh yes! And you really need to learn how to shop the straw markets. Ever seen the sponge markets? So, tomorrow around ten I will call on you at the Royal Vic and you will get to meet Penelope. We'll go to Government House, too. Yes? Good. Now Geoffrey, where are you taking me to lunch?"

Amelia was agape but amazed to know that someone seemed to care at the same time for her and the callous bureaucrat who was trying to spindle her mission on a pile of paperwork. *If I can't change his mind, maybe she can.*

"Good morning, good morning," Beatrice called from her carriage to Amelia on the portico of the Royal Vic precisely at ten the next day. Hitched ahead of her was a stocky, gray-tinged roan with ears sticking through a Bahamian straw hat.

"Before we're off to Government House I want you to meet Penelope," enthused Beatrice. "Now she may look like an ordinary horse, but she is of distinguished lineage. Oh yes! Her ancestors were bred by Spaniards on the Barbary Coast. Some were put aboard ships for the New World and at least one of them must have wrecked on the shores of Great Abaco island not so very far from here. They ran wild up there for years and years until some local decided to bring a few to Nassau and put harnesses on them. So, Penelope is what we call an 'Abaco Barb.' I thought she deserved a nice feminine name after all that running in the wild. Penelope, say hello to Miss Beach may I call you Amelia? Yes? Good!"

Amelia was to learn quickly that Beatrice Peters' words came in fusillades, with no way to pry open a phrase until she was inhaling to ready the next salvo. "What do horses eat here?" she wondered aloud. "You don't raise wheat or oats, do you?"

"Well, on Great Abaco they got along on cow grass," said Beatrice. "But Penelope needs her energy to climb up and down this ridge, so she gets extra treats. Loves sugar cane but too much makes her jumpy and so does barley malt but she loves it, too. But best of all she likes hibiscus. If someone has a hibiscus bush hanging over their front wall Penelope will stop everything she's doing until all the blooms are gone, but she's nearsighted I think so she'll start in on oleander which looks rather the same to her, but oh my, the tummy ache that follows!

"Now look across the street to Fort Fincastle before we go off," Beatrice continued without a hitch while bidding Amelia climb up the buckboard. "Built in 1793 after Nassau finally grew weary of pirates taking over the place. At long last the good folk of Nassau had more cannon than the pirates did. I read that in the last century there were over a thousand of them on the island at any one time. Blackbeard, Calico Jack Rackham, Stede Bonnet, all big stars on the criminal stage. Now I know some of these chaps visited America as well, but on Nassau we had governors of the crown who were worse than the pirates. Why in the sixteen hundreds when Cadwaller Jones was governor – maybe that's where the word *cad* comes from – anyway, the Assembly wouldn't pass a bill he wanted so he hired a pirate ship to train its guns on the Assembly building until they did. Pass his bill. He welcomed the pirates, embezzled the treasury and refused to recognize William and Mary as monarchs. So when the law-abiding citizens finally rose up and arrested him for treason, the pirates gathered a mob of rogues and had him restored to his full powers."

Beatrice, still with reins in lap, paused for a second to seek a moral to the tale. "Of course whenever some pirate fleet came in for provisions or to spend their loot, the people and the governor both welcomed them lustily. Sort of like right now, I would say, not that *you* all are pirates, but the motive of our local citizens is still the same.

"But you know what's strange?" she went on. "The only verified capture of Spanish gold by a pirate ship out of Nassau that I've ever read about was when one of them sailed off to Cuba and captured a Spanish ship carrying eleven thousand pieces of eight. And yet when the captain of that Bahamian ship died many years later, his will left the family only something like two quid, a gun and some fish hooks. So you have to wonder, why does the treasure always disappear?"

I hope not always, was Amelia's first thought.

"Well now, we're off to visit the governor," Beatrice continued, jerking the drowsy Penelope forward with a gentle rap on the rump. "However, the governor's not in. See the flagpole?" She pointed a half-mile to the southwest where the Union Jack fluttered even higher than the tall columns of Government House. "If the governor were in residence, his personal flag would be flying below the Jack. Must have gone off to the Assembly."

As they plodded along Shirley Street on the limestone ridge, past homes of barristers and bureaucrats, Beatrice become a bit more pensive. "The governor is quite likeable beneath all the ribbons and sashes," she said. "Yet I feel somewhat sorry for him. His wife is not well – or so she claims – and has been in England quite some time now for the purpose of regaining her health, even though one wonders how the fog and sooty coal dust of London could compare with clean ocean breezes here. Each month the poor soul sends his man Anson down to meet the Cunard steamer with hopes that she might have sent a letter, but most of the time he comes back empty-handed."

The carriage stopped at the foot of a wide stone staircase with a large statue at the top. A lone sentry with white pith helmet emerged from a guard box and seemed to recognize Beatrice with a nonchalant nod. "Signing the book," was all she said, and he waved her on with a white glove.

At the top of the long staircase they confronted a large statue of Christopher Columbus. "I suppose a lot of your Americans think he first landed on your shores," she said merrily, "but no, no, he made landfall in The Bahamas and, as you see, we have the statue to prove it."

"Well, I'm glad there's an engraving to tell me who he is," said Amelia. The New World founder looked more like an Italian pirate, with slouched cocked hat, a toga over one shoulder and a jaunty grin.

Looming behind the stone statue on the top of Mount Fitzwilliam – the Bahamians' wry name for the hundred-foot limestone ridge – stood the four-columned, two-story residence that Amelia had only seen distantly from the terrace of the Royal Victoria. "You see, all the buildings here were of wood until the English Loyalists came here after your Washington chap chased us out in that dreadful rebellion. This is the first building here to be built of stucco and coral rock. The pink and white is our own special touch."

Soon they were past another sentry and inside a vaulted foyer. "Here to sign the registry," Beatrice said, nodding to a custodian sitting by a wide marble table.

"Certainly, Mrs. Peters," he answered.

Mrs. Peters?

"Well, there's what all that riding and climbing is all about," said Beatrice, pointing to a white leather-covered guestbook. "Say something nice to the governor." Amelia settled for her name, home city and "residing at the Royal Victoria Hotel."

"Would you mind if I just showed the ballroom to our guest?" Beatrice asked the custodian.

"By all means please do, Mrs. Peters," he said.

They entered a columned, mirrored hall twice the size of the Royal Vic terrace. "Here is where the Governor's Ball takes place on the queen's birthday every May twenty-fourth," Beatrice said as she began a slow twirl about the dance floor. "Now you would think that this would be *the* most exciting ball to attend, but it more or less works in reverse in Nassau. The Governor's Ball is so stiffly formal, with none of the racier new songs, that it's boring – and with the stingiest of libations because they come from the governor's purse. Everyone who attends is a royal with a distant connection – or thinks he *might* become a royal snob by way of knighthood or the Victoria Cross – or feels he must behave so prim and properly as to eliminate all visible signs of mirth 'lest someone be *staring*."

She inhaled. "Next you have the Christmas and New Year's balls at the Assembly House. A little zestier because the libations come from the legislative purse – other people's money – and because you might actually find some real live breathing Bahamians there. Finally, there are the regular non-events at the Royal Vic, which everyone attends and anything goes. So you see, my dear, now you know how the social order is composed. Shall we continue our ride?"

"Will you join me for lunch at the hotel?" Amelia asked as they mounted the carriage again.

"I'd be pleased to, but first let's ride down George Street. I'd like to show you a special shop you might not find on your own."

They ambled downhill in the direction of Bay Street, then east along a narrow, parallel coral rock lane lined mostly with homes behind walls. Without a command, Penelope stopped at a gate with the sign SEA GARDEN GIFTS. On both sides of the gate the whitewashed walls were an embroidery of yellow trumpet vines, climbing red roses and purple bougainvillea.

Inside was a small courtyard and open-faced shop of decorative white bleached corals and shiny giant conch shells. Orange starfish and sponges embedded with tiny shells were suspended from the ceiling on strings, undulating in the late morning breeze. But Amelia's gaze quickly fixed on a table with shelves of artificial flowers exquisitely carved from some sort of bone.

"You are right to be drawn to these," said Beatrice. "Each one is carved from conch." Just then a young buxom black woman, no doubt the store clerk, emerged from a doorway of hanging glass beads.

"Good morning, Mary," said Beatrice. "I don't think I have any more room for your beautiful carvings, so I brought another visitor to see you."

"Well that's nice," she answered in a soft Bahamian lilt.

"I love your conch flowers," Amelia said. "I want a string of them for my windowsill at the hotel. When I return home, they will decorate our dining table. And I must have this large conch shell. And this purple sea fan. But tell me, Mary, where do you find them all?"

"In different places….in the sea gardens."

"In the coral formations on the sea bottom," explained Bernice. "But Miss Beach would like to know where."

"Ooh," Mary said with a giggle. "*That's* a secret."

"Oh, come now," scolded Beatrice. "I'm too old to go looking in the sea and Amelia here will soon be on a ship for home."

"I never know exactly," said Mary. "My brother, he goes sponge fishing all over and finds them. But I think maybe these come from the Blue Lagoon."

"The…where?"

"A lagoon on Salt Cay. A cay beyond Hog Island. Inside of it is the Blue Lagoon. But you would need a boat to go there."

"Well, for now I will be content with your treasures," Amelia said. "But perhaps before I depart, I will find a boat to take me to the Blue Lagoon."

Amelia was still digesting her Sea Garden experience when she and Beatrice sat down to tea and finger sandwiches at the Royal Vic tearoom. Beatrice was babbling about shopping when Amelia suddenly dammed up her stream of consciousness. "Beatrice, I don't mean to disparage any of the lovely sights of Nassau," she said "But don't you ever feel a longing to burst free of the confinement of… of womanhood? Of propriety?"

Beatrice: "Oh my."

Amelia: "I mean, here we are at noon on a tropical isle and I am already feeling hot and stifled in this, this *tent* I'm required to wear. The shoes take forever to lace up and when I'm finally finished, my feet hurt. Don't you ever feel the same?"

Beatrice: "Well, I, but we are expected to…."

Amelia, her words beginning to spin out of control: "You know what I'd like to do more than anything? I'd like to take off my clothes and go swimming in this beautiful water. You know, I've never had much interest in swimming because the waters around Savannah are brown and sort of sticky and full of crabs that pinch. But this beautiful blue water is the closest I can imagine to the cleansing waters of the River Jordan. Now, I know what a dead conch looks like, but I would love to see one moving along the bottom and pick it up and see what's inside. I'd like to see a sea fan actually swaying with the current."

Beatrice, gently, after a rare moment of reflection: "Amelia, you are young and high-spirited. I was, too, at your age, although I don't recall ever having an urge to jump into the waters at Brighton Beach with no clothes on. Tomorrow after lunch, let Penelope and me show you the busy parts of Nassau with certain insights that might escape a newcomer. We'll stop at the harbor so that you can say good-bye to your ship captain. Then we'll go by the swimming beach and show you why your, er, ambitions, might be a bit unrealistic."

Amelia: "Maybe we could just sit on the beach in our stuffy hot cotton. We could feed the gulls and watch the waves break. It would be exhilarating even at that."

Mid-February was cool, bright, with gentle breezes. But just when perfection threatened to become monotonous, the capricious weather gods would decree a day of cold, gray and bluster. On this evening, a gusty squall had blown glasses and napkins about the Royal Vic terrace, leaving only the hardiest of drinkers and dancers to navigate the slippery tile floor.

Charles Timmons arrived in a carriage with two officers from other ships. After a quick greeting, Charles shooed them into the bar and led

Amelia in the other direction.

"I think this would be a perfect time to find us a quiet table inside the dining room," he said. "No more consuls and governors for a while. I've been waltzing around the harbor all day in search of engine parts."

Luckily, they found a table by a window looking uphill towards Government House in the distance. Strains from a string quintet next door made for a pleasing backdrop. But any thought that Charles might have an intimate, romantic dinner in mind quickly faded. In her wittiest way, Amelia described the "rite of registration" at the Government House and splendid art creations at The Sea Garden, but Charles only nodded blankly.

"Charles, I learned today about the coral gardens at Salt Cay," she exclaimed. "They call it the Blue Lagoon. Won't you take me there one day when you return? It's somewhere near Hog Island, but you need a small sailboat to get there. If you can steer that big one, you can steer a much smaller one, right?

"Pardon?" He finally cracked open a smile at her persistence. "Yes, they train us on the little ones before we're allowed to steer the big ones," he said. "But that would be beyond my official duties," he said with his most officious face.

"*Pleeeze*?" she pleaded in a little girl voice, followed by a comical fluttering of eyelashes.

"Of course, of course," he sighed with a roll of the eyes. "We'll go to your sea garden."

"Well, then," replied businesswoman Beach. "Now it's your turn to tell me what's filling your head right now."

Charles buttered a piece of bread and ordered a bottle of Chablis. "Oh, it's a jumble of things, as it always is before a sail." Then he poured out his worries. "Everybody on board has specific tasks, but the captain gets handed dilemmas that don't have specific solutions," he said. "For instance, I sent word on a boat that left last week for Wilmington telling the captain to alert the command at Fort Fisher that we'd be running the gauntlet – that's the Cape Fear River – around twenty-two hours on the night of the twelfth. A good part of our manifest is a load of rifles that's supposed to have arrived here yesterday from London. If it doesn't arrive tomorrow, do I wait another day? If I do, the moon will be larger over Wilmington and the people at Fort Fisher will think I've diverted.

"Then I think one – maybe two – of our stevedores may have the beginnings of yellow fever. It's hard to tell because they're always sweating anyway. So, if I leave them behind, where do I find new ones without word spreading and everyone else jumping ship? And if I leave them here, they're both from Bermuda. What happens to them here?

"So that's the kind of worry that captains get and what can make them dull dinner company," he said while pouring wine. After they agreed on a cracked conch appetizer and stuffed red snapper, he added: "You know this fish of ours probably came from your sea garden."

"Stop it!" she scolded. "I want to hear more from your captain's worry list."

"Well, I worry that the Union navy will have more blockaders when we arrive. Word's going around that they're building something like forty double-enders, which could make things truly difficult."

"Double enders?"

"That's a fast ship like ours, but with rudders at both ends. You can reverse the engine and go just as fast in either direction. In other words, our ability to sneak around a blockader's stern is reduced if it doesn't have to turn around. Suddenly the stern just takes off after you."

"Well, maybe the construction's been delayed," said Amelia. "Why don't you ask your friend, the Union captain who wants more bales."

"Oh quite," he answered. "That would be treason, of course, and I don't think we're chums enough to get him hanged for some bloody bales of cotton."

When the entrees arrived, they ate mostly in silence – he, churning his thoughts and she fretting over just one worry that consumed her mind. Before meeting Charles on the portico, Amelia had stewed over how to transport two excessively heavy sea trunks to the Royal Bank of London vault without divulging their content or her purpose. She needed a confidant and the only plausible candidate was the man across from her. She had concluded that she would enlist his help if he showed enough charm or at least affection at dinner to prove – well, indicate – that he would be loyal and not just another buccaneer.

But the conversation had not led down that path. The meal was over. Charles excused himself "for a moment" and could be seen talking to his officers on the adjoining terrace. She knew that harbor duties beckoned, and by the time he returned to the table, Amelia had decided on a compromise based on half-truths.

"Charles, let's just finish this wine before you leave," she said when he was seated. "Because you've been so busy, there is something very important that I haven't told you."

"Yes, I'll carry letters to your father. Did you know that ship captains get five cents for each letter they transport?"

"Please, this is serious," she said, "something much more important to me – and my father. You know how you teased me about taking so many pieces of luggage? Well, the reason is that they contain gold. Gold ingots."

Charles cocked his head with an impish smile. "If I'd known that on the way here," he said, "I would have kidnapped you and sailed off to some Caribbean paradise."

"Please concentrate," she replied sternly. "My father and I are the only ones who know about this gold, which now resides in my room, which is not a very secure place, I can assure you. Much of it is designated for the Liverpool builder of the very ship you are about to sail tomorrow."

Charles: "But why gold? No, let me guess. The people in Liverpool won't accept Confederate dollars because of how the war is going and the inflation it's caused. And your father's only hope for having his pile eroded by worthless currency is to buy a ship with gold so that he can sell cotton across the Atlantic and get paid in pound sterling."

"I suppose so, Charles," said Amelia. "But all this commerce generates the same pound sterling that pays your fees. So it would seem that we're all in this together. I know how terribly busy you will probably be tomorrow morning, but I am asking that you have two of your strongest men with a carriage here at 9:30 to haul two heavy trunks to the Royal Bank of London down on Bay Street."

"How heavy?" Charles asked.

"I don't know exactly," she said with a trace of impatience. "All I know is that two of my father's dock workers carried them up the gangplank in Savannah."

Charles clearly wasn't rushing into anything. "Just curious," he mused. "Why can't the bank do this?"

Amelia gave an exasperated sigh. "It's because the bank – that Geoffrey Peters fellow we met last night – is wrapped up like a mummy in *exchequer* regulations," she fumed. "He's the only live person I've ever met who al-ready has rigor mortis. The official policy is that the bank might be held liable if its employees were transporting the gold and some pirates shot them and stole the loot."

"I see," said Charles softly. "Of course I will send you two men. At 9:30. Two strong men. Perhaps a few coins would cheer them."

From their table, they could see the *Sea Breeze* officers lingering at a distance as if ready to leave. "Yes, I see your men," Amelia said, "but I'd like one more favor. The music is playing again and I'd like just one waltz around the room."

They did so, and with no boat swaying under her feet this time. As they walked off the floor, she reached up, kissed him on the cheek and said, "Thank you for everything, Charles. I hope to see you off tomorrow afternoon."

The next morning just after 9:30, a gardener continued cutting yellow daisies as two sailors from the Sea Breeze hoisted two padlocked steamer trunks onto the back of a buckboard at the Royal Victoria portico. Neither the women ambling to market with a few pence to spend, nor the shop-keepers, who hoped for a ten shilling sale, turned a head as a wagon load – worth more than all of their dreams combined rumbled to a stop in front of the Royal Bank of London.

Amelia had followed at a respectable distance in a one-horse cab. Without asking anyone inside, she simply had the sailors barge in so boldly with the first trunk that it might have been discharged onto Geoffrey Peters' desk had he not instinctively opened the low gate that led to the bank vault.

"Good morning, I am here as agreed upon," she announced nonchalantly as the men went to the wagon for their second trunk. "If you will unlock that door there, I will complete the safety deposit and be on my way."

He did, and Amelia was soon back at the Royal Vic, pleased that bold-ness and bravado had prevailed over inertia and indecision. In fact, to cel-ebrate the occasion, she stopped in the hotel gift shop and treated herself to a copy of the popular novel, *Jane Eyre*, which represented another bold breakthrough – a book actually written by a woman.

After lunch, Beatrice and Penelope came calling and Amelia quickly lost the unease she had felt knowing that this lively, loquacious woman was the wife of a cold-hearted banker who all but disdained the trust she was thrusting upon him. "Do you like our hats?" she said in place of a greeting. Both wore broad brimmed gardening hats with white and yellow flowers affixed to the band. "Penelope tried to eat hers while I was putting it on," she added.

As they rode on, the people and buildings Amelia saw from her carriage took on different shapes and meaning when described by Beatrice. As they rode down East Street, the same one she had taken with the gold wagon, Beatrice pointed to the walled buildings and proclaimed that "One day soon all these walls will come down if Ambrose – Governor Fairchild – has his way. Do you know why, my dear? Because the walls were built during slavery times. But they tend to keep the air from circulating and make the homes hotter inside. We can have breezes again if we replace the walls with iron grillwork, fences and windows. Would you agree?"

Amelia had no chance to agree or disagree, because Beatrice had come to Assembly Square at the corner of East and Bay streets. "Now we are truly in the heart of The Bahamas," she proclaimed. "Here you have the legislature in one building, the Treasury across the street and in that third building a collection of offices such as the court, the post office, the surveyor general and assorted what-not. And over there the jail, so you can make laws, enforce them and punish offenders all within a short walking distance. See how civilized we English are?"

A block later on Bay Street they came to a large Anglican cathedral. "Of course the church of England was first to set up shop here a couple hundred years ago," she said, "Then came the Methodists, but the Baptist missionaries really started making inroads after slavery ended because I think the blacks just liked all that shouting and singing better than the stuffy old Anglican Church.

"Now this church, Christchurch Cathedral, gives you a perfect picture postcard of Nassau society today," Beatrice rambled on. "If you went in here on a Sunday you would see the wealthiest people sitting in high-backed pews at front and center. They actually pay rent for them. Poorer white people would be behind them in the center and on the side aisles. Then in the upstairs gallery you would see all the blacks – the people who were here on this island in the first place. But some would call it progress, because thirty years ago you wouldn't find any blacks. Are there blacks in your church, Amelia?"

Amelia was about to admit that all the blacks at her church were outside standing beside their masters' carriages, but Beatrice and Penelope were already clattering down Bay Street.

She pulled Penelope to a halt in front of an old stone building with an imposing Georgian two columned entrance and a tall opening on either side. It ran long like a basilica or open-but-roofed market house. It seemed to be the center of street vendor activity. Other people milled about, some with bottles in hand, some singing and swaying to the sound of a man beating a wooden drum.

Why is this so familiar? Amelia wondered. *Because it reminds you of the slave market in Savannah.*

Beatrice, with arms outstretched: "This is my favorite place because it's been here longer than the Assembly buildings and because whatever's going on inside is the most important commerce in Nassau. It started out as a slave market. Then when that business was outlawed, it became the center of the sponge and wrecking businesses. Now for the most part the same people do both. When there were no wrecks to salvage, they would go sponge fishing or try to farm. But it always seemed that the sponge fishermen were at the mercy of the merchants to sell their catch right here at Vendue House. The merchants fixed the prices they would pay. Let us say that a man was about to take a sponging trip of a month or so. The merchant would advance him money for provisions at ridiculous prices. Then when it came time to sell his sponges, the sponger wouldn't make enough to cover his advance. I remember one case that made the newspapers. Five men on a ship fished, cleaned and dried about eight thousand sponges in a voyage that took five weeks. When they took the catch to this building right here, all they got was eleven pounds between the five of them for five weeks' work. And it didn't match their advances, which meant they owed the merchant even more. That's worse than slavery, because at least slaves don't owe their masters money."

She looked at Amelia beside her. "Are you wondering what all this has to do with you?"

"Yes I am."

Exactly what Beatrice wanted to hear. "All right. When the war between the states, as you call it, started coming to Nassau in the form of all this trade you see out there in the harbor, the same people who were eking out a living at sponging and wrecking found they could make unheard-of sums as dock workers, sailors, waiters and so forth. Until three years ago a day laborer would earn about two shillings a day. Now they can demand ten. And they can get twelve shillings if they sleep right at the harbor on top of a bale of cotton."

"Shouldn't we applaud this as a good thing?" said Amelia.

"You might think so if it continued," retorted Beatrice quickly. "But your war isn't going to last forever. Most of these people have lost the skill or desire to farm or sponge. The young ones probably haven't learned at all. And when the war is over – they all do end, you know – and this place returns to poverty and idleness, it will be left worse than ever."

"Hep, hep, Penelope," Beatrice spoke to the horse as a man approached with arms rung with bracelets. Another was behind him with a tray of woodcarvings. "Time for us to leave," she said. "We've been spotted. It's getting to be mid-afternoon and I want to show you one more thing before we go down to that ship of yours."

The carriage clopped westward on Bay Street until the street sellers were left behind and only a few waterfront buildings remained. "This is where the beach gets nice and where you might be inclined to indulge your bathing fantasy," said Beatrice pointing to the water. Diving, frolicking and jostling one another were twenty or thirty Bahamian males, ranging from boys to sturdy young men judging from the size of their naked malehood.

"Now if you want to take your clothes off and plunge in there among *them...*" said Beatrice with cocked eyebrows.

"I see," said Amelia. "I mean, I understand. Drive on."

As the carriage reversed course and headed back east past Vendue House again, Amelia wedged in some words. "Beatrice, you speak of this coming 'regression into poverty' with... with a kind of bitterness... almost as if you were one of them... as if you feel it personally."

"I am sad, I suppose, because my husband and I see omens of the future that these people do not," said Beatrice slowly and somberly. "And, yes, I think it will affect my life personally, although I can't say for better or worse."

"How so?"

"Well, when the war ceases and we have no more economy, the Royal

Bank will have scant reason to stay here, will it. Nor, then, will Mr. and Mrs. Peters. Returning to England would mean being with our daughter, and that's good. But returning might not be so good for Mr. .... Oh, that is your *Sea Breeze* ahead with the crates piled all over the deck. Looks like they may have loaded, or is it *laded*, her full."

They drove in silence, both scanning the wharf for Charles Timmons. "I think he may be aboard," Amelia said at last. "I would appreciate your stopping here" – she motioned to a spot in the shade of a warehouse – "while I hand him two letters."

Beatrice pulled some sugar cane stalks from a tote bag and reached out to Penelope as the horse leaned back to snap them up. She could see Amelia stop a dock hand, then a sailor, and disappear up the gangway.

Charles was alone in the pilot house, bent over a chart table with some sort of calibration instrument. Instead of knocking at first, Amelia observed him for a few seconds through the glass door. He seemed sad and grim, no doubt feeling alone with his captain's burdens. But when she knocked lightly on the door, he stood upright and his face lit up almost as much as her heart.

She tried to be the business representative of Huxley and Beach, handing over her letters, asking as to sailing times and cargo manifests, but when she asked him about the status of the new Union "odders and enders," they both broke out laughing at her malapropism.

"Now I have something for you that I could not give out there on the wharf," he said.

"What is that?" she asked.

"This," he said. He clasped her tightly in his embrace and kissed her long and lovingly until they ended it only to inhale another breath.

———

Beatrice was quiet for a block or two on the uphill return to the Royal Vic. Then she said: "Well, did you make your delivery?"

"I did," said Amelia, determined to volunteer no more.

Beatrice: "It would seem that he delivered something in turn."

"Beg your pardon?"

"Well, your hair is quite out of place."

"The wind, I'm sure," Amelia parried. "You know how Penelope flies through the streets."

"Of course. But I was young, too, and I remember tingling all over once upon a time."

When the carriage arrived at the Royal Vic portico, Beatrice announced: "I shall accept an invitation to take tea, especially because it is four o'clock precisely."

"By all means," said Amelia. "But let's do something different. Let's climb the steps to the cotton tree across the path and asked to be served on the platform."

"Why not?" said Beatrice. "And since it offers a splendid view of the harbor below, we can at the same time observe the departures of certain vessels."

"Indeed," said Amelia. "Nothing escapes you."

Two folding chairs and a tiny round table on the deck that girded the massive tree proved quite adequate to satisfy Amelia's whim. Beatrice, who had already read *Jane Eyre*, was discoursing on the character of Mr. Rochester when Amelia interrupted. "Leave some of the book for me to read," she said. "What I would really like to know is, why are you so attentive to me, a perfect stranger?"

Beatrice stirred her tea and took a long sip, as if deciding whether to deflect the inquiry with a joke or take it seriously. "Well, all friends were strangers once, were they not?"

"Yes, I suppose," answered Amelia. "I apologize."

The abrupt question, however, seemed to have left Beatrice pensive. "I guess it's in part because you remind me of my daughter Claire in Brighton," she sighed. "She'll have a baby before long and I'm stuck here. And I have little else to do. No one to talk to. Sometimes people are more candid with strangers than with people they see all the time. And you'll soon be far away in Savannah."

Amelia would have been relieved to let the subject drop, but Beatrice began churning her innermost thoughts like an organ grinder. "Having a husband to talk to would be nice," she said, studying Amelia's face for a sign of empathy. "You probably haven't had time to know the real Geoffrey Peters. You've probably seen the very primly proper rectitude he displays just like the bankers who trained him. But behind this stiffness is a stiff."

"Another cup?" Amelia tried to change the subject, but Beatrice went on.

"You're fortunate you met Geoffrey before noon. He can manage until then, but by the time he's finished his usual lunch of whiskey sours at the Wellington Club, he has to sleep it off with a long nap. Then by cocktail time he's ready to go to the Royal Vic and sail three sheets to the wind again."

Amelia: "Would going back to England be...*healthier*...for him?"

Beatrice stared into her teacup. "Geoffrey had a choice: come to Nassau or be sacked," she said without looking up. "He was held responsible for a perceived impropriety in which he as branch manager had to pay for an underling's mistakes. Does he want to return to England? I don't know and I don't think he does. At least he's *somebody* here in Nassau. Back there he might be re-assigned to a branch in Whitby or Scarborough where right about now the wind would be whipping in from the North Sea and blowing up my bloomers. But I don't know if he can recover his reputation and his sobriety. We do know that if he's to return, it can't be as the head of a failed branch in Nassau."

Beatrice sighed, gobbled a ginger snap and finished her tea. "Meanwhile, I guess I'm in limbo," she said. "Just like you."

Chapter Eight
NASSAU, MARCH-APRIL, 1864

Vendue House, Nassau

As The Bahamas eased into its most glorious time of year, Amelia Beach had found the rhythm of her life swaying as leisurely as the foxtail palm fronds in the seductive hilltop breeze. With azure skies and balmy temperatures day upon day, it was effortless to fall into a routine of morning strolls followed by piano practice, lunch in the Orangery, an afternoon of reading, tea at four and mingling with familiar faces during evening soirées. In fact, Amelia had become a fixture at the Royal Victoria, along with a few elderly convalescents who had sailed on Cunard from England for the winter.

But whenever she strayed from her routine, Amelia's mind would wander quickly down troublesome pathways. There had been no letter from the Royal Bank of London and none from her father. Worse: no visit from Charles. She struggled to visualize his face. And the kiss that had lingered so long was beginning to recede into the misty place where old memories go to hide. She struggled to let logic remind her that the passage to Savannah was impossibly dangerous and that all hands were needed for the Bermuda – Wilmington run. Her patriotic self lectured the selfish girl that the North Carolina port was crucial to the rail line that supplied the desperate rebel force in Virginia.

When Amelia could also sense increasingly that the debonair fabric of The Royal Victoria was becoming ever so fragile with each passing day. *Maybe it's just my being here longer, like wearing an old dress that was exciting the first time you put it on. But maybe not. Yes, I have it: the air is no longer festive, as with the certainty that this is the most exciting place to be on earth. Why? Fewer ships arriving with lavish cargos. Fewer huddles of traders concocting fortunes on the Royal Vic veranda. Almost as if everyone is waiting like me – waiting for a ship to arrive with newspapers headlining,* SOMETHING DECISIVE HAS HAPPENED.

But there are none. And so, the orchestra plays cheerful music, like an ornate music box, while porcelain couples, with frozen smiles, waltz around and around.

March 24 began like any other: breakfast, stroll, piano, reading, lunch, perhaps a game of whist, more reading, and tea with Bea at four. Just after lunch, Amelia found herself a shady spot overlooking the harbor and had begun reading when she noticed a large number of dockhands swarming about a wide-beamed ship she'd never seen before. It flew the Confederate flag, and, unlike the sleek blockade runners that usually tied up, she counted six large cannons on this one. Five minutes later into her book, her head jerked up to see the governor's carriage rumbling down Parliament Street. It was quickly followed by an escort of six grim-faced horsemen with pistols holstered on their hips.

Oh my! Amelia arose to ask anyone she could find in the lobby what they might know about all the commotion. There she was stunned to see her friend Beatrice in fervid conversation with Felix DuBois.

Their heads turned at seeing Amelia. "Beatrice, aren't you a bit early?" was all she could manage.

"No, this is something else," said Beatrice distractedly. "I should be back for tea at four."

"Well, don't I get a *hint?*"

"I'm surprised you don't know all about it," Beatrice answered. "That's the *Saint Augustine* down there. That's not a blockade runner. It's a Confederate raider that has sunk who knows how many commercial ships in the Atlantic, and Ambrose – the governor – is pretty exercised about its being here."

With that she exchanged a few more muttered words with the hotel manager, strode out of the portico and was soon headed downhill in one of the Royal Vic's fleetest carriages. When Amelia looked back, DuBois had disappeared as well. Standing alone in the driveway, hitched to Beatrice's empty wagon, was Penelope, probably as puzzled as Amelia.

Beatrice was her old bubbly self when she appeared back at the Orangery for tea. "Well, I have enough gossip for the two teapots today," she announced. "It seems that a few hours ago this big Confederate cruiser pulls into port and muscles its way alongside the wharf. Well, everyone got into a frightful frizzy because it's not where it's supposed to be. On top of that the man who comes striding down the gangplank is John Tyler Wilkes, who's supposed to be anathema to the crown, to your North, and even some in the South, I'm told. Have you heard of him?"

"Oh, yes, Beatrice. He's one of our greatest heroes."

"Well, then, it seems that your hero swaggers down the gangplank and demands a load of coal – and a big one it would take, I'm sure. Anyway, word of his, shall we say – demeanor – travels up Parliament Street and pretty soon the governor himself is down there with some armed soldiers to scare him off.

"Now Ambrose demands that the ship leave because it would violate the queen's strict law of neutrality. He unfurls a copy of the prime minister's proclamation, as if to rub the captain's nose in it. They have words, and I understand that this hero of yours threatened to shell Nassau into rubble unless he gets his coal. Well, the two men glower at each other for a while and the governor finally says he will deliver an answer within an hour. And the next thing I know, Anson, the governor's driver, is knocking on my door with a note."

"You? Why you?" Amelia asked incredulously.

Bernice straightened in her seat, poured a topper of tea, and quipped: "Perhaps Ambrose thought a lady's charms would have a calming effect on the man, although I don't know if I could take that as a compliment what with him having been at sea for so long. At any rate, I came up here to confer with Felix. Then I went down to the wharf to meet with this Wilkes."

Amelia: "And then?" She was struggling to envision Beatrice in this military tableau.

"Well, he was becalmed by my charms, no doubt, but especially because I gave him my word that he could get his coal rather expeditiously if he would come to the Royal Vic at seven to meet Felix DuBois and attend a little reception in his honor. The reception was my idea, and I invited some of the various ships' officers who were standing around watching all this. But you'll have to help Felix round up some more of your compatriots. And by seven."

Amelia tried to gulp all of it down as Beatrice sat back and took another sip of tea. "Me round up my compatriots?" exclaimed Amelia. "You're not putting me in charge of this little scramble, are you?"

"Well, I'm not a proper Southern lady," she said, slathering a portion of a scone with clotted cream. "Besides, this would give you a chance to meet this Captain Wilkes and give him another letter for your father. Perhaps you'll convince him to ramrod that big cruiser right up your Savannah River and deliver it to your father himself."

Amelia sat for a while in stunned silence. "I'm utterly astonished by your surprises," she said as if exposing a carnival medicine man. "Why you in all this? Why Felix DuBois? Are you some sort of spy?"

"No, my dear," answered Beatrice between chews. "A spy is someone who works for one side and gets paid for it. I'm just a plain gossip who takes in and gives out information."

"But surely you have some purpose in all this."

Amelia's supposed friend cocked her head in thought. "Well, I'd say it's all to keep the system in balance," she said with a regally benign smile. "Each night we see the heavens above spinning by in perfect synchrony. On our little planet right now, we have a balance that you and your father and this Captain Wilkes are trying to preserve. African kings sell their captured enemies as slaves because they need the money to buy cotton for their turbans and robes. You buy the slaves and then grow the cotton that gets sent to England to make dresses to ship back to you and garments for the African kings. So you see, it all swirls about the Atlantic Ocean in majestic order."

Amelia stared back intently throughout the soliloquy. "You're not making much headway," she said.

"Ah, but wait," Beatrice answered. "We have the same firmament to balance on our little island to keep us peaceful and prosperous."

"But where do you and Felix DuBois fit into the firmament?"

"Ah, Felix. Things are not always as they first seem, are they?" said Beatrice with a gloriously emotive sigh. "Felix and the governor maintain a balance like twin planets orbiting one another. When Felix arrived here, he had been the superintendent for the French absentee owner of a sugar plantation on Martinique...."

"Wait a second," interrupted Amelia. 'DuBois told me he's from French Guinea."

"Martinique." Beatrice plowed on. "About six or so years ago, just after the sugar harvest was sold, Felix appropriated the cash and helped himself to whatever he could carry away from the manor house. Then he set the whole thing afire and ran off with some of the slaves. Today these same people live in their own little settlement on Hog Island.

"Do you know why?" she asked, coyly enjoying the intrigue. "No, you don't. It's Because they live next to the coal yard."

"Please keep going," said Amelia. Her tea was becoming as cold as the clotted cream.

"All right," said Beatrice. "I'm going to wander a bit from the point again, but I'll come back as always. Now Ambrose – Governor Fairchild – could have put Felix and his chums in chains, but he saw something special in him. To be sure, he liked the money Felix had arrived with. But he also liked the cut of this well-groomed, well-spoken man who stood before him at their first meeting. Felix looked and acted the part of the refined gentleman – an example of what Ambrose thought all freed Bahamian men could aspire to become.

"But secondly, Felix arrived here just after the governor himself, and soon after he had gotten the Assembly to authorize the building of the Royal Vic. Mind you, Ambrose wasn't entirely altruistic. His estate in Yorkshire had been in the family since the days of Henry the eighth – that's three hundred years ago – and the buildings were falling down faster than he could restore them. And the sheep herd, which was the backbone of the family wealth, was nearly wiped out in the big blight of '54, which you'd be too young to remember. So, Ambrose Fairchild's clubby chums in the House of Lords restored the balance in his firmament by prevailing on the queen to name him governor of the least of her domains – The Bahamas."

Amelia found herself hanging on every word as Beatrice continued. "Well, my dear, the advantage of being so far away and so little-noticed meant an ideal opportunity to right the balance in that part of Yorkshire by some judicious plucking of the Bahamian bird of paradise, if you will.

The problem was that the bird was almost too scrawny to yield but a few feathers – a bar license fee here, a portion of wrecking booty, the granting of fishing rights, and so forth.

"But this man, Ambrose Fairchild, was imaginative and resourceful," said Beatrice. "The same year he arrived here, he persuaded the Cunard steamship line of Canada to make a monthly call to Nassau and deliver mail for a fee of, I believe, a thousand pounds a year. When the ship *Corsica* started coming around on its way south from New York, he dazzled the Assembly into authorizing the construction of a glorious resort spa that would attract people from northern climes in the U.S. to his land of sun and breezes. The same law gave the governor the power to appoint a manager for the hotel.

"Well, Ambrose couldn't appoint himself, could he? No, indeed. But there was nothing in the law that said he couldn't appoint a firm to manage it. So just to be sure, he, in 1861 I believe, got the Assembly to pass the Partnership Liability Act. Everyone was told its purpose was to facilitate the creation of various business ventures.

"Now I'm coming into the home stretch, my dear," Beatrice said while signaling for another pot of tea. "The management contract for the Royal Vic was given by the governor to a limited partnership with an obscure name, but owned by Felix DuBois and Anson Brown."

"Anson, Anson," said Amelia. "Why is the name familiar to me?"

"Anson Brown is Ambrose Fairchild's long-time valet – the same one who brought the message to my door today. I doubt that Anson Brown knows anything about the papers he put his X to."

"Then," interjected Amelia, "the war came along and the Royal Victoria was suddenly busy beyond anyone's wildest expectations."

"Yes, but this created one more problem, which quickly became another opportunity," said Beatrice. "The queen's order to enforce neutrality made it so that the coal yard on Hog Island could not sell coal to Confederate flag ships that were bringing in all these goods and customs fees."

"So, let me guess," said Amelia. "The governor and Felix DuBois formed another of these partnerships to sell coal to blockade runners. But how could they sell to Confederate ships if it violated the order issued by the very same governor?"

"Well, you *didn't* guess, did you?" chortled Beatrice. "In building the hotel, they used a large old scow to haul lumber from the forests on Great Abaco island to Nassau. When the hotel was finished, the partnership bought the scow and made it into a coal barge. Now then, when your Master Wilkes' ship comes in demanding coal, the governor of the Bahamas, in front of a great crowd on the wharf, stoutly defends the queen's neutrality edict. Then Felix's people on Hog Island load their barge up with coal and float it off into international waters. There, mostly at night, I imagine, Mr. Wilkes and his battleship will be waiting for the transfer. And all quite legal. Everybody gets their coal. Nobody gets harmed and the queen is left in peace instead of having to muster up a fleet to defend the honor of her little colony."

"Again, peace and harmony are preserved in the world of New Providence," snickered Amelia. "And, I suppose, should Felix DuBois try to steal more than his share, the governor can turn him over to the French authorities."

Beatrice, with a raised hand: "Of course. Yet, if Ambrose Fairchild does so, Felix could visit the Assembly prosecutor with a litany of misdeeds by the royal governor. But that would be double suicide, wouldn't it? Instead, our twin planets are spinning in perfect synchrony."

Amelia nearly rose to begin preparing for the Wilkes reception, less than just two hours away. Then she sat back and decided to pursue the discussion while her gossip was still wound up.

"Beatrice, from the way you cast about the name Ambrose, you must know him well."

"I help him preserve the balance," she said, looking away.

Amelia: "*How* well? This…all in the name of balance? My, the weight of the cosmos must be upon your shoulders. Let me guess again: the governor's wife has been away for some time for her health and you have offered your companionship to a lonely man. You gave him more than gossip – and all for the good of the firmament?"

Beatrice pursed her lips for a rare moment of silence: "For the good of Geoffrey Peters and the Royal Bank of London as well."

"I see. How so?"

Beatrice had turned from clever – almost flippant – to humorless and defensive. "When the Assembly created the Bahamian government bank, it was largely because no British bank of any size would take the risk of coming to this sleepy little island," she said. "Then, two years ago, the Royal Bank of London took the gamble. Ambrose and the Assembly regarded the new bank as an unwelcome upstart, a latecomer trying to cash in on the

American civil war. There was much talk of regulations to make it rather unpleasant for the Royal London to operate here. My involvement has helped keep that movement at bay and it has saved my husband's position. He can ill afford to return home with the stain of banishment on his record."

Beatrice stood at the table, looked at the timepiece in her purse, and said: "By the way, this 'gossip' also may have saved all of Nassau today at the docks. When I arrived, your John Tyler Wilkes was still bellowing about shelling the city to smithereens if he didn't get his coal. It was I who softened his heart by inviting him to a reception at the Royal Vic. And it was I who pledged my word of honor that Felix DuBois would give him his coal."

"Again," Amelia pressed, "I'm wondering…why are you telling *me* all this?"

"I told you, my dear, I'm a compulsive gossip. A gossip requires someone to gossip to.

"Oh, and one thing more," said Beatrice, assuming a sugary smile. "The rules are that my gossip is for you alone. If I learn otherwise, your gold might just vanish. Poof!" She raised her palm and blew as if on an imaginary dandelion.

Amelia was shocked. "How did you know about *that*?"

Beatrice, still sickly sweet: "When one's husband is in his cups, there can be quite a slip between the lip and the cup. Or is it the cup and the lip?"

Back in her hotel room, Amelia sat at her writing desk, forcing her pen to scratch out yet another letter to her father. So far, three of them had gone unanswered. As before, she wrote in an improvised code, referring to the gold deposit as "my trousseau." *But does it really matter anymore, Daddy? Are you in Savannah to answer me? Has my mother forgiven us both? Do DuBois and the governor know about the gold?* She could only hope that it was not in the interest of Beatrice and her husband's bank to tell possible predators. Besides, there was no time at the moment to think about it.

At just after six Amelia put on the green and gold satin gown that she wore on special occasions and headed for the lobby. Just inside the main portico she saw Felix DuBois in amicable, animated discussion with three men, all hatless and in plain black evening coats. The one at the center of attention appeared to be in his mid-forties with a trim black beard. If the stranger were indeed the famous John Tyler Wilkes, he looked more like a mild-mannered apothecary a blackguard. Yet, this nephew of Jefferson

Davis, who could have had a cabinet post in the Confederate capital, had chosen to captain a ship that made daring raids on Yankee shipping and kept rebel hopes alive with each newspaper headline.

Amelia passed by at a distance and found a sign – WILKES RECEPTION – in front of a meeting room adjoining the dance floor and veranda used for larger functions. Inside, it was still empty save for two waiters stacking glasses and bottles on a side table. The room was familiar because she often practiced mornings on a spinet piano in one corner. Still inside the seat was *Papillion,* a songbook of spritely dances by Robert Schumann. At twenty of seven she sat down and began to play from the Schumann scores, speculating that an open bar and the sound of music would siphon off some of the naval officers, brokers and bureaucrats who were headed to the restaurant and dance hall.

By ten of seven, Amelia Beach was still the only one in the room. In fact, she had already noticed that a few couples had been drawn like moths to flame by the WILKES RECEPTION sign, only to recoil and hasten away. *Yankees on vacation, I can tell. How odd. Some might even own ships sunk by John Tyler Wilkes. Maybe some are parents of sailors who drowned. Maybe some of their sons are marching on Savannah. Enough! Who is in charge of this thing anyway? Perhaps it really is me. You are what you think you are. Tonight, it seems I am to be a hostess.*

Amelia returned to the lobby and found the same three men still huddled with DuBois. She hovered with a smile and arched eyebrows until Wilkes looked up and said: "It seems a handsome young lady is trying to get our attention."

"Indeed, she is," replied Amelia with Beatrice-like bluster. "I am Amelia Beach of Savannah, Georgia, and I'm here to escort you to a reception in your honor. But we need the honored guest present in order to have a reception."

After introducing his two officers, Wilkes extended a firm arm. As they strolled to the reception room, it was easy for Amelia to play the star-struck schoolgirl. "Have you really sunk thirty or more enemy ships?" she asked.

"Well, we usually try to capture them first," he answered. "But I suppose the answer is, yes."

"Are you really the nephew of President Davis?"

"I am indeed," he smiled. "But it's difficult for me to think of him as *President* Davis. My brothers and I have always called him Uncle Jeff since we were little. Back then I played in his barn, swept up the stable. Never thought of him as a statesman."

"And you see him now?"

"Yes, I go back and forth to see him in Richmond. I was a lawyer before going to sea, so I do special projects for him in the capital. Deliver messages for him and so forth."

By the time they reached the reception room, a few Confederate officers were already helping themselves to the bar and canapes. Amelia invited Wilkes and his men to do the same, then stood in the corridor outside beckoning like a carnival barker to anyone she knew even remotely who had the slightest Confederate connection. This included Beatrice and Geoffrey Peters, who merely nodded on their way to the bar if to say, "You're on your own, dearie."

With Wilkes now the center of a dozen or so male admirers, Amelia felt the odd woman out. So, her refuge was the piano. She sat, played a few Chopin works she knew by heart and then launched into the Schumann dance pieces. The crowd had grown to a respectable thirty or so, but the music was smothered by the clinking of glasses and roars of laughter when a joke reached its punch line.

All the while, Amelia had noticed one of the officers from the *Saint Augustine* studying her at the piano as he stood alone with a glass of red wine. "May I get you one of these?" he called out.

She nodded and they were soon toasting Captain John Tyler Wilkes. "Introducing Malcolm, his loyal bursar," he said.

"Introducing Amelia, player of inappropriate music," she announced.

"Well, perhaps so," he replied. "This is a military crowd, it appears, and when they've had a few snorts they're ready to burst into a lusty song."

"Well, I know several," she said, "but you do know, of course, that we are in a land of strict neutrality, as you were so haughtily told on the docks today. Do you think I really *should*?" she added mischievously.

"Fire away!"

She embarked upon *Rebel Boy* in a lady-like fashion, but with no apparent effect on the cluster of imbibers.

"Do *Bonnie Blue Flag,* only louder," he said with hands raised like a conductor.

She did, and a few heads turned her way.

Malcolm the bursar was enjoying the conspiracy. "Now for *Dixieland.* I dare you," he commanded.

"Only if you'll bring Captain Wilkes over to me later," she said. "I have a business matter of some importance to discuss."

"Done!" he declared with a clink of their glasses.

Amelia emptied her wine glass and put her heart into it.

> *I wish I was in the land of cotton*
> *Old times there are not forgotten,*
> *Look away! Look away....*"

By the third *Look away!* The discussions had snapped to a halt and the crowd faced her with glasses raised. To a man they were singing:

> *Then I wish I was in Dixie! Hooray! Hooray!*
> *In Dixie Land I'll take my stand, to live and die in Dixie!*

By the fourth verse, the "reception" had turned raucous, with voices bursting into the hotel corridors, stopping promenades in mid-stride, turning the stiffened necks of English bluebloods and causing tongues to cluck.

An unintended result was that it seemed to signal a return to duty aboard ships, much like the singing of *God Save the Queen* at the end of a cotillion. It was enough, anyway, Amelia concluded – a songfest that could be explained as "all in good fun" before some ninny could start rumors that Nassau was under siege by a hostile navy.

True to his word, Malcolm the bursar was approaching with John Tyler Wilkes at his side. "It's a pleasure to have met so talented a young woman," he said with hand outstretched, "especially one who reminds me of some-one very dear."

Another woman in his life? "Yes," he said. "My daughter Emily. I have four daughters, you know, and you look about Emily's age."

Purged of any romantic impulses, Amelia turned to business. "Captain Wilkes, I know you must leave soon, but since you mentioned delivering messages as part of your duties, I wonder if I could prevail on you to deliver a particularly urgent letter." Without pausing for an answer, she continued: "Have you heard of the firm of Huxley and Beach in Savannah?"

"I have," he said.

"Do you personally know my father, William Beach?"

"I do not."

"Well, he sent me here on company business over two months ago. I have attempted to send letters to him three times and have never received a reply. I know that the Savannah River is closed, but I thought perhaps you might know a way to reach him."

She tried innocent charm again: "Why just today a lady friend of mine said she would wager that you could just ramrod that big ship of yours right up that Savannah River and park it right on Daddy's wharf like you did here today."

Wilkes wouldn't bite. "Well, ma'am, I'm afraid my duties currently take me elsewhere," he replied. "But I believe the railroad is still running from Richmond to Savannah. That might be your best chance of getting through. So, yes, I could deliver your letter to agents of the Confederacy in Wilmington or Richmond who are headed to Savannah by rail."

"Thank you, thank you," she said with a spontaneous kiss on the cheek as she pressed an envelope into his hand.

"Perhaps you could honor me with a letter of introduction in the event I encounter your father myself," he added.

"I already have," Amelia replied. "The letter tells him all about your arrival here and thanks you for your part in my reaching him. I know he will be very grateful."

Wilkes turned to leave, she pressed for just one more favor. "My father's ship, the *Sea Breeze*, has been going back and forth between Bermuda and Wilmington. Do you know its captain, Charles Timmons?"

I have only heard of the ship," he replied. *I believe I saw the name* Sea Breeze *in Bermuda on a yellow fever quarantine list, but I'll not alarm the young lady with uncertain information.*

"Would you please take this letter to Captain Timmons under your care just in case your paths should cross?"

Silently the captain slipped the second envelope into his coat as Malcolm the bursar whispered in captain's ear: "Night falls and duty calls."

"Yes," said Wilkes, "but just one more rendition of *Dixieland* and we will take the pleasant memory of this fine evening with us."

Amelia played the first verse and chorus. No one sang, but the dozen men remaining in the room stood in solemn attention until she finished.

Then she was alone in a quiet room as the musical strains of her other world floated back from the Royal Vic dance floor.

Chapter Nine
NASSAU – JULY, 1864

As she entered her sixth month in Nassau, the life of Amelia Beach had become wrapped up in worry and weather. The cool, clear days of winter and spring had dissolved into a monotonous repetition of tolerable mornings followed by hot, sticky afternoons in which tall white clouds billowed into flashing thunderclaps that burst with a downpour. Even the finest room at the Royal Victoria was scant refuge because any breeze that might waft in through open window shutters could also bring gusts of rain that could soak a bed already damp with night sweat.

All this left Amelia in a gray spirit mixed with a debilitating sense of powerlessness, as if she were an Anne Boleyn, peering out from her cell in the Tower of London, wondering when and how others would decide her fate. And her worries had more fronts than a war that now seemed as far off as China. News by way of London was always a month old. More current news usually flowed by way of Wilmington to ships' crews docking in Nassau to the officers who made their way uphill to the Royal Vic soirées. And so, through the news-gossip-rumor funnel, Amelia found herself peering through a kaleidoscope that produced a blurry scene of Confederate retrenchment: Vicksburg gone, a ravenously aggressive general named Sherman ravaging Georgia, and Petersburg – the Union's "back door" to Richmond – now under a siege of uncertain duration. And scarcely a week passed without news that one of the famous English-built blockade runners had been captured or sent to the bottom by a Yankee gunboat.

When Amelia would eagerly ask new arrivals about Savannah, news of her home was invariably shrouded in shrugs. She knew that the port was still barricaded by a picket of gunboats, and that trains were still running from Atlanta, but no reports from anyone who ever rode on one. How she longed even for a letter of girlish chitchat from sister Lucy. She prayed often for a letter saying that Joseph was back home and safe after a humane stay in prison camp. Her frustration with the lack of any correspondence from her father had produced a simmering fury and the absence of Charles Timmons a dull ache.

Nassau itself was its own Tower of London, waiting for a hopeful sign that the good times would waltz on, but witnessing daily omens of disappointment. The Customs Office was still reporting an undiminished number of cargo ships arriving, but they had mostly become older and smaller sailboats from Jupiter, St. Lucie and other unfamiliar inlets on the Florida frontier. All seemed to be skippered by scruffy men in overalls who had doubtless been farmers until realizing that hauling forty bales of cotton would make them four times as much as a whole year's crop of beans or barley.

And, of, course, the Royal Victoria was the barometer that best displayed the economic weather for Nassau. The band played on, three nights a week, but to fewer paying guests. And bookings for the next winter were so few that the Cunard Line was rumored to be dropping the monthly run from London.

Even teas with Beatrice had become dull and predictable, with Amelia shuttering her ears before the well-worn stream of chatter could trickle inside. But on Tuesday, July 19, Beatrice was bright and bubbly again. "Instead of meeting for tea on Thursday," she said, "allow Penelope and me to take you on a special trip that morning. Shall we say nine when it's still a bit cool? No fancy dress, my dear. It'll be just us girls."

"Well, that means I'll have to cancel my whist game that morning," said Amelia in mock despair. "My ladies will miss me; I'm the only one young enough to read the tally sheet."

"You'll have something interesting to tell them the following week," assured Beatrice. "And by the way, don't wear a lot of folderol under your skirt."

Beatrice's flow of conversation matched her high level of excitement on the appointed morning as Penelope, in a new pink straw hat, led the carriage down Bay Street and westward through downtown. After passing the public swimming beach that had turned Amelia's eyes away, they trotted beneath Fort Charlotte, built on a limestone ridge in 1788, its forty-two guns never having been fired in war.

In a minute, they stopped before a walled military compound, guarded by two ebony sentries, resplendent in white shirts, red vests, red pantaloons and red boots. The guards seemed startled at first, but lowered their arms when Beatrice handed them an envelope. Amelia could spot the governor's large gold seal on it but wasn't about to spoil her surprise.

"You've just been greeted by proud members of the West Indian Regiment," Beatrice announced. "They are the queen's best – and actually, only – fighting force in The Bahamas. And you are now on the grounds of Graycliff. Ever heard of it?"

"Yes. Nassau's oldest hotel?" said Amelia.

"Right you are." Beatrice pointed to a solitary two-story mansion set among gnarly oaks on a low rise above an expansive beach. "Built in 1776 for guess whom – the American navy when it had the audacity to occupy Nassau before you were even a nation. These days it's been leased as a residence for the officers of Fort Charlotte and Fort Fincastle."

When Penelope plodded to the front entrance of Graycliffs, Beatrice bounced out of the carriage and went inside, bidding Amelia to remain seated. Soon she was climbing back in the carriage with a large covered basket and clearly enjoying her passenger's suspense.

Amelia: "Where are all the officers?"

Beatrice: "Oh, they're off doing their day duties. Won't be back until evening. We have the whole grounds to ourselves."

With that she dropped the reins on Penelope's rump and they were off downhill. The carriage came to a drop-off of a dozen or so feet with coral steps leading down to a broad white beach that sloped to a waterfront of sparkling turquoise. A jetty marked the eastern boundary of Fort Charlotte, and alongside where it met the beach were several large coral boulders as tall as the two women. The boulders and limestone ridge above them projected patterns of shade from the mid-morning sun.

Beatrice fed Penelope some sweet treats from a box on the carriage floor and motioned for Amelia to bring the large wicker basket and set it on the sand. Removing a blanket from atop the basket, Beatrice spread it carefully on the smooth sand and observed with a self-satisfied grin as Amelia nestled opposite her.

'Well, now," she said. "You once told me your fondest wish was to frolic and splash about in the water and play with the fishies and do whatever suits your fancy. I just had to find you a place that was free of young men with their plonkers and bollocks flopping all about."

Amelia held both hands to her eyes to hold back the tears, then let them flow. "Oh," Beatrice," she exclaimed with sheer joy. "This is the nicest thing anyone has ever done for me!"And how did you do it?" she asked after her eyes took in the white beach and sun-dazzled Caribbean beyond. "I must say, I suspect the hand of Governor Fairchild in all this. Did you sell your soul to get us in this place?"

"Well, I did mention that we wanted to go swimming somewhere in private," Beatrice said, immensely pleased with herself. "Ambrose looked rather shocked or at least surprised, so I said 'Just do it. Get us inside Fort Charlotte, and while you're doing so, order the mess at Graycliffs to make us a lunch.' And as he was writing the note for me, he said 'I suppose I can indeed order the troops at Fort Charlotte about – at least for ceremonial purposes.' And I said 'Well, this is ceremonial, to be sure.'

"So, you see, Amelia, we are having a seaside ceremony," she said. "Now get on with it. I'll be your lookout."

Amelia cautiously gathered her broad calico skirt in her arms and waded into the knee–deep water. Her method of exploration was to move her toes across the bottom until they struck something rough, then stoop over to pick up the shell or sand dollar that she'd discovered.

But it wasn't exactly efficient. "You're getting your bloomers wet," Beatrice shouted when Amelia stumbled and nearly fell over.

"I can't stand this anymore," Beatrice yelled after watching a second stumble.

With that, Beatrice moved the picnic basket and whipped the blanket free with one sweep. Holding the blanket like a bullfighter's cape, she commanded: "Take your bloody clothes off and jump in with your bare bum. And be quick about it!"

Amelia looked wide-eyed at her benefactor with feigned shock. Then she quickly tossed away three years of proper etiquette at Miss Hucklebee's Preparatory School for Young Ladies and discarded everything in a heap on the blanket. Soon she was floating and crawling hand over hand walking in shallow water with her bare bottom bobbing up and down – and no concern for how it might have looked to a sailor in the crow's nest of a passing ship. Ere long she was tossing newly-discovered treasures up on the beach for Beatrice to fetch. Whelks. Coquinas. Sand fleas. Sand dollars. A hermit crab was granted its freedom for being "cute." Floating by was a small thatch of Sargasso weed, the first observed up close since spotting a huge blanket of it from the stern of the *Sea Breeze*. And, from under the Sargasso blanket, the first sting ray she had ever seen undulated slowly away as if only mildly inconvenienced. Above all, Amelia would always remember the clear, clean feeling of the languid Bahamian water in mid-summer.

In time, she heard a shout: "Amelia! I'm getting hungry!" Beatrice had even thought to bring a large towel, and Amelia gratefully wrapped herself in it while wishing she never had to climb back into her hot, scratchy layers of cloth. Without unwrapping, she plopped down on the blanket to see that Beatrice had already prepared plates of sliced chicken breast, sweet pickles, cold sweet potatoes and carrot sticks. 'And if you're a good girl and finish your meal, we have cookies," she clucked.

"Oh dear, I almost forgot," Beatrice added. "Look what else we have!" She pulled out a bottle of French Cótes du Rhone from the basket and two small glasses. "I brought this from home," she said with a wink. "We wouldn't want any swill from the army mess to spoil our meal."

The wine staved off a chill that had come over Amelia, and she was just about to lay back on the blanket and nod off when Beatrice winked again and said, "one more treat." She pulled out two cheroots from her sack and cupped her hands as she lit one with a long fireplace match. "Naughty but delightful," she pronounced. "You really must!"

At first, Amelia recoiled with the same curled lip that would greet a dose of Caster oil. But not to spoil the party, she struck a second match and swirled some smoke inside her mouth until she coughed uncontrollably. "Beatrice," she rasped, "it makes me think of how a cow pie would taste if you tried to chew it. You've done this before?"

"Oh yes! And how many cow pies have you tasted?"

"How could you ever kiss your husband?"

"Just like he's kissed me."

"Well" said Amelia, "maybe it's like garlic. The only defense against garlic breath is to eat some yourself."

Amelia stuck her cigar in the sand with hopes it would die out. Now dizzy with smoke and drowsy with food and wine, she lay back on the blanket and let the sun warm a perfect moment. Something told her it was *too* perfect, but instead she allowed herself to think of nothing but watching the changing patterns of the wispy white clouds that passed overhead.

After what couldn't have been forty winks, she heard soft words calling out, as if from the cave of a Delphic seeress: "Amelia, Amelia, can you hear me?"

"Yes." She opened her eyes and blinked in the sunlight.

"The gossip has some important information you need to know."

From the ominous tone of voice, Amelia was already certain it would not be good news. She sat upright, pulled her arms around her knees, and merely nodded.

Beatrice began. "Each month Geoffrey and all the branch bank managers receive a confidential report. It's intended to alert them as to loans that might be in jeopardy due to impending bankruptcies. It also alerts them to loan applications they should avoid, or to thieves who might be trying to deposit illicit money. It covers changing political conditions in other countries and developments that might affect the outcome of a war. Do you understand?"

Amelia: "And you have something to say about the War Between the States?" The sun was directly overhead, but she felt a chill.

"Yes, I do," answered Beatrice. "This week Geoffrey's report stated that a large portion – or perhaps even all – of the Confederate government's supply of gold is missing. It has been kept in Richmond, Virginia, as you probably know. The speculation is that it could have been entrusted to some merchants in payment for war supplies. Or it could have been moved by the treasury itself in anticipation of Richmond falling to the North."

"So thus far you have speculation."

"Yes, my dear. But cannot you see that this casts a suspicious eye on the gold you have stored in our bank in Nassau? Can you offer any proof – any documentation – as to the source of this gold?"

So...Beatrice the friend is now Beatrice the banker. I wonder what else.

Amelia, guardedly: "It belongs to Huxley and Beach. The company has spent over thirty years trading in cotton and other merchandise. It does not rob government treasuries."

Beatrice now stared at her with a hard look. "Yes, but the question again is how they came about this gold. Companies that sell to English buyers get paid in pound sterling. Gold is not what one gains in the course of normal business."

Beatrice leaned forward with her most earnest demeanor. "Please, my dear," she pleaded, "I have confided in you many more times than you have in me. Please believe that I am your friend, trying to protect you. I think you owe me your trust."

Really? You drove me out here and set this trap. But now I am snared with no way out save my wits.

"You are partially right, Beatrice," she answered. "Most of this gold was found by my father on the ocean floor off North Carolina when he was barely seventeen. He used it for credit to build his business."

"Oh, Amelia," Beatrice sighed, sinking back on her heels. "That is so difficult to believe."

Amelia stiffened with suspicion. "I daresay that whatever gold the Confederate treasury had was in bricks or bullion. The ingots you are storing have the markings of the Spanish crown in the sixteenth century."

Beatrice: "But all gold shipments are documented so that banks know they are not contraband."

Amelia: "If you had found a gold necklace right here in the sand, would you ask it for proper documentation, or would you rejoice and put it in your jewel box?"

Beatrice fell silent, stuffing the stub of her cheroot in the sand.

"Has Geoffrey heard from London about this gold?" Amelia asked. "Is that why we are here talking right now?"

"Yes and no," said Bernice. "Just as you have petitioned the British government to have your deposit released, so have the Wainright people – the shipbuilders in Liverpool. So far, they have been held up by the same, shall we say injunction, that you have faced. But it may be now that they've worked out a way around the problem. Under this proposal, the British government itself would claim – *seize* – the shipment, ship it to England and then allow you and the ship builder to petition for release of your rightful shares."

Amelia let the words digest, leaving her fuming in silence. "Oh, that would be ducky, wouldn't it?" she said at last. "Your bank offers no receipt for the gold, and later, after your government takes possession, it demands documentation that it knows we cannot produce. No, Beatrice, my father did acquire the gold as I explained and I'll not release it to anyone unless I hear from him directly. Your bank and your government are taking advantage of a war that has disrupted communications."

Beatrice had been packing the picnic basket as they parried. Now she held up the blanket again as Amelia shook sands from her undergarments and began dressing. Neither spoke until Amelia was a Victorian lady once more and they were sitting in the carriage under the shade of a large live oak.

"Amelia, I don't wish to alarm you," Beatrice said softly, "but do you know how easy it would be for the Bahamian government to seize the gold for violating some banking regulation or the neutrality law?"

"Does this mean your Ambrose knows about it?" she asked. "I can't imagine that you two have any secrets."

"No, he doesn't," said Bernice, looking into her eyes. "This should prove, if nothing else, that I am your friend with your best interests at heart. In fact, that leads me to one other possibility you might consider."

Beatrice stared away this time, then straight ahead, as if she'd just thought it up. "You could simply avoid all this doubt and commotion by shipping it to England as the property of the Royal Bank of London. Or better yet – why didn't I think of this earlier? You could find a way to make Geoffrey and me the property owners – a mere formality, I assure you – and then convert it to pound sterling once we arrive. All three of us, of course."

So, the viper has shown its fangs at last! They were sitting in an open carriage, but Amelia felt as if a room were collapsing on her. All she could think of was to delay...extend the intrigue until she could sort out an escape plan.

"Well, if things are that precarious," she said, "I think I'll just withdraw the deposit and watch after it in my hotel room until I receive further instructions."

"Oh?" said Beatrice with raised eyebrows. "You think you'll be able to keep it from Frenchy?"

"Frenchy?"

"Felix Delecourt DuBois, the man who runs your hotel."

"You mean to say he knows all about our little *safe* deposit, too?"

"I really don't know," answered Beatrice, "but little happens there that he doesn't find out about. One doesn't get to stay on as a maid at the Royal Vic without agreeing to notify the managing director about anything that might be converted to cash, bribery, blackmail and the like.

"And probably more so now than ever," added Beatrice. "While you're playing whist and taking tea, have you noticed that occupancy and quality of service at the Royal Vic have been declining of late? And with yellow fever running about the docks, I know word is already getting back to the wealthy clientele in England to find themselves another balmy island for the winter."

Amelia had been willing to let her newly-exposed adversary run on while her mind swirled with possible escape plans. Now she had one: deception and delay. She turned to Beatrice and instantly became the adoring, surrogate daughter. "I just want you to know how much I appreciate the lovely morning you showed me by the shore," she said with a thick spread of syrup. "I loved everything but the cigar. And I appreciate all the concerns you showed for my troublesome little dilemma. Your offer of having you and Mr. Peters help me directly is most thoughtful, and I do see its merits. I assume there would be a fee of some sort paid upon safe arrival in England?"

Beatrice, with a shrug: "Well, I suppose… something commensurate with the time and effort expended."

Amelia: "Certainly. That's to be expected. But, of course, I would need approval from my father. Huxley and Beach, you know, is a large business just like the Royal Bank, and it has its procedures."

Beatrice: "But, if you'll pardon me, how can you be expecting a letter from your father when one has not been forthcoming for so long?"

Two pythons intertwined and squeezing ever tighter. But I will squeeze more.

"I am already close to a breakthrough," Amelia lied. "And once again, Beatrice, the credit for it belongs to you. When you so skillfully arranged for that reception for Captain John Tyler Wilkes, you said it would afford me the chance to send him back with a letter for my father. I gave him one that night. Among other things, I suggested just such a stratagem as yours. Captain Wilkes promised to deliver it personally and return here soon with the answer. So, Beatrice, this is just another example of your kindness and concern at work."

You conniving old Cassandra! And to think: all those teas and carriage rides were just part of cultivating a scheme whereby Geoffrey and Bernice could retire in luxury to some pleasant country manor. Oh, well. As long as it remains your obsession, my deposit will be safe from threats of government confiscation – if they were ever real at all.

One late July morning, Amelia was sitting alone at breakfast, ruminating on the realization that her twenty-fifth birthday had come and gone a few days before like just another torpid summer day in Nassau. The only person who would have gladly celebrated – no doubt with a mawkish display of some sort – was Beatrice, but that was the best of all reasons for letting the date roll by quietly.

Suddenly her thoughts were disrupted by a porter bringing a handwritten note:

Docked here early today. Can I see you soon as possible? – Charles.

Amelia walked to the balustrade and looked downhill at the wharf – something she once did daily but had long since ceased. Sure enough, she could make out the sleek gray hull and twin masts of the *Sea Breeze* at dockside, nearly straight down Parliament Street. Either unloading was already completed or there was nothing on board to unload in the first place.

Within minutes she was bouncing down in a cab, not sure which of her many conflicting emotions would first greet Charles Timmons: a longing for his embrace or the scorn of a woman so long ignored. Actually, neither had a chance to display itself because she encountered him at the foot of the gangway signing some papers for a Bahamian customs official. She waited as he offered a sheepish smile over the man's shoulder.

What erupted was a mock lecture by a school marm to a naughty boy. "Where have you been and what have you been about?" she said with pointed finger.

"Where haven't I been?" he replied. He looked somewhat haggard and perhaps not in the mood for repartee after a long night at sea. "You look lovely as usual, and I probably look ten years older," he said.

Instead of a dashing sea captain disguised in farmer's work shirt and straw hat, he resembled a tired farmer impersonating a sea captain. Behind him Amelia could see that a large section of the once-smooth hull was now *crinkled,* as having been clumsily repaired after being dented like a sardine tin.

They agreed to meet again at eleven – not in the Orangery where Beatrice might pop up, but on the platform around the big silk cotton tree where the ocean breezes were certain to fan them. As Charles began climbing the gangway, she called out: "Do you have letters from my father?"

"Yes," he answered. "I would have preferred to set the stage a bit first, but I know that won't do." Soon he was back with an envelope and up the gangway again.

"Just one?" she called.

"Just one."

Amelia pried it open with a fingernail and was already trying to read as the carriage bounced along the uneven coral street.

March 4, 1864

"MARCH FOUR?" Amelia shouted out, making the driver jump in his seat.

My Dear Amie,

I deeply regret that your ship was fired upon as you left the Savannah River, but immensely relieved that you made it safely to Nassau. Captain Timmons has told me of your bravery under fire and that you have found comfortable surroundings at The Royal Victoria.

I can report that Lucy is healthy and precocious as ever, and that your mother is well, but continues to be unhappy with wartime circumstances, which, she seems to be convinced, I personally created. I wish I could report word of Joseph, but none has come. Keep up hope and prayers.

As to the business at hand, none of us here realized that the port of Savannah would be closed to trade so soon. It has taken time to find the right agents in Wilmington, so far away in North Carolina, and to secure warehousing and railway connections to Savannah.

I wish I could offer sound advice as to the disposition of your trousseau, but for the moment I cannot.

I will write soon regarding this matter as our choices become clearer. Meanwhile, I know you will continue to use the same good judgment you have shown so far.

Sincerely,

Your Loving Father

When Charles walked up the wooden stairs to join her at the cotton tree, her first impulse was to shout again: *MARCH FOUR? All you have for me is ONE letter dated five months ago? And such a bland letter!*

But his apparent weariness stopped her. His hair was neatly combed, but his dark blue frock coat seemed cut for a larger man. He smiled gamely, but she sensed a hardship story coming.

As he joined her on the bench that girded the tree, Amelia reached up and offered a conciliatory peck on the cheek. "I suppose I seemed impatient and demanding when I first saw you," she said. "And I confess that I was."

"You were entitled to both feelings," I'm sure, he said.

"And that one letter was so... *so general.*"

"I haven't read it, of course," he said. "But you should realize that in this very intense war of yours, there are many spies who snatch up other people's letters and read them and seal the envelopes back up. Especially on trains and ships where they're lying about in sacks guarded by poorly paid people. And some of them who don't mind receiving a shilling or two for looking the other way. A great many battle plans are found out that way, and it's probably why your father is so *general*, as you say."

"Well, can you fill in a few blanks for me?" she said.

"Where to start?" He hadn't given up chin-stroking. "Well, the first time into Wilmington we got in all right, although it's a long ride up the Cape Fear River – not like Savannah. The problem we ran into once we docked is that the supply chain is all backed up. Most of the military stores are meant for Richmond and Petersburg up in Virginia, but the Yanks have besieged them so strongly that the warehouses there are damaged and don't have room for more goods, even though the troops probably need them desperately. What you get is trains that can't unload up in Richmond and warehouses in Wilmington that are groaning with backed-up supplies. And all this can mean that it's better for ships not to unload than to create more piles of stuff on the wharves for the rains to soak. So, we were there for quite some time, which is when your father arrived with his letter. Wouldn't even have that if we hadn't been delayed."

He looked Amelia over and chuckled. "I daresay, you may be the only one in this whole bloody mess who's got any money. It sure is a lot more difficult than it looked when they built these ships."

"That was your only run?"

"No," he continued. "When we did finally unload, we took on some cotton and turpentine bound for a German freighter in Bermuda. We were clear of the Cape Fear River and just into sea on a perfect foggy night, but suddenly it lifted and there was a bloody searchlight staring right into our starboard. It came from a big gunboat that was probably just as surprised as we were. Kaboom! Kaboom! We had two holes at the waterline before we could fire up the engines. These runners have only a very thin sheet of steel on the hull to protect them – I didn't tell you that on your ride to Nassau – but that's what you do when you're building for speed.

"And that's when our troubles began," said Charles with a weary sigh that indicated a reluctance to describe them.

"Well, you may as well get it over with," said Amelia. "Just remember who was pacing back and forth in her room all those weeks, trying to imagine where you were and what you were doing."

"Would have told you if at all possible," he said, "but Bermuda is a thousand miles from Nassau. Actually, getting back to Bermuda was not so much the problem, because we have those water-tight chambers I told you about. It's what happens when you dock the boat and encounter human beings with politics and rulebooks."

"Is that why the hull is so, um, crinkly?" said Amelia, wrinkling up her nose.

"We spent weeks in a Bermuda boatyard just waiting for sheet steel from England," continued Charles. "When it finally arrived, some infuriating bureaucrats told us – after all that waiting – that the *Sea Breeze* really wasn't a British flagship because it was built to serve a war in which we were neutral. The real reason was that a navy ship claimed to have first priority on sheet metal. Needed it because they were installing a new *galley*, mind you. Well, they had some scrap metal about the place, and by soldering it here and there, they could re-cover the damaged parts of the hull. But they could have hired chimpanzees and done better work."

Charles was actually squirming on the bench at the retelling, but Amelia felt entitled to know all – for Huxley and Beach if nothing else. "The rest hasn't exactly been swashbuckling adventure on the high seas," he continued. "I believe I told you that a couple of my men had signs of yellow fever when we were in Nassau last. Well, we had six more come down while we were in dry-dock – I swear you get it from being in still air rather than when you're at sea with the constant breeze. And the same colonial government that wouldn't let us have steel, decided that we had to go into quarantine. I'm certain they just wanted to put this 'Confederate' troublemaker out of sight."

"And that takes you up to today?" said Amelia.

"Well, up until a week ago. We were released after sixty days. You could say that we had nowhere else to go but Nassau, but I truly thought our chances here would be better. We still need engine repairs, but already I'm hearing that the machinery that makes the repairs in Nassau is itself shut down for repairs. We need some rigging, too, but word is that what they have in stock here is being held back in case a hurricane hits and they need it for their own ships. And the longer we have to wait, the greater the chance the authorities in Nassau will slap us into quarantine," he added glumly.

Amelia remained silent for dramatic effect. "Was there perhaps any other reason you came to Nassau?" she said with head bowed.

"Well, of course, of course I wanted to see *you*," he answered, "but I thought I was supposed to be reporting to Huxley and Beach. I will confess, though, that if you had been in our shoes after all that sitting about, you would want to sail off to Nassau just to feel the wind in your sails again.

"This isn't sounding right, is it?" said Charles with a clownishly crooked grin.

"It's all right," she said quietly. "And it's enough explaining for now."

At first, Amelia had guessed Charles to be tired from a sleepless night of sailing. Now she could feel the full brunt of a fatigue and frustration that had plunged him from lofty dreams of glory to the indignity of impoundment in Bermuda. And perhaps something else. *Are captains excused from yellow fever?*

"I think you could use some well-earned rest," declared Amelia abruptly, rising and taking him by the hand. She led him down the wooden steps from the silk cotton tree and across the carriage road to the Orangery, where they ate lunch in the near-empty room. Afterwards, when he appeared drowsy, she rose again and said, "I have just the remedy for you." She walked him to her room and announced: "What you need most is a good nap without deckhands and customs people barging in on you. We have here a large feather bed. I have a book to read on the veranda, and I'll look in on you from time to time."

Charles said not a word. He nodded, pulled off his shoes, swung into the bed and was asleep on his back as Amelia picked up her book and locked the door behind her.

As Charles slept, Amelia sat mostly with an open book in her lap, thinking what was best for him, for her and the two of them together. At four o'clock, after watching gray clouds roll in and speculating that Charles could well be caught in a thundershower on his ride back to the wharf, she rose again, returned to the room and found him still face-up and mouth open, his shirt damp with the heat.

"Arise, Charles," she called from the chair next to the bed. After he had awoken and sat facing her on the edge of the bed, Amelia announced in a commanding voice: "I have decided that in the interests of Huxley and Beach, and in the interest of our beleaguered vessel, I shall be your care-taker while in Nassau. I order you to begin a regimen of fresh air, exercise and rest. You shall have all day tomorrow to go about arranging this and that repair. You shall also rent or steal a suitable sailboat. On the second day at nine a.m. you shall meet one Amelia Beach at the wharf. We shall then escape your prison of fetid air and feverish crew by sailing off to Salt Cay. There, we shall swim in the Blue Lagoon and explore surrounding beaches, but not before you have delighted me with a fine picnic lunch, because I'm growing weary of gristly, over-cooked chicken at the Royal Vic."

Oh dear, I'm sounding just like the scheming Beatrice.

Charles had been bent over tying his shoes when Amelia began her monologue. Now he sat upright with the first genuine smile she'd seen since his return. "Well, it started out sounding like a stern work order, but I do like the way it ended," he said. "Salt Cay?"

"You know where it is, of course."

"I know indeed. They say pirates would lurk there after being banished by the governor in years gone by. Maybe we'll discover their buried treasure."

"I've had enough of that already," she said.

For late July, the morning was almost cool, yet clear and sunny. A gentle breeze made the Union Jack on the *Sea Breeze* fluff like a tablecloth being shaken free of last night's dinner crumbs.

"I'll be right down," Charles called down from the deck. "Just waiting for Saint Matthew to finish packing the cracked conch salad. He went out on our little cat boat just after daybreak and dove for them himself. He wouldn't do that just for me."

The Bahamian cook emerged long enough to wave at Amelia with a wide smile before disappearing inside. Soon Charles was down the gang-plank carrying a large woven basket like the one Beatrice had brought to Graycliffs. He opened the lid with a flourish. "Here we have fresh water, the aforementioned conch salad, a loaf of sweet Bahamian bread, and a papaya and mango dish. And you will observe, milady, no gristly chicken to be found anywhere."

"And this?" Amelia asked, pointing to a brown bottle that hadn't been described.

"Ah, yes, Saint Matthews' medicinal rum preparation for those who might experience a chill after braving the icy waters of the Blue Lagoon."

"Where is our yacht?" she asked, offering her own hyperbole.

"Right in front of you," Charles laughed.

As they walked past the bow of the *Sea Breeze*, Amelia saw the top half of a sail sticking up from the foot of the pier. She bent over to see a beamy boat of not quite twenty feet with a single sail already raised and tapping gently against the wooden pilings.

"That's it?" she asked with feigned disdain.

"It is the cat boat I told you about," Charles answered. "Best little transportation you could have for a short trip, which is why Saint Matthew's brother built it. I steer from the tiller in the stern and you recline upon the bow like Cleopatra on her barge. When we hit the island, I can pull up the keel and run her right up on the beach so the queen doesn't even get her feet wet. But first the royal personage must descend that ladder there to reach her bark."

In a few moments, they were cutting through the calm harbor waters, the *Sea Breeze* shrinking as the harbor receded in the distance.

Amelia squinted to seek out Salt Cay. "Where is our island?" she shouted from her place in the bow.

"About forty-five degrees," he hollered back.

"All I see is a little speck."

"Well, that's how little islands look when they're four miles off."

"Awfully tiny."

"Well, big enough to have a blue lagoon inside, I suppose."

Amelia's thoughts turned to swimming, a delicate subject that had occupied her thoughts for much of the previous day. The very idea of making it socially acceptable for gentlewomen to parade about public beaches had only recently challenged the imaginations of fashion designers in New York and London. Amelia had paid calls on two ladies emporia in Nassau and had found a dreary, disappointing selection of concoctions described by sales clerks as "bathing costumes." All four that Amelia perused seemed to be slightly truncated versions of satin or silk evening gowns that displayed skin only below the elbows and knees. Immersing them in water, Amelia reasoned, would be akin to toppling a boat under full sail.

Her lifeline turned out to be a one-piece chemise-bloomer in robins-egg blue that she saw on a dummy in the lingerie section. Charles would be shocked at first, of course, but she could explain it to a clueless male as the latest swim fashion from Paris. And the robins-egg blue might just soften any notions that she was wearing underwear. Which would be the case, of course.

"Charles," she hollered aft, "I never asked if you could swim."

"Well… yes and no."

"Don't they make sure you can swim at the naval academy?"

"Didn't go to a naval academy," he shouted as Salt Cay loomed a mile or so off. "Didn't have one when I joined up."

"You just became a captain overnight?"

"No, no. Long story. When the Royal Navy began a few centuries ago, all officer candidates started off as midshipmen. Earned their stripes on the quarterdeck of a war ship with the captain ready to flog 'em for every infraction. Then around 1700 Parliament created the British Royal Naval Academy, which was supposed to teach young laddies to become officers by reading books for four years. But there were so many rich snivelings or mother's little darlings enrolling that the captains didn't want them aboard. So, they went back to training midshipmen like me at sea.

"Like I said, a long story. So, back to your question of can I swim. Well, when you're a beginning midshipman in Portsmouth harbor and they ask if you can swim, naturally you say yes for fear of being sacked. And then they say 'All right then, take off your clothes.' And before you can say Jack Sprat, you're plunging into twenty feet of ice cold water. Well, I shot back up like I'd been fired from a Parrot gun. So, I guess I can swim. This nice warm lagoon of yours should be a cinch."

A brief silence. "Can *you* swim?" he shouted into the breeze.

"Well, yes and no," she said. "Let's just say I have my own methods."

"A couple of dolphin we ain't," he called back.

Soon Salt Cay loomed into full view, perhaps no longer than a half-mile from end to end. Much of the perimeter was jagged coral, but as Charles slackened the sail, the west breeze and tidal current pushed the cat boat into a natural inlet shaped like a horseshoe. Not a trace of humans. A white, powdery beach and coconut palms surrounded an oval aquamarine jewel of still water. Charles sailed the cat boat to a wide beach at the far end, pulled the wooden keel up and let the momentum push them ashore. As they alighted, neither spoke a word. The only sound was of palm fronds being caressed by the morning breeze.

Charles reached into the small cuddy cabin, pulled out a piece of sail cloth, and spread it between two palms. Then he brought out a jib sail and stretched it overhead between the trees. "We may need some shade later," he half-whispered, as if feeling guilty to have been the first to break the silence.

"Let's explore some," said Amelia. They ambled around the perimeter of the Blue Lagoon, discovering that others had partaken of this Garden of Eden often enough. Among the wire grass and prickly pear cactus behind the beach were a few abandoned camp sites with the remains of fire pits littered with charred wood, broken conch shells and discarded bottles. The largest camp site, overlooking distant Nassau, included a crude lean-to of driftwood boards that someone had stacked around a palm tree like an Indian teepee. "Arrgh, mate," said Charles in pirate's guise, "here be the place where the treasure map says to dig."

"Dig if you must," Amelia answered. "I think I'll go swimming."

When they returned to their "camp" by the beached cat boat, Amelia darted behind a large sea grape bush and removed her long cotton dress. All that remained was the robins-egg blue chemise. This could go horribly, she thought, but it's now or never.

Amelia emerged from behind the sea grape and the first thing out of her mouth sounded like an apologia. "A little showy," she said, "but they tell me it's the latest swim fashion from Paris."

Charles merely looked on with barely-disguised mirth. "Well, the blue certainly matches the lagoon," he said at last.

That was all? Men!

"And what bathing attire do captains of the Royal Navy wear?" she said while dangling a toe in the water.

"What a proper English gentleman wears," he exclaimed while unbuttoning his shirt and belt buckle. "The latest fashion from the beaches of Blackpool!" And with a flourish he climbed out of his trousers, revealing blue and gray striped shorts and a matching top with shoulder straps.

"Well, at least our colors don't clash," Amelia said. "But I hope the sea gulls aren't laughing at us."

She waded in quickly as if eager to hide her unease beneath the surface. He followed. Both found the slope steeper and the water deeper than they'd expected. Before long they were holding hands in an effort to stabilize each other, but soon both were flopping about in water nearly over their heads. "I do confess," he shouted, "this is more difficult than Portsmouth Harbor. I know why! There's more salt in the water up there to keep you afloat."

"I think the fact is that you can't swim," she declared.

"And what is it you think you're doing?"

"Amelia crawled ashore and sat half in the water, catching her breath. "Well, I could if it weren't for these stupid bloomers...I mean this stupid bathing costume," she answered crankily. "It's all water-logged and it wants to pull me down."

Charles threw his head back, laughing.

"What's so funny?" she demanded.

"I can't help thinking how your derriere looks like a duck's when it goes into its plunge."

Now he was standing over her. "Well, why not just take the stupid thing off?"

"I'd really like to," she said, surprised that she had let her emotions do the talking and knew fully where it would all end.

"Well?"

"I will walk in and do it," she said, "But not until you do the same. Fair is fair!"

"But I'm not waterlogged."

"Fair is fair." She smiled up at him.

"Well, then, here we go!" he declared. "Adam and Eve!" And with that, off came his top, with the shorts flying off next, and with everything dangling just a yard in front of her.

"A lady requires more modesty," she announced, crawling back in the lagoon. Quickly she was upright in shoulder-deep water and struggling to be free of her cotton burden. "Good riddance to Parisian fashion!" she said, flinging it up on the sand.

By then Charles was already standing in the water beside her. "What do we do now?" he said with the same crooked grin that had been on his face since Amelia emerged from the sea grape bush.

"Well, I just think we should take a moment to enjoy the freedom of being here like your Adam and Eve," she said as if it were an academic exercise. "We may never be in a paradise like this again and in such circumstances."

Both looked all about the lagoon to make sure they were, in fact, alone in these circumstances.

"Well, let's see you swim now," he said.

Amelia tried, but as she walked into deeper water she began flailing about as before. "Here, stretch out and let me hold you," he said, putting his forearm just under her breasts. "Now move your arms like a swimmer."

The result was a sort of wrestling match that left them both doubled over in laughter. "It's like one of those theater tableaus gone wrong," Charles quipped. Then they were upright, locked in embrace, with Charles ever so upright against her.

Then they were on the beach blanket embracing again on their knees. "Am I still on official duty?" he asked when they pulled their lips apart to breathe.

"Let me see," she murmured huskily. "I am on duty as director of your recuperation program. So, you see, you don't have to be on duty – or even be an English gentleman."

And I am also 'on duty' because I am a twenty-five-year-old woman who is determined to know love – in one form or another – even if I must I go through the rest of my life as a spinster.

So, they made love on a deserted tropical isle on a blanket of sail cloth beneath a sail cloth canopy strung between two coconut trees. Afterwards, they got goose-bumps lying in the shade and had a mug of Saint Matthew's remedial rum preparation just to warm up. Then they devoured the cracked conch salad, savored bites of mango and papaya, had another mug of medicinal rum, and made love a second time.

A few months later, Amelia Beach would look back upon it as the happiest day of her life.

Chapter Ten
AUGUST 24, 1864

As they sailed away from Salt Cay, Amelia and Charles promised each other they'd return often. But as ship repairs and requisitions and illness intervened, days rolled by until the memory had begun dissipating like the wispy clouds they had watched from their beach blanket.

The engine rod, for example. When the blockader's grape shot had ripped through the hull of the *Sea Breeze*, it had also bent a piston rod that drove one of the side paddlewheels. A new rod had been forged from scrap steel in Bermuda, but it kept bending at high speeds, making the giant wheel lurch on each rotation like a soldier marching with a wounded hip.

While Timmons recited a list of similar worries, Amelia fretted over her captain's health. Upon his return from Bermuda, she had attributed his fatigue and weight loss to sleepless nights during the crossing. But after Salt Cay Charles showed little appetite and sweated profusely even while sitting at ease. Amelia could now observe him each day when he returned from the docks because she had persuaded him to share her spacious room at the Royal Victoria, insisting that the hilltop breezes would keep him cooler at night.

The drift of the war added to the malaise. Although news from the American continent was now an unbroken story of Rebel retreats, hopes had been buoyed by a navy that made daring blockade runs and high seas captures of Union merchant ships. But now came word that would mark a symbolic turning of the tide against the navy as well. Somewhere off the coast of France, the Union gunboat *Kearsarge* had surprised and sunk the *Alabama,* known to all as the Confederacy's swiftest and most heavily-armed warship.

Other troublesome indicators arrived almost daily from the crews that ran the gauntlet to Wilmington: reports of blockade runners run up on the sandy shoals that gave Cape Fear its name.

Then came another wave of complaints that soured the evening festivities at the Royal Victoria. Wilmington, people buzzed, had become infested with outsiders interested only in making obscene profits by importing expensive luxury goods. It seemed that military needs had become secondary – to the point where one Confederate admiral was urging the navy to take over all transport of war materials from abroad.

And so, England and its Bahamian colony began to drift with the current. Reacting to another directive from London, Governor Fairchild had ordered that no war ship could dock in Nassau for more than twenty-four hours, nor obtain more coal than necessary to reach the nearest port.

On the afternoon of August 24, Amelia was reading on the hotel veranda when she heard the thuds of distant cannon fire. It was not so unusual given the scripted hounds-and-fox chases that Charles had explained, but on this occasion the combustion seemed excessive.

Within the hour her heart quickened as she spotted the unmistakably broad-beamed *Saint Augustine* cruising past Hog Island lighthouse on its way to the harbor, wisps of black smoke still trailing from two starboard guns. Several minutes later, two carriages of soldiers clattered by the hotel on their way to the waterfront from Government House as if bent on repeating the first encounter.

Amelia, now standing at the balustrade overlooking the wharf, was surprised to see no sign of commotion or confrontation. A few soldiers stood near the gangway, apparently chatting calmly with a bearded man who could only be Captain John Tyler Wilkes. After another minute or two, the clutch of Nassau soldiery returned up East Street in their carriages, joking and jostling one another as they passed the Royal Victoria.

Four o'clock tea with Beatrice followed, but this time the latter had no compelling news about what went on at the wharf. "I wasn't consulted and wasn't there," she said with a dismissive air. "But I can imagine you are tingling with anticipation at receiving the instructions you've been expecting from your father. Can we assume Captain Wilkes has contacted him?"

"I'm not assuming, but certainly hoping," replied Amelia, reflecting bright anticipation but revealing nothing beneath it. For the past three or four teatimes, she had forced herself to keep up a chirpy chatter about books, food and flowers, but nothing that might reveal a glimmer of gold. For her part, Beatrice parried with sweet insouciance, but punctuating her patter with word pictures of castles and gardens and tearooms they "really must visit together when you come to England." But Amelia only smiled through the perfidy. *Might this be our last tedious teatime?*

When she returned to her room, Charles had already arrived and was removing his sweat-stained farmer's shirt. "We are invited to dinner on the admiral's flagship," he announced, using his private pejorative for a man he'd declared to be egocentric. "We're due at seven."

"Oh, that sounds exciting," said Amelia, "a thousand times more than my tea with Bea. Did you ask about news from my father?"

"I did indeed," said Charles, falling into the bed on his back. "He has something for you. But he says it's all part of presenting some terribly sensitive information, which is why he wants you aboard the *Saint Augustine.* Everyone at the Royal Vic has rabbit ears, he's convinced."

"I suspect you'd rather not go if you had a choice," she said, "but perhaps *this* will revive you." She motioned for him to roll over and began rubbing his back with hot cloths. The mix of the drying heat with the ever-present ocean zephyr streaming through the louvered window could be relied on for a cooling of tired muscles.

"Were you there when the governor's soldiers came down to see Wilkes?" she asked.

"Yes, in the background, but able to hear."

"Well?"

"It was all over in a minute. The officer in charge began reading the edict about having to depart in twenty-four hours, and Wilkes said that would be no problem as they intended to comply all along. Then they said he could only have enough coal to reach another port, and he said that would be fine. I heard one of his officers muffle a laugh and I learned that they already had eighteen days' worth of coal. This would just be a welcome topping off, if you will."

Amelia continued kneading his back in silence. "I can tell you're mulling over something," Charles said at last.

"Yes."

"Well?"

"I'm trying to sort out something. The *Saint Augustine* arouses all sorts of combative instincts in Nassau. Therefore, some people who don't like the *Saint Augustine* must be watching it day and night. And that would be the Union consul, John Flemming, or one of his lieutenants. If they saw Amelia Beach going aboard, it would confirm to Flemming and his people that the Confederate spy they're so worried about is up there plotting some wicked scheme. Could they arrest me, Charles? Or am I becoming too melodramatic?"

"Well, they'd first have to convince an English magistrate of some sort. They'd need an arrest warrant."

"But what if they captured me and dragged me before their own court in some cold northern city? I mean, could they *kidnap* me? They did others, you know."

In the end, they agreed that to allay her fears, Amelia would dress in the same planter garb that she'd worn on the trip from Savannah. Charles would fling an old officer's cloak over her shoulders. Then the two would walk out a side door and amble down back streets to the waterfront. If someone identified two officers climbing the *Saint Augustine* gangway in the haze of a sinking sun, it would be a matter of pure luck.

To Amelia Beach, John Tyler Wilkes did not behave at all like a blustery egomaniac. He was courtly, soft-spoken, and solicitous of the most frivolous feminine banter. Especially because Amelia again became the star-struck and enthralled girl as soon as he greeted her with both hands outstretched on the deck of the *Saint Augustine.*

"So, have you enlisted in the Royal Navy?" a bemused Wilkes asked after looking up and down her strange attire.

"I know I must look ridiculous," she answered, "but you need to know that the Union consul and others seem to think I am some sort of secret Rebel agent They've seen me residing at the Royal Vic for far longer than normal and concluded that I must be up to no good. So, I do believe they have people watching me."

"They're also watching *me*," he said. "Very well, I'll make it official by declaring you a secret agent. But seriously, you will need to tell any inquirers that you were simply invited aboard by a friend of your father for a tour of the ship."

"So, you *have* seen my father," she said anxiously.

"Yes. He is well and I know you must be eager to learn more, but if you'll indulge me for a moment, let's make sure this Union consul sees us taking that tour," he replied in a fatherly tone. It had become clear that John Tyler Wilkes would conduct the evening's agenda on his own terms.

"Overall," he said, "we are about the same length as Captain Timmons' vessel just down the wharf. We also have the same maximum speed – about seventeen knots. Correct, Captain?"

Charles nodded at their side. "The difference is that we're far beamier – wider – in order to accommodate all the artillery. That's why it requires a crew of over one hundred to run the ship compared to…?"

"Twenty-six," answered Charles, "if we're lucky to find that many." He'd planned to tell Wilkes about the effects of the yellow fever scare, but Amelia interrupted.

"By the way, where is everyone?" she wondered aloud.

"Yes, we are a bit spare, aren't we," laughed Wilkes. "There's only myself, the cook and a sentry fore and aft. Since we've been at sea for two weeks, the crew charged over the hill there to some place called Grant's Town for local entertainment. I believe the officers, at least the gentlemen among them, went to the Royal Victoria. And there's the irony. They're probably all dining on lobster and red snapper, whereas all I can offer my guests from the Royal Victoria is a plate of roast beef and potatoes from our last stop in Havana.

"But back to the tour," he said, leading them forward just past the twin smokestacks where two rows of artillery were mounted on chasses. "What you see here are one eighty-four pounder, two thirty-two pounders and two twenty-four pounders. Each one requires five or six men to service, which is why we have such a large crew."

"I know I'm going to look silly," said Amelia, "but why would it take five or six men to fire one of these things? I should think you would just put in a cannon ball, light a fuse in the back and off she goes."

Both men burst out laughing. "If you can invent a gun like that, you could save the navy thousands in payroll costs and mountains of beef and biscuits," said Wilkes. "Let's just stop here and have a look at this thirty-two pounder and I'll try to explain. It's called a Dahlgren gun, or some-times a 'soda gun' because it more or less resembles a soda bottle. It can fire projectiles of up to thirty-two pounds for nearly a mile. Now if you want to batter the walls of a fort, you would select a solid cannon ball. If you want something to explode and start a fire when it hits, you would use one of these shells. They look like cannon balls but have a charge of gunpowder inside. Or, if you are passing by a hostile ship at short range, you could fire a third type of cannon ball, which is filled with small musket balls – or sometimes even nails or bolts. That's called grape shot, and it's like firing a very large shotgun."

"Yes," added Charles. "And I do believe the average tar would rather try dodging a cannon ball than facing grape shot. You could lose an arm, an eye and even a leg and still live, if you still wanted to by then."

"So, you asked what we do with all these men," said Wilkes, turning to Amelia. "Please remember that sailors train for years at these very demanding and dangerous jobs, but I'll give you a tourist explanation. The gun commander is called the Number One. He aims the gun. Number Two is the sponge man. He cleans the bore of the cannon with a sponge to douse any embers and remove other debris. Number Three is the loader, who inserts a bag of gun powder as well as the projectile itself. Number Four fills a vent hole with powder and some unrelated tasks you needn't worry about. Then when Number One gives the command, Number Five fires the gun with a slow match.

"And there you have it," said Wilkes with a theatrical flourish. "Simple as one through five, except that you may have to do it twenty times in rapid succession while keeping your wits about you despite the deafening noise. And if you don't, the gun can blow up on everyone around you. Did I leave anything out, Captain Timmons?"

"Actually, the British navy usually employs six gunners on each piece," Charles replied with a slight bow. "We really must study your techniques."

After a further walkabout on deck, Wilkes declared it time for a glass of wine and ushered them into the paneled officers' mess room, with a large, well-polished oaken table in the center. "I feel as though we are three mice in a royal banqueting hall," observed Amelia.

"Yes, I agree," said her host. "But I should tell you that a bigger reason for sending the crew out frolicking was the need for absolute privacy on what we're about to discuss."

Amelia felt a chill as Wilkes leaned across from his seat at the end of the table and examined his guests from side to side. Again, she realized that her strong urge to ask about her father would be satisfied only when the nephew and special emissary of Jefferson Davis deemed it appropriate.

After pouring three glasses of French rosê and taking a long sip, Wilkes began. "Less than a month ago I was in Richmond," he said with lowered voice. "I met with President Davis and members of his cabinet. I feel I have as accurate and recent picture of the war's conduct as any general in the field. The cabinet in Richmond sees the current Battle of Atlanta as decisive and that the city, I regret to say, will fall sometime in early September. When that happens, we are certain that the reckless and aggressive General Sherman will take his sixty thousand troops on a march toward Savannah. Along the way, it will be very destructive to everything in their path.

"Meanwhile, Petersburg continues to be under siege. The railroad from Wilmington continues to be the major supply link, but the tracks are constantly sabotaged and we are having to rip up track on other railroad lines to replace them."

"Does this mean that surrender is just ahead?" Amelia asked.

"No, not if you mean capitulation," Wilkes replied quickly. "We may not be able to win territories, but we can still put ourselves in a position in which some of the more southern states can form a new government. Or, we could inflict more damage so as to be in a stronger position to sue for terms that would allow us to retain our culture and traditions. And this is where you become so vital to the outcome."

Amelia took a long sip of wine in hopes it would sooth the sudden ache in her stomach. *How could a young woman who started out on a two-week trip to look after some luggage suddenly become vital to a nation of nine million?*

But what came out of her mouth next was....

"Are you saying that President Davis and his cabinet know who I am? And who my father is?"

"Very definitely," answered Wilkes with a vigorous nod. "And now let me give you a letter from your father before the cook arrives with dinner."

As Amelia unsealed the envelope with her butter knife, the two men sipped wine from crystal goblets no doubt purloined from a Yankee merchant ship.

July 25, 1864

My Dearest Amelia,

I think about you every day and realize with great sadness and regret that circumstances have kept you in Nassau for so long. I am further distressed at learning that Captain Timmons, whom I had expected to look in upon you often and keep you informed, has himself been delayed in Bermuda for so long.

Savannah remains free of hostilities, but we fear the possible oppression of enemy occupation should Sherman move south from Atlanta. The blockade of the Savannah River is still in force, but we have been able to move some goods to Wilmington by rail and onto other ships. If, perchance, you should see some HB bales on the docks of Nassau, know that each one bears my love.

Meanwhile, know, too, that I have been in personal communication with the bearer of this letter. I urge you to listen carefully and respectfully to his suggestions with regard to your trousseau.

I want you to know that your mother and I pray for your return every day – although separately, I must confess. Lucy does, too, of course, although much of her time has been occupied by being with child. The father is a Confederate officer, but thus far not a gentleman in our household. We hope that time will heal.

Again, if you heed the suggestion from the bearer of this letter, we shall be re-uniting quite soon.

With love,
Your father

With a dismissive wave, Amelia passed the paper to Charles and took an unladylike slurp of the French rosê. Her first impulse was of annoyance – even anger. "It's so *general*," she said disdainfully, "so vague as to what I'm supposed to do. I'm told to follow what 'the bearer of this letter suggests.' Suppose your cook had brought it to me?"

Seconds later, the cook had brought something else: plates of roast beef, boiled potatoes and turnips, smothered in a rich brown gravy that was more Savannah than anything she had ever tasted at the Royal Victoria. As all took their first bites in silence and the gravy warmed her insides, Amelia regretted the flash of temper she had aimed at the nephew of Jefferson Davis. But it was too late.

Wilkes put his fork down and looked at her with scolding eyes. "I expected that you would feel this way about the letter," he said sternly. "But I want you to know how *I* feel. We went through combat three times in the two weeks since we left for this destination. We had to shoot our way into this harbor today. At any time, had our guns failed us, the enemy could have boarded this ship, killed me and found in my belongings a letter addressed to you. If it were the one with the explicit instructions that you seem to have preferred, the plans for the survival of the Confederate States of America would have been exposed and quickly put in the hands of Abraham Lincoln."

The cook reappeared seeking approval and was quickly sent away with compliments from the visitors. Wilkes refilled the wine glasses but shoved his dinner plate aside.

"I am prepared to tell you, right now, everything your father and I discussed," he said in tones indicating that even a hungry man's tasty dinner was of scant consequence compared with what he was about to say. "But you must remember that everything I say here is top secret. You, Captain Timmons, are not a citizen of the Confederacy and I have no control over what you might say, so I can only rely upon your word as an officer and a gentleman. May I do so?"

"You may," said Charles, raising his wine glass as if toasting Truth.

John Tyler Wilkes: "As I said, I did meet personally with your father. It was three weeks ago in Florence, South Carolina. Why there? Because Florence is accessible by railroad from both Wilmington and Savannah. I can say with certainty that he will be in Wilmington to meet you on the date we agree upon. I believe his greatest concern right now is where he should locate for the remainder of the war."

Amelia: "What do you mean by 'locate?'"

"He has asked that you bring the gold to him. If he wishes to be close enough to reassure himself as to the security of the loan – and a loan is what it is, may I say – President Davis has assured me that he will find a suitable place of residence for your family in Richmond. However, the president has also stated his preference that Mr. Beach remain at your home in Savannah. The city's leaders are already discussing how they will react when General

Sherman arrives at their gates with sixty thousand men. Since the prospects are dim for armed resistance, the city fathers appear to have concluded that they will turn the city over to the Union in exchange for a minimum of disruption to everyday life. This would mean housing the general and his top officers in the leading homes of Savannah – one of which would surely be yours. Now then, the president is asking that your father remain there so that he might observe conversations, plans and the like that can be reported back to Richmond via secret courier."

Amelia:" You mean spying?"

"I suppose so."

"For which they hang people?"

"If caught."

Amelia: "Are you familiar with the cases of Rose Greenhow and Belle Boyd?"

"I am," Wilkes answered quickly.

"Both were hunted down and imprisoned. Then one of them drowned escaping a Union blockader. Correct?"

"Yes."

Amelia, emboldened by wine and rectitude: "Well, let me tell you, sir. I have already been approached by the Union consul in Nassau and warned that I am risking arrest and who knows what else if I am confirmed to be spying, which is what they already think I'm doing here in Nassau. As I said, this is why I dressed this way for our meeting tonight."

"I see, Miss Beach," said Wilkes, his eyes fixed on hers. "Although I am an attorney, I am not an expert in such matters and am certainly not *your* attorney. I suggest that you bring up the matter with your father when you meet in Wilmington. I might add that I personally am on so many 'wanted' lists for piracy, murder and mayhem that I have ceased to worry about which charge shall snare me. And that brings me back to my very important mission here, which is to develop a plan for transporting this gold to Wilmington."

Amelia knew by now that she had exhausted any reserves of good cheer. But she pressed on. "Before we discuss the 'how' of this plan, may we discuss the 'why'? The manager of the Royal Bank of London here has shown me a report saying that the Confederacy's gold supply in Richmond has either been spent or pilfered or something similar. Is this true?"

"It is mostly true," said Wilkes, his eyes still riveted on hers. "The remaining gold reserves have shrunk to just over sixty thousand dollars in value, but not due to theft. It has simply been spent down to provide security to merchants and to meet the all-consuming costs of the war."

It had now become dark outside and a lone oil lamp cast eerie shadows over the oaken mess table. Wilkes reached inside his jacket, but quickly drew his hand back.

"If you were thinking of a smoke, please go ahead," said Amelia, hoping for a speck of gratitude.

He nodded, drew out a cigar, lit it and exhaled. "We are now entering a very delicate, confidential area," he said softly. "The Confederacy has been negotiating a crucial, confidential loan with a large European financial institution. The amount is over $25 million, nearly enough to see us through to achieving the objectives I explained to you earlier. The loan is contingent on being backed by a certain level of gold reserves. Because the European institution has come upon the same information as your Bank of London, they are preparing to release only part of that amount now. The rest will depend upon a personal inspection of our reserves by their emissaries.

"Hence, it is vitally important that your *trousseau*, as your father and you call it, be physically present in Richmond within the month. As I said, it is a temporary loan, to be repaid once the war ends, with significant profit to his firm. Meanwhile, I want to impress upon you, Miss Beach, that this gold is more important to our nation's survival and success than anything I can think of. That includes me, my ship and all my crew, for example. And this explains why we have come all this way at our peril."

Charles had been mostly silent throughout the evening, but now he broke in.

"In no way do I mean to impugn your reputation as an officer and a gentleman," he said, "but how do we actually know that the letter comes from Amelia's father? If our roles were reversed, would you not ask for some further evidence?"

"Perhaps I would," answered Wilkes. He leaned back in his seat, pulled a velvet pouch from his breast pocket, and handed it to Amelia. "This is what I was about to reach for when you thought I wanted a cigar. Upon my honor, I would have given you this under any circumstances, but I thought it best to wait for a moment such as this."

Amelia reached in the pouch and pulled out a double-stranded Spanish gold chain with a locket. She knew without opening it that inside would be a cameo of the Virgin Mary, the twin to the chain and locket she had kept at her bedside since first sailing on the *Sea Breeze*.

When she had composed herself, she said, "Thank you. This means everything to me."

Wilkes, pleased at regaining her trust but chagrined at using melodrama as a rapier, let some silence sink in as he refilled the wine glasses. "Now, if we may discuss logistics," he said quietly. He produced some maritime charts and spread them upon the table.

"As usual," he began, "everything centers on the phases of the moon. The next new moon over Wilmington is September 1, just a week from now. Since the *Saint Augustine* must skedaddle by dusk tomorrow or be disintegrated by the governor's bluster, I suggest we rendezvous in the early afternoon of August 29, just outside the neutral zone, after you've coaled up at Hog Island. You will carry the gold, of course, because the *Saint Augustine* isn't going to run the gauntlet up the Cape Fear River. Rather, we will escort you as far as we can towards New Inlet. If we are spotted and they send up rocket flares, the *Saint Augustine* will immediately go hard to port and draw the guard dogs eastward. We are a prize catch to them, so you can expect two or three of them to go chasing after us. Wait until the last of them has given you its wake and then put your boilers on full blast towards New Inlet."

Charles Timmons piped up again. "So far, the *Sea Breeze* has only gone by way of the Old Inlet," he said.

"The Old Inlet is full of shoals outside," said Wilkes with a dismissive wave. And once you find your way in, it is fifteen miles longer up the Cape Fear River to reach your port."

Timmons wouldn't be dislodged. "The New Inlet is said to be finicky because it was created by a storm only twenty or so years ago. I'm told it draws only eleven feet. We draw ten or eleven depending on our load."

Wilkes again: "No. It draws thirteen, I'm reliably informed. It also has Fort Fisher sitting at the entrance. Recently fortified, too. Its guns can hit an enemy ship four miles out. And it has a new navigational light atop the hill that will shorten your guesswork. You get within four miles of the fort and you're nearly home free."

"All right," said Timmons, "but I will not go when above-decks are load-ed. We'll be too slow and heavy."

"What if you loaded only below decks?"

"I suppose we could manage fourteen knots."

"Well, then, you are still two knots faster than the Yankee lot."

Timmons: "How many blockaders can we expect to be guarding New inlet?"

"Probably more than you've seen before," said Wilkes. Our intelligence shows that they're building their fleet gradually for an invasion of Fort Fisher and eventually Wilmington. But they're far from ready at this time. The ships you'll encounter are more or less in a single straight line from east to west. At Old Inlet they now have two or three rows. You have to zigzag between them, and that's where you can run up on the shoals."

Timmons: "Well, then, I am not going to carry explosives. I'll pack some rifles, but no Minié balls or gunpowder."

Wilkes: "And speaking of things in the hold, how are these gold slabs – or whatever you call them – now stored?"

Amelia: "In two steamer trunks."

"I strongly suggest that you remove them from the trunks and bury them in the bottom among the ballast," said Wilkes. "If someone boards you and they see two chests in the hold, they'll think they've found Blackbeard's treasure and fly to them like dogs to steak bones. And that reminds me: if you are unlucky enough to be chased down and boarded, your captors will be happier upon discovering luxuries like whiskey and fine clothing in the hold and not go prowling among the ballast."

"I have another problem: yellow fever," Charles interjected. "Our crew normally numbers twenty-six. We arrived here with nine and I worry about further desertions."

"Well, in the next few days, I'm sure you can round up a few more," said Wilkes. "I suggest you tell them that the fewer the men, the greater their shares from all these luxury items."

John Tyler Wilkes clearly didn't want to discuss earthly barriers to cosmic plans.

It was now approaching ten o'clock, and the three could hear the first shouts and whoops of men stumbling up the gangway from their evening's revelries. "Are we understood then," said Wilkes. "Late afternoon of the 29th at the north end of Great Abaco Cay."

Timmons and Amelia nodded. They stole down the gangplank and walked up darkened Parliament Street to the Royal Victoria, where they could still hear the strains of dance music from their room.

Amelia, exhausted after her mental skirmishing with the president's personal emissary, was ready to plunge into her pillow. But Charles sat sprawled upright in the easy chair, wanting to joust more with Wilkes than he'd done at dinner.

"I just don't trust him," he said. "I tried not to get in your way, but he just doesn't fit into the balance of things."

"I don't understand," said Amelia, peeling off her planter's garb. "He seems the true patriot to me."

"Ah, that's precisely it," Charles sighed. "I don't see this mission through the same lens as you. I don't know how to deal with a bloody *patriot!* Word out there among the sailors is that he takes no shares for any ships captured. His crew lives strictly on navy pay. They say he has no regard for his own life or for others around him on both sides. He's been known to charge into the middle of a Union fleet with guns blazing on both sides. Nobody does that. And they say he sank some unarmed whaling ships off New England and let their crews flounder about in heavy seas. This kind of person is dangerous."

Charles nearly seemed to wobble in his chair, with legs spread before him. Whether from too much wine or from the mysterious malaise that Amelia had come to call *the plague* for short, his speech was slurred and his demeanor sour.

"Wilkes is calling for too small a margin of error," he went on. "Pilots from Cape Fear have told me it's eleven bloody feet deep. Could he be talking *high* tide or *low* tide? I just don't know. What I do know is that I don't think this man is our friend. I think if we hadn't shown up for our rendezvous he would have come in here and snatched us up at gunpoint."

By the time Charles had finished ruminating, Amelia was on her side, sinking into sleep. But she had decided that Charles was behaving like a different man and she had just put her finger on the reason. The dashing captain she had fallen in love with had always met the worst of news or the most cutting remark with a jaunty wit that deflected the arrow from its target. But suddenly, Charles Timmons seemed to have lost his most endearing gift – his sense of humor.

Amelia awoke the next morning in a sweat of her own. Charles was dead asleep, but she shook him anyway. He rolled over, blinking. "What? Are we sinking?"

"Charles," she whispered huskily, "what if Geoffrey Peters refuses to re-lease the gold? Could you and your men force its release? Pry it out of there somehow?"

Charles blinked some more and rubbed his eyes. "Well, hardly," he said, squirming to the edge of the bed. "I can picture Saint Matthew and Jimmy in there with guns they probably don't know how to shoot. In any case, I would no doubt be indicted for bank robbery in my own country, get sacked by the navy, and spend the rest of my life a beggar."

"I understand," she said. "I came to the same conclusion. That means our only other source of help would be the crew of the *Saint Augustine*, which leaves tonight."

Over breakfast they devised a plan. Charles went to the docks and con-ferred with Captain Wilkes. Amelia donned her market dress, took a han-som to the Royal Bank of London office and bid the driver wait for her early return.

It was just opening time when she entered the bank office and found it empty save for the usual teller at his window and Geoffrey Peters at his desk in the rear.

"Good morning, Mr. Peters," she said as cheerfully as she could force herself in his depressing presence. "May I have a word?"

Amelia swung the little grilled gate open without asking and seated her-self beside his desk. "Mr. Peters," she said with her sweetest smile, "it would seem that your wife – my friend – Beatrice and several others have learned about the two trunks that lie in your vault. I've decided that I would like to re-assume all security risks and store them at the Royal Victoria again. Therefore, I would like to call again today at a suitable time and…"

"I see," he replied quickly. "I will need documentation of ownership and receipt of deposit, of course." Peters had already thought about and rehearsed such an event.

"You gave me no receipt," said Amelia. "Oh dear, I think we may be about to repeat an old conversation. But do you personally doubt that there is gold in those trunks and that it belongs to me?"

"Well, Miss Beach, there seems to be a very legitimate question as to whom it belongs," he said, squinting up through his spectacles.

"You have received no letter from Huxley and Beach?"

"No, indeed."

"I see," she said calmly. I thought you might have received one by now."

"Likewise," he replied, "I thought perhaps one would have arrived on that big gunboat that docked here yesterday."

"I'm sorry, no. I'll try to straighten the matter out as soon as possible. Thank you, Mr. Peters, for your time and trouble," she said, rising to leave. "Please give my very best to Beatrice and my favorite horse."

Amelia continued in her cab along Bay Street, then turned into the wharf and rode past the *Sea Breeze*. When Charles appeared, looking out from the deck, she held up two fingers. Charles nodded. He would soon visit Captain Wilkes.

———

At 3:45 pm, fifteen minutes before the Royal Bank of London was to close for the day, five burly men entered, looking quite patched together in old civilian clothes. One stopped at the teller's window. The others approached Geoffrey Peters' rear desk, one carrying a small square box and the other shouldering a long narrow box with *Wilson Window Blinds* stenciled on it.

"You are here to make a deposit?" Peters asked nervously. His hands had already begun trembling in anticipation of resuming their love affair with gin and tonic after work.

"Naw suh," said the largest man with an unconcealable southern drawl. "We are heah to *remove* a deposit. From the vault behind that door over there."

Peters struggled for a response that would signal resistance, but nothing came out except banker jargon. "And you have proper documentation, of course?"

"Suh," replied the largest man. "Rather than waste yo-ah valuable time, let me do some explaining." He opened his tattered coat long enough to reveal a revolver stuffed into his belt. Then he reached into the square box and produced a wooden tripod, which he placed on Peters' desk. "This, suh, is a fine oaken gun rest, which we will need, because we have heah"

– another ruffian removed a large heavy rifle from the window blind box – "a new Henry repeating rifle. Its chamber contains sixteen 44-calibre shells. I'm using the tripod for safety reasons. The gun is very jittery and some- times, when you just touch the trigger, it can sort of cut loose and spray all sixteen shots at once. But if I place it snug-like on the gun rest, it should be able to blast right through that steel lock on yo-ah vault. And if not, we'll have fifteen other tries at it.

"Now suh, would you please open that wooden door that disguises your vault?" said the large man politely. "We'll be quick about it because we're very good at this sort of thing."

Peters had now been struck speechless, his jaw merely moving up and down like a hooked fish sucking in air. He glanced to the front of the room and noticed that the intruder up front had placed a CLOSED sign in the window. The teller was now standing in a far corner, face to the wall like a naughty schoolboy, struggling to muffle his whimpering.

"Or," added the large man, "maybe y'all would prefer to open it right fast with yo-ah key. That way you can still have a safe place for other deposits."

Peters nodded almost joyously. After he had unlocked the vault and the accomplices had carried off the two trunks. He and the teller were poked and prodded inside the steel-plated room and told not to reappear for an hour be- cause two of the men would be waiting outside with drawn pistols if they did.

An hour later, when Peters rushed out to the Magistrate's Court office in Parliament Square, he found it closed for the day, with bureaucrats already enjoying *their* gin and tonics.

An informant for the American consul, keeping watch on the berthed *Saint Augustine*, reported seeing three men on a buckboard pull up to its gangplank and struggle aboard with two heavy trunks. He observed the *Saint Augustine* pulling away from its berth just before sunset. He saw it pass alongside the *Sea Breeze*, and stop for less than five minutes, but could not see what might have transpired between them. By nightfall, the *Saint Augustine* was well out to sea, a fox hunting hounds.

On the afternoon of the next day, Amelia heard a firm rap on her ho- tel room door. A well-dressed Bahamian man solemnly asked, "Are you Amelia Beach?"

"Yes," she said warily. He looked like an undertaker and her first thought was that someone had died. He quickly tapped her with a roll of parchment paper. "This is a summons and you have been served," he said. He had hastened away and disappeared around the promenade before she could get a word out.

As Amelia had feared, the parchment announced, in lavish olde English, that she was to appear at a *Hearing of Inquiry* on the following Monday before a panel appointed by the Magistrate's Court to decide whether one Amelia Beach had committed an indictable offense as an accessory in the robbery of the Royal Bank of London on the twenty-fifth of August instant. If so, and the alleged crime involved less than five thousand pounds sterling, she would be tried by the Magistrate's Court. If more than that, she would appear before the Supreme Court of The Bahamas.

Well, it's certainly more than five thousand, she said to herself. Her first thoughts were of Rose Greenhow and Belle Boyd, both spies dead at a young age. Were their crimes worse? She felt her heart race, as it always accompanied unpleasant surprises. *Need to find breathing room.* She took a half-read novel to the terrace where she so often enjoyed the late afternoon shade while awaiting Charles' return.

But her eyes would not focus on the words. Instead, thoughts came rushing into her head, all twisted, knotted, and clamoring for attention. *What is an 'accessory?' The same as a bank robber? Would that Times reporter find out and splash my name all over London? Oh yes, he would mix me in with infamous female spies. Do I find a lawyer? But we're supposed to leave on the same day as the hearing. Charles will know what to do. Or will he? Could he abandon me here because he doesn't want his navy career besmirched by association? Is Charles in league with Geoffrey and Beatrice Peters to sail off with the gold? No. Peters can't leave here or he'd be an accessory as well. But Charles and Wilkes plotting together? No! No! Can't think such stupid thoughts because you'll only replant them in places where they shouldn't be. Stop it! Cease! I love Charles and I need him. But I can't let him be seen in that court. I'll have to do it myself.*

By the time Charles arrived from the docks, Amelia greeted him with a tight squeeze and a kiss on the lips. She had decided on a jaunty, defiant mood as she pointed to the parchment of legalese on the bedroom table. "This is nothing," she said, "just Peters trying to rescue his reputation by telling his bosses that he did something about it. I wasn't there holding any gun. I'm a wounded victim of a heinous crime, just like the bank. In fact, I'll threaten to sue the bank for failing to protect my deposit."

Charles watched her bravado with bemusement. "Well, I haven't received any summons," he said, "so I don't think they'll be searching the ship. Or will they?"

Amelia put her finger to her lips. "Just tell me we're still sailing on the 29th," she whispered. "That's all that matters."

"Damn it all," he declared. "I no longer like the looks of this place. I'm tired of whispering in this room because it has inner hallways and walls with ears. I don't feel like going out there tonight and dodging all the Beatrices and Geoffreys and Flemmings and newspaper people lurking about the dance floor. Let's take a cab to the ship right now. Tomorrow you can get your things and check out. You'll be safer on the *Sea Breeze* for the next two nights. And you'll be closer to your trousseau, which, by the way, is stuck among a lot of limestone rocks in the hull."

"Oh, yes, yes!" she exclaimed with a hug and another kiss. "I'll be a mouse in whatever corner you wish to stash me." *Thank you, my darling, for sheltering me. And shame on you, Amelia Beach, for ever thinking he might desert you.*

At ten a.m. on Monday, August 29, Amelia, clad, despite the stifling humidity, in a fulsome dark blue dress, entered the lobby of the stately Magistrate's Court and, grasping her summons, began to search for room 104. As she walked down the nearly-empty hallway of chambers and hearing rooms, she saw the unmistakable plumtitude of Beatrice Peters standing at the end. "Well, we meet at room 104," Amelia said acidly. "And what have we here?"

A hand-printed sign:

MAGISTRATE'S INQUIRY 1207 [BEACH] CANCELLED

"What? Why?" exclaimed Amelia.

"The charges have been dropped," said Beatrice grimly.

"And you're here to tell me why?"

"Yes," Beatrice answered with eyes lowered. "Perhaps Geoffrey acted a bit hastily. You might have as well had you been threatened and frightened and humiliated. But we have come to realize that since no receipt for the gold was ever issued, no bank assets were lost. Therefore, there was no robbery and no reason for you, Miss Beach, ever to file an insurance claim or suit against the bank."

"I see," said Amelia. "And therefore, no news will reach the headquarters of the Royal Bank of London that could upset people in high places and cause the dismissal of one Geoffrey Peters."

"I think we've both done too much confessing," said Beatrice. "But I also believe we now have an understanding. In light of the fact that your ship is loading up and ready to sail, I suspect that this will be the last we see of each other. I also came here to say that I have sincerely enjoyed your company."

Beatrice extended her gloved hand and Amelia took it, struggling to say something pleasant that wasn't a lie. "I will always remember you for making possible my first swim in your lovely blue waters," she said. *There. That will have to suffice.*

They walked out of the courthouse in silence and Amelia gave Penelope a playful pull on the ears as Beatrice boarded her carriage. Just as she pulled away, a wiry bearded man in a derby moved from behind a courthouse pillar, his face darkened by the strong sunlight. "John Flemming at your service," he said.

"Ah, dedication to the Yankee cause takes you everywhere," Amelia answered stiffly.

"I seem to be the only one to be disappointed that the hearing didn't take place," he said with a tip of the derby.

Amelia began walking towards Bay Street. She could see the *Sea Breeze* at berth in the distance, but Flemming had fallen in step with her. "I just want you to know that I am not stupid, nor am I done with you," he said with rancor. "For five or six months, you have been the social belle of the Royal Victoria, flitting between Confederate sea captains, soldiers and merchants, passing information this way and that. We know that it took three strong men a great effort to move two large sea chests onto the pirate ship, *Saint Augustine*. What could be in just two trunks that made the ship come to Nassau for just one day? Maybe you are exporting anvils, but I am convinced you are smuggling *gold*."

Amelia knew she had the upper hand but was walking as quickly as her high-top leather shoes and stiff satin dress would allow. Now Flemming lurched in front of her and whirled about, blocking her path. "Mark my words," he barked. "You are known to the War Department in Washington, and wherever you go in the continental United States, you will be hunted down and tried for treason. And your deeds will become even more infamous than those of Belle Boyd and Rose Greenhow."

As Flemming stood lecturing with pointed finger, Amelia realized that the derby probably added several inches to his height and that, without it, he was a good four inches shorter than she. *Such a little man in all respects – perhaps even pathetic.*

"Mr. Flemming," she said, "would it make you feel kindlier toward me if I told you that the gold belongs to my father and that it is to be used to pay for a new merchant ship? And what if I said I am as distressed as you are about the theft of this gold by these bad men?"

Flemming seemed to take her seriously because he pressed on, like a beggar grateful for any scraps she could fling at his feet. "Do you think this loss will cause your father's business to stop shipping military supplies to and from Nassau?" he asked.

Amelia halted and faced him four-square with hands on hips. "This is ironic indeed," she said with all the acerbity she could muster. "You have warned me of the perils of sharing military information. Yet the very man who wants to prosecute me for spying seems to be imploring me to share military information. You should know by now, sir, that my answers to your questions will always be framed by what response will best serve the Confederate cause."

He nodded, as if recognizing the stalemate, and shuffled up Bay Street, perhaps in search of more compliant spies.

Chapter Eleven

As Amelia watched the Union consul Flemming stalk off, she could already see Charles at his usual position at the base of the gangway, a frown frozen on his face as he signed some forms for a waiting harbor official. "I know I'm in the way," she said upon reaching his side, "but I wanted to report a great victory. The inquiry has been cancelled! Peters withdrew his charges. No jail for me!"

"Jolly good. I don't think they wanted to take your fire," was his sole comment. "Now if only you could fly out to Wilkes and demand that he grant us another day."

"Problems?"

"Manifold." Charles signed another form and waved off the Bahamian bureaucrat. "So far we have a crew of nine – same as when we arrived. I sign one man up and another deserts. Malaria, fear of yellow fever, or just plain fear."

"Why fear?"

"They talk to other sailors. They don't like the idea of being sunk or being captured and sold as slaves. Imagine that."

He looked up from his fistful of papers for the first time. "Amelia, I'm assuming you and Mr. Beach will approve my doubling the crew pay to fifty dollars a day. Plus their cargo shares, of course."

"Well, whatever you need to do," she answered.

"Good," he said, "because we have an even bigger money problem. Coal. Oh, I can get bituminous, but DuBois seems to have quarantined the anthracite from Pennsylvania and I'm not sailing with soft coal. We'll be three knots slower and they'll see our smoke from ten miles out."

"Then why is Felix DuBois hoarding all the good coal?"

"He won't take Confederate dollars and he wants fifteen dollars a ton U.S. Says the Yankee captains are ready to pay it. We need a hundred tons and we don't have fifteen hundred U.S. And I think the price is going to go up as the day goes on.

"In fact, as soon as the rest of this stuff is on board, I'm going up there and plead with DuBois. May have to trade our gold for coal."

"*What?*" Amelia stared up at him, mouth agape.

"Bad joke," he said. By then two shipping agents were waiting to get the captain's ear, and Amelia turned away. She began wending her way through the remaining crates of cargo scattered on the wharf, each with a manifest label affixed. Fifteen dozen "fine shirts." Fifty dozen umbrellas. Assorted cases of Cuban cigars. Stationery, soap, sardines, riding boots, and, as a lone gesture to the military, five hundred Enfield rifles, but without ammunition. A hundred cases of French brandy. She recognized the labels *Hennessy Three Star Cognac* and *Calvados* from revelries at the Royal Vic and remembered her father's lament that essential war materials were being replaced in cargo holds by black market luxuries.

Edgar, the quartermaster, passed by and noticed Amelia studying the labels on stacks of crates.

"What's this over here?" she asked, pointing to several boxes of wood chunks. "They look like the knots you see on boards."

"You're quite right," said Edgar. "When you need a sudden burst of speed, you toss them into the furnace. You can use cotton for the same effect, but of course we have none on this trip. But if we run out of pine knots, we can always toss in a can of pork fat. That's the best yet."

By one o'clock the ship was packed and Charles walked up East Street to the Royal Victoria. Amelia returned to the captain's quarters, which Charles had insisted she occupy, since he could have the pick of three empty officers' berths. After finding Joseph's plantation trousers in the bottom of her suitcase, she changed into her sailing garb, topped by the summer wedding hat she'd refurbished for her maiden voyage dating back a lifetime of seven months. She had time on her hands, but not with a book this time.

She climbed the ladder to the roof of the pilot house and sat cross-legged, trying to capture, for the last time, the rhythm of a place that gathered in its embrace both Victorian etiquette and mankind's most primitive displays of exuberance. Whereas once it had shocked her, it now absorbed her.

Along the quay, a British flag steamer had just arrived, and a dozen naked boys were already diving into the harbor waters as a cluster of elderly ladies with silken parasols laughingly tossed coins from brocaded purses with sparkling marcasites. Just beyond, Amelia saw Vendue House, where fruit and straw market ladies were no doubt debating whether to stay open to snag the new tourist arrivals or shutter their stalls for the usual noon rest so they could regain enough energy to survive the afternoon heat. Up on the hill beyond Vendue House stood the stately Government House with the tall, bare flagpole signaling that Governor Ambrose Fairchild was elsewhere.

Amelia swiveled around on her bottom and faced Hog Island across the harbor. She studied the driftwood shacks of the coal workers, where children darted among hung-out wash fluttering like multi-colored flags while clusters of women sat in doorstops chatting. *Who is happier, a woman wearing nothing but a skirt and blouse, or one wrapped in suffocating layers of modesty? Did an English matron ever sing and sway her hips as she walked?*

Amelia gazed southeast across the sea towards a tiny cluster of palm trees that she now knew to be Salt Cay. *I know there are conch on the bottom of the Blue Lagoon, if only I had known how to dive for them. Someday, perhaps. Does Charles remember it as I do?*

By one o'clock the caressing morning breeze had stiffened, making empty dories in the harbor dance on their mooring lines. No sign yet of Charles. *DuBois must be raising the price as predicted.* Amelia fixed her gaze on the Royal Victoria, still elegant on its aerie atop the ridge on East Street. *I will miss the tropical gardens. Two hundred varieties, they say, and I only took the trouble to learn a dozen or so. Most of all, I will miss the big silk cotton tree under which Charles and I so often held hands and smelled the jasmine scent that the night breeze brought. Will he remember it the same?*

By two o'clock the ship was fully ready for departure and the sparse crew had nothing more to do except look up at Amelia and ask what she might know that they didn't. All she could do was shrug.

At three, Amelia had been joined on her perch by Jimmy the sailor and Edgar the quartermaster, both with spyglasses. They had observed some activity around the portico of the Royal Vic, and now saw a two-horse buckboard wagon pull up. "That's not the captain," said Edgar. "There's two people in there with the driver and some luggage in back."

However, the wagon lumbered straight down East Street, and soon Jimmy didn't need his spyglass. "That's Capt'n Timmons," he declared, "and he's got a black man in a suit and tie with him."

"That's Felix DuBois, manager of the Royal Vic," said Amelia. "This should be interesting."

As the buckboard reached the gangplank of the *Sea Breeze*, all three atop the pilot house were now on deck, expecting important news. Charles quickly silenced any questions with a finger to his lips as Felix DuBois mounted the gangway, giving a quick nod of recognition to Amelia before disappearing into one of vacant officers' cabins. Two crewmen struggled to carry his large steamer trunk into the small room as well.

Now alone with the inquisitive three, Charles would only say, "Long, difficult negotiations regarding coal. Suffice it to say, Mr. DuBois will be traveling with us on vacation and in search of another business opportunity. We will now shove off and do our coaling at Hog Island. If Mr. DuBois wishes to tell you more, I will leave that to him."

It was only when the *Sea Breeze* pulled alongside the coaling dock on the north side of Hog Island that Amelia got the next sighting of Felix DuBois. As all aboard felt the gentle thud of the ship meeting the wharf pilings and heard the clank that accompanied the gangplank's deployment, DuBois quickly emerged from his appropriated officers' quarters and strode down to the coal yard. Since there had been enough time at the Royal Vic to pack a trunk, he could have changed into comfortable traveling clothes, but DuBois was dressed precisely the same as when greeting hotel guests. Amelia stared from the deck transfixed as he began addressing a cluster of men in ragged, sweat-stained shirts while attired in highly polished black shoes, gray/black striped trousers, starched white shirt with high collar and French cuffs, a silver silk vest, and black puff tie with pearl stickpin, all carefully coordinated in a black, brushed cotton frock coat.

Within a few minutes, DuBois remained in discussion with two of the men while the others set to filling large cast-iron carts from a twenty-foot-high pile of coal. One group would then shovel it into an opening in the hull while others loaded another cart at the mound of coal. The two men disappeared into the thicket behind the coal yard and DuBois was again up the gangway and into his quarters. In a minute, he reappeared with a book in hand and went into the empty galley.

Amelia's curiosity was more than she could bear. She had long realized that Charles, the fiancé of her aspirations, became reserved and formal the moment he walked on the deck of his ship. This she respected and admired, but Amelia Beach had her business responsibilities as well.

Charles was alone, leaning idly on a deck railing, when Amelia approached. "Captain," she said evenly, "I believe that I, as Huxley and Beach representative, should be consulted when you have unplanned expenditures."

She could see irritation all over his face. "Really? Well, I had to use my wits. And it was a race against time. If I'd had to break it off with DuBois at the hotel and go back to get your opinion, I don't think we'd be here right now."

"All right, I understand, but why is DuBois here?"

"How do you think we got all this coal? That's anthracite they're loading, by the way."

"So, what's he getting in return? You told me he wanted fifteen hundred dollars U.S. How did you come up with *that*?"

"He was willing to trade the coal because he wants to go to New York."

"A hundred tons for a trip to New York?"

"All right," said Charles with palms up, "I also promised him a share of the profits."

"Crew shares?"

"Officers', Amelia," he added. "Every man has a little treasure hunter in him. He's no different despite his fancy folderol."

"And that's all?"

"Not quite." Just then, the two men DuBois had been huddling with emerged from the woods and shacks behind the coal yard, each with a bundle over his shoulder. Soon they were on deck and down the stairs to the engine room. As they had reached the top of the gangplank, one man was a head taller than Charles and probably twice his weight.

"I told you we were way short on stevedores. Absolutely couldn't have left without extra help, and DuBois says these are the best of the lot."

"And I suppose they come at a pretty price?"

"Well, coalers also like treasure hunting, so they're getting crew shares, of course."

"Any more surprises, Captain?"

"No."

"Well, I shall trouble you no further," said Amelia, "but you did say Felix DuBois was free to talk about his situation. I still think there's something more to this 'vacation.' Maybe it's woman's intuition, but I'm going to pay him a visit."

Amelia paused at the entrance to the galley to see Felix DuBois, still fully and formally dressed, seated at the crew table and reading a book by a stream of light that poured through a porthole. "Ah, Miss Beach," he said. "When we met, I never imagined I would be sailing one day on your ship."

Me neither, she thought, *but only because a slave owner in Savannah wouldn't be inviting a man of color aboard.* "Mr. DuBois," she said instead, "I know I am interrupting, but…."

"But if *you* deem it important to do so, it is not an interruption."

I've heard him say that a dozen times to bothersome hotel guests, but he always makes me believe he means it. "First, it's stuffy in here. If you'll just allow me to open the porthole, you'll get a lovely breeze."

"I am grateful," he said. "I have much to learn about my new surroundings."

Amelia: "Oh, I see you are reading a book." *How stupid.* "In French, I see." *Even stupider.* "What about, may I ask?"

DuBois: "It's about the history of the fork."

Amelia: "The *fork*?"

DuBois: "Yes. We use so many of them in my business that when a history of forks appeared, I resolved to read it. I confess that was three years ago. Now I have the time."

Amelia: "I never thought about forks having a history." *Truly stupid remark.*

DuBois: "Oh yes. We homo sapiens have been using knives and spoons forever, but forks for only a few centuries. I just finished reading a passage about a Venetian princess in the twelfth century who was so loath to touch her food with her fingers that she had a goldsmith make an instrument with two prongs that could spear her food – but only if her servants cut it into *très petite* pieces. Her courtiers all thought it must be the new fashion, so they had forks made as well. But when the princess suddenly died of the plague, everyone admitted how *stupide* it was in the first place, and so they threw away their forks."

DuBois had lowered the book as he spoke, and Amelia noted that the words seemed to be in couplets. "The history of the fork is written in French poetry?" she wondered aloud.

"Forgive me, Miss Beach," he replied. "I have indeed begun the history of the fork, but that book is back in my room. I thought that it might be a more interesting subject to you because the book I have here is a French translation of poems originally written in Latin, Greek and English."

"It's true, I don't speak French, Greek or Latin," said Amelia, "but do not assume that I would be more interested in forks, which reside in kitchens, just because I am a woman. I have long ago ceased to assume that you are a slave because of your skin color – especially because you are the most elegantly-dressed man I have ever encountered."

"*Touché* on both counts," he replied. "Well then, I am reading here *Childe Harold,* a long poem by George Gordon Noel Byron. You have heard of *Lord* Byron?"

"I have read poems by Lord Byron in the very garden of the Royal Victoria, which you so carefully maintain."

"Splendid. Then we have a bond. I am especially intrigued by the question of why a young Briton would eventually give his life at a young age fighting in the Greek war of independence."

"I was taught in English Literature," she answered, "that he was incensed because the Turk occupiers were demolishing so many ancient Greek statues. But perhaps you'll never really find the answer to your question. I remember another poem in which Byron also wrote: 'The tree of knowledge is not the tree of life.'"

DuBois folded his hands across the open book. "Another reason I read poetry, Miss Beach, is that one can find insights hidden away in this stanza and that epigraph, like finding gems on a roadside. When you walked in, I was reading that if one could compare the universe to a book, someone who has only seen his own country has read but just one page."

DuBois had presented a segue. "So, you are now adding pages to your life's book," Amelia said. "Captain Timmons told me your ultimate destination is New York. Are you not concerned that you'll be kidnapped in Wilmington and sold into slavery?"

DuBois: "Concerned, *oui,* but I am a French citizen with a proper visa, which is valid on trains serving both sides of your war. I have some intriguing business possibilities in New York, which I would like to see anyway before I am done residing on this world."

Amelia: "There's something else I'd like to ask you, and I do so as the representative of Huxley and Beach. Who are the men who just came aboard?"

DuBois: "The large man is Antoine, who can do the work of two men in the engine room. The other man is Felipe, the best fireman I know. He knows when and how to burn coal efficiently. If Byron is correct that one can find poetry in everyday life, then Felipe is the Cupid who ignites the passions of coal and furnace."

The *Sea Breeze* headed north from Hog Island as if on a leisurely holiday sail, but more deliberately to conserve coal and the energy of Antione and in the boiler room. The sun was low when the ship left the last of Great Abaco Cay to port, its compass set on fifteen degrees northeast as John Tyler Wilkes had instructed. And as forecasted, they soon spotted the *Saint Augustine* wallowing in the choppy sea, waiting patiently for its scheduled appointment.

On the third day, September 1, tensions rose with the first sighting of the distant mainland. The wind and sea were rising as well, with swells that sometimes obscured the view of one ship from another and caused their captains to widen the distance between them.

Hurricane or a passing summer storm? Timmons had asked all aboard to keep alert for frigate birds, which traditionally arrived from the Caribbean as harbingers of approaching hurricanes. But as darkness began to envelop the third and final night, no frigate birds had been seen.

The two ships rode due east in tandem, swinging wide past the Old Inlet with its shoals and blockaders. In another fifteen miles, the cloudy sky had become moonless and pitch black when a rapid blinking light came from the *Saint Augustine*. It signaled a turn to zero degrees north, which the *Sea Breeze* followed. Then it began to rain, with heavy drops driven across the window that fronted the wheelhouse.

Knowing that her only duty was to stay out of the way, Amelia tried reclining in the captain's quarters, but the ship's heaving in the sea swells made her stomach churn. She retreated to the galley, only to find Felix DuBois still in formal dress and reading his Byron or biography of the fork. This time he didn't look up to make conversation, so she stumbled and groped her way along railings to the wheelhouse, where she found a stool in one corner and sat silently. "No sitting outside *this* time," was the captain's only comment.

The only people in the wheelhouse were Charles the navigator, Edgar the pilot, and the mouse on the corner stool. Amelia saw sailor Jimmy perched outside as usual atop the crossbeam, but this time in a whaler's black oilcloth. He'd have trouble earning his five dollars for spotting a blockader on this night.

She noticed that the crew hadn't covered the paddlewheel housing with the usual tarp to muffle sound. The wind and waves would be sufficient.

All was eerily dark and quiet in the wheelhouse until Jimmy raised his arm with a pointed finger and Edgar spoke up at the wheel. "That's the light atop Fort Fisher," he said. "I reckon us to be about seven miles from New Inlet."

The *Saint Augustine,* just a shadowy form a quarter mile away, abruptly turned to port and steamed west two hundred seventy degrees. It was the signal that the *Sea Breeze* should follow tightly in its wake. But in these rolling and rainy seas Timmons left a three-hundred-yard leeway between the two lest they topple into one another.

Amelia knew by now that the expected line of blockaders – three, five, ten? – would be positioned somewhere between their present location and four miles northwest. To station a blockader nearer land than four miles would put it within range of Fort Fisher's heavy cannons.

So now it begins, seven months reduced to a few minutes.

Amelia reckoned roughly that if they were gaining ten miles an hour, each mile would require six minutes.

Six long minutes passed with nothing but rain and heaving seas.

Six more minutes passed with more rain and heaving seas, rain splattering against the pilot house window.

Amelia was just counting the beginning of another mile when the ship rose in the crest of a swell and all could see a black form about a half-mile away.

The *Sea Breeze* dove into the trough and rose again to see a blockader close enough to count three cannons on its port side.

When they plunged and rose again, the sky was lit with rockets, and Jimmy shouted, "Holy mother of Jesus, Oy see five of 'em all lined up at port! A reg'lar picket line!"

Suddenly the closest ship was under full steam, making a diagonal cut across the bow of the *Sea Breeze* in an obvious effort to head off the *Saint Augustine.* Within seconds a single volley of fire came from a *Saint Augustine* cannon, the signal for the *Sea Breeze* to begin its charge through the picket line.

"I figured more would chase Wilkes," was all Timmons said for the first few seconds.

The *Saint Augustine* and the pursuing blockader were steaming south, trading cannon fire.

"We're heading into the middle of the squadron," Timmons shouted to his pilot. After riding two crests of the rolling waves they had agreed on four blockaders and a likely fifth. "We've run into their right flank," said Timmons. "All sterns facing us and the wind from the northwest."

When they rose to the top of the third swell, more rockets had lit up the night like high noon. "Hard to starboard," Timmons commanded. "Maybe we can run around the other flank."

As the *Sea Breeze* cut sharply to the east, Amelia blinked in disbelief. Two of the blockaders were racing toward them, stern first.

"Damn! Double-enders," shouted Timmons. "First time I've seen them."

Instead of losing time and distance to the *Sea Breeze* while they turned about, the two Union ships had simply reversed their paddle wheel direction and made the most of having rudders at both stern and bow. Both blockaders were now a hundred yards off the port side of the *Sea Breeze* and were already opening fire.

"Full steam!" Timmons shouted down the horn to the firemen below. "We can't let them face us abeam or we're sitting ducks."

It meant heading away from New Inlet and the squadron line, but soon the *Sea Breeze* would be offering only its narrow backside to the pursuers and outracing them.

Jimmy jumped down from the crossbeam just in time to hear Timmons shout: "Jimmy, get some crew men unfurl the forward sails. We'll have the west wind behind us."

Timmons would have raised the aft sails as well, but the skeleton crew consisted of just three sailors working in a driving rain.

As each sail was hoisted, Amelia could feel the ship thrust ahead like a racehorse making a stretch run. Suddenly Edgar yelled, "Captain, look aft!" They saw crewmen from the nearest double-ender loading what looked like a Dahlgren Gun on its forward deck.

A missile whined well over the topsail.

This time as they rose, a second shot exploded as it hit the topsail, tearing a hole in the canvas and scattering pieces of spar on the deck below.

The men on the blockader were reloading their forward gun as the *Sea Breeze* hove into their view again. A loud thud. The whine, with Amelia holding her breath as always. Then, the sharp *crack* of hardwood splitting, the main mast collapsing on the deck, and a bulky lump, but not wood, landing on the wheelhouse roof.

"You lucky bastards!" Timmons shouted into the splattering rain on his windshield.

As the ship pitched with the next swell, a lifeless body tumbled from atop the wheelhouse to the deck in full view of the mouse in the corner.

It was all legs and arms with no head. Blood pulsed from what had been the neck.

Amelia was struck dumb, beyond screaming. She stared away. When she looked again, the spurting of blood had abated, leaving the body undulating in a wash of blood, ooze, rain and seawater.

"Should we run her up ashore?" asked Edgar the pilot. "The people there are Rebs. They'd work hard to salvage her."

"Absolutely not," shouted Timmons quickly. "The ship's worth more by far than the cargo. Your so-called patriots would just keep all the liquor and cigars. We're going to outrun the bastards. Give it all you've got," he shouted down the trumpet to the engine room.

The *Sea Breeze* charged through the rain and waves, aided by the wind and Gulf Stream. The blockaders were clearly losing ground, but still within sight of their quarry.

On the chase went through the black outer space of the sea. By ten-thirty the *Sea Breeze* had led its chasers some thirty miles from their posts around New Inlet, but their pursuit continued, leaving their lights on as a defiant reminder of their grim determination.

By eleven o'clock the lights of the pursuers had not been seen for several minutes. Just as Timmons had concluded that they had surely turned back at last, a husky voice from the engine room called up: "Capitan, the engines is overheatin'. We need to shut down for a while."

Timmons left the wheelhouse, calmly stepped over the body on the deck and began climbing down the ladder to the engine room, where he saw the steel door already open, clouds of steam hissing from inside. Antoine, the giant, was leaning against the ladder, mopping his sweaty torso with a soot-stained towel. Timmons could see Felipe inside the inferno, sloshing a bucket of water into the furnace.

"We got goin' too fast for too long," shouted over the din. "And we been usin' the pine knots, which made it extra hot."

"How long do you need to cool it?" asked Timmons.

"Can we give it a half hour? We're all het up, too, Captain."

"Twenty minutes," he shouted back.

Meanwhile, Amelia hadn't moved from the stool she had commandeered when she first entered the wheelhouse. Edgar, the stout, bearded Englishman, was seated at the chart table with arms folded as if awaiting the next command. Earlier, Amelia had managed to learn that Edgar had begun on a gunnery crew in the Royal Navy and eventually worked his way into a quartermaster position. He'd signed aboard the *Sea Breeze* expecting to earn just enough cash to buy a tidy cottage on the harbor front in a seaside town named Weymouth.

But now all Amelia wanted to know was: "How could all of you just leave a man's body lying out there with no one to attend it?"

Edgar: "Well, it's what happens in war."

Amelia: "But it's as if no one cared. Didn't anyone know him? Did he have a name, a family? Did he have friends here?"

Another voice: "Maybe yes, maybe no." She looked up to see Charles standing in the open door to the wheelhouse. "Edgar, could you find someone to bring the remains below decks? Thank you."

Now they were alone. "The likelihood is that no one knew him much at all," Charles said. The charming, tender lover on Salt Cay had hardened into an overburdened ship captain who wore his cares on his sweat-soaked forehead.

"He was one of my new sign-ups. He did so because he knew there would be risks to making more money than he had ever seen before. The fact is, they tell me, that he was up there clinging to the main mast well after the others had finished with the sails. They think he may have been drunk. I was in here with you. All I know is that Edgar is right. It's what happens in war." His voice showed irritation.

But Amelia wasn't willing to become the punished child. "Tell me, Charles, why did you pull away so quickly at New Inlet?" she asked with a sharp edge. "We've probably taken more fire than we might have, had we just plowed on through the squadron."

"Oh, so the owner's daughter is now captain as well," he scowled. "Well, let me begin by saying that I never would have sailed this ship with a mere nine crewmen had it not been for you and this Wilkes insisting that we had to reach Wilmington on this particular night. And I have a hundred other thoughts playing in my head right now. Would you like to hear them before your court of inquiry? Or, should I say, court martial?"

"A civil reply is all I asked for," she answered quietly.

"You do recall rain and heavy seas at the time we turned away, do you not?" Charles snapped. "Besides the fact that I could scarcely see through the rain, we had the swells. If we had gone into a trough inside New Inlet with its eleven-foot depth we could have slammed our hull on the bottom or even capsized."

Amelia turned aside, ready to dismiss the outburst. "But I'm only beginning," he said, glaring down at her while standing at the wheel. "Do you recall Wilkes saying he would draw off two blockaders? Well, he managed to attract just one, didn't he, leaving five or who knows how many more all lined up and quite eager to sink your father's ship.

"And speaking of the ship, your father will thank me for bringing it back to Bermuda or Liverpool so that everyone can get paid properly instead of being killed. Interesting, Amelia, that you never asked me about my own pay. The fact is that during all those months since you first sailed, I was paid just once, and that was months ago after that first run to Wilmington. And I never mentioned it the whole time you were sitting on your precious gold in Nassau."

"No, I didn't know." She felt her defenses breaking down.

"Speaking of Charles Timmons, did you ever consider that I cannot afford to be captured and drummed out of the Royal Navy for getting mixed up in somebody else's stupid war? Did you know that they're now tossing crews of English blockade runners into military prisons with the rest of the Rebel soldiers? Confound it, Amelia, can't you see that I'm sick? No, not yellow fever. Malaria! If they take me, I'll die in one of those filthy camps like your brother did."

He saw her gasp but hadn't run out of invective. "That's right. He's already dead, sorry to say. Wilkes said not to tell you, but that's war, Amelia. It's what can happen after all those boys march off with all their brass buttons gleaming and all the girls cheering. Sorry, but you needed to know. Those aren't gentlemen's clubs the Yankees are running back there."

Charles, having released all his frustrations in one ugly burst, mopped his brow and turned to drawing lines on a chart. Amelia sat dumbly, unable to summon thoughts or words in the midst of pervasive hurt that gripped her.

After a long silence, she rose and stumbled into the blackness on deck, scarcely noticing that the rain and waves were abating. Nor did it register with her at first that someone had removed the nameless, headless sailor. Aimlessly, she made her way towards the galley, noting, as she passed the engine room, that no more steam wafted upward from the furnace. Her mind staggered like her feet, trying to picture her brother's face and capable only of repeating *Joseph gone. Gone forever.*

As Amelia entered the galley, the only light was the low flame of the lantern over the mess table. At one end, on the same bench where she had left, sat Felix DuBois, the same book in his hands.

She sat at the darkened other end of the table as DuBois continued reading. *I should have known...should have asked more about Joseph all along. Should have asked Charles if he'd been paid. Should have realized his career would be in jeopardy. Should have known more about malaria. Need to return to the present moment.*

"Mr. DuBois, you are exactly as I left you," she said across the table. "During all the shooting and commotion, you read your poetry."

"Yes, and sometimes I meditated," he replied. "Byron faced the same dangers when he crossed the Hellespont in a warship."

"Perhaps not as calmly, I daresay."

"Well, you must remember that I am a paying passenger, not a crewman."

"Is that why you remain fully dressed?"

"It does no harm to remind them."

"Can you tell me the time, Mr. DuBois?"

He took a gold pocket watch from his vest. "Nearly midnight," he answered. Just then they felt a belch from the smokestacks and heard the paddlewheels begin to slap water again. The ship heaved forward. Two men rushed by outside and were soon hoisting the small aft sail.

"Where is there for us to go?" Amelia wondered aloud.

"New York, or perhaps Baltimore," DuBois said. "We are still an English merchant ship."

"I'm going to find out."

The last place she wanted to be was with Charles Timmons in the wheel-house, but she returned to find Edgar at the wheel with the captain looking aft through his spyglass. "Look behind you," he said abruptly when she entered.

She saw the lights of two ships, perhaps two miles off.

"Yes, it must be the same two bloodhounds," Charles said. "Must have seen our smokestacks quit and thought they'd find out why. We're making only nine knots and they're gaining."

"Aft sail isn't helping much because the wind has fallen off," said Edgar at the helm.

By now Amelia well knew the symptoms of true danger: a fluttering heart and churning stomach. No one spoke as the twin paddlewheels slow-ly churned through the water. Again, she thought of the condemned Ann Boleyn in the Tower of London, awaiting her hour.

She caught Charles staring at her on her corner stool. "I'm sorry for hav-ing given you such bad news," he said in a husky voice.

She shook her head in silence, then looked back at the lights growing larger and brighter in the blackness.

By the time the clock on the chart table read twelve-twenty, the pursuers had closed to within a mile.

Charles called for Jimmy, his all-purpose crewman from Liverpool. "Jimmy, find a mate. Go into the hold and break open a case of Enfield rifles. Set six of them aside and pitch all the other cases overboard as se-cretly as you can. Then bring the six rifles to the crew quarters. Don't look for bullets because there are none. But we may need the rifles for show in the event we have a dialogue with these chaps."

The stalking continued. As the bloodhounds closed to within a half mile, Amelia could make out a large gun on the forward deck of the lead ship.

Charles left to confer with the men in the engine room. Returning, he told Edgar, "I told them we had nothing to lose with full ahead, but I could see we're already beginning to overheat again."

Charles turned again to Amelia. "I don't mean to alarm you," he said, "but the seas are now calmer and if these blokes open fire, their aim will probably be better. I want you to go below to your quarters."

"No. Can't. And won't." She felt icy with fear, but she had already made up her mind that she wasn't about to die from sea sickness or by drowning inside a windowless wooden box.

Suddenly there was no longer time for conjecture. All three jumped as the lead ship's cannon exploded and a cannonball went skipping past the port side.

The second ship swung wide and maneuvered so that the two were at right angles to the *Sea Breeze,* one at zero degrees and the other at ninety. "They're looking to hit the hull or paddlewheel," said Edgar. "Do I face with stern or bow?"

It was too late. Fire erupted from the same forward gun and the *Sea Breeze* shuddered as a cannon ball glanced off the top of the port paddlewheel, sending shards of wooden baffles flying into the night.

"Just what they wanted," said Charles. "Looks like they aim to cripple us enough to board us and then tow us back to their base. So now I look for them to come by for a chat."

As he predicted, the ships ceased firing. They approached cautiously, maneuvering into position not a hundred feet away, one lying opposite the stern and one alongside the wheelhouse on the port side. As they swung into position, lamps were illuminated so that those on the *Sea Breeze* could see a cluster of Parrot guns and Dahlgrens facing them nearly point blank. On one ship a crewman held a large oil lamp beside a flag that showed blue and yellow vertical stripe.

"Lovely," said Charles, turning to Amelia. "It's a kilo flag, meaning he wishes to communicate. Edgar, show him a delta flag."

Edgar walked out of the wheelhouse and held up a blue rectangular flag with yellow stripes on top and bottom.

"Maybe he enjoys a jolly good joke," said Charles. "It means 'Keep clear. I am maneuvering with difficulty.' They should understand why."

But no Yankees laughed. The ship opposite the *Sea Breeze* wheelhouse allowed itself to drift within fifty feet. A man with captain's stripes and thick black beard stood at the deck rail with a bullhorn. "I am captain of the *USS Iona,*" he yelled. "Prepare for boarding."

Timmons was ready with his own megaphone. "We are the *Sea Breeze,* a British merchant ship. You have no right to board," he yelled back. As he spoke, Jimmy, Antoine and Matthew strode forth from their quarters with Enfield rifles and stood at the railings.

Timmons continued: "We are a British flagship with civilian merchandise. We have no military ordnance or ammunition whatsoever!"

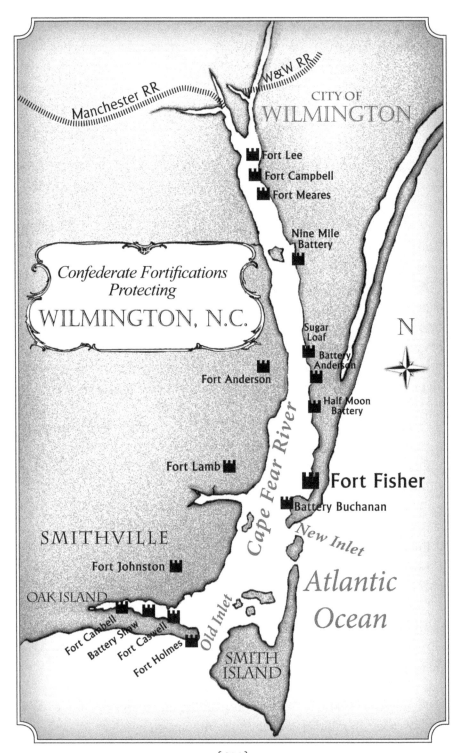

Confederate Fortifications
Protecting
WILMINGTON, N.C.

CITY OF WILMINGTON

Manchester RR

W&W RR

Fort Lee
Fort Campbell
Fort Meares

Nine Mile Battery

N

Sugar Loaf
Battery Anderson

Fort Anderson

Half Moon Battery

Fort Lamb

Fort Fisher

Battery Buchanan

Cape Fear River

New Inlet

SMITHVILLE

Fort Johnston

Atlantic Ocean

OAK ISLAND

Old Inlet

Fort Campbell
Battery Shaw
Fort Caswell
Fort Holmes

SMITH ISLAND

The *Iona* captain cut him short. "We have heard that story before. You are disguising piracy under a neutral flag. Prepare for boarding."

The captain signaled for a lifeboat to be lowered. Timmons nodded to his crewmen, who raised and cocked their rifles.

"I repeat," yelled Timmons. "We will not be boarded. It is you who aspire to be thieving pirates! We have nothing for you. Go to hell!"

The *Iona* captain whispered to one of his companions, then rolled his arm as a signal to winch the lifeboat back onto its trestle. "Very well," came the deep megaphone voice. "Only it is you who are going to hell!"

The big guns facing the *Sea Breeze* were already loaded. Timmons scanned the clusters of men in motion on the *Iona's* deck. "Cover yourself!" he called. "Grape shot!" Timmons dropped below the ramparts. Amelia dove to the floor inside the wheelhouse. Edgar was still at the helm when a cannon ball full of Minié balls shattered the windshield, creating a cacophony of clanks and pings as they ricocheted among the instruments. Amelia, splattered with glass fragments, saw Edgar collapse and crumple to the floor beside her. She reached out with a hand, but his eyes were open in wide-eyed surprise. Edgar was dead.

As Amelia struggled to rise among the shards, she fell back as the ship shuddered from another blast towards midships. A cannon from the second ship had torn a hole in the hull and seawater was already pouring in.

Amelia crawled on all fours across the shattered wheelhouse doorway. Charles sat on the slick deck floor, arms around his ribcage. She called his name, but he seemed too dazed to respond.

She lifted her head above the rampart just in time to see the *Iona* captain bring his arm down. A Dahlgren gun fired at such close range that she felt the impact before she heard the gun's explosion. Black smoke began to belch from the hole that it tore in the ship's thin steel plating.

The engine room, of course. Oh no! "There are *men* inside there!" Amelia shrieked. And just as she did, a fiery form shot out from the metal furnace room, its torso enshrouded in an orange and yellow corona that lit the night like a large oil lamp. It bleated "*Leo, leo, leo*" as it rolled around amidst the blood and watery ooze that had once been inside the unknown sailor. This one had a name. It was Felipe. He was burning to death and she knew not what to do. Later she learned that he had been begging for "L'eau," or "water, water, water" in French.

The sight of the human torch ignited a rush of reckless energy that Amelia had never known. *If I am going to die, it will not be as a lamb led to slaughter.* She drew herself above the railing and screamed across the night: "Stop! Stop, you savages! You see we have no cargo on deck!"

The inferno and the madwoman shrieking at them caused a brief exchange between the *Iona* captain and the two officers at his side. "Then tell your captain to surrender," came the subdued response.

"He is too wounded to talk," she yelled wildly. "We have only a few passengers. We have a French citizen. You have killed three men! How many more lives do you want?"

"Then show us these passengers!" shouted the captain.

"They are afraid of being killed as well," she shrieked back. "We have no military materials. Those rifles you saw don't even have bullets."

Amelia ran in a frenzy to where the crewmen had dropped their rifles when they'd scurried to escape the cannon blasts. She snatched up an Enfield and held it over her head. "You want *this*?" she screeched. "Here take it!" She flung it into the sea between the ships. "You want *this*?" She repeated the scene twice more, then stood foursquare in front of the Yankee officers with hands raised and palms open.

"There is NOTHING MORE!"

Both guns and voices went silent on the *Iona* as Amelia watched the captain and two other men in earnest discussion. After an endless minute or two, the captain raised his megaphone.

"We are leaving," he simply announced.

Then in an apparent afterthought, he raised the megaphone again. "We are also leaving your lifeboat," he said. "Tell your captain it was to be our next target."

Amelia stood erect with both hands on the port railing as if to shoo away the double enders as they reversed propellers and churned away. Soon the blockaders were but twinkling stars on the horizon. Then there was no horizon, only the moonless night, the light west wind in her face, and the aimless roll of the sea.

At her feet, Charles was stirring, mumbling to himself, chunks of shattered paddlewheel and shards of glass at his side on the deck floor. Jimmy and Matthew stood by, clearly awaiting orders from one of them. "Help the captain into the pilot house," Amelia said, but Charles waved them off. He was now on all fours, breathing hard.

He extended a hand. "Careful. Broke some ribs I think," he gasped. When they guided him upright, pieces of broken window fell to the deck.

"Need to get our bearings," Charles mumbled as they steadied him on his feet. "Get me to the chart table."

Then he saw Edgar's body, crumpled on the floor. "Oh, oh, I didn't know," he mumbled. But the sight seemed to sober him like a pot of black coffee. As the other two men gathered up the corpse, they exposed a blood-soaked shirt, where one of the exploding Minié balls had struck. "He probably turned at the wheel when he heard the gun go off," Amelia said.

Charles stood swaying at the chart table as Amelia did her best to brush away the shards and splinters on top, some from the shattered face of the ship's clock. But the hands had survived intact. They read twelve-forty.

"Did you know Edgar well?" she asked, as if just gauging his sensibilities.

"Knew him well," said Charles. "Five, six years together. Crimea. South China Sea." His words came in short bursts, as if speaking were painful.

"Did he have a family?" *Good to get him talking.*

"Here we go again," he said. "You wouldn't make a good captain. Captains have no time for mourning."

He spoke with eyes affixed to a nautical map. Then he declared, "Britannia rules the waves. Know why, Miss Beach? Because we trust in God and the British Admiralty Chart.

"Behold, before me...the Hydrographic Department's Chart of the Carolinas. You know, of course, that before I became a pirate captain...I was a navigation officer. Pretty good with a sextant, too. But no stars tonight... so... am obliged to rely on experience...intuition...sagacity. All that rot."

Was he trying to be the old Charles? Witty and affectionate? Or was he just rambling as he tried to gather his faculties about him and plot a new course?

Charles paused after working some numbers and a divider. "I would put us at forty, forty-five miles northeast of Wilmington. We are more than twenty miles from shore because we cannot see a single light. Our first port would be Beaufort...but that means defying the guns of Fort Macon, which the Union captured some time ago. Then we have Cape Hatteras, but no. The Yankees got that lighthouse and everything around it. Just up the road is Ocracoke Inlet. Don't know about that one, do you, Amelia?

Now call for Jimmy...would you please?"

Charles was rambling, reeling. Perhaps even delusional? But he was their only captain and Amelia shied from seeming to contest his authority at such a moment.

"Jimmy," he said when the sailor appeared in the doorway, "take an assessment of our damage and report back on the double."

Then he continued weaving a strategy of escape. "Not too far around the bend from Ocracoke is Norfolk," he said, talking more to himself than Amelia. "Now think about it. Lots of waterway, many docks. Yes, Yankee territory, but held for so long that the blockade might be looser than Wilmington. So, we have no more weapons. Now totally a merchant ship. We share some of our liquor with any blockaders who want to board. We limp into port, an innocent English flag merchant ship, wrongfully shelled by privateers. No: *Confederate* raiders. All shot up and seeking refuge. Kindness of strangers and all. More liquor for customs people if we must. Yes, I like it, Miss Beach. And you know why?"

"Why?" she said, trying to hide her doubts.

"Because Norfolk is so close to Richmond. We bring the gold in our luggage. We stay at a hotel. Later we take it out in the countryside. Yes, bury it like Blackbeard's treasure chest. Then we send word to Richmond. Your Jeff Davis sends a few brave soldiers on a secret rescue mission. Ah, maybe Wilkes himself! Even better than putting the gold on a train in Wilmington."

Charles sounded even jocular through the pain in his ribs. "You know why Amelia? Because Wilkes already said it's getting dangerous to put anything on a train. So we have an even better stratagem than before. Agreed?"

Before Amelia could answer, Jimmy returned. "Well, Cap'n, a four-foot gash in aft hull. Foremast shot to hell, as you know. Mizzenmast still up and catchin' a haul wind, maybe good for a knot or two. One paddlewheel housing shot out, but some of the baffles is good if we can get 'em to turn. Engine room fire pretty much doused. Tryin' to coal up now."

"Excellent," proclaimed Timmons jauntily. "Stay right here, Jimmy. I am appointing you helmsman of the *Sea Breeze*... with a commensurate share of prize money."

"Well, Oy dunno,' said the old salt. "Never been that high up before."

"Damn it man, I'm tripling your wages," Timmons rasped so loudly that he cradled his rib cage in pain. "All you do keep the wheel on forty degrees northeast until I tell you otherwise."

He turned to Amelia and his conversation with himself. "I know things may not look so pleasing to the eye...but remember... we've still got almost two hundred feet of freeboard...maybe a couple of watertight compartments," he ruminated. "Still got the cargo. And your *trousseau*, Amelia. We've got the Gulf Stream pushing us at six knots an hour. Wind blowing us another one or two. Even more when we get the paddlewheel moving again."

He laid a beam compass alongside the chart and measured. "From forty miles east of Wilmington to Norfolk, Virginia is, maybe, a hundred and sixty miles. At eight knots, it becomes just over twenty hours. Less than a day, anyway. We have food and Saint Matthew in the galley. We can make it. Right, Jimmy?"

"If'n you say so, Cap'n," said the new helmsman.

Well, at least it's a plan. Amelia needed hope like a tonic for upset stomach.

⸺

By one o'clock the ship had begun to list to port. But a cheer went up on deck as the stacks began coughing smoke and the shattered paddlewheel began to turn slowly but erratically. As the portion with the missing baffles hit the water, the ship would pause, then lurch forward when the intact paddles made contact.

Charles now sat at the chart table, holding his side and apparently dozing. "Jimmy," whispered Amelia, "let me hold the wheel while you go and have a look at how much water we have in the hold."

Jimmy returned several minutes later. "Well, Oy'd reckon about half full," he said.

"I don't know what that means," she answered. "How far from the waterline to the bottom where the ballast is?"

Jimmy waggled his head while counting to himself. "Well, Oy'd say five to six feet."

"Is any of the cargo still dry?"

"Well, Oy sure seen some brandy cases on top."

"Go back, Jimmy, and see anything useful that you can bring up on deck. You *do* know how to read?"

He nodded quickly and stepped out onto deck.

"He doesn't," muttered Charles, still with eyes closed, "but he'll find the spirits."

———

By two o'clock Jimmy had rescued five cases of cargo and stacked them behind the wheelhouse. Amelia would soon learn that all were of French brandy.

Within the next hour the outlook for the ship's survival had deteriorated. A broken piston arm had shut down the already-crippled paddlewheel. The portside list had worsened.

The hold had nearly filled with seawater.

The gold at the bottom was submerged beyond rescue.

Captain Charles Timmons, bracing himself against the starboard wall, continued working calculations at the chart table as Jimmy grappled to hold the wheel steady. Finally, Timmons broke the tense silence. "Looks like we're passing Beaufort Inlet."

Amelia did her own calculating inside her head. "That's not halfway to Norfolk," she said. She waited for a stern rebuke, but none came.

———

The clock read three-thirty a.m. when Charles next spoke. "I think we're going under," he said with no emotion. "Never had to abandon ship before. Jimmy, leave the wheel. Tell crew to prepare the lifeboat. Get the cargo you salvaged and tell Matthew to bring whatever he can from the galley. Then tell everyone to gather no more than an armload of belongings."

He turned to Amelia. "So sorry for all this," he said with a wan smile.

Two inches of seawater now covered the deck from the pilot house aft. The port-side list now required hanging onto hand railings when moving anywhere.

Soon Amelia had joined the cluster of men watching the lifeboat being winched over the port side. A twenty-five-foot yawl, it was normally indispensable in ferrying men to wharfs and between ships. But it was also kept ready for emergencies, thus equipped with jugs of fresh water and several buoys of kapok for tossing to anyone who got washed overboard.

They stood in the darkness as water lapped at their ankles: Amelia, a lone woman dressed in a man's clothing; Jimmy, his career as a helmsman cut short; Matthew, holding two baskets of provisions; Antoine, the large fireman, stained with soot; Felix DuBois, his striped pants soggy at the tip but still retaining their press.

The captain stood apart, holding his bullhorn and a leather portfolio case of maritime charts. His face displayed the shame of trading his pride and authority for the rule of a lifeboat.

All carried little bundles and bags of personal effects. All but Felix DuBois. "I require a steward," he announced.

All blinked or stammered as if not hearing correctly. He addressed Timmons. "Perhaps you forget that I am a paying passenger," he said with an overbearing mien. "A bargain is a bargain. This lifeboat is still your vessel, albeit smaller."

Charles studied the erect DuBois. "Very well," he said at last. "Antoine, go to your friend's cabin and help him bring his things."

Antoine reappeared a minute later carrying a steamer trunk over his head like a wild game hunter's porter.

"We can't accommodate all that," Timmons said with a weary shake of the head.

"You must," answered DuBois. "It contains very valuable goods."

"Such as?"

"Books and clothing. I'm not obliged to explain beyond that."

Charles tried to throw up his hands but winced and simply rolled his eyes. "Perhaps you will read to us as we row," he said.

It was just after four a.m. when all six were afloat in the lifeboat, being rowed by Antoine and Matthew. The wind was light and the seas tolerably calm. They had rowed hard to be free of the ship's undertow should it capsize. Now, when they paused to look back, the once-sleek *Sea Breeze*, built to resemble a luxury yacht for holiday cruising, now listed like an old derelict, its middle shooting sparks through the engine room cavity. Almost directly overhead, the sliver of the new moon also listed to port as if pulling the ship's cargo of gold down to where Blackbeard had lost it off Shackleford Banks a century and a half before.

Charles raised his bullhorn to speak, the pain in his ribs having sapped the strength of his voice. "We have abandoned ship, but we are not to abandon hope," he intoned like a vicar from a pulpit bow. "We have sailed past Beaufort Inlet and are somewhere off Shackleford Banks… a long barrier island, mostly uninhabited. We are approaching Cape Lookout Light, which is dark but occupied by Union troops. We must row a wide berth around

Lookout Point, lest we be discovered and captured. We are going to try our luck at Ocracoke Inlet… just a few hours north. There is no Union garrison there. Chances are the locals will take us in. And when dawn comes, a friendly ship may rescue us as well.

"Again, do not despair," he added. "Saint Matthew here has tasty snack of dried fish and bread. Bought it just this week in the Nassau market."

"And Cap'n, sir," interrupted Jimmy. "May Oy suggest we uncork this 'ere bottle of cognac to warm our chilly bones?"

"All right, Jimmy," said Timmons, "and as we do, let each say a silent toast to the *Sea Breeze.*"

The bottle of cognac went around, as there were no glasses. Black, white, English, Bahamian, French, American, men and one woman all took their turn tugging at the same bottle. As the ornate bottle came to Amelia, she squinted to read the label, *Hennessy,* with its three stars, *Âgé de six ans,* and fondled it for a moment as an elegant souvenir of a life at the Royal Vic that she could still taste. She took a long swallow that burned her throat but warmed her insides.

As Amelia passed the bottle to Charles, she noticed for the first time a rip in her sleeve revealing a purple-encrusted line where one of the flying shards must have cut. Her dead brother's trousers were streaked with more blood and her leather shoes sloshed inside with the oily seawater that moved across the boat's hull with each pull on the oars.

Amelia turned to Charles, seated beside her on the lifeboat's forward bench. Now spent, he sat slumped against the gunwale, arms again cradling his midriff. But now, in the cold, heavy air, she could see him shivering and shuddering beneath his woolen planter's coat.

Malaria was back and in full display.

The two had lived with it and could again. But could they live with each other? *Do you still love me, Charles? Did you ever say those words? I can't remember. Tell me!* But all that came out was: "I can't believe I just chased two ships away like that."

"Yes, quite a show – what I heard of it," Charles answered, his gaze fixed on the listing *Sea Breeze.*

Was that a compliment?

"I'm sure they didn't relish shelling all those passengers you told them about. But remember, they were forty miles from home. Easier to let a ship sink on its own than lose a night's sleep escorting us all the way back to Wilmington."

They sat in silence, watching the smokestacks of the *Sea Breeze* dip into the sea as it finally disappeared into the black after a final burst of sparks from the engine room. "Sink, damn you, sink," Charles muttered.

Amelia's thoughts turned to survival. "You told me earlier you didn't know if Ocracoke is friendly," she said to Charles.

"Give them hope," he answered. "It's even better than food and brandy."

Then he leaned against the gunwale again and closed his eyes.

Amelia found hope elusive. She felt empty and alone again as she drew around her the same tattered officer's jacket she had borrowed to visit John Tyler Wilkes. Cognac and Saint Matthew's bread had warmed the ache in her stomach, but they had not begun to fill the ache within her soul. And as the minutes ground on, the silence allowed a cacophony of thoughts to come screeching and scolding into her head.

You lost the family fortune it has taken your father years of hard toil to amass!

You failed John Tyler Wilkes!

You failed President Jefferson Davis and ruined his plan to save the South!

You fell in love with the captain of your father's ship!

You helped sink the ship before the builders were even paid! And now three men are dead!

You may have caused this captain to be sacked by the British navy!

You have no brother to come home to! And had he gone to Nassau instead of you he wouldn't have let all this happen!

Your mother was right all along and she'll never take you back! And you have shamed your father!

Maybe no one will take you back because you'll be arrested by the Yankees and thrown in jail as a Confederate spy!

Maybe this lifeboat won't make it to Ocracoke.

And maybe it will be for the best.

Chapter Twelve

Terra Firma?

No sight was ever more welcome. The first glimmer of gold seemed to Amelia like the eye of God peering over the horizon to remind the weary occupants of a tiny lifeboat that they weren't forgotten in a vast space. And soon the rising sun became a prism for a dazzling spray of light that magnified each puff of cloud into a gallery of gold, orange, yellow and white.

No one spoke as the rowers continued the same slow slap at the calm ocean that had kept the boat heading northward with the Gulf Stream, even when they were dozing. For over eight hours Antoine, the muscular foreman of the coal yard at Hog Island and the bulwark in the engine room from Nassau to Wilmington, had insisted on maintaining his oar while others alternated at the other. Every hour or so, Felix DuBois would rise, massage the big man's shoulders as he rowed, and speak French words softly into his ear. *How strange, but at the same time touching,* Amelia thought.

Breakfast was uncooked hardtack with some jam smeared over the top. Stale, stored-up water from a canvas bag made do in place of morning coffee. Everyone was stirring but Charles Timmons, who had never budged from his original leaning position against the gunwales. His shirt was soaked and his breathing was rapid and shallow, as if unable to inhale deeply.

By ten o'clock they could make out a short white lighthouse at the entrance of an inlet surrounded by a cluster of small buildings. The only sign of maritime life was a small craft a mile or so outside the inlet. As they approached it, they could see two teenage boys fishing with hand lines from a weathered skiff.

Charles startled everyone when he sat up and raised a hand to signal the rowers to approach the boys. The lifeboat glided along the Gulf Stream until it was bobbing in the calm sea nearly bow to bow with the skiff.

"Ahoy, how's the fishing?" Charles called out in a friendly voice.

"Not bad," said one cautiously.

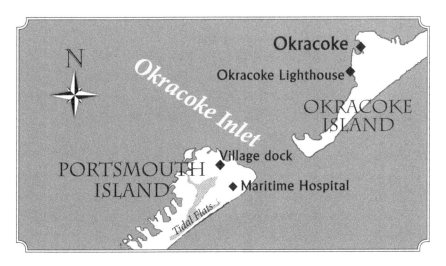

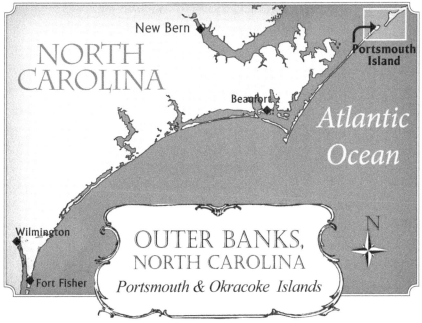

"Bluefish?"

"Yep. It's bluefish season awright."

"That lighthouse there. Is that Ocracoke?"

"Sure is." The lad was wary but not unfriendly.

"You live there?"

"Yep."

"Can you tell me who's in charge there?"

"Well, no one, unless you mean the Yankees."

"I need to know because we're from a ship that just sunk last night."

The second boy looked up from studying his hand line. "Well, there's a hospital for shipwrecked sailors. But it's over on Portsmouth Island. That's on the left side across the inlet. You can just about see it from here."

"Who runs it?" asked Charles.

"Don't rightly know. Never been there. The government, I think."

Charles dug deeper. "How do people in town feel about the war?"

The first boy scratched his head. "Well, the war [he pronounced it wo-ah] is kinda funny. My daddy was grabbed up by the Union army and he run away and came back here. My friend here, his daddy wound up with the Rebs, but he come back too. I guess we just wish the whole thing would go away."

Charles was just about to signal the oarsmen when the second lad finally got curious enough to ask, "You Rebs?"

"No. I thought you could tell by my funny accent," said Charles. "English. From The Bahamas."

The two boys showed neither comprehension nor curiosity to learn more. The lifeboat was soon beating through gentle swells towards the inlet, with all aboard wondering if the boys even knew whether the words "England" and "Bahamas" were places or just gibberish.

As they rowed into the Inlet, Charles remained seated upright and was no longer shivering. Malaria had skulked away from the sun's warming rays. And in the bright light they could now glimpse Portsmouth Island on the south side with its white hospital building and, behind it, a church steeple poking out of the tree line. On the north side of the inlet, a lighthouse marked the entrance to a large harbor that formed a perfect semi-circle, ringed with boat sheds, houses and stores. "That certainly looks more inviting," said Charles. "But now there's a surprise!" He pointed up the inlet to the stone ramparts of a fort in the distance. "Those boys said no one occupied the place."

But they were too weary to change course. Now well inside the inlet, the lifeboat headed toward what might be a ship's chandlery or fish market. Amelia could make out a dozen or so people sitting or ambling this way and that. "Nobody seems to notice us," she remarked. "Maybe they're all in their houses having lunch."

Said sailor Jimmy: "If'n this was Cornwall, you'd see people rushing down to meet a bunch of survivors. Up in the cottages they'd be getting out extra blankets and boiling tea."

"Seems like not many people for the number of buildings," said Amelia. "Care to guess the population?"

"An ol' sailor trick is to count the church steeples first," he said. "Oy see four here. Then you figger about two hunnert per church, which makes it eight hunnert, then add a couple hunnert more for sinners like me. So mebbe a thousand.

"But rich they ain't. You can always tell how well off a town is by the paint on the buildings. Lookee there. They got faded white paint, faded gray paint and no paint a'tall."

They approached the longest building, which looked like it might be a ship's chancellery or fish market. It sat along a wharf with bowed, weathered planks. Two white-haired men in loose faded overalls sat on a bench mending a large net, apparently oblivious to a boat approaching with six shipwreck survivors.

A steep ladder awaited them because the tide was low.

"I think I should be inconspicuous," Charles whispered to Amelia. "English ship captain with no documents. Don't know if this is a port of entry. They could demand visas and all. Don't know if that fort is Union, ready to throw us in irons. Besides, don't know if I can climb that ladder."

"Who should go?" she asked.

"You go."

"Oh lord," she said. "I'm a woman dressed like a man. They might think I'm a pirate."

"But you talk like one of them," said Charles. "Take DuBois. He looks impressive. He also has a visa."

After a brief huddle and a hushed conversation, Amelia struggled up the rusty ladder with Felix DuBois behind. The net menders still had not moved nor said a word.

"Good afternoon," Amelia said brightly. "We come from a merchant ship that sank at sea just last night. We came from Nassau."

Both men looked up, but with blank stares.

"Nassau, Bahamas," she added. "An English colony. Is there a store here that would take English pounds?"

Both cocked their heads in thought. "Don't rightly know," one of them volunteered.

The door to the building opened and a large, elderly woman stepped out. "Not here, anyways," she said, having heard everything from behind an open window.

"Well, is there a bank here?"

"Not since the fort closed up. Only in New Bern nowadays."

"And how far might that…"

"Fifty miles thataway," the grim woman said, pointing to the expansive waterway beyond the inlet.

"You mentioned a fort," Amelia said.

"Built by the Rebs three years ago. Then the Union fellers came and spiked all the guns. Tore up the walls. Nobody there now."

Amelia pressed on. "Is there a doctor hereabouts? One of us is sick."

"That'd be Doctor Drummond," she said. "But he ain't here now. Sailed over to New Bern yestaday."

Just then the door opened again and two men joined the scene, both younger than the net menders. They stood with stony faces and arms folded across stained coveralls.

"Is there a hotel in town?

"This town or *that* town?"

"This one."

"No," said the woman. "And leastways not for coloreds," she added with a nod towards the silent Felix DuBois. The men flanking her seemed eager for an excuse to maneuver both intruders to the dock ladder.

"Madam," Amelia lied, "this gentleman is the French consul to the Royal Bahamian government, a very important official."

Muffled snickers. "Well, he ain't no o-*fficial* here," the woman said at last. "You really best go to that hospital over there," she said, pointing across towards Portsmouth Island. "It's there 'specially for people like you. The same doctor runs it. Doctor Drummond. He'll be back soon enough."

Suddenly, the prospect of immediate food and rest that had buoyed them since first spotting Ocracoke Lighthouse had vanished, leaving spirits spent. Their strength waned as well as they left the harbor behind and rowed against a strong outgoing tide to cross the inlet. Arriving at the bleak town dock on

Portsmouth Island, they disrupted a dozen screeching seagulls, leaving only a jumble of old wooden crab traps leaning against a weathered, windowless shed.

Inside the shed they surveyed a crooked stack of fish pots, a box of rope, a fish cleaning table and a pile of old sailcloth. Amelia pulled off one of the canvas remnants and announced that she was too tired to go further, was going to drag a piece of sail out into the afternoon sun and take a nap. Within a minute, all six were collapsed on canvas tarps, warmed by the sun, but cooled by the steady breeze that flew up the inlet

Riding in a carriage. Bumpy road. Passing pink, blue, turquoise houses. Purple and red Bougainvillea hanging over walls. Looking up. Wide stone steps. Government House but no one home. Guard house with soldier standing inside. Red, white uniform. He comes out with angry look. Raises rifle. "Go! Leave! Big stone statue. Christopher Columbus? Can't make out face. Father? Daddy Beach! Daddy! But its face is stern. Scolding eyes. His arm points. Go!

Amelia sat up as if to run, then lay back rubbing her eyes and trying to make sense of her dream of rejection. She could scarcely believe that she had been in Nassau just three days before, able to choose between marmalade and fresh peach jam at the Orangery and idle away minutes in her wardrobe closet deciding which one of ten gowns to wear at the ball that evening.

Within a few minutes all had re-assembled, carrying their pitiful packs, Antoine uncomplainingly shouldering the steamer trunk of Felix DuBois. They had argued over what to do with the five cases of brandy on board but decided to leave them under the aft seat and hope the place was too forlorn to attract thieves. Then off they shuffled in the eastward direction of the hospital, which made a convenient landmark even when a mile away.

Portsmouth Island was hardpan flat, almost like an extension of the seabed. Amelia had known the flat coast beyond Savannah, but that landscape was camouflaged with tall grasses, pines and majestic live oaks. This place was a tabletop of lichens, spikey stunted grass and a few gnarly trees that centuries of storms had spared, perhaps only as an expression of God's mercy. And as if to prove that the sea was only inches away from covering the island at will, the path eastward moved through a twisted labyrinth of shallow tidal creeks.

Houses just as wooden, weathered and gray as those on Ocracoke were spaced out along the creeks as if no one could countenance being within shouting distance of his neighbor. In a few minutes, the path led to a cluster of three hardscrabble buildings: a shack with a hand-lettered sign, FISH MARKET and a Closed sign on the door; a whitewashed one-room schoolhouse and an overgrown shed with peeling paint. A sign above on its roof read: U.S. POST OFFICE AND GENERAL STORE.

The refugees now harbored scant hope of help and were not contradicted. As the six approached the school, a door opened and a dozen or so barefooted children from toddlers to teenagers emerged and stood dumbly in their gray dresses and overalls until a young teacher shooed them back inside.

A query at the store/post office produced an encore of the Ocracoke scene. Goods for English money? "No. Don't have much to sell here anyway except what local folks need. You go on up to the hospital. They'll take care of you. You g'wan now. Hospital's right up the road."

As the hospital building loomed larger on the path, the only other sign of Portsmouth civilization was a Methodist church, fronted by a tall wooden steeple that would have been the pride of any town in New England. Atop it was a weathervane with an iron crosspiece that turned in the wind as if meant to show that the cross of Christendom faced wherever one's journey led. A few yards away was a farmhouse and a few outbuildings. A lone cow was tethered behind one of them and the sight of it brought Amelia up short.

That's what makes this place so eerie. Where are all the horses, sheep, goats, chickens and ducks that would be out clucking and peeping and grunting on any other farm area like this one?

The hospital lay just ahead, almost at the line where ankle-high vegetation gave way to sand and sea. The building was easily the largest and newest of any they had seen since landing in Ocracoke harbor. Painted white, its two stories ran perhaps a hundred feet long, with tall windows. On the perimeter were several outbuildings. Congregating outside one of them were a half-dozen colored men and women sitting, standing and staring at them. The second sign of life was a young man, wearing the trousers of a Union uniform, who seemed to stagger at a half trot from the hospital building to another outbuilding. Another followed him into what was certainly the latrine.

The survivors paused at an outsized round brick cistern debating what to do next. Just then they heard a woman's voice on the path behind them. "Greetings to thee," the voice squeaked cheerfully. "Comin' to visit somebody in the hospital?"

All heads turned to see a wisp of a woman who looked sixty but might have been twenty windblown years younger by the calendar. Her thin face was partially masked by a floppy bonnet. A faded gray skirt seemed an extension of her gray complexion. Her apron and blouse were tired remnants of gingham patterns. And from a milkmaid's yoke on her slender shoulders hung two pails that twisted in the air when she walked.

All six stared at her dumbfounded before realizing that maybe they weren't lepers after all. Someone had actually spoken to them. Charles pushed Amelia to the forefront again. The apparent friend studied the young woman's clothing for an instant but broke into an amused smile as Amelia poured out her story of shipwreck and rejection. And in turn, this harbinger of kindness revealed herself as Rachel Ruth Staley, wife of the pastor of the First Methodist Church of Portsmouth, displaced from her New Hampshire roots "because we go wherever the bishop sends us."

"Well, what's in the pails?" asked Amelia. "Are you bringing milk for the patients?"

"I sure wish Eliza – that's my cow – could produce that much," said Rachel. "No, what I got in this here one pail is biscuits, if ye could call 'em that. They don't leaven much, so the men up there like to dunk 'em in beef tea. That's what I got in the other pail. Tonight it'll be more like dinner because they're just about out of rations in there."

"Are you in charge of feeding everyone in the hospital?" Amelia asked, incredulously.

"Well, yes and no," said her new friend. "Ye see, this here was built as a maritime hospital. Before that, ships would come into Ocracoke harbor with goods for towns up and down Pamlico Sound. If some had sailors with ailments like scurvy or what we might call social diseases, they would just let them off – abandon them – in Ocracoke. Then you had shipwrecks, and what to do with the survivors who washed up on shore? So, the government [she pronounced it *gummint*] built a half-dozen marine hospitals up and down the coast. Everything was working pretty well 'til the war came along and the hospitals had no way to get supplies all the way down here."

Tiny Rachel bent over the low brick cistern, ladling water into one of the milk cans. "Well, at first we had the Ladies Aid Societies here and from Ocracoke that would bring out food," she said. "Our Portsmouth Methodist would do it two days a week because we was so near. But with the war the

Union started sending patients up here from Fort Macon. It just got to be too many mouths to feed, and the Ladies' Aid groups just sort of dropped out along the way."

Rachel straightened up and began attaching the full pail of water to her yoke when sailor Jimmy insisted on carrying it. "Thank thee," she said, "Now I feel light as a feather. Well, then, when the ladies fell off, the stealing started. When you got hungry patients, you got some of them going out at night and stealing chickens and ducks, pluckin' people's peach trees and such. I even caught one of 'em tryin' to milk Eliza. Then someone broke into the general store.

"But you can't really blame the ladies aid people for *that*," she continued. "The diseases in there would scare anybody off. You get typhoid, malaria, dysentery, measles and what-not. We don't have no measles now, but when it happens every couple of months or so it just flies from bed to bed."

"And now you're trying to feed the whole hospital?" Amelia asked again.

"Well, I'm a Christian," said Rachel with a shrug. "That's what we're supposed to do, ain't it? But I'm only one Christian woman and I've got to help my husband with the church. Now I've got it so I can cook for him and the hospital, too. On Wednesdays when we have a potluck at the church, I'll bake two, three extra pies and that's the day's delight for these men in there. Now, ye wouldn't think three pies wouldn't feed fifty men, but truth is, a lot of them can't really eat. So, some just sniff at the smells. I suppose me and the pies just remind them of their mothers."

Amelia dabbed at something wet in her eyes and realized that tears were trickling down her salt-stained face. *Have I met someone with more misfortune than me?*

"How do you do it all?" she blurted out.

The little woman peered up sideways so her bonnet covered one eye. "Well, ye just git up in the morning and ye put two feet over the bed," she said with a crooked smile. "Then thou say to thy feet, 'Let's just git on with it.'"

Rachel advanced a dozen steps and stopped again. "Speakin' of pies, I told those contrabands over there they wouldn't get no pie if they did no work. Now they're spittin' mad at me."

"Contrabands?" asked Amelia, who'd begun walking alongside her new friend.

"That's what we call the freed coloreds. That's them hanging around the linen shed and the dispensary. They just showed up two, three months ago. Three men, four women, maybe more if they'd all come outside at once. Came down here from some farm in Carolina because some Yankee soldiers told them they was free. But their owner didn't quite agree and went huntin' for 'em. They wound up begging for mercy at Fort Macon, which didn't know what to do with them. So, they got dropped off here, just like shipwrecked sailors.

"Dumb as dirt and you can hardly understand them," Rachel said with a low voice and a glance back at the men of color walking behind them. "Someone told 'em they could get a boat to Washington, DC, where *Mister* Lincoln would give them free houses and free everything else. Well, Doctor Drummond – he's the hospital superintendent – he said they could stay in the linen house until their boat came to take them to the promised land, *if* they'd wash the sheets and towels. But no, they don't have to work because they're free, they say. And I say, no pie."

They were now in front of the two-story hospital portico that faced the sea. "Can you find us space for the night in the hospital?" Amelia asked.

"No, I wouldn't do that," Rachel said with a firmness that wasn't to be trifled with. "All sorts of disease. Did I mention smallpox? And yellow fever? Best ye wait for the doctor."

"But we're just about dead in our tracks," Amelia said with pleading eyes. "We've rowed a lifeboat at least from Beaufort and haven't slept but two hours in the last day."

Rachel reached up and put a thin arm around Amelia's waist. "Well, I suppose ye could sleep on church pews if ye wish," she said. "We don't have enough blankets, but I can give thee some coats to put over thee. But what shall I do about supper?" she wondered aloud.

She was loud enough to perk up Matthew the cook, who had been walking behind the two women. Rachel had begun lamenting that she had only one bluefish and two potatoes for her and the reverend that night. "Lady, if you will give me the fish and the potatoes, I can make a fish chowder for all of us," he said.

As soon as they had laid down their belongings in the fellowship hall behind the sanctuary, Matthew departed for a long beach walk. As the sun began to cast shadows on the waves that rippled over the shore, he returned with a sack and began putting its contents into a large kettle. Rachel was intently interested and the two were soon in animated conversation.

"This is all from thy walk along the beach?" asked Rachel, peering out from her floppy bonnet.

Matthew: "Yes, lady. To go with your bluefish and potatoes we now have here some whelks, mussels and clams."

"Mussels? Them black things?"

"Oh, yes, lady, very tasty when you boil the whole mussel."

"Well. Here God was providing all along and I didn't see it."

Matthew: "Yes, lady. When you are on a long trip looking for sponges and have no money, you learn to take what the Lord hands out." Next, he began cutting some stalks that looked like white pulp.

Rachel: "My goodness, what is that?"

"This, lady, is the stalk of the saw palmetto, which you have growing along the path. Very tasty when you boil it in a pot like this."

Finally, he produced a kerchief full of corn kernels and tossed it in the pot. "Now this is just some corn that was on the ground in your garden," he said.

"But that was from our corn crop last month."

Matthew: "Yes, lady, but in my life, I see rich people who only shake the low branches of any fruit tree. What falls to the ground they leave for people like me. This corn will be tasty after we boil it for a while."

Matthew began slicing some small apples. "Them apples," Rachel said, "they look nice when ye see them cut up in pieces, but they looked pretty rotten and wormy when they was on the ground."

Matthew: "They were when I found them. But God provides for both man and worms, I think. I see a worm in the apple and I say, 'Mister worm, you can have one half of the apple, so I cut your half away and leave you on the ground. I take the other half and make something nice for me.'"

The sun was setting and lamps were being lit in the social hall as Matthew carried in a steaming pot of chowder. Just then the door to the sanctuary opened and in walked a middle-aged man with a trim beard and wire spectacles, clad in a black vest and white clerical collar. Rachel introduced her husband, the Reverend Hiram Staley, and said he was just in time to say the blessing. After the brief and perfunctory ritual, he took even less time to ladle himself a bowl and disappear on grounds that "I am working on my Sunday sermon and hope ye will visit us to hear it."

It was just as well. Seated at a long table made from old ship's planks, the weary but reinvigorated refugees greedily consumed a tasty stew of fish, whelk, mussels, clams, potatoes, corn and hearts of saw palmetto. They took the last of the two-day-old Bahamian bread and dipped it into the chowder broth until the last drop was sopped up. Then they applauded as Rachel brought out a surprise apple pie.

The others had already begun to stake out sleeping pews in the adjoining sanctuary when Amelia found herself at the sink washing dishes with Rachel. "How many people do you have here on Portsmouth Island?" she asked.

"That's anyone's guess," Rachel answered. "We been here only ten years. They say that the 1850 census showed about six hundred. In 1860, I read it was about five hundred. But now with the war, so many got dragged off to fight on one side or the other, and some just got so tired bein' caught in the middle that they moved out, too. One man in our church had a fine, new-built schooner. He was so afraid the Yankees would take it that he sailed it up a freshwater creek around New Bern and just sunk it. Figgers he'll raise it up when the war's over and start up again. I think that just about sums it up for most folks around here.

"Of course, that hospital over there couldn't go nowhere," said Rachel. "I guess it just sort of fell to Hiram and me by default, like folks thought it was part of the church or something."

Rachel kept her eyes on her washing and scrubbing, but she clearly needed someone to talk to. "It's not all Drummond's fault," she said. "See, the first doctor was John Potts. He got a contract from the government that was supposed to cover his pay and everything for the few patients they expected. But after just a couple of years Potts couldn't make ends meet, and Drummond agreed to take it over. That was a dozen years ago. He never expected that all these sick people would be jammin' up his hospital.

"Far as I know, he's not a doctor," Rachel continued. "He runs cargo schooners up and down the sound. But people started coming to him from here and Ocracoke, and I guess he just learned doctorin' along the way. And I suppose if people believe a doctor's gonna cure 'em, enough of 'em will get better. Anyway, Hiram says it's none of our business. But now he's gettin' older. Almost seventy, I reckon."

They were finishing up, a lone lantern flickering in the darkness. Rachel was quiet for a few moments, then started up again.

"Hiram didn't show much of himself, did he," she said. "Well, it wasn't about working on a sermon. He's just not sure what to do with ye. See, this church was built on land donated by Doctor Drummond. That creek ye crossed to get here is called Doctor's Creek for him. He sits on our board of trustees, and ye might say that no one else does anything unless he says so. So, ye can see why my husband is not eager to cross Doctor Drummond."

All the dishes and cups were back on their shelves. The big stew pot had been scrubbed clean and Rachel stood on her tiptoes to blow out the lantern flame. "Open that door to the church, will ye," she said. "I need to go the house and collect some covers for our guests."

Amelia opened the door to the sanctuary slowly and peered out at the twin rows of pews from behind the pulpit. Felix DuBois was sitting off to the side, squinting down at a book in the dim light, Antoine sitting silently beside him with arms folded. The only other person in the sanctuary was Jimmy.

"Where is Charles?" Amelia asked. Jimmy held a finger up to his lips and pointed below. Amelia walked over to see Charles, lying on the hard pew, his farmer's jacket pulled across his chest, and using his leather chart case for a pillow. His knees were drawn up. His face was perspiring and he was shaking. His eyes opened and he managed a wan smile.

He's only a captain at sea. Now he's just a tired, sick boy. He's in a strange land and wants to be lost in it until the sea takes him back. Will he ever become the same man that I knew only a few days and weeks ago? Forgive me for what I've done to him and for having to see him this way.

Amelia straightened up and walked aimlessly back to the pulpit. A few yards across the room she noticed for the first time a small square organ not much bigger than a spinet piano. Atop a carved music stand was an open hymnal, perched above a single keyboard shorter than a piano. Behind the music stand was a bronze plaque with the engraved words, *American Harmonia Company*. Amelia sat on the round stool and pushed some keys. No sound came out. She looked down and saw two flat boards meant to be pushed by the feet.

When she did so, she was startled by the brief squeaks the little organ produced. Realizing that one must pump the two boards continuously, she began playing the first thing that came to her mind, the Chopin polonaise that she had played the previous Christmas in Savannah. Her fingers were stiff and her clumsy footwork only produced an embarrassment of hurdy gurdy wheezes.

Something simpler, perhaps. She looked up and found it in the chords of the song in the open hymnal and began playing.

Amazing grace! How sweet the sound
That saved a wretch like me.
I once was lost, but now am found;
Was blind, but now I see.
'Twas grace that taught my heart to fear,
And grace my fears relieved;
How precious did that grace appear
The hour I first believed.

Through many dangers, toils and snares,
I have already come;
'Tis grace hath brought me safe thus far,
And grace will lead me home.

The Lord has promised good to me,
His Word my hope secures...

The organ emitted a muffled, muddled chord as Amelia's hands went limp on the keyboard and her feet froze beneath her. She rocked back and forth, sobbing silently.

Someone touched her shoulder. "That was sweet," said Rachel softly. "No one has played that organ since Miss Barnett passed a year ago.

"Now ye come with me," she said quietly. "I have a room just for thee."

"Just a moment," said Amelia. She walked over to the pew where Charles had lain. Jimmy was gone, but someone had put a blanket over Charles and he was fast asleep when she whispered his name.

She dried her tears and followed Rachel, the rush of emotion having drained her last drop of strength. They walked across the moonlit yard and entered the back door of the farmhouse. Just off a sitting alcove was a starkly simple room with a small whitewashed bed. "This was my daughter's until she got married," said Rachel. It had only a pine armoire and round wicker bedside table with a pitcher and catcher on top. On a wall beside the bed was a painting of the Virgin Mary that someone had cut from a book and framed so long ago that the face was wrinkled and the halo tarnished.

"Now say thy prayers," whispered Rachel, softly closing the door.

Instead, Amelia sat on the edge of the bed debating whether remove her clammy, salt-and-blood-stained clothes or sleep in them. In a few seconds, she toppled over and plunged into a trench of deep sleep.

The crinkled Virgin Mary was staring down from the sunlit wall when Amelia finally opened an eye. As she looked around the strange surroundings, she blinked in disbelief was to see a cotton dress, apron and bonnet on a hanger inside the door. The dress was the predictable faded gray, and the apron had stray threads hanging at the bottom from too many scrubbings, but she decided it was the nicest gift she'd ever received – even better than the surprise beach picnic orchestrated by the scheming Beatrice Peters.

Amelia was last to enter the social hall at the rear of the church and her companions made a great fuss over her new dress – especially over the bonnet that she had donned at first for comical effect. Matthew, it seems, had gone out foraging at sunup and had returned with another pail of field corn, a few mushy peaches and hard crab apples that had long since fallen to the ground. The result was a lively discussion with Rachel over how to make "hoe cakes," a term that baffled the Bahamian.

"Ye know about cornbread?" she asked him.

"Yes, lady."

"Well, hoe cakes is nothing more than corn, water and salt laid out flat like cow chips. They call 'em hoe cakes because when slaves are out weedin' in the fields, they build a fire and cook them patties right on top of their hoes."

Matthew added his own touches – a paste of crushed peaches and crab apples that, when spread over a patty in the oven, made it a tangy, tasty breakfast staple.

"If all of ye will just be patient," said Rachel after breakfast, "Doctor Drummond's boat should be along soon. Elseways, nobody over there will have any food a'tall. And 'til he does, I have a chore or two for ye to earn thy keep."

On her orders, Jimmy was soon feeding kindling to the fire pit. Matthew and Antoine were dispatched to the hospital cistern to fill a kettle with water and build a fire under it. Then they were off to the cow shed to lug back a crate full of soiled sheets and pillowcases with so many indelible stains some had come to resemble floral patterns. Into the kettle they went like a laundry chowder while the men were conscripted to take turns stirring long pine paddles. As the chastened bed linens were fished out, Rachel and Amelia began hanging them on clotheslines.

Peering between the hung-up sheets, Amelia could see Charles walking slowly towards the beach. *Sea air will do him good – if he doesn't begin dwelling on his plight,* she thought. The only other male not doing Rachel's bidding was DuBois. He sat on the church steps with a book, but several times Amelia caught him looking their way.

"Strange fellow" said Rachel. .

"A very important man in Nassau," mumbled Amelia with a mouth full of clothespins. "French aristocrat," they say.

"Oh, Mister DuBois," Amelia called out cheerfully. "Oh, *Monsieur* If you help us here, no one in Nassau will find out."

"Can you help?" squeaked Rachel. "I'm too short for some of these lines. Besides, I'll see that ye get no supper!"

The wall of dignity cracked with the first smile Amelia had seen – more revealing than the ones he manufactured when helping new Royal Vic guests from their carriages. DuBois stood and removed his wrinkled frock coat. Then he was at Rachel's side, bowing and smiling. "Under the circumstances," he said, "I am at your service, Madam." He reached to kiss her hand and Rachel jumped back. "That's enough!" she sputtered. "Now, do ye know how to use a clothespin?"

Just before noon, the two women looked between their fluttering sheets to see a lanky old man plodding alongside a mule cart. "Just as expected," announced Rachel. She hurried down the path towards Doctor's Creek and could be seen gesturing and pointing to her visitors.

When he reached the farmyard, Doctor Drummond stopped, seemingly sizing up the newcomers. He wore a gray shirt and black vest over rumpled black trousers – just enough to make anyone think twice before complaining that he didn't dress like a doctor. There was something else that Amelia realized only later: a mole on his cheek that made him resemble the Abraham Lincoln she'd seen in newspapers.

"Came by way of shipwreck, did you?" he said. Before inquiring about anyone's health or exchanging a pleasantry, he asked if the lifeboat at the dock was theirs. "Right sturdy and beamy. Think you might want to sell it?"

"Our captain's off on an errand," Amelia said, "but I certainly doubt it. Can you provide us with some quinine? Captain Timmons is in need of some for malaria," she said.

"Haven't got any," he answered. "Ran out of it some time ago. But if you'd part with that lifeboat, I might be able to find you some up in New Bern."

Amelia switched to her next pressing request. "Can you tell me how I can get an important letter to my parents in Savannah? They need to know I survived."

"Don't see it as likely," Drummond posed in thought for a moment, then shrugged. "Hasn't been any mail to this place to or from the South in a couple of years." Rachel gave a vigorous nod of agreement, seemingly eager to learn more about her new ward. "The way it works nowadays is that if someone from here is headed up to New Bern, they'll collect letters from here and take 'em along. Then you got to wait for someone later to go up to New Bern and bring back whatever mail they find. That could be two months, and only if it's all within the Union."

My God, and Beatrice used to complain that it took two weeks to get a letter from London.

"But you're talkin' about a letter to *Savannah*," Drummond chortled. "Union Post Office don't deliver anything below the war line. I hear tell that up in Washington D.C. they have a whole Dead Letter room just for mail like that."

Seeing Amelia's forlorn face, he said, "There's one other way, but I don't think it's any good for you."

"Please," she pleaded.

"Well, it's called Flag of Truce mail…mainly for prisoners of war. I've never tried it, but seems you send a letter to your kin folk and you include a second envelope with their address as well. You could drop it at Fort Macon and they would deliver it up to a fort on the Virginia border. They have people there that do nothing but read letters from Rebs. They cross out what they think is seditious and what's left goes to the person in the Confederacy."

"I understand, sir," replied Amelia, "but even so, they would know I am alive."

"I suppose so," said the doctor, jabbing his mule in the rump to resume their journey. As he was speaking, Amelia had sized up the cart's cargo: sacks and crocks of basic staples, she presumed, but none she could recognize.

"Rachel and young lady, I got to go now and feed some hungry patients with God's bounty," he said. "I'll try to think on your situation, so why don't you meet me in my office in about an hour. And ask your captain about that boat."

U.S. MARINE HOSPITAL
Portsmouth Island, North Carolina

The plaque hung over the porch that served as front entrance. The porch faced the sea, which made for ideal rocking and recovering during good weather. The square building was elevated on cement blocks so that during storms the ocean would just wash on through the opening instead of undermining the structure.

Because Charles could still be seen sitting in the sand on the beach, Amelia asked Felix DuBois to accompany her. The moment they swung open the front door, the two visitors recoiled as if they had gotten too close to an iron smelter – only in this case it was the overpowering smell of urine and feces and open sores. A cockroach nonchalantly strolled by their feet and exited into a crack in a dirty baseboard. Groans seemed to escape from several patient rooms down the hall. In the last one a voice loudly rasped, "Oh, oh, oh, oh, oh" without ceasing.

Thankfully, they needn't walk down the corridor. A sign above the first door read *Superintendent's Office.* Apparently Doctor Drummond had not yet finished distributing God's bounty, so they gingerly nestled into two unsteady wooden chairs that faced a scarred and stained mahogany desk. A bookcase against one wall contained just a few medical-looking books on one of its three shelves. Atop the desk was a paperweight anchoring a thin pile of invoices and receipts, and next to it a *Ledger Book, U.S. Treasury Dept.,* the size of a parlor Bible. Amelia looked around, then quickly flipped open some pages. The last entry was dated May 12, 1863.

"Well, well, here we are," said the lanky physician, wearing a once-white smock and stethoscope around his neck. "And you again are?"

"Amelia Beach, from Savannah."

"And you?" he turned to her debonair companion.

"Felix DuBois, a citizen of France," he said with a bow of the head – always a bow because in this strange land he was unsure who would take the hand of a man of color.

"Mr. DuBois is too modest," said Amelia. "He has been French consul to the Colonial Government of the Bahamas. And most recently he has been managing director of the largest hotel resort in Nassau, the capital. You have heard of the Royal Victoria Hotel, no doubt?"

"Mmm," hummed Doctor Drummond.

Amelia: "You were kind enough to invite us here so you could perhaps help us return to our places of origin, I believe."

Drummond: "I don't think you understand. When the war began, the Union sank two schooners in Ocracoke Inlet so that no seagoing ships could come and go. A blockade without gunboats, they reckoned."

Amelia: "Are railroads available?"

Drummond: "Not anymore. When I was up to New Bern, I was able get some coffee beans for our hospital. The reason I could find that scarce commodity was that the rail line to South Carolina was blown to bits and the train turned over. Seems that ever'body from thereabouts was out scooping up coffee beans in jars because the train had been hauling a bunch of sacks from some blockade runner. Somebody asked if I wanted to buy some, and I said to myself, well, I would do it to brighten up my boys here."

Amelia: "Well, what about Fort Macon over in Beaufort? Don't ships come in there?"

Drummond: "Some, but they don't come here much – maybe once a month just to look us over or drop a sick soldier on us. Besides, if you go over there and tell 'em you're from Savannah, they just might could put you in a POW camp. Now I'm not sayin' that ship you got sunk in was a blockade runner, but if they thought so over at the fort, it could be even worse for you."

To Amelia, the "doctor" seemed to take some satisfaction in blockading all of her exits. Beginning to boil inside her cotton farm dress, she decided to poke at his own vulnerabilities.

"When you go traveling like that," she asked, "who stays at the hospital to care for these poor patients? Is there no nurse?"

He squared away behind his desk and faced her with a paternal smile. Or was it a smirk?

"There *could* be," he said. "And I think that should be you."

"*Me?* I'm no nurse!" Amelia felt her heart sink, as when the *Sea Breeze* began to go under. DuBois coughed and shuffled his feet in protest.

"You're young, you look like you're from good stock, and you're the only white woman around," Drummond said sternly. "And I don't see this here *diplo-mat* about to get his hands dirty. There's plenty of women nursin' in this war that never had no training when they started out. Besides, I surely don't see you – and your group – going anywhere until the war's over."

"I think we could stay at the church and help Rachel out on the farm until we find transportation," she countered.

"Naw, I don't think the church trustees would cotton to that," he countered. "Besides you all could do more to help Rachel by working over here."

He was approaching checkmate and she could think only of diversion. "How could you possibly entrust all these sick patients to people with no medical training," she said scornfully.

"You really make too much of it," he said. "In the first place, I didn't abandon all these people. I took over a contract from a physician who couldn't make ends meet. I reckoned on feeding six or eight at a time – sailors from ships run aground in storms – and sendin' them on their way. When the war broke out, it was suddenly fifty, with no way to change the contract. Supplies got harder to come by and prices went up. To make ends meet, I had to go back to lightering ships and running supply boats for the locals."

"And leaving patients for days at a time," she parried.

"That's the other thing," he countered just as quickly. "Your talk about medical training seems to picture battle scenes where doctors are sawin' off legs and nurses are wrappin' gunshot wounds. The men here are almost all with various diseases that they can recover from in a short time."

DuBois spoke up. "But where would we obtain medicines?"

"That's the first thing we ran out of around here," said Drummond. "But again, we get along just fine without them. You make too much of all this snake oil."

He reached over to the shelf and began thumbing through a rumpled manual. "Now this here's the handbook from the U.S. Sanitation Commission – that's what supplies Union hospitals. You can see right here on the cover, its motto is 'Prevention rather than cure.' It says right here inside that the most important thing is good food, clean clothing, clean water, shelter and good personal hygiene.

"You see? All this talk about 'modern medicines' is just sellin' so much snake oil," he lectured. "You read papers from all these fancy pants doctors up in Boston and New York that diseases are caused by little bugs that you can only see under a microscope. But that's been shown to be bunk. These 'germs' are just blood cells rebuilding themselves."

Drummond is sounding like a snake oil salesman himself.

"Now I ask you," he implored, jabbing the air with his stethoscope probe to make his case, "what hospital is in a better position to heal men than right here on Portsmouth island? We have fine sea breezes to sweep away the swamp vapors that cause malaria and typhoid. We have the biggest fresh water cistern for miles around. We have the best-built hospital in North Carolina, with a fireplace in every room, mind you. And where everyone else in both North and South suffers from lack of meat, we have all the fish and oysters we can catch.

"And salt," he exclaimed. "It's in short supply everywhere, which is why I couldn't bring us more meat. But we have all the salt we can make from seawater if we just make the effort."

Doctor Drummond was foremost a businessman. "Now with all these things in your favor, all you really need to do is feed those patients, change linens, say encouraging words to them and help them write letters home. I assure you they will recover with just this extra touch."

"If there are no medicines, then feeding them is the most important curative," spoke up DuBois.

"Yes," echoed Amelia. "And the quick look I had inside that cart downstairs did not seem to indicate healthy eating. May we have another look at what you brought from New Bern today?"

The doctor frowned and sighed as if victory had just been torn from his grasp. "Very well," he said. He led them down the front steps and around to a locked storeroom. The crates and jars were still in the mule cart.

"What's in that one there?" said Amelia, pointing to a red substance packed in salt.

"That's meat. Can't hardly get any these days and I was lucky to get some."

"What kind of meat, Doctor?"

"Mule meat. It's what everyone's eatin' these days. And when you boil it, you can use the broth for beef tea."

Amelia pointed to a crock of brownish goo.

"That's sorghum," he said. "These parts haven't seen sugar for months, so now there's a new molasses mill over in New Bern. When I got to New Bern, they was having a Sorghum Festival to promote sorgo while I was there. It's a fine sugar substitute and I was lucky to be there. They were selling sorgo jams, pies and the like. Your patients will enjoy sorgo pie, which you make with flour and walnuts."

"And where might the flour be?" DuBois asked.

"Right now, wheat flour is going for twelve hundred dollars a barrel," said the doctor. He pointed to an open sack of white, caked granules. "This here's rice flour. You use it to make what we call Secession Bread just like your momma's probably doin' in Savannah right now. And pretty soon the gardens around here will have pumpkins, which make a good bread, too. You just boil 'em until they get all mushy. Then you strain it through a sieve and add some rice. Makes for right tasty bread. Not like your fresh warm wheat bread, but good enough if you're in a hospital bed. These boys ain't exactly gourmets, you know.

"Now over here's the special treat I mentioned," he said pointing to a crock of brown beans with a stir sick protruding. "Them's the coffee beans I bought in New Bern."

Amelia couldn't resist stirring, which revealed a swirl of brown beans, large tan chips and finely-chopped greens.

She frowned, but Drummond was prepared to stir more rhetoric. "No one here drinks *pure* coffee these days," he declared. "What you do is add chicory root and some chopped up dandelion stems. You can hardly tell the difference from true coffee. Brewed some for my boys today and they were grateful. I said *grateful.*"

Amelia had planned to utter something non-committal and bolt for the pathway to the church, but Drummond blocked the way with his tall frame it and steered them back into his office. They settled uneasily into their rickety chairs again as the doctor sat, chin resting in a cupped hand, and eyes gazing heavenward as if in search of a divine revelation.

"Well, here's the way I see it," he said at last. "You probably ain't goin' no-where until the war ends or somethin' big happens to change the balance. So, I'm going to propose a fair solution. You let me use that lifeboat of yours to haul some goods around Pamlico Sound. What I will do for you is let you run this hospital."

Both opened their mouths to protest, but he held up his hand for silence.

"My contract as superintendent of this hospital calls for eighteen hundred dollars a year, paid in quarterly installments. I will pay you half of that for as long as you stay. You can clear out some space in the hospital and some of the outbuildings where you and your people can stay for no charge a'tall. And I will continue to help with supplies."

"I should think two-thirds of the fee would be more equitable," said DuBois.

"And I can't authorize you to use the lifeboat," added Amelia, *although, come to think of it, I come closer than anyone to being its owner.*

Drummond sat fiddling with his stethoscope, then resumed. "All right then, we can put off discussing the boat for now," he said in a hurt tone. "I can't give you two-thirds because I will still have food costs. But I will give you sixty dollars now. On October first when the quarterly stipend arrives, we will begin regular monthly payments of seventy-five a month. I will also go over to Tyron's General Store in Ocracoke and tell them to let you buy anything you need on credit until that next government payment comes in."

Hearing no further protest, he pressed on. "Now then, you, Miss Birch..."

"Beach."

"Miss Beach will become Director of Nursing, a very prestigious title for one so young."

"Again, I have no such experience," she said firmly. "Mr. DuBois here has extensive experience in organizing and managing large institutions."

"And I'm to call him Director of Nursing?"

"No. Managing Director, the same as he was at the Royal Victoria Hotel just three days ago."

"Very well, Managing Director. And you, Miss Beach, you can become Matron of Hospital in charge of providing patient services. And I have something that will help you in your glorious calling." He reached into his desk drawer and handed her a large brass broach. It was an unlikely design: a staff with wings and two snakes wrapped around it.

"That's a caduceus," he said. "It's your badge of authority and your patients will respect its power to heal them."

She held the thing in her cupped hand, her mind too confused – jumbled – to respond.

Is it possible that this is God's judgment – my penitence – for all the harm I have caused? Is this to be the hell I deserve?

"But for no fixed period of time," she heard DuBois saying. "Only until we are able to leave."

Doctor Drummond reached for a cracked leather satchel on the floor behind him. He pulled out a large, worn breast pocket billfold and slowly counted out six ten-dollar greenbacks. Amelia felt shame at the worthlessness of Confederate money as the man who looked like Abraham Lincoln carefully laid down each Union bill bearing an engraving of the enemy president.

With that, Drummond suddenly rose, announced that he had "business" in Ocracoke that afternoon, and would return the next day to "walk you around."

Amelia stood between him and the door. "Is there not some sort of procedures manual or nursing book I can be studying until then?" she asked. He turned to the yellowed books slouched on the adjoining bookshelf and handed her a thin pamphlet and medical textbook. "Here," he said. "Tell you all you need to know. Now I must go."

Drummond all but shooed them onto the portico outside the main entrance. At that point, he loped down the stairs and untethered his mule. After walking briskly down the pathway as if to outdistance anymore questions or shouted misgivings, he swung his long legs over the mule and clopped towards Doctor's Creek without looking back.

As they stood on the portico watching in puzzled silence, Amelia turned to DuBois with a frown. "I am shocked that you agreed to this so quickly," she said.

"The church pews are too hard to sleep on," he said. "The cook snores."

"And that is why you agreed?"

"Not entirely. I always look forward to a challenge," he said. "The Royal Victoria is one example, but it is not as difficult as supervising the quarters of a hundred cane cutters on a sugar plantation. And the odors in their settlement are not unlike here. This place is so sorely neglected that it intrigues me. And if we can help these patients get well through better management, it will be a good thing."

Yes, but if you fail, you can't burn the place down and run away.

Chapter Thirteen

Chaos

A melia Beach, Matron of Hospital, sat on the edge of her small farm-house bed turning the pages of the slender *Manual of Directions Prepared for the Use of Nurses in the Army Hospitals* as the late afternoon sun made light patterns on the white wall. *Published by the Women's Central Association for Relief*, read the cover.

But hardly a bible of practices and procedures, she thought. *Mostly recipes with ingredients no one has around here. The same for all the medicines it prescribes.*

> **TOAST WATER.** Cut a slice of stale bread about twice the usual thickness; toast it carefully until thoroughly browned; put into a quart of boiling water and let stand until it is quite cold; the fresher it is the better. A little currant jelly or a slice of lemon are grateful additions.

Currant jelly? Lemon?
Maybe in the writer's house in New York, but not here.

> **MUSTARD POULTICE.** Mix ground mustard with hot water alone. Flaxseed meal or crumbled bread may be used with the mustard where active counter irritation is not required. They should be spread very thin on brown paper or coarse muslin and may be applied directly or with the interposition of fine cambric. A very moist plaster is much more efficient than a dry one.

How can I do this if I don't know what they are talking about?

> **VAPOR BATH.** Place the patient in a chair, and a vessel of boiling water by his side. Then envelop the patient, chair and vessel with blankets. The evaporation may be increased by placing one or two hot bricks in the water. The procuring perspiration will be great if the patient covers his head with the blanket so as to breathe the vapor.

And be suffocated in the process?

ENEMATA. The instrument best adapted for the administration of injections is the self-acting flexible rubber injecting tube. The pipe should always be carefully oiled and inserted at least two and a half inches. Useful purgative enemata are:

- Warm soap suds.
- Warm soap suds with the addition of molasses.
- One ounce of castor oil, beaten with an egg yolk and mixed with a pint of water.
- Injection of tobacco, sometimes used to relax muscular contraction, made by infusing a dram of boiling water for an hour, and straining.
- An ounce of turpentine, beaten with the yolk of an egg and mixed with a pint of water.

Amelia imagined a wan, hungry soldier, who hasn't seen an egg in weeks, watching in wide-eyed disbelief while a nurse mixes turpentine with an egg – all so that she can shove it up his hindquarters. It seemed so ludicrous that some authority up in Yankeeland could be urging all this on someone in remote Portsmouth Island that she began laughing so hard that she fell back on the bed. Then remorse. *Oh, God in Heaven, forgive me for being such a rich man's pampered daughter that I can't understand what they are trying to tell me. I haven't even begun and already I am making fun of people in authority. Please, God, don't let me kill anyone else through my ignorance and arrogance!*

Perhaps she would find the medical textbook, *Macintyre's Therapeutics, 1857,* more illuminating. The first thing Amelia searched for was a cure for malaria. Quinine, indeed, was the agent of choice. But what else might work? There, on page 82, it read,

"Some generals have found that turpentine treatment is amply sufficient to interrupt the morbific chain of successive paroxysms, one application only being required in the majority of cases. Other substitutes include a tonic brewed from the bark of the dogwood poplar and willow trees, dissolved in whiskey."

"Tree bark and whiskey!" she nearly shouted. "That alone was worth the whole book!" Amelia searched for more medical knowledge.

TYPHOID FEVER. The signs are gradually rising temperature, rose-colored skin spots, then diarrhea, delirium, stupor and death. Treatments recommended are cathartics or mild purgatives, diaphoretics, narcotics and counter-irritants. If the patient lapses into delirium, a paste of ground and powdered beetle (Spanish fly) should be applied over the patient's shaved scalp."

Purgatives? The answer came on the next page.

PURGATIVES. The mucous glands that line the intestines can be stimulated by irritants, thereby flushing out any poisons believed to have caused organic inflammation. The preferred oral purgatives are calomel, colocynth, jaipp, rhubarb, croton oil, sulphate of magnesia and saline solutions. If the oral route leaves something to be desired, the other end could be pumped with warm water or up to two pounds of gruel.

Two pounds of gruel? Oh please! I see it coming out like buckshot! Oh Lord, there I go again. Well, I certainly have many choices of enemas. But the only purgatives I know are rhubarb and saline solution.

Out her window she saw Rachel strolling across the yard to the cow shed with her milk pail. Amelia caught up with her, settled on her wooden stool, ready to relieve Eliza's bellowing.

"Rachel, can we grow rhubarb here?" she asked.

"Why sure. Good for early spring, and one of the few crops ye can grow in late fall. Why? Ye hanker for some rhubarb pie?"

Amelia told her of her medical discovery and the little lady nearly fell out of her stool laughing. "Well, we can grow a crop for that purpose," she said, "but we can also go out and get some saltwater. That's a lot easier."

Then Rachel abruptly changed the subject. "I hear ye will be at the hospital a while."

"Who told you that?"

"Felix. Just this afternoon."

"You call him *Felix?*"

"Well, I sure do. He calls me Rachel. Tit for tat. Anyways, it occurred to me that maybe ye would like to stay in my daughter's room for your visit here. 'Course there might be a price to pay. We sure could use ye to play the organ on Sunday mornings."

"Well, that's sweet," replied Amelia, "but I think I'd need a place big enough to care for Charles. I've been reading about some ways to treat his malaria besides quinine."

"Ye betrothed?" Rachel looked up and into her eyes while still pulling and tugging on Eliza.

"Not exactly, not yet," she stammered. "We were planning to announce it in Nassau, but we got interrupted by a little inconvenience."

"And that would be?"

"Our ship sank." Amelia allowed her point to settle in. "Rachel," she said at last, "this may seem forward of me, but Charles and I might could just clear out the tool shed and make enough space for one big bed. We could put the tools over here in the cow shed."

"Mmm, well, I don't know," Rachel replied without looking up. "The Reverend Hiram might have a problem with ye bein' unmarried. We have a sayin' back in New Hampshire. Two cats can curl up in the oven, but that don't make 'em biscuits. Pastor's got to look pure and chaste for his flock. But I'll ask him."

Supper time that night was consumed by so much conversation that Matthew's steamed clams and oysters slid down without the usual accolades. One topic was what to bring the patients for an evening snack, Drummond presumably having served them the main meal that afternoon. A second, more heated, discussion, was who should deliver the food. Should DuBois and Amelia use the occasion to introduce themselves while delivering God's bounty? But Rachel held fast that the newcomers should not intrude until Doctor Drummond could properly introduce them the next day. Hence, they a compromised. Matthew would heat up some hoe cakes with peach puree and Rachel would deliver them.

But while Matthew was still turning the hoe cakes, Amelia and DuBois questioned Rachel about the patients they would greet the next day and how the men might greet *them*. "Well, I'd say that some of 'em is truly bad sick," she replied. "Some is maybe not so sick. Then there's some who may just be hidin' out, maybe afeared that if they get better they'll get sent off to be shot up somewhere else.

"But there's something else goin' on that keeps 'em all edgy-like. Right from the start the Yankees took over the ground floor and ordered all the Rebs upstairs. So now they're still fightin' the war from their beds. Not good for their health," she said sadly.

Back in her room that night, Amelia sat on the edge of her bed, squinting beneath a flickering oil lamp, determined to resume her medical education. She had just opened the book when a folded newspaper fell out. It was a page from the *Baltimore Herald*, already yellowed from the humidity. The date on top was December 3, 1863. Amelia unfolded it carefully and read the headline, *The Unsung Heroines of The Union*. It told about the volunteer nurses who toiled selflessly in the rows of hospital tents after a great battle, treating Rebel and Union soldier alike amidst the agonizing screams of pain that followed bloody gunshot wounds and the amputations.

The reporter had focused especially on just one such nurse, a young Quaker woman of twenty-five named Cornelia Hancock. She had left a comfortable home in Salem, New Jersey and headed west because her brother-in-law, a doctor, had told her that soldiers in a farm town called Gettysburg were suffering after a great battle and were desperate for help.

Amelia looked at an adjoining photo of the girlish Cornelia in a plain dress with her hair pulled back and parted in the middle. She had simply packed up and left for Gettysburg despite having no nursing experience.

But she did have determination. The reporter wrote that it had been only a few months since Dorothea Dix, a feisty, five-foot mental health pioneer, had burst into the Army Surgeon General's office in Washington and insisted that he end the practice of banning females from army medicine. When she finally left, it was with the newly-invented title of Superintendent of Female Nurses for the Union Army.

However, once in charge, Dix decreed strict rules for new applicants. They had to be over thirty, wear simple dresses, "unencumbered with bustles," and have "physical features that will not turn a man's head."

Amelia looked into the black windowpane and it reflected a hair style that still suited a dance at the Royal Vic more than a farmhouse on Portsmouth Island. Then followed a paragraph that she would come to read often:

"Miss Hancock recounts that she was turned down upon arrival in Gettysburg and was told to appeal personally to Dorothea Dix in Washington. Her in-law, Dr. Henry Child, accompanied her, only to see her refused again. Miss Dix said she was too young by five years

and was also encumbered by 'rosy cheeks'. But not easily swayed, Miss Hancock left and got on the next train to Gettysburg while Dr. Child was still pleading her case. She simply showed up, said she'd been approved, and was put to work.

"'I learned a lesson then that I have never forgotten,' Miss Hancock says. 'If your cause is righteous and you encounter bureaucratic barriers, just crash right on through.'"

Amelia read slowly in the dim light, savoring each experience of a kindred soul who might have been her sister. She learned that Cornelia Hancock had already left Gettysburg and was, when the reporter called, nursing in a Washington "hospital" for contrabands. She kept a journal that she mailed to her mother, and in her letters, she begged shamelessly for whatever the good Quaker ladies of Salem, New Jersey could send her way. The article quoted one entry:

"Here are gathered the sick from the contraband camps in the northern part of Washington. If I were to describe this hospital, it would not be believed. North of Washington, in an open muddy mire, are gathered all the colored people who have been made free by the progress of our army. Sickness is inevitable, and to meet it these rude hospitals, only rough wooden barracks, are in use – a place where there is so much to be done you need never be idle. We average one birth a day and have no baby clothes except as we wrap them up in old pieces of muslin, that even being scarce. Now that the army is advancing, it is not uncommon to see from forty to fifty arrivals in one day. They have nothing that anyone in the North would call clothing. This hospital is the reservoir for all cripples, diseased, aged, wounded, infirm, whatsoever the cause. And all accidents happening to colored peoples in all the employ around Washington are brought here."

Amelia read to the end, re-folded the article, tucked it back in the medical book and resolved to remember:

I will never feel sorry for myself again. I will help wherever I can regardless of North or South. I will try to keep a journal and write letters begging for help if I must. I will no longer dress up to please Charles but dress DOWN to un-please strange young men. I will remember Daddy's words: "You become what you think you are."

And I will crash through unreasonable barriers. I really must write
all this down, but sleep comes too quickly.

The next morning, September 3, broke with clear blue skies. After break-fast, Jimmy decided to lead the men down to the beach for a swim in the gentle rollers and to wash the clothes they'd been wearing since leaving Nassau. Amelia and Rachel dried the dishes in the social hall. Felix DuBois, wearing a clean suit of impeccable formalwear from his bounteous trunk, sat at the dining table, charged with watching out the window for Doctor Drummond to come down the footpath.

"Does he ever not show up on an appointed day?" Amelia asked Rachel.

"Well, sometimes," she said. "Maybe if he can't get across the Sound in a bad storm. Maybe if one of his boats has trouble." She kept her eyes lowered.

"Well, I will give you my opinion," said DuBois. "I do not think he is coming at all, or until the day comes when his next payment arrives from the government." He looked hard at Rachel and said, "Could it be that you are not telling us something?"

Rachel paused long enough to reveal that he was right. "Well, yesterday, after ye met in his office and he was passing me, he shouted, 'Rachel, I for-got to tell them that the key to the storehouse is in my middle desk drawer.' He had never said that to me before."

"He is not coming today, or maybe ever," reaffirmed DuBois.

They heard sounds of commotion down the path and stepped outside to look. The cluster of contrabands outside the linen dispensary were shout-ing something, pointing to their midriffs and signaling in the universal language of raised palms.

"They're hungry and we should do something," Rachel said, quite happy to change the subject. "I will go at once and make some of that new coffee. They will probably think it a special treat. Maybe Matthew can make them a stew from what's in the storehouse."

"Yes," agreed DuBois. "That mule meat we saw is only good for stew anyway."

Early that afternoon they had reassembled at the hospital with a push-cart containing a stew pot and coffee urn. On the first floor, which "be-longed" to the Union men, the new managing director and his fearful cohort encountered two rows of rooms divided by a central corridor. Each room had two beds flanking a fireplace. Each fireplace had a common hearth that also served the two patients in the opposite room.

The plan called for Rachel to enter first and begin serving. She would introduce DuBois and Amelia. Antoine would wait in the corridor in case of trouble.

"Sounds like the slop cart," they heard a voice inside say.

When Rachel entered first, a young man raised up on his elbow. "Hey, skinny bitch, where you been?" he yelled before seeing the others. "You bring that whiskey and tobacco I ordered up?

"And what we got here?" he smirked when DuBois appeared in the doorway. "You got yourself a butler? You dressed up a dusky just for us?" The man in the other bed chortled but didn't seem able to sit up.

It was obvious that Rachel had long endured such talk, so DuBois spoke up. "Now pay attention," he said softly but firmly. "Doctor Drummond has gone away for a period of time. I am Felix DuBois, the new acting managing director."

"Well, I'll be damned," said patient number one.

"You will address me as Mister DuBois. Not Duboise, but *Dubwah*. Can you repeat that for me?"

The lad mumbled something, which DuBois ignored. "Allow me to present Miss Amelia Beach, who is your new matron of hospital."

"Pretty fine filly for a matron," the first patient snickered.

"Now then, the first rule here is to show respect," said DuBois. "Besides calling me Mister *Dubwah*, you will call this lady Miss Beach and you will refrain from all forms of cursing and slander as regards either of these women. Is that clear?"

Neither patient said a word, but DuBois did. "Stop the service," he said to Rachel as she was dipping her label in the stewpot. "You will not be fed today, or until I hear you both say yes."

"Hey, I didn't do nothing," patient number two shouted as they rolled the cart outside. "You dumb smart-alecky sonofabitch," they could hear him shouting at his roommate as they entered the next room.

"Wasn't that a bit harsh?" Amelia whispered to DuBois as they paused before the second door.

"Yes, it was," he said. "But because food is our only real curative, we must see from the beginning that it is served properly. You ladies can try again later, but I am prepared to be the devil incarnate."

The next fifteen room visits produced a cascade of similar instances, but the reception seemed to become more docile as word about the threat of no food passed through the open fireplaces between each room. Meanwhile, Amelia's head was swiveling with first impressions, trying to pinpoint the odors that seemed saturated in the walls and floors. Filth was everywhere: men holding out mess kit dishes overlain with caked old food. Filled and unclean chamber pots sitting beneath beds. Once-polished hardwood floors now stained with all shades of spilled food and feces. And towels…where were the towels and rags so necessary to any hospital? *At least Cornelia Hancock's hospital had muslin.*

For the remainder of the visit they climbed to the second-floor, which the banished Rebels seem to have barricaded like a besieged fort. Again, it did not begin well.

"Oh, I thought them Yankee buzzards stole our food again," carped a gaunt lad of twenty or so years. Shirtless, he sat barefooted on the edge of his bed, boils or carbuncles up and down his left arm and side. He listened open-mouthed to the refined speech of Felix DuBois and cut him off when asked to pronounce *Dubwah* properly.

"I don't care how yuh say it," he sneered. "I ain't gonna pronounce nuthin' no way before some niggra paradin' around in a white man's costume, no matter if I starve to death." He glared at DuBois sullenly. Then he grabbed the ladle from the stewpot, scooped out a portion, jumped off the bed and flung it out of the open window.

"There's your dinner!" he snarled. "Now what do ya think of that?"

"I think it shows me that you are well enough to jump out of bed and walk about with no problem," said DuBois calmly. "And you will not eat again until we see that you have cleaned your mess kit properly."

When the maiden visit was over, Rachel scampered off to milk Eliza. Amelia, DuBois and Antoine placed the half-full stewpot back on the mule cart. "Well, that didn't go so badly," said DuBois, straightening his cravat.

"Oh my God, how can you say that after the way they talked to you?"

"Well, it went better than if I had walked in there in overalls," he replied with the dry wit she was coming to appreciate. "But you see, I always have Antoine to help me validate my words. If that man had flung the food in my face, he would no longer have a face."

Then he was business again. "I think before we finish the day, we should inspect the condition of the various outbuildings," he said.

The nearest was the cookhouse, a detached structure built of stone blocks for fire safety reasons. "There is nothing wrong with this place." DuBois declared. Next to the hearth and stove was a low stone wall and an empty alcove. Said DuBois: "A proper plantation cookhouse has a space like this so that someone – usually an apprentice cook – can sleep next to the kitchen in case of fire. I think Matthew would be happy to have this all to himself instead of a church pew."

They walked several yards away to a low, once-whitewashed wooden structure from which they had seen patients going back and forth. The stench announced its purpose. "Now there's the main source of our malefaction," he said to Amelia. "Please remain here while Antoine and I make a closer inspection."

They opened the door to the latrine and stood with their backs to Amelia as they peered in. Only then did she notice a long stick leaning against the shed when Antoine grabbed it and began poking in a place she didn't want to think about. In a few seconds they slammed the door and bolted away, laughing as they held their noses. "This will never do," declared DuBois. "Somehow we will need to replace it. I don't mean dig it out. I mean build a new one. Fortunately, we have here in Antoine a plantation foreman who has built some very nice ones."

The next out-shed had been built to the same dimensions as the latrine. When they opened the wooden double-door, they were startled to see an array of mops, brushes and wash pails that looked as new as when issued by the government. "I have never been more shocked," said Amelia. "Here we are in this den of filth and this doctor of ours has overlooked the means to make it right. Now I hope he doesn't come back!"

Barely discernible, down a weedy path from the far end of the hospital, was a low, squat structure. As they approached, they could see a dozen crude gravestones behind it. Closer inspection showed only two with names crudely carved on them. The others were merely fieldstones, dragged in as markers. Amelia peered inside the structure, no taller than her shoulders, and gave a start at seeing a pine casket with a raised compartment along the outer lid.

"I know this place from reading about a Union nurse in the war," she said. "It's called the Death House." Antoine, who was said to know little English, nodded and said "Oui, la couloir de la mort."

"Well, it seems that not all of Doctor Drummond's patients get better," Amelia continued. "According to this nurse I read about, if the patient is a person of low station, he simply gets buried out back with a marker like these. If he is an officer or someone prominent, the casket in there has a compartment where you can pack ice or salt while it's being shipped back to his family."

"We should complete the tour by seeing the linen shed and its current occupants," said DuBois as they began the walk back to the church. "Yes, I agree," said Amelia, "But you and Antoine go. I have an urge I can't explain that I must satisfy."

"What kind of urge, mademoiselle?"

"A strong desire to do something that actually involves nursing. I can't explain it. I just want to talk to a few of the patients. I never had a chance to find out what ails anyone. Don't worry, there's plenty of daylight left. I'll be back in time for supper."

"One hour," said DuBois, "or we will come back for you."

"Just give me the key to the storeroom," she answered. "If anyone gives me trouble, I'll just tell them Antoine will kill them."

Yes, I am frightened. Why did I have to ruin a good beginning? Because it's not enough to dress like Cornelia. I must have her courage. You become what you think you are.

Amelia found herself inside the storeroom where the pail of mule stew was still covered, still warm enough to sate a gnawing stomach. Into the house of chaos she went, up to the second floor, where her Rebel drawl might be more welcome. On the way up, she rubbed the caduceus broach that she had pinned on her dress. *Maybe it's just a good luck charm, but it gives me confidence, perhaps like I'm part of a strong sisterhood.*

She knocked softly, then opened the door slowly to see the irascible, iconic Rebel in dirty pajama bottoms, still sitting on the edge of his bed, but now playing cards with a youth from another room. Both had scraggly chins that needed more months of cultivation before harvesting full beards.

"I thought you might like something to eat after all," were the first words that came out.

He eyed her suspiciously. "Where's that other fella?" he asked.

"Mister DuBois? He's not here. I had some beef stew left and I thought you might like some after all."

"Well, maybe I would," he said, his rancor melting. "Guess I did sorta waste some rations a while back there. But that dressed-up nigger kinda spooked me. I mean here I am in rags and he comes 'round with his airs and all. You know what I mean?" He felt around under his blanket and produced the same stained mess tin that she reluctantly filled.

"I know what you mean, but that doesn't make it right," she replied in her softest diplomatic demeanor. "Mister DuBois is a very learned man. He's French and has been in charge of some very big institutions in Europe and the Caribbean. His purpose is only to help this place improve and help you get healthy in the process. Why, he has even brought with him a cook whose whole purpose is to fatten you up. I think it's the French helping out in the war the way they did in George Washington's day."

The young man was eating far too greedily for someone so willing to heave his ration out the window an hour before. "Well, we sure wasn't gettin' fat with Doctor Death," he said between mouthfuls.

"We call him that because he looks like an undertaker," added his companion. "And sometimes he is."

"You sure you're not working for Drummond?" said the first man.

"I'm sure."

"He's gone?"

"I can't say forever, but he's asked Mister DuBois and me to oversee the hospital in his absence."

"You know about him stealin', don't you?"

"Can't say that I do."

"Well no one of us can prove it beyond a shadow, as they say, but each month a whole bunch of food gets delivered here from Fort Macon and I damn well guarantee you – 'scuse my French – that only a part of it ever gets into this hospital."

"That's for sure," said the other. "'Cuz every week or so we see that mule of his pullin' an empty cart up to the storeroom right below us, and when that mule heads back down the path, it's pullin' crates from that same storeroom back down to the dock. And where do you think it's headed? On his boats, right up to New Bern! We'd wager on it anyways."

Amelia filed the information in her mind and changed the subject. "Well, I'd better take this stewpot down the hall while it's still warm enough," she said. "A few others down there were just as brassy as you this afternoon. But I'll stop on my way back if that's all right."

Amelia fed three more Rebels who had changed their minds about going hungry. Along the way she counted heads – sixteen in all – and tried to take a quick census of illness. There were no charts on beds. When she would ask men about themselves, the diseases most often described – doubtless repeated from Doctor Drummond – were dysentery, malaria, and consumption. Almost all of the Rebels looked gaunt and frail, but most were standing, walking or sitting in bedside chairs.

Emboldened by being received as a nurse, Amelia left her stewpot in the hallway and entered the long corridor on the first floor. As she walked about and introduced herself to Union patients, no one seemed to mind her Southern accent – perhaps because they were too sick to notice. Unlike the second floor, the great majority here were bedridden. The thirty she counted had a witch's brew of lice, typhoid, tuberculosis, malaria, gangrene, bed sores, and unexplained tremors. Some asked for her help in writing letters to loved ones. Amelia left after her walk-through with an impossible-to-remember list of needs that she knew little about fulfilling.

She knew it was drawing near her hour "curfew," but she climbed the stairs to the second story and knocked again on the first room she had visited. Patient One and his visitor were still playing cards at bedside. Patient Two was out of bed and squatting over a bedpan, but she'd already seen that twice on the other floor and knew that she'd betray her caduceus if she flinched.

"Just back to say good night," she said. "I never did introduce myself properly. Amelia Beach from Savannah – Nurse Beach to you. And you?"

"Lucas," said the sated one. "Jeremy," said the other. "Two peas in a pod." "How so?"

"Well, we both from South Carolina. Met up in the Battle of the Wilderness in Virginia. That was in May, I guess, even though it seems like years. Anyway, we was layin' side by side behind a big oak log one day shootin' away at Yankees and the sergeant gets up and yells, 'Ever'body charge.' Well, three, four seconds later that sergeant was shot right through the head. Now, Jeremy's already got some buckshot in his leg. And I says to him, 'You know what, that's one damn charge too many. Why don't we go squirrel huntin'?' We got, what, sixty-five thousand men. The other side has, what, a hundred thousand,' and I says, 'they ain't gonna notice two less Rebs.' And Jeremey here says, 'That's just two less mouths to feed.' So we went off backwards like, squirrel huntin'."

Just then Jeremy shifted his weight and Amelia winced as she saw a dirty cloth wrapped around his left thigh, a yellow liquid seeping through. She realized how helpless she was to do anything and simply ignored it.

"Trouble was, there wasn't enough squirrels left out there," said Lucas. "So in time we met up with a like-minded bunch of Rebs and we became what we called the Rebel Raiders, tryin' to disrupt Yankee trains and warehouses and the like. But the months went by and we couldn't find enough farms or warehouses to feed ourselves no more. Our captain said we had to fend for ourselves, so there we were again."

Lucas looked up and gave Amelia a hard stare. "You working for the Yankees? I mean you bein' a nurse and all, it's sorta like a priest, ain't it? Everything confidential?"

"Confidential," she said, pointing to her caduceus pin.

Lucas nodded in approval. "Well, by July something, we had wandered down to the North Carolina coast because it was more peaceable and there were still some nice farms that armies hadn't trampled over," he added. "But now the trouble was that the Yankees had damn near taken over the whole state. Just like the Rebel Raiders, we had to sleep by day and raid chicken coops by night. By then Jeremy's leg was oozin' and then late one night somebody's henhouse got a bit noisy and I got hit with buckshot, and now I'm bleedin' all over my arm and side. By then we was too tired of bein' hungry and we heard about Fort Macon over at Beaufort Inlet. So one day we just knocked on their door, you might say, and hoped they had a doctor and some food."

"And then you wound up here," said Amelia. The room had grown dim and she feared that DuBois and Antonine would barge in and start a ruckus.

"Well, I could tell right off they didn't know what to do with us," said Lucas. "We was Rebs trying to surrender accordin' to all the official rules of war – we even showed up with a pillowcase on a stick to surrender proper like – but I could hear 'em fussin' and arguin' among themselves. We later figgered out that the nearest POW camp was Point Lookout up on the Chesapeake. Well, they just didn't have no way to get anyone there, 'least of all a couple of Reb privates.

"So, they kept askin' about how we got shot up, and we'd explain all about the Battle of the Wilderness, which was pretty famous by then. This officer looks at me and says, 'that don't look like no combat wound.' I says, 'Oh yessir.' I had this yarn all in my head about how I'd crept up to this general's camp to spy on a meetin' they were havin' and how his orderly got me with a sawed-off shotgun. So then they said, 'Well, you belong in a military hospital and we're takin' you to one just up the coast.'

"And that's how we got to this place, which really ain't military, we found out."

"Would you say there are others up on this floor in your same situation?" Amelia asked.

"More or less, I suppose," said Jeremy.

"Could you say they might be lying low until the war ends?"

"Well, it could be part of it. At least this place has a bed for ever'body. They say in those POW camps they stack you up like cordwood and some don't even have beds."

"That might be right," interrupted Lucas. "But some of 'em that come in healthy-like now have diseases they never thought of before. Diarrhea is somethin' you just seem to catch around here. Same for malaria. I swear it's all from northerners. And them coloreds, too.'"

"Look around," said Amelia. "It's from all of you. But I'll see you again tomorrow. And I'll try to do something about that leg."

<hr />

The sun was setting as Amelia entered the church social hall and the other five "survivors" were seated about their usual dinner table. "Supper's done, but we saved some for you," said Matthew as he finished wiping the dishes.

"Surprise!" she said as she lifted the lid over her plate. "Beef stew! Why didn't I think of it?" She tried to convince herself that "mule meat" was only a figure of speech, because it was indeed what troops on both sides called all red meat of undetermined sources.

"Miss Beach, you look radiant tonight," exclaimed Felix DuBois, who had never before commented on her appearance. "Does this mean you had a successful visit?"

"If I look 'radiant,' it certainly has nothing to do with my plain appearance," she said. "I have met with some of these patients, and I just have a confidence that we can bring them back to health despite their present sad state."

"I quite agree," said DuBois, who had already removed his frock coat and rolled up his French cuffs. "That is why I have called what I believe is an important meeting. We must begin with a plan."

"Proceed," she said with a wave of her fork.

"Our first and greatest priority should be to raze the latrine and the filthy building that encompasses it," said the managing director. "It is not as difficult as you might think. We begin by attaching chains or ropes to the shed and pulling it over on its side. That cow over there might even be able to do it with help from some of us. But before we do that, we dig out the new latrine, haul the dirt to where the present one is and then fill it up with a lye mix. We clean the old building, repair it with new wood and put it upright over the new, pristine site."

"Hear, hear," they chorused.

"I am beginning to make a list of necessities that we will need for a trip across the inlet to this general store in Ocracoke that is prepared to grant us credit," continued DuBois. "The first item on the list is three dollars each for clothing. That does not include me, as you can see. You have soldiered on gamely, but one must be properly attired to perform one's tasks."

"Hear, hear," they shouted again.

"The next items in regard to the latrine are some pine boards, nails and lye," he said. "To these I add three dollars."

"Next should be quinine for Captain Timmons," Amelia piped up.

"All right, I agree, but I have no idea how much we can afford," answered DuBois. "I will put a question mark beside quinine."

"The second priority, in my view, should be to scrub those vile floors," said DuBois, "and we do not seem to lack for brushes, mops and the like. We only lack for someone who is an expert at scrubbing – perhaps of ship decks?" He gave Jimmy a long, wry look and the old sailor gave back a snappy salute. "Aye, aye, admiral," he said. "Am Oy to have any mates?"

"I am just coming to that," said the managing director. "The third priority should be to make patients responsible for the condition of their rooms – at least those who are able to move about. By this I mean their mess kits, chamber pots, and bed sheets to the extent that they should be required to strip them off every few days and pile them in a place designed by our hospital matron here. As to floors, yes, each patient should try to help Jimmy in his initial efforts. After that, they should mop once a week themselves."

DuBois paused and continued. "Now, at this point let me pose a question that all of you must be thinking at the same time. None of this has ever happened so far. How are we to compel these patients to do all this on their own?"

Shoulders shrugged. "One way is food," said DuBois. "Those who don't comply simply get no ration that day. Cruel but effective – and necessary if you stop to think that keeping the place clean can do as much to restore their health as good food. Similarly, one can reward good performance with little treats – a piece of fresh pie to be savored while one's bedfellows salivate with jealousy. It works everywhere I have been."

"I have one more possibility," said Amelia. "In the nursing and medical books I've been reading, there are recipes for drinks made with whiskey and brandy. And one nurse keeps referring to giving her men 'stimulants' before dinner. May I remind us that we have nearly five cases of fine brandy stashed in the lifeboat. I think this could also be doled out as little rewards."

"And to *us* what deserves some," Jimmy chimed in to a chorus of laughter.

"Excellent, magnifique," DuBois responded. "And one more thing. I intend to bestow titles on certain people to give them prestige and authority. As you may be aware, people in these parts address some respected men as 'captain,' even though they may not have held that rank in the military. It's akin to the Spaniards, who address a respected person as 'Don Pedro' and so forth. I can envision a 'captain' of the Confederates and a similar position among the Union men.

"Next, I turn to our sainted Matthew," DuBois said. "I do so lastly because you are the most important. When we go to Ocracoke with our market list, what is it you most require restoring health among these men?"

"Chickens!" quickly replied the Bahamian.

"Chickens?"

"Yes. If I have enough chickens, I will have many eggs. And if you have eggs, you can make many dishes – omelets, soufflés, batters, cakes – and you can add eggs to other dishes to give them that rich taste that makes a man want to eat."

"Chickens it shall be," said DuBois, "even if we have to go begging from farm to farm. Should anything else be on our shopping list?"

"Beans of all kinds," said Matthew.

Amelia: "What of the linen room? Did you and Antoine look in there and talk to the people living there?"

"We did," said DuBois with a grimace. "They still have sheets piled up on some shelves, but I think we discovered why there are so few towels and rags at the hospital."

"Well, why?"

DuBois and Antione looked at one another and grimaced again. "Let me simply say…. we discovered a, er, pile of soiled towels in back of the building that had been used for, ah, wiping themselves."

Silence all around.

"Did you tell them to stop it? Or were you unable to be understood by them?"

"Perhaps it is you who needs to understand," DuBois said. "They say our Doctor Drummond forbade them from using the latrine. And one thing more. Yesterday I overheard someone I shall not name describe these people as stupid because they could not read. I'm told that in your plantations a night patrol visited every cabin to see if the slaves were using any books. Some had hidden books in hollowed logs in the walls and would read by moonlight after the patrols had gone. If they were found out, they were beaten."

Clearly the meeting needed to end on a brighter note and Jimmy played it. "Ooh Oy'm so sad," he emoted. "Everyone gets to be a captain but me. What can Oy do after Oy've swabbed all the decks so that someone will give me a *stim-u-lant*?"

"Jimmy!" Amelia called out. "You have been on ships for longer than I have been alive. You have seen treatments for all sorts of sickness. Would you go with me on my rounds and help me so that I don't kill someone in my ignorance? And maybe you can make someone laugh like you do us."

"Mebbe Oy can," he said, making a funny face. "Doctor Jimmy at your service."

"Well, that leaves our captain," DuBois said. He turned to Charles Timmons, sitting quietly at the end of the table, his arms wrapped around his waist.

It's been only three days. He is ill and is still mourning the loss of his ship and maybe the loss of his naval career. Give him time.

Charles made it easy. He turned aside with a dismissive wave. "Felix, I was the captain while we were on the ocean. You can be the captain on land."

"Thank you," answered DuBois, "but I thought we still might ask two things of you. Since you are spending a good bit of your time on the beach, perhaps you could search for valuable objects that we could use. In my native land, we would find things like brass lanterns, fine driftwood, wood and such from passing ships. Once in my youth I found a French officer's shaving kit. I still have it."

Charles shrugged with what seemed like acquiescence. But DuBois had one thing more in mind. "Could you also investigate the possibility of making our own salt from the sea? If we could find a way to dry seawater in large pans or ponds, we could even make enough to sell what we don't need. That way we could buy Saint Matthew more chickens."

Charles nodded wearily and the gathering broke up in near darkness, Amelia relieved that the leadership torch had been passed without incident. She departed full of resolve to "get up and get on with it," as Rachel would say.

Swinging a small oil lamp by her side, Amelia made her way across the farmyard, determined to read the Cornelia Hancock article one more time before the morrow. As she placed the lamp beside the darkened bed, she sensed something different. She swung the lamp over the bed to see two skirts, a blouse and an apron – all faded gray, of course, but evoking more joy than any Christmas morning in Savannah that she could remember. Then she saw a note on top of the apron.

1. Hiram said noe to the cohabittaton of the unwed.
2. If your going to be in that hospital everday, you
   will need more cloths. These are from my dautter.
3. Can you play Amazing Grace in church next Sunday?
   Service at 11.

Chapter Fourteen
LETTERS FROM THE FRONT

September 4, 1864

Dear Mother and Daddy,

I feel like a ghost from the past, but here I am, alive, and not injured or impaired in any way. Perhaps you have learned by now that the ship was sunk attempting entry to the Cape Fear River near Wilmington, North Carolina. My trousseau went down with it. There is not much else I can tell you about that because they say that all mail during this time of war is scrutinized and censored. So, I will save the censors the trouble by saying that I am saddened beyond measure at the tragic turn of events.

Actually, I have no idea if or when this letter might reach you because, as you no doubt know, mail from one side to the other goes only through one central point at a Union fort in Virginia. To make matters more complicated, I am on Portsmouth Island, North Carolina, which is across from Ocracoke Inlet, and very difficult for mail service to reach. It comes, when it comes, via boat from New Bern, which is over fifty miles away.

Captain Timmons is among our six survivors. So, ironically, is Felix DuBois, the manager of the Royal Victoria Hotel, who happened to be journeying with us as a passenger on vacation. Currently we are staying and volunteering our assistance at a small government hospital that desperately needs help. We care for both Confederate and Union patients who have been sent here with a wide assortment of illnesses.

I am vowing to keep a journal of my activities and hope to send you a little bundle of my jottings when I can find enough paper and envelopes to fill them up. I hope you will save them for when they arrive home, as I think this is a time I will remember for the rest of my life.

I am certain you are under great difficulty and regret that I can only send my love and prayers at this time. Let us all hope that the war ends soon and that we can reunite. Your loving daughter,

Amelia Beach

Amelia's Journal

September 6, 1864

I arise each morning in an enthusiastic state. I am actually doing some good. Replaced a bandage on the thigh of a Rebel private named Jeremy, my first case. Didn't have bandages, so I asked Felix (although I always call him Mister DuBois by sight) if we could cut up just one of the sheets in the linen house. A big argument ensued, but I won and Jimmy made several strips out of it. Took off dirty yellow bandage, washed with hot water and put on new wrap. Didn't know what I was doing, but it certainly looks better than the old one, and Jeremy, the Reb private, seems to feel better, or at least is grateful that someone cares. I do.

Jimmy is an English sailor among our survivors and he is taking charge of what all of us now call "swabbing the decks." Although we have new buckets and mops in the shed out back, we have no soap, cleanser, etc. So, we boil water in a kettle, pour some on the floor, let it settle for a while, then brush and scrub. Maybe no soap, but so much better! Put soap on shopping list.

Fears of being assaulted or insulted by salacious young men have subsided. Could be my plain appearance (hair straight and parted in the middle), but I think it's because someone is finally caring about them. They think of me as sister, maybe even mother. Helped write two letters home for patients today despite slipping and sliding on wet floors. Now on to sleep.

Sept. 8, Thurs.

Already falling behind with my "daily" journal. Floor "swabbing" finished yesterday. For using only boiling water it has done wonders, and enough patients helped so that there may now be some pride in keeping things clean. Odors are much reduced, but I wonder if they notice. Tomorrow all will be ordered to pile their mess kits in the big sink at the end of the hall so they can be given the same boiling water treatment. Next will be the bedpans, etc., but I suspect everyone will say they are too sick to do it.

Jimmy, our English sailor, is becoming everyone's "chum" on both floors, Rebels on top and Yankees on bottom. He's old enough to be their father, but he acts like a private. Tells them of his colorful life aboard ships, mostly balderdash, but they love it, and it keeps their attention while I'm doing something that could cause pain.

But Jimmy is also part of the swearing and cursing that goes on around here. I have chosen to ignore it or else I would be fighting battles every day in every room. Sometimes, like measles, it spreads to me, and I just hope I will not blurt out something shocking back home at the dinner table.

I am finally sorting out diseases, enough to know that patients with the same illness would be better off segregated in similar locations. But the Yankee-Reb division is just too sharp and contentious to unscramble at present. Some would rather die than be placed next to the enemy, which is what might happen if they aren't.

As to the challenge of recognizing this or that condition, the most difficult is delirium. One man tosses and cries out all day and will scarcely accept my entreaties. But I have persevered and today I leaned over him and may have discerned the source of his misery. He said after the battle of Plymouth, not too far from here, he lay immobilized in an army hospital. A soldier in the bed next to him had been shot in the spine and paralyzed from the waist down. Some hospital person placed the paralyzed man's feet by a fire to warm him at night and then went off and left him. During the night, coals flew from the fire and burned his feet black like charcoal while both lay helpless to do anything about it. So, the patient here plays this horror over and over in his tortured mind and recoils from the sight of anyone like me.

Then there is the delirium that signals the last stages of typhoid. We have two such cases and they are uppermost in mind. Both are even more tormented by the lice in their hair and thanked me with tears for combing out what I could.

But of all the conditions that one can contract, the saddest for both nurse and patient is chronic diarrhea. It comes about in so many ways, but all converge toward the same end: men become emaciated and become blacker than one of our contrabands. They have absolutely no appetite and defy all curatives, yet require more care than all the others. I read my meager *medical texts and pray for insight.*

I try to talk to Charles every evening after dinner to keep up his spirits. I tell him that Macintyre's Therapeutics suggests that in lieu of quinine, turpentine should be applied "externally." But as to where and in what amounts it is silent and Charles recoils from the idea anyway. The book also recommends a "tonic" brewed from the bark of dogwood, poplar and willow and dissolved in whiskey. We do have brandy in the lifeboat and the island is supposed to have dogwoods, so Charles has agreed to find some. We must give something *a try.*

Sept. 10, Sat.

The new privy is all dug out, but further progress is at a standstill. We have too little lumber or nails for a new enclosure, so we have to somehow pull down and move the present "shack," which is a flattering name at that. Felix thinks we can hitch up the cow at Rachel's, but I want to be there to see such a miracle. I have never seen this cow do more than stand munching in the field and then amble lazily to the milking shed.

Living arrangements have been settled. Very delicate. Matthew the cook in the cookhouse. Felix in a large room at the end of the main floor, with Antoine supposedly as bodyguard against patient mischief. Charles agreed to an end room on the Reb floor with Jimmy to watch over him. That leaves me in my regal abode in the farmhouse. It may measure all of ten feet by eight, but it is all mine. I feel some guilt, but my colleagues insist that the hospital is "no place for a woman," meaning lack of privacy, undergarments lying about and all. Even so, they gave me a cowbell that I am supposed to ring loudly should an intruder threaten.

I continue to write letters to patients' girlfriends and families. And here one sees how alike all young men are despite the bitterness that divides them. The common fear is that the girlfriend has gone off with another man or that they will be too maimed, disfigured to be accepted. Also common is the fear of expressing their heartfelt love lest they be guilty of "sissy talk." Hence, most will instruct me to say in the beginning that the letter is being dictated to a nurse, which I suppose relieves them of being held to account for the nurse's literary flights of fancy.

But I must also read letters that come to patients. One Yankee showed me a response from his betrothed in which she told him bluntly that she was about to accept the hand of another because she could not marry a "cripple" and be deprived of the chance for a "stable home." He was inconsolable that day and I remained with him until assured he would not try to harm himself. But the next morning he was all smiles and even singing. "I reckon I've had a lucky escape," he said. "That trifling girl never would have made me a good and faithful wife."

I also read letters from mothers who may not realize they are writing to someone who is laid low and powerless. I saw one of them at the bedside of a typhoid patient. I suppose he had written saying how he longed to be home with her. I borrowed the letter with her reply: "No, my son, your place is not by me. You are needed yonder. Go and avenge your brother. He did his duty to the last. Don't disgrace him and me. Come son, don't cry anymore. You're Mother's son, you know." How out of touch with reality of his condition!

Practiced on the organ after dinner. Mustn't embarrass Rachel and the reverend tomorrow morning. Foot pedals cause me more trouble than the notes.

Sept. 11, Sun.

Raining this morning. Jimmy serves "coffee" and hoecakes for breakfast while I go to church. Forty or so showed up, mostly old people with stony faces. "Amazing Grace" had too many squeaks and wheezes, but the singing was also squeaky and wheezy, so I consider it a draw.

Surprised to see even this many people, because you don't come across them during the week. I think they stay away from the hospital or pretend it isn't there. Oh what their help could mean! Just a chicken here, some butter there. Wore my caduceus pin to remind them.

Our supplies from Drummond running low. Tonight we had another seafood stew, only this time with something new like cut-up clams. Matthew wouldn't say at first, but then said he had decided to get rid of the frogs that frequent the cistern. It's what they do in Nassau, he said. Felix says the French grill them and dip in butter. No butter, says Matthew, which led to a discussion about rowing over to Ocracoke tomorrow for all manner of supplies. The list grows: chickens, beans, clothes, wood, nails, towels, sheets, or even a bolt of any fabric that can be cut up.

No Drummond at church and The Rev. Hiram doesn't know his whereabouts either. Hiram thanked me but remains distant. Only he can rally his congregation to support the hospital, but a difficult request because it's supposed to be operated by the Almighty government. I did ask him about the

Christian Commission, which donates supplies to the hospitals mentioned in the article about my nurse friend, Cornelia. If he can find their address, I will write to beg for help.

Charles might be making a real contribution. When Felix asked him to look for ways to make salt, I thought it was a kind way of letting him go beachcombing. But this afternoon Charles led me to a narrow eddy where seawater comes and goes with the tide. On the edges lies white foamy stuff called brine, which is high in salt. He says all English navy officers are taught to scoop up brine, dry it in the sun and boil it, leaving salt crystals. Now he wants a kettle of some sort like they use to make molasses. Probably too costly, but onto the shopping list it goes.

SEPT. 13, TUES.

Matthew came back with some leaves and twigs from a dogwood tree. Made him cut them up and brew a pot of "malaria tea" for Charles. Took a sip and it tastes like dirty hot water but I kept a cheerful countenance while making Charles drink a cup for his health. He did it only to make me stop badgering him. We shall await to observe its effects.

Food shortages getting beyond even Matthew's ability to forage. Feeling hunger myself, but so did Cornelia. Tomorrow is shopping day in Ocracoke, we agreed at another group meeting. We decide to go to Tyron's, the largest general store, and put as much as possible on credit, then spend up to twenty dollars for things we can't get at Tyron's. That should leave something to put toward transportation out of here, should it ever appear.

Felix wants the delegation limited to himself, me, and Jimmy. Can't have too many "coloreds," he says, or we might not get served. Sad, but probably true. Emancipation doesn't change a small town overnight.

Mess kit sanitation improving. Not quite so for grooming our "iron horses," as they call the bed pots. Not so easy with diarrhea "running" amok. With that joke, I retire for the evening.

On a bright but blustery morning, DuBois, Jimmy and Amelia found themselves at dockside on the inlet, their lifeboat tugging at its tether, its deck chalky white after too many visits by seagulls. Also intact were the five cases of brandy, still stashed in the bow. Antoine had been added for rowing and would stay to guard the boat in Ocracoke.

On their first visit as shipwreck survivors, they had rowed straight for the building with the longest wharf. Now they went beyond and saw that most of the town was laid out in a long curve along the harbor. As the three took a surveillance walk among the morning shoppers and strollers, it was quickly apparent why Portsmouth Village was but a shadow of its neighbor across the inlet. Among the expected saloons and eateries, they passed an apothecary, a blacksmith forge, a farm feed store, a dry goods emporium, a bank with a *CLOSED TEMPORARILY sign on the door* and, their first objective, Tyron's Mercantile.

Tyron's was every general store in the Carolinas that hadn't been ravished or eviscerated by waves of soldiers. A long look down the worn pine plank floors indicated an attempt to show every barrel and bin, even though some were nearly empty. The dusty shelves behind the counters were a façade of bottles and cans spaced to hide the absence of spares behind them. It was a Civil War survivor trying to avoid surrender.

A portly man with a fringe of white hair encircling his bald pate was wrapping a package for two women. Amelia waited her turn, again pushed into the role of spokeswoman by DuBois for her "friendly Southern accent."

The shopkeeper looked up at Amelia and beamed benevolently. "And what can I do for *you*, young lady?" he said.

"Sir, you are Mr. Tyron?" He nodded. "Perhaps you've heard of us." Amelia nodded in turn to DuBois at her side and introduced themselves as the new managing director and matron of the marine hospital on Portsmouth Island.

The shopkeeper kept his cordial smile, but with no sign of the expected recognition. "Doctor Drummond said you would be expecting us. We've come to buy supplies."

Tyron cocked his head for a moment. "Oh yes, you must mean Drummond the schooner man," he said to their relief. "That's right. You would know him as the hospital manager. But we've known him here as the man who ships us supplies on his way up to New Bern. Then he buys other merchandise in New Bern and brings it to stores down here."

Amelia: "He told you nothing about appointing us to manage the hospital? Nothing about extending us credit until our monthly stipend arrives from Fort Macon?"

Tyron: "Haven't seen him for over two weeks, so he couldn't have told me about you."

Amelia: "Do you know that he gets a monthly payment from Fort Macon over in Beaufort?"

Tyron: "No. Never asked."

Amelia: "Did he tell you that he gets supplies from Fort Macon as well?"

Tyron: "No. Never asked. With that schooner fleet, he probably goes all over tarnation to get his merchandise."

Amelia excused herself just as another shopper advanced to the counter. The three retreated to a corner of the store. "Our plan's already thwarted," she said. "And he probably doesn't have a lot of things on our list anyway."

"Excuse, if you will," said DuBois. He approached the counter, where Tyron had been eyeing their conference while seated on a stool, his arms folded across his white apron. "Sir," he said, decorously. "Is there anywhere in this fine city where we might purchase some live chickens?"

Tyron lifted his chin from his chest. "Mr. Barkley of the feed store just a few doors down," he said. "Has a big coop out back and he might just sell off some for the right price."

DuBois returned to the huddle. "Since we agreed that Matthew's chickens were *a priori,* we should go first to the feed store," he said. "Next, we'll go to the dry goods place and buy clothing. Miss Beach, I'll ask you to guess at sizes for the others. We will spend up to twenty dollars for chickens and clothes. Then we will go and spend thirty at this *bon marché* for whatever we can get. We will still have ten left over for transportation and we can add to that when Fort Macon pays up on the first of the month. That's your managing director's decision."

They left Tyron's with a promise to be back and were soon in front of an equally rotund Mr. Barkley, whose stacks of newly-baled hay cast a dusty cloud through the store. "Well, I do have chickens," he said, "but them's wartime chickens. Can't buy 'em for a song these days."

Not knowing the first thing about chicken prices, they were sure that Saint Matthew would be pleased with paying eight dollars for the two hens, one rooster and four hatchlings they delivered to Antoine on the wharf for safe keeping.

That meant twelve dollars to clothe five shipwreck survivors. Plain cotton pants and shirts for four men took up eight dollars. Amelia was about to ask DuBois to spare two dollars so she could buy a pretty dress to wear at church, but she caught herself up short. *No, save the two dollars for some quinine and ask DuBois for extra if it costs more. Better to play the organ in something that might arouse sympathy for our cause. The hand-me-downs from Rachel will suit the purpose.*

Back at Tyron's Mercantile, they entered to see the shopkeeper in fervid conversation with a tall, erect woman in a black dress with white polka dots. Her black hair, pulled back and parted in the middle, accented a large, sharp nose. *Oh dear, does my hair look that plain? Maybe it makes my nose bigger.* The conversation must have been about the "delegation" from the hospital because it stopped as they approached the counter.

DuBois asked Amelia to keep a careful count with pencil and paper. At the end, when everything was piled up by the counter, her list showed:

50 lb	corn meal, $1
1 bu.	beans, $2.36
40 lb.	lard, $2.20
50 lb.	rice, $6
20 lb.	smoked ham, $3.60
30 lb.	dried fish, $1.50
5 gal.	molasses, $2.89
10 lb.	brown sugar, $2.60
1 bu.	peas, $1.90
doz.	pine boards, $4
10 yds.	brown sheeting fabric, $2.50
10 yds.	bleached sheeting fabric, $2.50
20 lb.	soap. $1.60
2 gal.	saffron oil, $3.50

"Thus far we are just over thirty-eight dollars and I think we have everything," said DuBois after checking her arithmetic.

"Nails!" said Amelia. "We forgot nails for the new latrine."

DuBois looked up at Tyron the shopkeeper, who, with his presumed wife, had been staring at them without letup. "Yes, I have some ten-pennies," said the shopkeeper.

"I don't see them," said DuBois.

"I keep them behind the counter. They're so scarce, people steal them from the bins out front."

"How scarce?"

"Forty cents a nail."

"Forty cents? *Mon dieu.* In my home, they might be a penny. What is the reason?"

"Wartime. I didn't start it, you know. Somebody up in New Bern bought up all the nails and now makes us pay dearly."

Amelia: "Would you mind telling me who sells you the nails?"

"Drummond, I think." He looked at his wife, who nodded.

Amelia put paper to pencil again. "Well, that would mean we can buy only seven nails," she said.

Throughout the whole buying process, the sharp-nosed woman had scarcely stopped staring at the strangers. *Something bad is going to erupt.*

"Then this forty dollars should cover it," said DuBois.

Oh no, it won't," said the woman, bustling past her husband to confront DuBois. "The price is sixty dollars. Those prices you see on the goods are for the local people of Ocracoke. We charge outsiders fifty percent more."

DuBois took a step backward as if someone had knocked the wind out of him. "And how do you rationalize that?" he asked at last.

"Didn't my husband tell you about war shortages? We got to keep enough in stock around here to serve our locals. You know it's also hurricane season, do you not? One big storm could wipe out this place and the town could starve."

Amelia moved beside DuBois. "Now let me tell you something," she said hotly. "Patients at that hospital are going to starve without this food. Would you like to come and see for yourself?"

"It's none of my business," said the rigid woman, jutting forth her equally-chiseled chin. "That's a government hospital, so you should complain to them. Besides, you're lucky I'm not charging you double. I hear you got Rebs and all manner of outsiders over in that place and that's what we charge them. And I don't know what in tarnation *these* two are," she said, pointing at Jimmy and DuBois.

Amelia knew the time had come. She had carried the necklace in her purse from Savannah to Nassau to this bleak place with the bedrock belief that it would only be used to buy her way home if all else failed. With the identical necklace Wilkes had brought from her father, it was the last of the fortune she'd been entrusted to protect. *Without this food, none of these patients will ever trust me again if we come back empty handed. And some will surely die. I will not be responsible for more deaths.*

Amelia reached in her purse and removed the velvet pouch. "Mrs. Tyron," she spoke up, "I am going to show you a valuable Spanish gold chain and locket that is at least two centuries old. At one time, it belonged to Blackbeard the pirate."

As Amelia spread it on the counter, she continued: "This is worth several hundred dollars, whether in American currency, English pounds or French francs. I am asking you to hold this in collateral for one month until we can get our next payment from the Union government."

The woman turned over the heavy rosary chain in her hands, opened the locket and gave an impressed nod at viewing the Virgin Mary inside. She stared down at it for an eternity of seconds as her fingers explored its golden strands. "All right," she said at last. "We'll let you go with these goods, provided that you pay the twenty dollars owed within thirty days."

"I'd like a receipt for the necklace," said Amelia.

"We don't do receipts," she answered stiffly. "We're here. You have witnesses. We ain't going anywhere."

DuBois gave a sideways glance that let Amelia know they had gone as far as they dared. He asked Tyron if he had a cart to help carry the merchandise to the docks, and Amelia noticed the two in conversation as they stepped off the front porch. When Jimmy went with them to help load the lifeboat, Amelia told him she would join them soon.

She strode down the street to the storefront with the *Apothecary and Sundries* sign. Behind the counter was a woman – girl – younger than herself, with strawberry hair and a thin face full of freckles.

"Do you have any quinine?" Amelia asked.

"Sorry, we don't," said the young apothecary with a shrug. "It's very scarce. We get some at the beginning of the month, but we have heart patients already waiting for it. And some send it to soldiers with malaria."

"When your shipment arrives at the beginning of the month, does it come from Doctor Drummond?"

"Yes, Doctor Drummond. You know him?"

"Only slightly." Amelia was about to turn on her heel and leave, but something drew her into further conversation, perhaps if only to speak with a female her own age or thereabouts.

"As you have probably deduced, I am a newcomer here," she said. "I have just joined the hospital staff on Portsmouth Island. Can you tell me how to distinguish yellow fever from malaria?"

The girl – a few years younger – seemed to have difficulty assembling her answer. "They say both are caused by foul air and stagnant water, but you can tell the difference soon enough," she said softly. "Malaria can go on and on, with the sweating, chills and all. But yellow fever can kill in a week – headaches, pain in the joints, black-looking vomit." And with that her voice cracked and she turned away.

"What troubles you?" asked Amelia in the comforting nurse's voice that now came reflexively. "Are you not an apothecary?"

"Yes….no," said the girl as she fought back tears. "You, being a stranger, don't know the sadness that has enveloped my hometown of New Bern. I was studying in pharmacy school when I learned that my brother had been carried off to heaven. He was the first to die of it."

"It?"

"Yellow fever. It struck New Bern in late August and now the whole town is in the grip of the epidemic. They say three hundred have died since my brother succumbed. And that is why I am here."

"How so?"

"Our family owns the main apothecary shop in New Bern. We had just opened this place in Ocracoke when John was stricken. My other brother moved from here to New Bern to take his place and now here I am, a mere student, being asked questions about things I haven't studied yet."

Her voice trembled and the tears ran down her cheeks again. "And now I can't go back there because my own family says it's too dangerous."

Amelia reached over the counter and took the girl's hand in hers. "I know something of what you are going through," she said. "I have been thrust into a nursing position I know little about. But together we will just imagine ourselves nurse and pharmacist, and somehow, we will prevail."

"May I call on you again?" she said, looking into the girl's watery eyes. "My name is Amelia."

"Mine is Jane, and next time we'll have tea."

Amelia arrived at the dock to see the lifeboat already packed and DuBois counting ten-penny nails from a paper sack. "Where did you get all those," she asked in amazement.

DuBois explained with a coy smile: "When Monsieur Tyron and I were bringing the cart down, I mentioned that we had an exquisite bottle of French cognac aboard our vessel. He averred that he didn't touch spirits. I averred in turn that despite his abstinence, it might be useful to have some spirits on hand for medicinal purposes. He agreed it would be wise – in exchange for another twenty nails."

"Well, with that wife," said Jimmy, "he could use some of them spirits right off."

❦

The Beach Beacon
(FORMERLY AMELIA'S JOURNAL)

Sept. 15, Thurs.

We have nails, we have wood. So today, while patients watched from their windows, we had Eliza the cow hitched to pull the horrible old latrine over, with Antoine and Matthew pulling a rope on the other side. Antoine and Matthew are sweating, the cow is doing nothing and I am doubled over laughing – shame on me. Suddenly Antoine shouts something in French to Felix and we all ask what he said. "He said you have to hitch the cow so it's facing the latrine." So, they turn Eliza around and reattach the harness. Then suddenly Antoine jumps up and down in front of the cow, yelling something in French. All this scares Eliza. She lurches backward and the whole shack falls down!

Now we have soapy water to scrub down the dirty thing and some boards to cover where old ones had rotted through. Tomorrow they will do all that in the morning and drag the "new" shack over the "new" ditch in time to empty pots from the night before. I am being a part of Progress!

Progress in the linen shed as well. Felix visited there yesterday and gave this very large contraband woman the title of "Captain of Linens." He says she has already taken charge, bossing everybody about, but imposing some order in the way sheets etc. are washed, folded and stored. I think she is sweet on Matthew, who now lives just up the path.

Anybody who reads this should disregard the "1866 Ledger" printing on back of this journal. I had run out of paper until I remembered the big fat ledger book in the hospital office. I have torn out some sheets in the back and apologize to whatever bookkeeper is here in 1866. More shame on me, but I need the paper for *The Beach Beacon!*

SEPT. 18, SUN.

Church again. Am working through the hymn book. Played "Battle Hymn of the Republic," which I don't like because Christians shouldn't be marching into battle and killing – also because each side in this war thinks the hymn is meant for them.

But there are angels even in war. Rev. Hiram surprised me with the address of the U.S. Christian Commission mission in Fayetteville, NC. Without fail I will write them a heartfelt letter tonight! The Rev. agreed to putting his address on the envelope and Rachel will mail it. Don't trust the P.O. people and fear that Drummond would toss it overboard if it were carried in his boat.

Warmer than usual after church, so I walked the beach with Charles – a rarity that I take time to notice the beautiful shoreline. Not Nassau blue, but a wild, windswept beauty all its own.

Charles wanted to show me the pile of assorted copper, lumber and iron that he had salvaged here and there – a steel pipe, a small anchor, a copper platter, a ship's bell, a battered brass barometer still attached to a wormy board. He's anxious to see what a blacksmith in Ocracoke can do with it all. But Charles is not looking stronger. Sits and shivers a lot. The dogwood "malaria tea" shows no effect, except on the poor denuded dogwood tree. I now know where to get quinine and will be there when it arrives – in a few days, I hope!

Forgot to report on the latrine. All cleaned, patched, put upright and promoted from "shack" to "shed." Jimmy reports that patients are showing it more "respect," which I must accept on faith because I won't go near it.

More progress, I think. Matthew and Rachel were doing dishes and he asked if he could keep his rooster and chicken family in her coop. In turn, he promised to feed them all and clean up whatever chickens do in their coops. Will the incumbents rebel? Another civil war? Will Matthew appropriate eggs from alien chickens? To be revealed in the next issue of The Beach Beacon.

SEPT. 21, WED.

Too busy, too tired to write much. Having new sheeting fabric means having to cut many strips, then take off old oozy bandages. This is real nursing and I am of marginal value, because all I have is soap and water. Jimmy had to tell me how to tie off a bandage. Jimmy a blessing. He's there beside me, joking with patients and telling stories so they don't notice my blundering. Overall, better food and sanitation are making a difference, but there's a limit to our resources and to our time here.

Sept. 24, Sat.

Seems like everybody stops at the chicken coop to cluck over the chicks. You can already notice the growth. Big hen has laid three eggs. Will we get some for breakfast?

Felix has named two "floor captains" at the hospital, one for the Union floor and one for the Rebs. Held a formal ceremony. Grumbling among losing contenders indicates they take it seriously. The Reb captain (2nd flr.) already claims that he is "over" the Union capt. I hope he is joking.

Felix announced at dinner that he will start using stimulants (spirits) as rewards for good deeds, etc. Big discussion as to what to mix with cognac, which is our only stimulant. Jimmy won the day. He piped up and said, "Tell them they'll be getting The King's Grog." We asked what it was. He said, "It's what they give sailors in the British navy when they sink a ship or win a battle." We asked what was in it. He said equal parts of brandy, sorghum molasses and water. We said "That's nice because we have the ingredients. What does it taste like?" Jimmy said, "I have no idea. I just made up the whole thing. But if you believed it, so will they."

And so, The King's Grog is born. Matthew will serve us some tomorrow night.

Chapter Fifteen
DEVASTATION, SEPTEMBER 28, 1864

A t first it swept in as just another blustery fall day, with heavy dark clouds rolling in like unruly ocean waves. As Amelia and Jimmy made their rounds of the hospital's second floor, they observed Charles Timmons standing on the balcony facing the sea, his arms wrapped around his torso, hair blown back as his uplifted face scanned the sky. After several minutes, he returned and had difficulty slamming shut the louvered doors to the balcony. "I saw three frigate birds," he said. "Something's up out there – a big storm, maybe a hurricane."

By mid-morning the sun had been blotted out by a gray blob of a sky and the wind came in from the south in warming gusts of disarray. Then it was Rachel, walking briskly up the foot path with Felix DuBois trying to keep pace.

They gathered in the tidy office DuBois had salvaged from Drummond's dishevelment. "We got a big 'un comin' up from the south," Rachel declared breathlessly. "Don't know how bad, but the animals already know something's up. I got two cats under the bed and I can't drag Eliza out to pasture. Ye must make fast thy shutters and put thy stores above ground. Git yerself extra water from the cistern," she admonished. "Y'er gonna need hardtack and other plain staples, because ye might not be able to make fire from wet wood. And pay heed to me when I say *wet*, because this whole land can flood as far back as Doctor's Creek and then some.

"Now I got to git home and do my own boardin' up," Rachel dithered, nearly spinning around. "Hiram's shutterin' the church. I got to figger what to do with all them chickens. Need to tie the goat in the milk shed."

"Let's all be calm," said Felix DuBois, seated at his desk. "Jimmy, get the two floor captains and put all able hands to work securing shutters. Matthew, you can help Rachel look after the chickens and whatever else she needs. Jimmy, go to the outbuildings and secure what you can. I will have Antoine go secure the cutter as well."

"And me?" asked Amelia.

"All you have to do is keep forty-six patients calm and content."

Amelia had never experienced a hurricane. Neither had most of the patients, who seemed to anticipate something of a welcome diversion from their interminable purgatory. All were soon sobered by new and strange sensations. The first thing Amelia noticed was the darkness that followed the shuttering and the lack of lamps to brighten spirits. Then came the pelting of rain, as if the furies were heaving buckets of water against the outside walls and shutters, leaving dribbles to find their way through the slipshod government construction and puddle among the trunks and bedpans. With it came a cacophony of sounds – wind howling outside, hissing through seams between walls and windows, screeching its way down the many fireplaces in chilly gusts that made calloused young men clutch their bedclothes like nurslings.

Amelia, however, had determined that she would dispense good cheer from room to room despite also dispensing an unpopular porridge of lukewarm peas and smoked ham. With Jimmy at her side, Matron of Hospital Beach declared that the King's Grog, which hitherto had been dispensed sparingly for caring deeds and good conduct, would now be offered to one and all in "celebration" of the hurricane.

When innards and hearts were warmed, patients were soon clamoring for Jimmy to do a hornpipe and sing a bawdy song. Despite flickering oil lamps that would barely illumine a room, young men were clustered about, bantering insults and sharing campfire stories, all while clanking their cups at Amelia for "just another snort."

But as the darkness of night made the rooms even dimmer, the lamps were snuffed and men were again drawn back into their blankets and into the clutches of their battlefield fears and ephemeral images of loved ones at home. And as the night howled on, Amelia found herself at the bedside of those too sick for any levity in their fragile lives.

One was Charles Timmons, who had taken to his bed and who expressed little interest in conversing – only in asking Amelia for more wraps of any kind to quell his shivering.

Could malaria be so terrible that it makes him shut me out of a loving relationship? Does this rain outside and the dampness inside make it all worse?

Can malaria lead to yellow fever?

Downstairs in the Union camp lay a typhoid victim who had already required much of her "nursing" time. Stanley, a twenty-year-old infantry private from Pennsylvania, had suffered at first from headaches and pain in his muscles. Soon these became secondary to his inability or unwillingness to eat, which could only be due to his constant stomach pain, caused, in turn, by an impaction in his bowels, which, in turn, had brought about painful hemorrhoids. The primary means by which Amelia had learned to gauge the severity of typhoid was by the small pink spots that the disease displayed on his back. And on this night, his scrawny torso displayed more pink spots than ever.

By then Amelia was no stranger to enemas. She begged Stanley to allow her to try a saline solution, but he turned his backside to the wall in protest. What if Jimmy did it? Refused again. So, Amelia settled for just sitting beside him, offering gentle words of encouragement and begging him to take sips of water. Midnight passed and outside the storm howled on.

At four in the morning, Amelia had gone down to DuBois' office just to relax at his desk for a spell. When she awoke with a start, she realized she had been fast asleep in the chair with her head on the hard desk. Spotting a streak of daylight in the hallway, she rose, opened the office door. Hearing no howls nor shrieks of wind outside, she walked to the end of the corridor and carefully opened the door to the front porch. Still in a half-dreamlike state, she encountered only a gentle breeze. Day was breaking and Amelia found herself staring from the rail of a ship into an orange and blue sunrise that made the glassy ocean beneath her glisten with gold.

She blinked and realized that the "ocean" beneath her "ship" was instead a floodtide of water that had passed beneath the raised portico of the hospital. From the front balcony, Amelia gazed back towards the church, Rachel's farm and Doctor's Creek. All the trees, bushes and buildings stood amidst a shallow sheet of water that had fused with the ocean surf.

Was the tide headed in our out? If still coming in, water would lap into the first floor of the hospital and leave all their scrubbing and cleaning a stagnant mess of silt, salt and sand.

Stagnant water, the curse that breeds the twin scourges of malaria and yellow fever.

Amelia focused more intently on the watery scene all around the hospital.

White sheets or squares lying in the water, resembling giant mushroom caps or the soggy sails of capsized dinghies. *They are sheets, blown askew from the linen shed.*

Water saturating the new latrine.

Water over the graves and into the death house.

Water washing away the eddies of brine from which Charles had hoped to make salt.

The cross atop the church steeple leaning over precariously.

Water covering Rachel's chicken coop in the distance. Chicken wire fence down. No sign of chickens.

No more Doctor's Creek beyond the farm. Just a swampy slurry stretching from the ocean to as far west as the eye could see.

A cloud of panic was beginning to envelop Amelia when the door opened behind her and Felix DuBois emerged, immaculately dressed for another day of business.

"I've got to go over there," she said, pointing to the church. "We need to get these patients some breakfast."

"You don't want to wade through all that," he said.

"I'll just take my shoes off."

"I know you aren't fond of snakes. No. Matthew is ready to serve coffee and hardtack from the storehouse below."

"I fear this will be our undoing," she said aimlessly.

"You have been up most of the night," DuBois countered. "What you need is more sleep and things will be better."

He motioned Amelia to follow him down the hall. They entered the last room, which, she realized by then, belonged to DuBois and Antoine. It was spotless, with clean clothes hanging neatly from a railing. Two neatly made-up cots stood side by side, each with a small bedside table. Atop each was a glass vase with plumes of sea oats and blooms of yellow jessamine.

"Antoine picked these just yesterday," said DuBois, unfurling a blanket. "He's up and over at the linen shed, so no one will bother you. Please get some sleep now, and you will feel much different when you return to normal."

"Normal?" she mumbled. "We could be finished." But she hardly finished the sentence before she was fast asleep.

༺༻

The Beach Beacon

Sept. 30, Fri.

Weather clear, calm and beautiful, as if The Almighty wanted to apologize for the ruckus He created. Maybe there is a change in our fortunes as well. After my "enforced" rest, as I walked back onto the front porch, looked out and saw the contraband women wading out in the swampy water gathering up the sheets and towels that had been blown about. Later they scrubbed them in the inlet with soap and hung them out to dry. No dry wood for a kettle fire. I was not one to make a fuss. Making do.

Inside the hospital men are carrying mess kits, blankets and the like in the corridors amidst great commotion. DuBois beckons me in his office and says it's supposed to be a surprise for me, but I awoke too early. The floor captains agreed to re-arrange room assignments so that each room has one weaker, infirm patient and one (relatively speaking) able patient charged with looking after the other. In the process, they are more paired by type of ailment, though no change in the Mason-Dixon Line between floors. How did DuBois (and the floor captains) get the men to change? I suspect that the able ones were proffered promises of The King's Grog, but I think more are realizing they can't just lie there whimpering and expect to return home healthy.

Oct. 1, Sat.

The flooding recedes into slippery mud, so we pray for bright sunshine to dry it. Food still the number one problem. Matthew had moved the sacks of grain in the storehouse off the ground, but a lot of rainwater blew in during the storm and made things like peas and cornmeal soggy and starting to ferment. Not all the way through, but enough to increase our worries about survival if Doctor Drummond is delayed with the Fort Macon rations. We watch for him by the docks each day.

At a meeting after dinner we discussed the food situation, which led to talk about going over to the general store in Ocracoke, and then how to raise the twenty dollars needed to retrieve my gold chain from the "pawn" lady. The pawn here is me.

Felix says we should try to raise $20 by doing fix-up chores for people in the church who have storm damages. Rachel attended and said someone needs to straighten the cross on top of the church. Jimmy volunteered – said if he could climb a rigging with a ship swaying in big waves, he could toss a rope over the cupola and scramble up there. Rachel and Matthew decide to go on a chicken hunt. They will call on houses and ask about strays, but also to gauge who might have extra stores and who might need various repairs. Rachel said she will prevail on Rev. Hiram to make an announcement in church about the "chicken mission" and our offer of repair help. At least it may get these people to notice the hospital!

Oct. 2, Sun.

Over sixty at church today. Maybe the hurricane has brought them together to share stories of their suffering and their various needs. Rev. Hiram made his announcement and Rachel said two members came up to her afterward and asked for a visit. A start. Played "Blessed Be the Tie that Binds" in hopes someone might see a blessed tie to themselves and the hospital.

Oct. 3, Mon.

Two chickens found sitting in the branch of a tree out along Doctor's Creek. May need to buy more in Ocracoke if theirs haven't flown the coop as well. Meanwhile, Rachel thinks she and Hiram should pay a visit to the Drummond house. She says the wife lives there alone and might know of her husband's whereabouts. Rachel thinks there may be food supplies in a storehouse there.

But a sad event occupied us much of the day. Stanley, the typhoid patient from Pennsylvania, was dead in his bed when Jimmy and I brought around the evening supper. I feel the anguish of any nurse or doctor who knows not the exact cause, or who has not been privy to parting words. I will forever believe that poor Stanley simply grew tired of being ill in so many places.

I hastened to the church and Rev. Hiram dropped his business at hand and went over to say some final words as a few others looked on. Jimmy and the Union floor captain took him to the Death House and put him in the coffin that lies therein. I doubt that he will be allowed to rest there long, for it is supposed to be reserved for officers. And Jimmy points out that the ground is still soft for digging after the storm, so "the sooner we dig, the better." I will compose a letter home, a eulogy to his bravery and so forth. I hope that from this Charles learns the importance of self-preservation and "pluck," as his countrymen call it.

———————

On another clear, calm post-hurricane afternoon in early October one of the Rebs hollered down the corridor for everyone to come watch "something you ain't seen before." A cutter-sized boat with a single mast in the bow was heading straight towards the hospital with two sets of rowers straining to thrust it up on the beach. When it scraped into the sand, two men in Union blue jumped over the sides and stood knee-deep in the gentle surf, pushing at the gunwales to give the boat a few more feet of dry land beneath it. Then, to the cheers of a dozen patients gathered on the portico, the soldiers began unloading sacks and boxes of provisions and stacking them on the sand.

As the four men labored, a tall man in his thirties with a black mustache strode to the main entrance. His long black riding boots accentuated his height. He was coatless, with blue shirt and suspenders, but he needed no epaulets and stripes to convey that he was in command.

"I am Captain Benjamin Hawkes, First Artillery of New York," he announced stiffly to DuBois and Amelia, now standing before him as an audience watched from the balcony above.

"We have had people watching for you at the town dock," said DuBois. "That is, we were expecting Doctor Drummond and his ship. You came on another one."

"Yes, what you see there is a buoy tender, which happened to stop at Fort Macon," answered Hawkes. "The army more or less appropriated it for this mission while the navy did a little shore time in Beaufort. As for the amphibious landing, my oarsmen gave me a hearty cheer when I suggested that we could save two miles by unloading directly on the beach. Besides, we were worried that you might still be in a flood zone where we'd have to slosh all these goods through a swamp."

"And you are?"

The managing director and matron of hospital introduced themselves and extended their hands, but the captain held up his palms with a shrug. "I sincerely regret that I cannot take your hands," he said, "but with the great pestilence sweeping New Bern, all are under military orders not to shake hands – a great hardship when in the presence of a pretty lady."

They showed Hawkes to one of the porch chairs by the entrance and offered to draw him a glass of water but were told that "I can't even accept a Good Samaritan's gesture – only canteen water from Fort Macon."

"And the Fort is free of disease?" asked DuBois.

"Thus far, but at the expense of breaking all contact with New Bern."

"Including Doctor Drummond?"

"As far as I know," said Hawkes. "If he is attempting to administer to the afflicted, then heaven help him. Then again, he could have sailed off to speculate in a more promising land."

"Does your shipment include quinine?" asked Amelia, anxious to end the perfunctory patter.

"It does not," said the captain, conveying a touch of surprise. "Every bit that can be shipped from the manufacturer in Washington is being diverted to New Bern."DuBois got to the point as well. "Did you bring the monthly stipend from the government?"

"I did not."

DuBois, showing some pique: "Why, if you please?"

Hawkes, with equal irritation: "Because I don't have it. The funds you mentioned have always come from the Marine Hospital Service, with the army acting only as intermediary. And even then, we are authorized to pay only Drummond directly. We have no official record of who you are and neither, I suspect, does the Marine Hospital Service. We know nothing of the arrangement you have made with Drummond. I don't even know if we should leave these stores in your care."

Hawkes saw them slump dejectedly in their chairs. He saw Amelia dab at her eyes.

Finally, DuBois spoke up, not hotly, but evenly. "That was a most officious statement," he said. "You are correct, nonetheless. The truth is that we are shipwreck survivors – the sort that this facility was built to accommodate. We were dragooned by Doctor Drummond, one might say, because we had no other place to stay and no means of egress. But we have worked very hard to improve the lot of these poor wretches he so willfully ignored."

Now it was the captain's turn to collect his thoughts as the late afternoon sun sank below the building. "I regret that I have brought you bad news so heavy-handedly," he said. "Perhaps I was upset because we have gone to much trouble to secure and deliver these stores."

Continued Hawkes: "Let me say some things that you may not have been aware of when you so recently were washed upon our shores, so to speak. The Marine Hospital Service, for one. It operates outside the purview of the army or navy, but rather as a part of the U.S. Collector of Customs. When the hospitals were created as refuges for merchant seamen, the supporting funds were to come from a twenty cent per month tax on each seaman's wages. But the war has filled these hospitals with every sort of soldier and sailor – as you are so acutely aware – and this 'hospital fund' has been completely exhausted. And all the marine hospital physicians, I can assure you, have been pulled away to various battlefields. I think the Customs Bureau in Washington has simply thrown up its hands and asked military installations to do what they can to support any of these hospitals in their areas.

"With all that in mind," he said, "I return to this Drummond, whom you insist on calling 'doctor.' I confess that he has played, shall we say, a useful role during this war. Because we have no ships at the fort, Drummond and his schooners brought us convenient supplies as he plied his way between Ocracoke inlet to New Bern to Fort Macon and Beaufort. We knew that he had bought up some items in great quantities and that his prices were usurious but we in the camps needed those items. A farmer can grow other foods or draw on his storehouse, but an army must rely on others or starve.

"Well," Hawkes continued, "our commanding general, Burnside by name, has always been a harsh disciplinarian and prides himself on being no man's fool. Before long, he reacted with an edict that suited his reputation."

Hawkes stood at the table and fished a single folded paper from his back pocket. "This is a copy of a poster that has been circulated all over the Beaufort waterfront. I am required to show it to all shippers."

RULES
REGULATING THE MARKET!

Provost Marshal's Office
Beaufort, N.C., August 28, 1864

ALL FRESH PROVISIONS WILL BE SOLD ON THE MARKET WHARF. MARKET BOATS ARE NOT PERMITTED TO LAND AT ANY OTHER WHARF, AND PERSONS ARRIVING IN SAID BOATS WILL REPORT IN PERSON TO THIS OFFICE. THE INTENTION IS TO ACCOMMODATE **ALL PERSONS,** AND TO THIS END SALES WILL BE LIMITED. NO SPECIAL PERMITS WILL BE GIVEN TO ANY OFFICER, SOLDIER, OR CITIZEN TO PURCHASE EXTRA SUPPLIES, AND SALES AT THE WHARF FOR PURPOSE OF SPECULATION ARE FORBIDDEN. THIS OFFICE HAS DECLARED **MAXIMUM** PRICES TO BE ASKED, AND THE GUARD WILL ARREST ANY PERSON VIOLATING, OR ATTEMPTING TO VIOLATE, THESE REGULATIONS.

DuBois and Amelia studied it and looked up.

"Now then, there are some other things you don't realize in your peaceful little enclave," he said. "Yellow fever has struck the entire city of New Bern – the six thousand permanent residents, the two thousand men at the army post and the two thousand or more freed slaves who continue to flock there, ragged and in total disarray. Despite that, this General Burnside recently ordered the torching of two major warehouses of food and other supplies. And this, of course, has further fueled price speculation by unsavory dealers like – yes –your Doctor Drummond."

"Why would they put the warehouses to fire?" asked DuBois.

"A very good question, sir," said Hawkes, "and my answer is meant to enlighten and not insult you. It is widely believed that ships, sailors, and supplies from Caribbean countries are what carry yellow fever. I'm not a physician, but that seems to be the consensus among them. And I will confess to you, sir, that when I first heard you speak with an accent that I took as Caribbean or French Indies, I declined to take your hand. There is no such order, at least not yet. I reacted from fear and resorted to a fabrication."

"But I *am* French and Caribbean," replied DuBois, "and I have no yellow fever."

"And there's the rub," said Hawkes. "These same physicians say that yellow fever seldom strikes people of color from the Caribbean. Only the whites get it."

"The revenge of the slaves, perhaps," said DuBois with a faint smile.

"Touché," said Hawkes with a shrug. Both reached out at once and shook hands.

It was late. Amelia had finished "watering" her patients, as she called her round of bedtime drinks. She had read a letter to a lad who couldn't read, changed bandages, mopped brows, found an extra blanket for Charles and snuffed out the last lamp. As she trod down the footpath towards the farm and church, she noted that the two tents pitched by the soldiers from Fort Macon were also dark. But one faint light glowed in the window of the church social hall. She yearned only for sleep but knew that oil supplies were running low and assumed that someone had forgotten to douse a lamp.

Instead of a neglected lamp, Amelia was surprised to see Captain Benjamin Hawkes slouched at the dining table with his long legs draped over two chairs. Atop the table were a brown bottle and a glass half-full. Some sheets of paper lay beside it, turned upside down.

What to say? "Your men are dead asleep," she bantered lightly. "You must have flogged them like Roman galley slaves."

"They have reason to be worn out," he said. "The sail gave way to the calm winds and they probably rowed the last dozen miles," he answered. "But in any case, I'm glad that you looked in on me."

"Oh, why?"

"It's always pleasant just to be in the presence of a lovely young lady," he said, looking up at her for the first time. "One gets weary of soldiers, you know. One doesn't share thoughts of the heart with them – especially an officer. So please sit with me for a moment so I can share a thought or two from the heart."

He took a sip from the whiskey glass, untangled his legs from the chairs, stood up and pulled out a chair for her. Amelia, torn between the discomfort of a male stranger's flattery and her fear of affronting the hospital's link to survival, sat down and faced him.

"Thoughts of the heart?" she said. "I had taken you for an officer charged with doing his official duties, no more, no less."

"Maybe I was, once," he replied. "I charged the picket line shouting slogans, running through anyone in my way, until killing became no different than shooting squirrels. Then, when I took a bullet for the first time, I began to wonder. The second time I found myself confessing my sins to a priest I didn't know who gave absolution to a Presbyterian *he* didn't know. So, by now, I am no longer unwilling to share my thoughts of the heart, especially when I've had a little Scotch and sitting before a woman who was no doubt beautiful until she began wearing her hair straight and parted in the middle to satisfy the medical authorities. Am I right?"

She turned aside.

"I thought so."

"You are partly right," Amelia said. "I am from Savannah, Georgia, a Rebel refugee in your conquered territory by way of shipwreck."

"Nonetheless, I see you as a nurse who is trying her best to save lives on both sides," he said. "And for that very reason, I am going to share some more thoughts with you that could greatly affect you and the men in this hospital."

Amelia rose, went to a kitchen shelf, and returned with another glass. "We'll, if I'm going to be up past my bedtime, you had better pour me a small nightcap."

"Capital," he answered. "The first insight I offer you has to do with the size of the food allotment we just delivered. You are correct that it is not enough to last a month, but you do not know why. The reason is that official orders from the military district are that no rations are to be issued to Confederates in army custody. That includes patients and prisoners."

Amelia was wide-eyed. "You intend to starve them to death?"

"Not exactly," said Hawkes. "Now here is where I want you to listen, because it gets complicated. North Carolina, as you know, at first declared for the Confederacy. But as the Union began to prevail in these parts, many Confederate soldiers switched allegiance to the Union and were organized into two North Carolina regiments called the 'Buffaloes.' I have no idea whence the name came. When some of these men were captured in battle by the Confederates, twenty-two of them were hanged for the treason of escaping their ranks in the first place. All this had a devastating effect on the Buffaloes who remained in the two Union regiments. They feared certain death if captured by the Rebels and feared for their families at home as well."

Amelia deemed The King's Grog better than her first sip of Scotch, but it jarred her attention.

"Now I am approaching some facts so important to your survival," Hawkes continued. "In April of this year, before you arrived here, we fought the Battle of Plymouth, in which the Confederates charged the Union garrison and captured some two thousand men. Some were these Buffaloes. They were so petrified of being shot for treason that a great many escaped into the rivers and swamps of Eastern North Carolina. Some even live openly in Beaufort, just across from our fort.

"Now, then, Amelia, our commanding general, seeks to 'shape up' what he sees as lax discipline in New Bern, which he cites as a major reason for the yellow fever epidemic. He's the one who ordered the two warehouses torched – a reckless thing to do. Just two weeks ago he ordered the provost marshal of New Bern – the head of our military police in the town – to 'shoot to death by musketry' six of these runaway Buffaloes. The provost marshal assigned to that dreadful mission was my friend, Major Henry Lawson, as fine a man as ever lived. He told me over a bottle, just like this one, how he went from man to man, each sitting on his coffin, receiving from each one parting words and little keepsakes for their families while all the time tears were streaming down his own face. Then he did his duty and had them all shot to death."

Hawkes took another swallow. "Just before coming here I learned that my friend Henry had succumbed to the pestilence," he said, "so I drink tonight to his memory.

"Now here is why I am telling you all this, Amelia," he said with a hard look into her eyes. "Two evils are racing to this very place and I do not know which will arrive first. One is the hand of a ruthless general, determined to capture and execute every deserter, whether hospital patient or not. And I know without even walking your corridors that some of your patients are Buffaloes.

"The other evil is pestilence itself," he said. "You still do not appreciate the extent to which it has destroyed one city, so I am going to read something to you – a letter I received from a cousin who should be teaching school on Long Island, New York, had it not been his unlucky lot to be part of a death squad in the hell hole of New Bern, North Carolina."

Hawkes took another quick sip and picked up the papers in front of him. "All of my warnings cannot describe that situation like someone in the midst of it," he said. "Hence, I want to read part of a letter that comes from a soldier who happens to be my cousin. He writes of 'nearly all places of business closed' and 'entire households carried off, leaving not one in the number to tell the tale.' The words of my cousin Alfred read like a ghoulish ode to both faith and folly:"

While the yellow fever held undisputed sway, and the destroyer reigned like a relentless tyrant, there assembled a little band of courageous, devoted men, drawn together by the most sacred impulses which can inspire the human heart. They formed a phalanx of "Good Samaritans" and pledged their lives and all for the great purpose of administering comfort to the sick and the last sad offices to the dead.

Hark! There's a sound along yonder pavement. Some members of the "Dead Corps" are on their way to an afflicted mansion. They reach the threshold, then pause for a while, and determine to enter. It is almost certain destruction to breathe the poisonous air within, and yet they falter not. These administering spirits hover around the prostrate forms, soothing their anguish, and silently essaying to mitigate their unutterable pain, caused by the stifling effluvia of the infection.

There then follows the soul-sickening and silent, solemn travel of hearse after hearse, with no accompanying friend, save the zealous, fearless minister of God, leading the way, and under the grand canopy of Heaven's erubescent sky, pronouncing the solitary service o'er the departed.

Wend your way through the empty streets of the crushed city and whom do you meet? None, save here and there an officer hurrying rapidly along, as though conscious of his peril. There, turning the corner of Broad and Middle Streets, is one who has just been seized by fever, trembling convulsively from head to foot, and his pallid visage hidden beneath the collar of his coat. Young man, speed thee homeward, or saffron's hue will soon o'ercloud thy face. The avenger has marked thee for his own.

Hawkes stopped and looked up and poured himself another splash from the bottle. "I think my cousin has described my concern better than I could," he said.

Amelia nodded solemnly and crooked her finger for another splash as well. Now a dozen thoughts began churning through her mind. Without sorting through them, she asked: "Is Doctor Drummond caught up in this scourge? Could he be dead by now?"

"Yes, he's known to be in New Bern, and quite possibly a victim."

"One of us here has malaria. Is it true that someone with malaria is more susceptible to yellow fever?"

"I believe so, yes."

"We still have many pools of stagnant water lying about after the hurricane," she said. "And these are known to breed yellow fever, I believe."

"So they say. But I am trying to tell you to move these patients out of here before they are killed by our zealous general or the pestilence – and before you become part of a Death Corps,"

"And how do you propose to do this?" she asked. "Doctor Drummond told us that the inlet is blocked to ocean ships and you said you have none at Fort Macon."

"All true," Hawkes answered. "But if the purpose is to transfer sixteen Rebel prisoners to the POW Camp at Point Lookout, I think I can arrange for them to be picked up by one of the tenders that go back and forth supplying the blockading squadron at Wilmington. We can ferry the passengers from your dock to the tender at sea."

"They say this Point Lookout is a death trap."

Hawkes shrugged and sighed. "It's an island in Chesapeake Bay. It has forty thousand prisoners living in tents. All I know is that they seem to prefer it to escaping, probably because they would otherwise be back on the battlefield, or left to our general's tender mercies, or to yellow fever. You will need to convince your Rebs, and perhaps the prospect of reduced rations will actually help you."

Another thought had ripened for expression. Said Amelia: "We still have our five other shipwreck survivors. Three are British citizens and two are French. Could they board this tender and go on to the port of Baltimore, perhaps? There they might find passage abroad."

Hawkes brooded upon the question. "Well, Baltimore is not far at all from Point Lookout," he said at last. "It might involve the civilians paying extra cost. Army rules and all that."

They agreed that Hawkes would bring down another round of food supplies in a month's time, and with it more precise plans as to locating a ship to take them north.

Amelia yawned and stood. Hawkes rose as well and loomed uncomfortably near her, almost a head taller. He seemed to sway a bit on his feet.

"And now I want to ask you for something unusual," he said.

"Oh?"

"I want only to hug you – to embrace you – for a moment."

Before Amelia could react, Hawkes put his long arms around her waist and held her tightly. But tenderly. It was a long "moment." When he released her, she looked up and saw a tear in his eye.

"Why did you do that?" she said softly.

He reached back for the whiskey glass and drained what was left. "It has been over two years since I felt the embrace of a woman," he answered. "Last February I learned that my wife and three-year-old child had died of smallpox. Alone in a Long Island farmhouse with no one to protect them. I was away, killing strangers."

"I'm so very sad," she said. *I should not do this.* She drew up on her toes and gave him a kiss on the cheek.

"Well, she saved my life in the process," he said with a forced laugh. "I came apart so wretchedly afterward that the army declared me too worthless for combat and shipped me down to peaceful, quiet Fort Macon where I would be artillery officer of a fortress that hadn't fired a shot. I didn't even want to live at the time, but now I've decided that perhaps my life won't be so worthless if I can do something to save others."

"Maybe tonight you have," said Amelia. She finished the dregs of her glass and left Captain Benjamin Hawkes alone again with a bottle and a lamp that flickered like his memories of a family laughing and loving on Long Island, New York.

Chapter Sixteen

Revival, October 1864

Antoine rowed DuBois, Amelia and Jimmy over to Ocracoke Harbor on a cool, gray morning with a modest mission compared to their previous visit. In the managing director's waistcoat were twenty dollars, scraped together by repairing roofs, fences and henhouses around Portsmouth Island. Their strategy for "multiplying" the twenty was to ransom Amelia's gold chain from the general store, then visit the feed store and convince the owner to hold it hostage for a month in exchange for as many chickens as they could pry loose.

The plan began dissolving as soon as they entered the harbor. Hulks of a half-dozen swamped boats leaned in the water at precarious angles. A tangle of battered and flooded dinghies hindered their efforts to secure a landing spot along the wooden town wharf. After they climbed the algae-soaked ladder and began to survey the main street, it was as if the hurricane had blown down Ocracoke's last façade of pride and pluck in the face of a grueling, grinding war. Broken glass and scraps of rotted fencing lay strewn in the road as if no one had enough energy left to tidy up the town. A scrawny brown dog cowered behind a rain barrel, unsure of whether to beg or bark. The porch of a saloon was caved in and CLOSED was scrawled on a board that had been nailed across the doorway. The wooden sign atop the fabric store next door had flown off to parts unknown. Steam pouring from an open door up the road indicated that the blacksmith was still in business. But not the clothing store beside it.

In what should have been the height of morning shopping hours, the only people walking toward them were two women in sun-bleached "succession" dresses who had emerged from the fish market. Neither looked up as one said to the other, "Well, I wouldn't be so hasty to complain. At least you got something for supper. I got nothing."

They were about to pass the Drug & Sundries store when Amelia remembered the pharmacy student from New Bern. She peered into the cracked front window and saw the same girl seated behind the counter, reading a book. Asking her companions to wait outside, she twisted the doorknob and the girl's head jerked up in surprise.

"Remember me?"

"Yes, I do. Amelia."

"You seem so surprised when the door opened. Not much business these days?"

"The truth is, I don't even open the place some days," the girl answered. "For a moment, I couldn't remember having unlocked the door this morning."

The only positive news from the quick visit was that Jane, the young proprietress, had heard from her family that the yellow fever scourge in New Bern seemed to be abating with the cooler weather and that there was hope she might return in the winter. The bad news was having confirmed the sad state of Ocracoke. "The day after the hurricane," she said, "the Carolina State Bank sent notices that it would close in one week for a 'bank holiday.' Everyone who wanted their money out had until then or they'd have to go to Greenville or Raleigh to get it. Now everyone is wondering if they will re-open here."

"I'm so surprised," said Amelia. "I had always thought of Ocracoke as an island unto itself that could survive on fishing and oystering."

"I had a fisherman in here the other day," Jane said. "When I asked why he wasn't out there on a pretty day, he said he couldn't get wood and caulking to repair his boat. And he said he hardly had enough fishhooks left to make it worthwhile."

Pointing to her waiting companions and promising to return for the cup of tea that Jane offered, Amelia resumed the walk uptown. The general store seemed intact, but its large sign now read TYRON'S MERCAN because the winds had torn off the TILE and tossed it away. The large front porch, however, was starkly bare of the wooden rockers and bins that had given it a homey look.

Amelia had a feeling of dread as they climbed the porch stairs. Inside it was dim and eerily quiet. A quick sweep of the eyes around the large room revealed a few cans on mostly empty shelves. The bins and barrels that once lined the store counter were also empty. Along the corridor were tables of lanterns, cups, saucers, dry goods and used books in an effort to assemble remnants of merchandise for display. In the far corner, they saw portly Mister Tyron surveying them while holding a broom and dustpan.

He said nothing, and Amelia, in turn, dispensed with any formal greeting. "We've come about the Spanish necklace," she said.

Tyron nodded and turned toward the doorway leading to a storeroom or office. "Gwendolyn, your hospital people are here," they could hear him say.

Having bypassed an obviously odious duty, he kept his head down and resumed sweeping. After waiting in silence, the three supplicants looked at each other and Amelia had begun striding towards the doorway when suddenly it was filled with the form of the angular Mrs. Tyron, wearing the same black dress with white polka dots and the same defiant scowl they had seen on their first visit.

"We've come for the gold chain," repeated Amelia as she began to open her purse. "I have the twenty dollars right here."

"Well, it won't do you no good," said the shopkeeper's wife.

"Why?"

"Bank's got it."

"What? The bank robbed you?"

The sharp chin jutted out in defiance. "Young lady, you ever heard of an act of God?" "Well, if you was in business you would know that ever contract has a clause that says all transactions are null and void if an act of God strikes. And that hurricane was a bona fide *act of God* if I ever saw one. It ruined our food stocks and kept suppliers from bringing more. Why? Because of the yellow fever over in New Bern, which started with a *war*, which is also another reason for making a contract null and void. Acts of *wo-ah*." Amelia's indignation was rising as well. "But we didn't have a written contract, did we."

"Same thing – written or oral. All the same."

Amelia: "What does a bank have to do with all this?"

The woman sighed and continued her tutorial. "This business has a line of credit. Act of God and act of war means no inventory, which means no sales, which means no money to pay interest on a bank loan. So the bank took the necklace."

"You mean you willingly *offered* it to them," retorted Amelia with equal fire. "It was small enough to hide. There was nothing about it in writing. You gave something of great value for a pittance, I'll wager. How much did you get?"

"That's between us and the bank," the shopkeeper's wife sneered back.

"You want it back, you go to Raleigh and deal with *them*."

With that she turned on her heels and disappeared into the back office again. Her husband went on sweeping, his eyes fixed on the floor. The three stood fuming. Amelia, her hands shaking with anger, took a swift step toward the back room but then stopped, knowing that she would only be ranting to a closed door.

At last they turned to exit, but on their way out, DuBois paused at a counter of dry goods and picked up a roll of muslin. "Oh monsieur," he called out. "Oh *monsieur!*" Mr. Tyron looked up from his sweeping, expressionless. "We are requisitioning this material for the marine hospital," he said. "If you have any problem with it, you may take it up with the government in Washington."

Tyron said nothing, his mouth hanging open as they left the store. They were well down the street when DuBois looked at Amelia with a sideways smile that always accompanied his sly sense of humor. "Well, at least we have twenty dollars for chickens," he said as they approached the feed store. Indeed, they felt fortunate to walk away with three chickens and a rooster, even though they had bought the same number for only eight dollars the month before.

On October 10, the shipwrecked six held another after-dinner meeting in the church social hall. This time Rachel was included as well. "Let us begin by adding up the pluses and minuses," said Felix DuBois. "On the unpleasant side of the ledger, winter will be here soon. We have enough food supplies on hand for – two weeks, Matthew?"

The cook nodded and DuBois continued. "And we don't know if and when supplies from Fort Macon will come. The principal harvests are *finis*. The fields are bare or flooded with saltwater and most of the men needed to till them are off fighting for one side or the other. New Bern is isolated and Ocracoke is crippled, all of which leaves Portsmouth Island and its five hundred people alone to face whatever may come."

He looked up from his notes. "Well now, are there any positive entries for the other side of the ledger?" he asked with the same sideways half-smile that signaled irony or sarcasm.

"Well," offered Amelia, "at least there are no battlefields in Eastern North Carolina anymore. Things have calmed down. I also think we should count as a positive the likelihood that the Christian Commission will send supplies our way. It's been two weeks since I wrote them."

The next voice was that of Rachel. "Planting," she declared. "It's past the usual harvest time, but ye can still plant garden beans, rhubarb, cabbage, beets and all sorts of vegetables that will be ready by Christmas time. I tell ye, some even have more flavor after a frost. And ye can plant herbs in boxes and bring them inside during cold weather."

Surprisingly, it was quiet Matthew who kindled the most enthusiasm, probably because his ideas envisioned more immediate rewards. "I think there is more food on these farms than we realize," he said. "I see little signs of it when we make storm repairs. People are afraid to bring their goods to the towns and they are afraid to go hungry, so they preserve jars of many things – apples, corn, beets, tomato sauce – that make me hungry to look at them."

Matthew brightened at realizing he had an attentive audience. "Last week Antoine and I went to fix the roof of what they call a root cellar. Through the roof, I look down and I see potatoes. I see turnips. I see carrots and I think of a beautiful stew I could make for everyone here. But there are two ladies living there and I know they must eat, too. But then I say, not *that* much."

"Let us love, not just in word or speech, but in truth and action," called out a voice from the behind the table where they sat. "The book of John, 3:18." The voice was that of The Rev. Hiram Staley, who had been listening from the doorway to the sanctuary. He strode forth and stood next to DuBois. In his hand was a King James Bible and he began fumbling through the pages.

"Listen to Isiah, 58:18," he intoned. "If ye give something of thine own food to those who are hungry and to satisfy those who are humble, then thy light will rise in the dark and thy darkness will become as bright as the noonday sun."

"Amen," echoed Rachel.

Continued the reverend, his face flushed: "Thanks to God's grace and glory, I overheard ye discussing the very subject upon which I will be preaching this Sunday. At the conclusion, I will invite one and all to a meeting after church to discuss how we might sow and reap a bounty to share among ourselves and our neighbors at the maritime hospital. And as the sharers multiply, so will the body of our church!"

All were taken aback by the preacher's sudden enthusiasm. But Amelia was not about to let a newly-gained asset slip away. "Our biggest problem, Reverend Hiram, is the lack of bounty at this very moment. Do you know of any other ready sources of food for our fifty patients? Manna from heaven?"

The preacher stood in thought with Bible clutched between his hands. Then he said: "I would go out to the home of Doctor Samuel Drummond. It's a long walk, a mile or more past Doctor's Creek. Perchance you'll find him there, or more likely his wife Agatha. But I say, call and ask and ye may receive."

"The big white house with the white buildings beside?" asked Matthew. "If that's the one, we went out there. The woman shooed us away like we were crows in a cornfield."

"Well, could be that she was frightened," answered the preacher. "I know a few things that a pastor must keep in confidence. Rachel, why don't ye and Miss Beach take a walk out there tomorrow and have a woman-to-woman visit? And maybe you can get her to come to the service on Sunday."

On a cool, foggy Wednesday morning, only after the two had milked the cow and rolled a feeding cart through two hospital corridors, did Amelia Beach and Rachel Staley set out on their walk to the Drummond home. "I feel so...so emancipated," declared Amelia as they walked the footpath towards Doctor's Creek. "Except for going to the town dock, I have not yet been beyond your barn since I arrived here." They walked through a carpet of rust-colored marsh cordgrass until they came to Doctor's Creek, where sea oats and oyster beds lay exposed in the muddy low tide. A heron begrudgingly gave way as they climbed into the decrepit rowboat that settlers kept tethered on shore as a common ferry. They giggled like schoolgirls with each pulling an oar as they zigged-zagged across, crabs darting this way and that below the shallow surface.

On the other side, the morning mist began to dissolve and another dimension of Portsmouth Island revealed itself: otters playing along the shore, a grove of cordgrass hiding nests of brown pelicans. They followed a narrow path that passed by groves of scrubby pine trees with small farm fields at rest. Suddenly Amelia was seized with an overpowering sadness that made tears run down her cheeks. She turned her back on Rachel to compose herself.

"Ye all right?" said the little woman from inside her bonnet.

"Yes," answered Amelia. "For a moment, I was back on the Savannah coast. I was a little girl and my father took me on a walk just like this." She tried to change the subject. "Rachel, why do ye – you – think your husband changed so abruptly last night? I mean to say, he had hardly seemed to notice the hospital the whole time I've been here. Suddenly he seems so enthused in his support."

Rachel walked straight ahead, her bonnet obscuring her face like a mare with blinders. "Well, some folks take gettin' used to," she answered at last. "But could also have something to do with Drummond. Hiram is having to reckon with the likelihood that Doctor Drummond may not be with us anymore."

"Would that be good or bad?"

"Maybe good *and* bad," said Rachel. "Bad because old Drummond supports the church with generous donations. He brought that organ ye play on and he brought bells for the church tower all the way from Baltimore when the old ones wore out. When the collection plate comes up short, he refills it."

"And the good?"

Rachel walked on, silently shaking her head from side to side. "The same ribbons on gift boxes can be ropes that bind if'n it's the wrong giver," she said at last. "He can boss around a man who's supposed to answer only to God and his bishop. And that's all I'd better say about *that.*"

They passed a tattered farmhouse rimmed by a once-pretty picket fence that had been partly blown down by the storm, and this time Rachel was eager to change the subject. "That's the Mueller place," she said. "They probably need repairs, but they're too proud. And ye know what else? Could be that they don't have *church* shoes or clothes they think are fancy enough to be seen in. People are so proud, so afraid of being seen as poor. In any case, I don't see 'em in church anymore. Pity."

Rachel led on, commenting on each farmhouse and its occupants that came into view. "They all like the space between them and the next place over," she said, "but I think sometimes there's so much space that they all live like hermits. Maybe it lets 'em pretend that there's no war out there or maybe they owe someone money, but overall I don't think it's good. People need people."

"Well, that's the Drummond place yonder," Rachel said a few moments later. "It sits on what we call 'Back Creek.' It's our deepest and the best for tyin' up his schooners."

Drummond had built a rare two-story home with two oversized brick chimneys. The white house was flanked by two large outbuildings. "That one's a barn and the other 'un's for storage for his business," explained Rachel.

As they turned off the grassy, rutted footpath towards the house, the grandeur seen from afar had already begun to fade. The iron gate they had opened had become rusty and unhinged. Two undernourished cows grazed nearby and Rachel noted that "there used to be a salt lick for them cows. Now there ain't."

Soon a white-haired black man limped from the barn and stood squinting uncertainly into the morning sun.

"That would be Rufus," said Rachel. "I don't think he sees so good. He don't know who we are." She called out his name. He nodded with a warm smile and they met by the shell of the salt lick.

"Well, Miz Rachel, how you and the parson?"

"Fine. This here's Miss Amelia. She plays organ at the church. Works at the hospital. You keepin' this place up all alone?"

"Still tryin'," he said, shaking his head. "But I can't see so good no mo'. Like someone done pulled a sheet over my eyeballs. Doctor Drummond's nephew was supposed to come over from Greenville to help with the harvest, but I guess the army must'a got him. Doin' what I can, but you know, it's time to butcher the hog and smoke some ham, but I can't even wrassle dat hog."

Amelia broke in: "Maybe we can get someone to wrassle that...." But Rachel cut her off. "Miss Agatha in there?" she said, nodding toward the house.

"Oh yeah, she don't go nowhere these days."

"I imagine ye keep busy enough just tendin' to her needs," said Rachel with a wave as she guided Amelia towards the house. "Wife died a year ago and I wonder how long *he* has left."

The two women stepped over a rotted floorboard as they climbed the front porch stairs and knocked. The ceiling of the porch was a jumble of cobwebs, matted with trapped mosquitoes and spiders. "Don't say nothin' about the hospital 'til I see which way the wind's blowin'," said Rachel as they waited.

Eventually the door opened enough to reveal a thin, white-haired woman, peering over her pince nez spectacles. "Oh, Miss Rachel from the church," she said. "And?"

"And Miss Amelia Beach, our new organist. We just thought we'd take a stroll and come calling to see how you are." Rachel proceeded to tell Miss Agatha how lovely she looked and how beautiful her farm appeared when they had approached from the road. She quickly became another personality, sugary and obsequious. When they sat in the drawing room, Rachel oohed and ogled as Miss Agatha brought out three cups of real coffee, explaining that it was "company coffee" and that she'd "soon be with my chicory again."

When Miss Agatha explained that she had been reminiscing over a collection of daguerreotypes that she'd brought out from a parqueted box on the parlor table, Rachel said she couldn't wait to hear the story behind each and every one of the tintypes. Amelia joined in the nodding and nattering as Miss Agatha narrated the trips and occasions that had produced likenesses such as Senator Henry Clay, an elderly Andrew Jackson, the New York skyline, and the Liberty Bell in Philadelphia.

The last of the tintype plates was of a serious Samuel Drummond standing over a younger Agatha looking nervously at the black box facing them. "That's Sam and me in 1840 when they first started making daguerreotypes," she said. "We went on holiday to Baltimore and took one of the first steamboats on the Chesapeake Bay. We thought it was very exciting when it ran aground in some mud and took half a day to get off."

Rachel had been biding her time. "We haven't seen thy husband in quite a while," she interjected. "We miss him and I see there's no boat at thy dock. Has he been home lately?"

Agatha assembled her daguerreotypes into their box. "No. I know he was going on a long run and would be bringing some supplies to New Bern, but I haven't heard a thing what with the mail the way it is these days," she said. "He told me not to worry, but of course I do. I worry about Rufus, too. I don't think he can keep up with everything."

"Miss Agatha," said Rachel, "I think ye could use some brethren to keep ye company – someone to talk to besides sitting here all by thyself. Why not come to church this Sunday and see some old friends?"

"I don't know," said Agatha, her gaze fixed on the cupped hands in her lap. "The walk is quite long. I'm used to Sam taking me by boat."

"I have a boat!" exclaimed Amelia. "We'll call for you at your dock."

"I don't know," she repeated. "The war has made everything so...."

depressing. Then came the hurricane. Everyone looks so forlorn. Besides, I don't know what ever to wear."

"Miss Agatha, *nobody* knows what to wear!" replied Rachel. "Don't ye see? Everybody's clothes is threadbare, so everybody stays in their houses and avoid going to church."

The thin woman sat still on her Queen Anne sofa, turning one hand over the other. "I can see your point," she said, "but I think folks expect more from me because I'm, I'm…."

"The wife of Doctor Drummond, our leader and benefactor," interrupted Rachel. "Ye are indeed, praise the Lord."

Amelia jumped in before Rachel fell to groveling again. "We need your leadership, but the way to show it at this time is for you to dress as plainly as all the other ladies and take part in something we're going to meet about after church," she said. "We need to show our resilience in the face of hardship."

Amelia knew not whence the notion came, but there it was. "We're going to bring old skirts, dresses and hats, and you'll make a new lace collar for your old dress out of some other lady's old dress and it will become a new dress for the both of you."

Agatha's eyes brightened. "Well, I *am* a proficient seamstress, if I may declare so."

Amelia saw it as a door cracking open. "There's a lot we can do for food, too," she interjected. "You see, I am the chief nurse – the only nurse – at the maritime hospital, and we have a feeding problem. Most of our supplies have come from your husband's generous deliveries" [*oh my, now I am pandering, too*] "and these have ceased during his absence" [*must choose my words carefully*]. "Thus, the church is going to plant some vegetables on a common plot and share the bounty with everyone, including the hospital patients. We will put up preserves together and share them too."

Agatha Drummond was now listening and nodding. "I certainly have some catching up to do in that area," she said.

"One more thing," said Amelia, not daring to wait for any admonishments from Rachel. "We're also going to help each other with hurricane repairs. You see, because we need food supplies for the hospital, some of our staff and patients are already out fixing up roofs on houses, putting up torn down fences and the like. All they ask in turn are some small coins and donations of food staples."

"Patients repairing roofs?" she heard from Rachel.

No matter. Ideas were taking flight. "For example, Miss Agatha, I saw a damaged board on your porch step that could trip you at any time – or maybe Rufus with his poor eyesight, which could, God forbid, put an end to his service to you. One of our men can have things like that fixed in a jiffy. As a matter of fact, I have an idea."

"Oh dear," she heard Rachel mutter.

"Before I exhaust your kind hospitality, perhaps I could walk about outside with Rufus and see what we might do to help fix things around the property until Doctor Drummond returns."

Hearing no command to cease and desist, Amelia rose, thanked her hostess profusely, and all but bounded to the front door.

"Youthful energy," she heard Rachel say before the door was closed.

Amelia cautiously opened the barn door and saw Rufus sitting on a bundle of hay, smoking a corncob pipe. "Why that sounds right nice to me," he said after she explained her purpose. "Fust thing," he said, pointing directly overhead, "is this hole in the barn roof. Hurricane blew off a lot of shingles. I got 'em all collected, but I c'int climb up there to put 'em back on. Ever time it rains we get wet hay, and I'm 'fraid that the fust winter snow gonna make mush outa all our bales."

"You're in luck," answered Amelia. "We've got a sailor fella at the hospital who likes to climb ladders to tall places. What else can you show me?"

At the far end of the barn was a small pigpen that had an opening for a slop yard outside. "All we got now is two sows and a daddy," said Rufus. "Used to have a dozen, but two summers ago the Rebel army come through here and took off all but two. I guess we should thank 'em, because now we got us another sow. Doctor says it's time to kill the oldest one, but I got no bullets and I sure can't chase it around no mo."

"I've got a younger man who can do that for you," she said, thinking of Matthew but having no idea as to whether he'd ever butchered a pig.

Next, Rufus led her outside and behind the barn, where a vegetable garden was nearly smothered by a blanket of weeds. "I just can't get at it no mo," he said. "My knees done give out."

"What's in the ground?" Amelia asked.

"Cauliflower, kale, onion, cucumber, cabbage, and jus' about everth-ing," he said. "Each day I goes out and pulls out one thing or another and takes it back to the kitchen for Miss Agatha."

"We need to get it all out of the ground and get it jarred," said Amelia in the farm jargon she'd learned from Rachel. "You got a root cellar or a storeroom?"

"Over there," he said, pointing to the other side of the property. Amelia followed as Rufus shuffled towards a low white building as long as the barn. He unlocked the door and Amelia gaped in surprise as her eyes grew accustomed to the dim warehouse inside. Silhouetted against a smoky, cobwebbed window was a row of bacon and smoked hams, all hanging neatly on twine from ceiling hooks. Below were casks of grain and stacks of burlap. The scene resembled the cornucopia she'd imagined during hungry nights in bed, but the room smelled anything like the ideal horn of plenty. It was a mix of mildew and charred meat, overpowered by the pungent odor of fermentation.

A closer look inside the barrels showed why. "What's this one?" she asked Rufus.

"That's wheat. Doctor wanted some for flour and some for the cows, but it just done sat too long."

"This one?"

"Cornmeal. Supposed to go on Doctor's boat to some store, but it got left behind and it's turned bad." Rufus hung his head, as if it were all his fault.

They went down the row of barrels and burlap bags with Amelia asking critical questions like a government inspector. At the end of it she concluded that barrels of peas, rice, beans and sorghum were salvageable if one dug out a foot or two of the spoiled layers on top. The hanging rows of smoked pork were so unlike anything Amelia or the hospital patients had subsisted on that she blocked them out of her mind like the forbidden fruit of the Bible.

As Rufus turned to lead her out of the storehouse, Amelia spotted another barrel by itself in a corner. She peered over it and glimpsed something craggy and brown. Then her jaw fell open. *My God, it's full of nails – ten penny nails, already rusted brown as coffee.* Without saying a word, she scooped her hand in the middle of the barrel and put a large handful of nails in her skirt pocket, trusting that Rachel was right about Rufus' eyesight.

When they emerged from the storehouse, Rachel and Miss Agatha were standing on the front porch chatting. As Amelia began explaining the condition of the various barrels and bins in the building, it became obvious that the doctor's wife had never been inside. The same was evident when Amelia discussed hay bales, hogs and the vegetable garden, so she became simple and maternal. "Our volunteers will fix the things I mentioned in exchange for parts of your food supplies that are too much for you and the doctor to eat anyway. The only other thing we ask is that you come to church on Sunday and give us the benefit of your leadership."

Agatha nodded and gave both a timid hug before they departed down the walkway to the footpath toward home. As they looked back and waved, she waved in return.

"I think we convinced her," said Amelia when they were out of earshot.

"Ye sure did stir up her mind," answered Rachel. "Ye won't know if she's sorted it out until that boat comes to take her."

It had been a long day, but it was only one o'clock and they had the afternoon milking and evening hospital feeding before they could afford to think about being weary.

Sunday began with signs that autumn would soon be pushed aside by chilly gusts from the north. The ocean current had shifted to a southerly drift and the bluefish were already riding it down to warmer waters. Before long there would be frost on fields and ice caps on milk pails.

A chill that caused a parishioner to appreciate the warmth inside his church was ideal for the liberated Rev. Hiram Staley and the sermon he planned to deliver, for he intended to kindle fire in their hearts. Attired in black and a newly-pressed clerical collar, he stood at the door greeting each parishioner with renewed enthusiasm and was buoyed by the fact that Rachel's visits to church sisters in the past three days had drawn out more of them than at any time since the last Easter morning.

At five minutes to eleven the preacher looked back from the entrance foyer and noted that more than half of the pews were occupied. Of these, at least two-thirds were women. Most of the usual male churchgoers (and "usual" might embrace all who showed up more often than Christmas and Easter) were in army camps, lost in war, held as prisoners, or absent for the many excuses he'd heard for not visiting The Almighty in his house.

To punctuate his sermon points, the Rev. Hiram had asked the shipwreck

survivors to attend. Now three of them sat uneasily in the back pew – a curious collage, indeed, that made parishioners gawk and murmur as they
passed by: gaunt Charles, in the remnants of his southern plantation garb,
outsized Antoine in colorless slave cotton, looking nervous at his first white
church service; and in stark contrast next to him, another colored man in
a black frock coat, white shirt and gray silk vest that surpassed the attire of
any white male in all of Portsmouth Island.

At eleven, as the preacher prepared to close the front door, his expectations were culminated when Agatha Drummond, looking sheepish in a
plain white blouse and blue skirt, wobbled up from the dock path with
Matthew and Sailor Jimmy trailing behind. He motioned for the two men
to join their fellow shipwreck survivors, then strode down the aisle and
ceremoniously seated Sister Drummond in the first pew.

At that point Amelia took her seat at the organ to play the Call to
Worship, but Rev. Hiram signaled her to wait. He then stepped over to her
with his back to the congregation and whispered, "Amelia" (the first time
he had not addressed her as Miss Beach). "When I finish my sermon on
sharing, I am going to introduce thy people. Then I will ask ye to invite
everyone to the meeting after church.

"The Lord bless ye because I must tell ye: there will be no Christian
Commission in Portsmouth. I received a letter this week saying that they
are putting all their efforts into the rescue of New Bern."

"Is that why you are suddenly helping us?" she whispered back.

His answer: "Drummond has always forbidden the church to help the
hospital. He said it was 'government business.' But I knew he feared that
his own business might suffer. Now I say, 'He that oppresses the poor to
increase his riches shall surely come to want.' Proverbs, 22:16. Forgive me,
for I have been that man."

The reverend's heart was on fire that morning. He began with the evan-
gelist's most powerful weapon: shame. "The war and the hurricane have
caused us to withdraw into our homes and into the cellars of our minds,"
he intoned. "We hoard from fear. We fear that the military will come along
and take what we have – or even our very neighbors. So, one hoards sugar
but has no coffee. Another hoards coffee but has no sugar.

"The Bible has warned us of this condition since the days of Deuteronomy.

In chapter fifteen, verse eight, we hear, 'If there be among ye a poor man of one of my brethren within any of thy gates in thy land which the Lord thy God giveth them, thou shalt not harden thy heart, nor shut thine hand from thy poor brother. But thou should open thine hand wide unto him.'

"And this word from God Almighty has continued in nearly every book from Deuteronomy to the end of the New Testament," said the reverend with a vigor that had riveted everyone to his words. "I cite John 3:17. 'But whoso hath this world's goods and seeth that his brother hath need, and shutteth up his bowels of compassion for him, how dwelleth the love of God in him?'"

After a smattering of "amens," he cautioned that "the words of God are not just for men. For it sayeth in Proverbs 31: 19-20 that the woman 'layeth her hands to the spindle, and her hands hold the distaff. She stretches out her hand to the poor; yea, she reaches forth her hands to the needy.'"

The reverend raised his arms expansively. "Sharing one's possessions, no matter how small, can create a bounty for all who do it. Yes, one plus one can become, not just two, but three, four or five. Did not our Lord and Savior demonstrate this when he fed the five thousand with just one basket of five loaves and two fish?

"I am going to show ye how we in this church can do the same thing," he declared. "Next week, on a plot right behind this church, we – all who join in – will begin planting a winter garden. Yes, a garden that can grow broccoli, cauliflower, carrots, kale, onions and dozens of root plants in summer can also grow them in frost and even snow. Sisters, ye might not have a man at home, but ye might have seeds to contribute. Brothers, even though the years may have bent thy back and made thy knees creaky, ye can help plant and hoe a small plot. If not, we will have some strong men to help. And when we achieve abundance, all who helped will share, with enough left over for those in need."

The amens became less inhibited as the reverend snapped the reins on his sermon. "Yes, there are some here who are in need, but there are others hungry and in need right next door to this church. I am referring to the marine hospital with fifty patients who have been abandoned by the government that is supposed to care for them."

The preacher cupped an ear theatrically. "Harken! Do I hear some whispering that residing therein are *enemy* prisoners? Yes, if ye are for the Union ye will find Confederate patients there, maimed by the ravages of war. If ye are of Southern persuasion, there are Union soldiers who were wounded fighting thy brothers and cousins. If ye were a slave owner, there are even newly-freed coloreds living there.

"But do we live by the word of God or sinful selfishness?" he said with a finger pointed heavenward. "Listen to the words of our Savior that begin in Luke, 6:27: 'Bless them that curse you, and pray for them which despitefully use you.' Jesus goes on to say that if ye love only those who love ye and do good only to those who do good to ye, what have ye gained? For even sinners love those who love them. 'But love ye your enemies, and do good, and lend, hoping for nothing again; and thy reward shall be great....'"

The Reverend Hiram left the podium and stood at the altar. His voice rose. "The great Saint Paul preached this as well after our Lord and Savior had risen. When sentenced to go before the emperor Nero in Rome, the ship carrying Paul sank in a storm with over two hundred souls aboard. When they washed up on the island of Malta, they included Greeks, Romans, Jews, slaves and all manner of survivors who were strangers to the Maltese. But did these Maltese shut up their doors or agree to feed and clothe only those of a similar ilk? No. They opened their hearts and doors to strangers of all colors and nationalities.

"Today we have the same situation right here on Portsmouth Island," he declared with finger pointed at the congregation. "In addition to the sick soldiers in our hospital next door, they include six persons who came to us two months ago as survivors of a shipwreck. And they are of all backgrounds. If you gentlemen in the back will stand up,"

They rose awkwardly.

"I would like the congregation to meet Matthew, a citizen of the Bahamas; Antoine, from the French Caribbean, Charles, the English captain of the ship that was wrecked off Beaufort; Jimmy, a sailor from the same ship; and Mr. Felix DuBois, a prominent French citizen and diplomat. All of these men are doing their best as volunteers to help the unfortunate patients of the marine hospital and they have graciously agreed to help us plant our winter garden and make hurricane repairs on our properties."

A ripple of applause broke out.

"Ah, I noticed that some of ye were counting the number of persons who stood up. I said there were six, didn't I. Well, the sixth is our very own organist, Amelia Beach, whose home is in Savannah, Georgia. And she is going to speak to ye now."

Amelia felt clumsy, oxen-footed as she made her way from the organ to the pulpit.

Pulpit too tall. Never made a speech. People just gawking out there. Knees wobbly. Just plow on through.

"Brothers and sisters," she began. *First time I ever called anyone that.* "As Reverend Hiram said, most people here have repairs to be made after the hurricane and some don't have the men or the tools and nails to do it. So, we have some men at the hospital who are skilled in all sorts of crafts and who are prepared to help. All they want in return is for you to donate a little food to the hospital. I am happy to say that we have a leader in this respect. Sister Agatha – Mrs. Samuel Drummond – has already agreed to donate some peas and rice to our patients."

Amelia saw a few people fidget in their seats and she held her arms up. "Now for a very important announcement," she nearly yelled. "We're going to gather in the social hall behind you right after the service so you can write down your needs on a sheet of paper. Then we're going to have a meeting. We will be planting the winter garden next Wednesday and we'll have sign-ups for that. But we're also going to have some important events where we share our talents and whatever else we can spare. So please come back and hear all about them."

At the conclusion of the service, most of the parishioners filed into the social hall, no doubt driven by the notion that they could get some free house repairs just by signing a paper. When the door was closed behind them, Amelia seized the small podium, having shed her stage fright.

"From now on," she announced loudly, "we are going to have a potluck supper after each church service. I know that fills some of you with dread because you think you're supposed to walk in with a chocolate cake made from white flour, or a beef casserole that won a blue ribbon at the county fair before the war. But that's not the purpose. And it's why we're calling these "Sunday Substitute Suppers." *I just made this up from thin air.* "The goal will be to make what you can from a substitute – such as a dessert using sorghum instead of sugar – to see who is the most clever and imaginative. The one with the best idea – and it must be pleasing to the palate – will get a special prize. And the special prize will probably be a surprise concoction as well."

A sprinkle of laughter. "And I almost forgot," shouted Amelia. "At each Sunday Substitute Supper, we'll also have a special prize for the best coffee not made from coffee beans. The intention here is that we can learn from each other and please our families until this war is over."

More buzzing. "And finally," shouted Amelia, "during the next month we will begin Women's Wednesday – *just made that up, too* – starting next week. On the first week, we will bring seeds and shoots and plant our winter garden. The second Wednesday we will have a clothing fair. Bring your old dresses or curtains or men's pants and together we'll make them into something new.

"The Wednesday after that we'll exchange ideas for shoemaking. Everyone agrees that shoes are the biggest single shortage in this war. So, we're going to bring old pieces of leather, wood, carpets and other materials and learn from each other how to make the best footwear possible."

By the time Amelia stepped away from the podium, women were clustered about her with questions and others were buzzing in the background. *All we need is a dozen to show up.*

When everyone had departed, Amelia picked up the sign-up sheet for hurricane repairs. She counted eighteen names. Rachel, who had been standing near the door and watching, walked up and looked over her shoulder. "How ye going to get thy men to do all that work?" she asked.

"Don't know yet," said Amelia.

"What is the hospital going to gain from all that work?"

"Don't know yet."

"When you gonna tell these women that they got to donate part of those crops they plant?

"Don't know yet, but before it's over I hope they'll be donating food, clothes and shoes. First, we get them out of their homes and busy. Then maybe Hiram will pray and the Lord will hear."

<hr>

The Beach Beacon

Oct. 26, Wed.

Weather holding fine. Chilly 45 degrees in morning, then up to 75. Today I saw eight men plant a plot bigger than the size of the church. Helped by ground still soft from the big storm. On a farm tilled by one husband, it might have seemed too daunting even to begin. But today eight men (two from the hospital) had it done by afternoon. Rev. Hiram there in person with pitchfork to set an example! Two plus two does equal five, he proclaims to one and all.

We have 18 "share" croppers. Some brought seeds, some replanted the runts of pumpkins, squash, sweet potatoes already picked this fall. We also have in the ground: green beans, collards, broccoli, onions, Brussel sprouts, kale, cabbage, turnips, beets. Probably other stuff, too. Some muttering at first about things like "them's what brung seeds should get more share than them what didn't." But Hiram says we all share equally like the first disciples. I chime in and say the hospital will get half of everything. People look at Hiram, but no one argues. Meanwhile, I get to look out from my bedroom window and watch things grow. They say onions will pop up first.

Felix DuBois taking more direct role at hospital. Jimmy and I not to do feedings anymore. Floor captains will do that plus make patients do clean-ups. I see the proffering of The King's Grog at work here. Now I'm only to make rounds before dinner to check up on patients, write letters, etc. Good that mosquitoes and bugs waning with cooler weather, but colder nights mean more need for warm clothes. I still worry about what I can't see.

Felix and Jimmy want healthier patients to help with storm repair projects and the like. When Rachel says we should cover the new field with mulch to protect against frost, Felix promises to have the "best" patients go out and rake up pine needles to spread on top. More promises of King's Grog, I suspect. If mulching works, Jimmy and Antoine will pick a few patients for repair work on farms. The goal is to get men moving again, thinking about life after the hospital. And that could be soon if Hawkes comes with the boat for the Point Lookout POW camp.

Oct. 30, Sun.

First potluck after church. About a hundred at the service today and about half brought dishes. Those who didn't were leaving church when Rev. Hiram 'intercepted" them at the doorway implored one and all to come to the social hall. Everyone took smaller portions as he urged them to share like the disciples. I saw almost no evidence of meat, as if people were reluctant to be seen as bragging about having such a luxury in their home. Instead, I saw a flask of oil from sunflower seeds, sorghum pie made with crushed peanuts, rice bread, cornbread, beet vinegar and several fruit cakes. The prize dish, Rev. Hiram decided, was a fruit cake made with dried cherries, dried whortleberries, candied watermelon and molasses.

The lack of enough to make stomachs full was outweighed by the lively conversations across the tables – neighbors who hadn't visited one another in months, some with Rebel leanings, some with Union. But they didn't talk about whose son killed another's. They talked about finding food and using "Secession" recipes. To wit: I sat next to a Mrs. Babb, who said she had so many wild sweet potatoes around her place she scarcely knew what to do with them. She told how she cooked them baked and mashed, then how she even ground them into flour and made "bread." She also grated them raw and mixed them in salt to produce a pancake she calls "potato pone." Everyone wanted her recipes, and the whole time they were talking they were drinking what they assumed to be coffee. Turns out it's Mrs. Babb's own sweet potato coffee. She cuts sweet potatoes into small cubes and bakes them a crisp dark brown. Then the grinds them in a coffee mill and adds hot water. People were astounded at the good taste and Mrs. Babb won the prize for best substitute coffee. In her excitement, she called me an "angel." If she only knew.

Charles sat next to me at our table. He no longer shivers and says he doesn't sleep under a mound of blankets. His charm and wit seem to be returning, for he entertained the ladies at our table with his old aplomb. When Mrs. Babb mentioned using salt in making "potato pone," his eyes brightened and he wanted to know how she came about the salt. Our jaws dropped when she said her husband (dead now) didn't use big kettles. He used a large piece of old sailcloth – stretched it just above ground between four stakes and cut a small hole in the middle for drainage. Then he would go out to the creeks, scoop up brine and spread it on the sailcloth to dry in the sun. Salt is what's left. She says she still has the sailcloth and Charles is eager to go give it a try. Whether or not it works, Charles is back with us in spirit and we need his enthusiasm. Whether back with me I know not.

Best part of the day is that a Mrs. Conley answered my call for hospital volunteers. Lives just up the road near the schoolhouse. She will visit us tomorrow and we will find some suitable work for her. She is the angel – not me.

Nov. 3, Thurs.

Had the first "Clothing Fair" yesterday morning. Thirty or so women bring-ing old draperies, curtains, damasks, velvets, pillowcases and such for mak-ing into "new" clothes. Much talk about wearing homespun dresses in public. Learned that whereas in the deep South homespuns are actually preferred, Richmond ladies won't be seen in them. But that was laughed at by the Portsmouth Islanders. One quoted a poem, of which I remember only two lines: "The dress I now wear for thee, was a curtain in old Philadelphee."

Alas, I saw more talk and gossip than work. In fairness, some had no nee-dles. But they love talking about making hats and bonnets, which is easier to do with the scraps they brought. Much imagination shown: use of grasses, leaves, straw, wheat, oats, wiregrass and palmettos. Once you construct the hat, then you add little touches such as chicken feathers or pieces of ribbon purloined from worn-out hats.

Was good to see such enthusiasm, but I saw no clothes being made for hospital patients to wear with winter coming on, so I suggested we have a Spinning Bee the next week. That prompted a discussion about how many looms could be brought into the church and what materials to use. Again, I am amazed at the human imagination. Women here are already combining old wool with rabbit hair, dog hair, horsehair – even old mattress stuffing – to produce a wool-like material for making clothes. Even more important, it seems, is making underwear that doesn't chafe and itch.

As the last of them were leaving and I was feeling rather empty about the results, Elsie Conley asked me to join her. This is the soft-spoken "angel" who has begun visiting patients. Although she is probably near forty, she is too pretty to meet the Union army nursing standards, but I am the Dorothea Dix here! We went outside to the buckboard she had ridden over on and it had an old trunk in the rear. When she opened it, she explained that it was her late husband's clothing – everything from overalls to a Sunday suit to one of his uniforms, which was Union, I learned for the first time. She asked if they "might be of use" to the patients, and I was already gushing tears of joy before she finished. It made the day a success.

Must remember this: wheat bran boiled with water then used to wash dresses restores "body" and prevents fading. But what isn't already faded?

Mrs. Salter gave me a poem from a magazine about the hat-making rage.

Who now of famine dare complain
When female foreheads teem with grain?
See the wheat sheaves amid the plumes,
Our barns have become our drawing rooms,
And husbands who indulge in active lives
To fill their granaries, may thresh their wives.

"Miss Beach, Miss Beach!" Two Union patients jumped up from their front porch chairs and hastened to the office where Amelia was in lively discussion with DuBois about which of their charges was fittest for farm repair work. "Looks like the supply boat again," one of them exclaimed.

They walked out and, squinting into the bright morning sun, made out the familiar form of a skiff being rowed ashore by four men as a large schooner wallowed at anchor in deeper water. *Back home if someone wished to pay you a visit, they would send a servant around with a letter announcing the time of calling. But not in the military. They just show up and expect you to pack up everything and jump on a boat before anyone has time to prepare. Yes, it's him again, just like last time,* tall, bearded Captain Benjamin Hawkes standing in the bow like that painting of George Washington crossing the Delaware. Amelia's heart jumped and her breath quickened, brushing aside the Better Judgment that was supposed to guide the Matron of Hospital.

As during the month before, the three sat on the front porch as Matthew helped Hawkes' men unload the provisions onto a cart that would lead them to his storehouse. But this time Hawkes accepted Amelia's offer of water from the cistern. "The yellow fever's subsiding in New Bern and our provost marshal at Fort Macon has ended the quarantine," he said. "But they count over three thousand dead in New Bern…people of all stripes."

They talked about the weather on the journey to Portsmouth Island, but Amelia could see that Hawkes kept a serious mien, as if wanting to end light talk quickly because he had information to impart.

"What news have you for us?" she interrupted at last.

Hawkes took a deep breath and straightened up in his porch chair. "At our first meeting I talked about taking your Confederates away soon," he said in a voice so low that the others had to lean in. "Previously, we were unable to find the transport to do so, but now I can say it with assurance. Sometime in mid-December a gunboat will arrive offshore to pick up all of your patients who are able to travel – sick or not. The Confederates will be deposited at Point Lookout and the Union men will be sent to Washington for redeployment or release to the care of their families."

"How can you say this with such certainty?" asked DuBois with a dubious frown on his brow.

"I can because it's all part of a military plan," said Hawkes. "Last month my superiors didn't know what to do with any of you. Now they do."

"Well, what are the plans?" asked Amelia. *He seems so cold and officious. Does he remember the warmth of that moment just a month ago?*

"These are military secrets," he repeated in the same hushed tones.

"You want us to cure and clothe all these men and convince them to leave without offering us a single explanation?" she said. *I know you have a heart, but you keep it hidden.*

Hawkes sat with his long legs extended on the porch, gazing out at the anchored schooner. "All right, I'll tell you just enough to convince you," he said. A Union patient had wandered out on the porch expecting some fresh air, but quickly turned on his heel when the captain motioned him away. "But any word of this to Confederates *or* Union and I will see you both arrested and prosecuted."

"I am a French citizen," said DuBois.

"I'm already a Confederate," said Amelia.

"And I will have been hung before you go on trial," said Hawkes. He looked comically sheepish and all three broke out laughing as if acknowledging together that three people on forlorn Portsmouth Island weren't about to influence the war.

"Your word then," Hawkes said, and they nodded. "You know that Wilmington is the last port open to the blockade runners and that Wilmington feeds the major railroad that supplies General Lee's defenses in Richmond. This is why the Union is assembling a massive armada of warships for an all-out attack on Fort Fisher. The War Department is betting heavily that Lee will be forced to surrender within a few weeks. The invasion date has already been fixed."

"So far Portsmouth Island remains uninvolved," DuBois observed.

"But it is," said Hawkes. "The battle's aftermath has been planned down to the detail and Portsmouth Island is one of the details. Heavy casualties are expected because the naval assault on Fort Fisher may include a land invasion as well. Union casualties will be treated aboard a hospital ship stationed nearby. But since there are no facilities for Rebel wounded, one of the gunboats will transport the worst cases here to this hospital until they can be patched up enough to be sent on to Point Lookout."

"The worst cases?" said Amelia, wide-eyed.

"Yes," he nodded. "This is war and it's the best we can do for them. The army hopes to assign a surgeon here – perhaps a Confederate if they can capture one – because most of these cases will be artillery and gunshot wounds. They certainly won't be the Buffalo Rebel cases you have now. General Burnside in New Bern wants them all gone, as I told you before. And if they aren't all personally accounted for on the gunboat to Point Lookout, the general intends to hunt them down. In any case, we need all possible beds here available well before the planned battle."

Now it was Felix DuBois who broke in. "Please tell me something. On your first trip you came with four men. This time you came with six and two of them are sitting over there against a tree, doing nothing. Why?"

Amelia had scarcely noticed two young Union soldiers, sitting hunched with arms around their knees, their forage caps pulled over their eyes.

"I am coming to that subject," answered Hawkes. "Just as the army began relaxing its guard against yellow fever, we found that these two men have come down with something else. They have been diagnosed only having something the medics described as 'eruptive fevers.' They both have lesions – skin rashes – that could be early smallpox, scarlet fever, or measles. Or perhaps even the world's oldest social disease, although they deny any such contact. In any case, the policy from general headquarters requires that they be quarantined and observed until something can be confirmed or they simply get better. We don't know where they got it. All we know is that we can't risk endangering five hundred men at Fort Macon."

"So you shipped them to us," said DuBois with a hard look.

"Yes. You run a hospital, so you've been telling me. We cannot jeopardize the men at Fort Macon at a very critical time when they are supposed to be fit for battle. You are on an island where these cases can be more easily isolated for a few weeks until everyone here departs."

"So we have an added incentive to get these men healthy enough to travel," said Amelia.

"Yes," Hawkes replied, again lowering his voice. "But I must order you not to tell them until they see the gunboat out there. We can't have any more Buffalo Rebels scattered out there in the woods."

Suddenly Amelia felt a heavy sadness. DuBois seemed to be brooding as well. A challenging, already-rewarding adventure was about to be interrupted before it had achieved a happy, healthy ending. Images flashed through her mind: Lucas and Jerome condemned to a filthy tent city with forty thousand lost souls; gaunt, morose Union boys clutching newly-issued rifles in another killing field; Amelia tiptoeing about her home in Savannah while Union generals spread maps over the dining room table and smoke smelly cigars.

Perhaps Hawkes was reading their thoughts. "It's better not to let word slip out and set anyone off ruminating," he said with a tight smile. "Townspeople start locking up their homes in anticipation of some unknown horror. And soldiers are unsurpassed at imagining the worst – I suppose because they are the first to be thrust in the path of death.

"This is why everyone from generals to field officers don't issue orders to break camp until the last moment," said Hawkes, his eyes careening between Amelia and DuBois with a pleading expression. "It's just what generals do and soldiers expect. If you want your patients prepared for their next journey in life, you must see that they are healthy, well-fed and in good spirits."

Both nodded silently with no expression. "I do have a little something to cheer you up," he said brightly. "Still sequestered in the boat is a case of whiskey that I appropriated at great peril to myself. We had a platoon transferred elsewhere last week and they left what I judged to be some excess inventory in the rations storage room. So I had it 're-deployed,' one might say, to another government facility on this island.

"And I brought something for you as well, Miss Beach," he said looking into her curious eyes for the first time. He reached into the satchel that stood at his feet and Amelia brightened at the thought that it was a letter from her parents. Instead, he produced a thick volume. "This is a new medical book published just this year – *The Practice of Medicine in the Union Army*. Maybe it can help you with these fellows," he said with a nod at the two still leaning against the same tree trunk. "One thing that amazed me was the author's contention that more than half of the fatalities on both sides have come from disease."

Hawkes opened the book, where he had marked a page with a scrap of paper, and read:

The fire of an enemy never decimates an opposing army. Disease is the fell destroyer of armies and stalks at all times through encampments. Where balls have destroyed hundreds, insidious diseases, with their long train of symptoms, and quiet, noiseless progress, sweep away thousands.

"So, you see," he added, "those two men were brought here because they might save hundreds. And you and your staff are the real heroes of the war. I can't award you medals – only whiskey."

Dinner that night was supposed to be a celebration of "fresh" food and new company, or at least a respite from drab, boring fare and predictable conversation. Instead, the new supplies consisted mostly of hardtack, beans and smoked fish, which even Saint Matthew could barely camouflage. As for conversation, Captain Hawkes quickly deflected questions about the war, even though most of them had come from his military counterpart, Captain Charles Timmons. When Charles pressed him for a date on which the shipwreck survivors might be taken off "this dreary island," Hawkes would retreat into vague excuses about "shortage of transport" and promises of "soon, I hope."

This left Amelia parrying with Hawkes about what to do with the two men with "eruptive fevers." Upon closer inspection, both were boys of eighteen and nineteen. Hawkes insisted they be quartered in their field tents, apart from the other four soldiers from Fort Macon. Upon his departure the next morning, Amelia and DuBois would be free to figure out how to quarantine and cure.

That night, as usual, Amelia donned a cotton nightgown, dabbed at herself with a washcloth from the catcher of tepid water on her small nightstand, and sat on the edge of her bed thumbing through her new medical textbook in the flickering light of her oil lamp. But her mind kept wandering away from medicine. Charles had sat by her side throughout the dinner discussion and, towards the end, had put his hand over hers as he conversed with Hawkes across the table. The open gesture seemed to be meant for Hawkes, who looked down the first time but continued talking as if it were of no consequence. Charles remained until there were only the three of them, and until Hawkes rose with some parting patter about having a hard day and needing to rise early for the next.

There would be no late whiskey, intimate confessions, no caress, no warming of the soul. And now the distraction that kept intruding on her reading was none other than her disappointment.

In her bedroom, the black metal doorknob was directly in front of her and Amelia suddenly reeled back to see it turning before her eyes. Her right hand reflexively reached back across the bed for the cowbell that had lain on the nightstand like an ornament until that moment. But before she could shake it, the door cracked open, revealing the face of Charles Timmons. He slipped inside with a finger to his lips, his boots dangling from one hand.

"I miss you tucking me in at night," he whispered, "so I came to tuck *you* in."

Amelia was breathless with the surprise. Charles sat awkwardly on the bed beside her, then put his arm around her waist and squeezed. "You see, I think my ribs have healed," he murmured.

She could feel him begin to nudge her down on the bed, but she sat ramrod stiff. "Why now? Why here?" was all she could manage.

"Well, that Hawkes fellow is leaving tomorrow," whispered Charles, re- laxing his hold on her. "We need to press for a fixed departure *now*. I think he may be waiting for us to offer money. The last time he was here he said that the boat captain would want money to take us to Baltimore."

"You think I have some money?" she whispered back. All she had to her name was the last of the two Spanish gold chains, and in her mind it was always reserved for her passage back to home and civilization.

"What about your parents?" he said. "Are you expecting any money from them in the mail?"

"It's possible, but I haven't asked them for any." Their voices were rising and she put her finger to her lips. "Charles," she whispered, "in any case I don't know if I can go to Baltimore until I learn what fate my parents have met in Savannah. And have you stopped to think about my own fate? I could arrive in Baltimore only to find that I am on a government 'wanted' list for being a Confederate spy. Have you forgotten that horrid American consul in Nassau?"

Charles hung his head, eyes on the floor. "Well, I have no choice but to go," he said. "If the navy hasn't already listed me as AWOL, I'm sure it will be a struggle to return to active duty. I was thinking that perhaps your father might enclose some of the back pay they owe me for the earlier runs."

'Maybe he will. I understand your situation," she said lamely. *Just tell him what you already know and it will ease his mind.* The thought repeated in her head as they sat side by side, but something held her back – something beyond just keeping "her word" to Hawkes. *It's the wheedling and the whining tone of voice. Does he love me at all?*

Just then Charles put his arm around her again and this time pushed her back on the bed. When she squirmed to resist, the bed squeaked, one of his boots fell to the floor with a *clunk* and the cow bell followed with a louder *CLACK*.

Both sat up rigidly, ears attuned for a response from Hiram or Rachel. It came quickly. A faint yellow glow came from the window of their bedroom down the hall, then footsteps and a knock on the door. The doorknob turned again and there was Rachel in a tattered robe with a lit candle.

"What have we here?"

"Our apologies," said Amelia with arms folded across her nightgown. "Just talking about things."

"Well, ye know how Reverend Hiram feels about unmarried couples in bedrooms," she croaked. "I suggest ye go down to the church and finish talking about these things – unless it ain't fittin' for God's house."

Chapter Seventeen

RESILIENCE, NOVEMBER 1864

A s Benjamin Hawkes' schooner faded from sight over the early morning horizon, so did his words of reassurance that the patients from Portsmouth Island would be transferred to "a better place." The medical textbook he had brought plainly indicated otherwise, and Amelia's spirits sagged as she underscored and re-read passages from a report by one John Wooley, a U.S. Army surgeon who had made a tour of prison camps.

The men are unwashed, their clothes filthy, bodies full of vermin, and heaps of garbage lie about. Especially needed is policing of latrines. Trenches are too shallow, not the requisite five feet deep, and daily covering with dirt is entirely neglected. Large numbers of men will not use the toilets but use instead every clump of bushes and every fence border. It is impossible to step outside the encampment without having both eye and nostril continually offended.

Although the book offered encouraging reports as to various medicaments, Amelia's readings always left her with a heavy sadness. *Am I – are we – merely fattening calves for slaughter? Or can I believe Hawkes that men made healthier here will be better able to survive the war and return home to resume normal lives?*

But then the bustle of the day would interrupt and set more immediate thoughts in motion. This Wednesday, November 14, was to be the first "Shoemaking Festival," and some thirty women, all oblivious to the ominous military secret known only to Amelia and DuBois, were filing into the church social hall carrying totes and carpetbags full of worn-out shoes and so many varieties of scrap material that ladies were laughing over who had brought the oddest assortment. And there was Reverend Hiram, escorting Agatha Drummond, who had arrived with Rufus. He was carrying an old leather saddle and battered riding boots.

Said one woman: "I must confess that I seldom go out walking anymore because I fear wearing out my only pair of decent shoes." Heads nodded and other tales of hardship poured out as women spread their offerings out on a long table. "Confederate dogs must be trembling everywhere," one of them observed as another produced a dog skin. "A shoemaker would pay a dollar for it if we had a shoemaker," replied the first.

Said another: "My husband says that no sensible man in the South would leave his horse tethered outside a store or post office. When he came out, he'd find the saddle had been appropriated to make leather soles."

All of which prompted more ideas on where to find and use leather scraps. Riding boots were most coveted because the tops could be made into ladies' and children's shoes. One could also make children's' shoes from the morocco bindings found in books and purses. Old leather reins could be cut into strips to make shoelaces or bind sandals.

Mixed in the table talk were admissions of ingenuity – caused by desperation – that would not have been forthcoming in earlier days. Using wood, for example. "I hear tell of a factory upstate that produces a hundred pairs of shoes a day," offered one lady. "They have leather tops attached to wooden soles. And they say they will last until the next war."

"Well, if you come into my house with them, you'll have to leave them at the door," said another. "My neighbor made some herself and they tear up my floors and carpets whenever she visits."

They moved on to carpets. A woman reported that her cousin in Virginia wrote that she had made her children shoes from an old carpet, lined with flannel. "Well, I've heard of shoes made from sail canvas, and Lordy, we still have enough of that," said a table mate. Talk drifted to stories about other people: using felt from old hats, knitting a foot wrap and inserting a sole made of pasteboard, or simply wrapping the feet oriental style. After the stories had petered out, one woman piped up: "My husband said my pie crust was so hard he could wear it on his feet as soles." Laughter, and then: "My husband said he was going to paint his feet black so everyone would think he had shoes and socks on."

In the midst of the cheerful chatter Amelia ventured that perhaps a half-dozen or so patched-up shoes could go to the Confederates in the hospital, some of whom had holes in their soles from their long treks as fugitives. Heads nodded in agreement with no peep of resistance.

Then came the squeaky voice of Rachel Staley: "We could use more volunteers over there once or twice a week, I think it's time to revive the Ladies' Aid Society. How many could volunteer once or twice a week?"

Four hands went up timidly. *Just like that*, Amelia said to herself. *That makes six.* Then another voice said, "Miss Amelia, maybe you could play some songs on the organ for us. It can get too quiet in here."

"Well, maybe I might could," said Amelia, having grown comfy with Carolina idiom. "But only if y'all join me in singing some of them." In a few moments, she and two of the heftier women had wheeled in the pump organ from the sanctuary, as was the custom for social events. They sang along for several minutes, but the volume gradually diminished because, as one woman put it, "I guess I'm just too dull-witted to make all my stiches and remember words to songs at the same time."

"I should bring over some of the boys from the hospital," Amelia mused aloud. "I hear all sorts of songs over there, and I don't just mean hymns. I hear Irish sea chanties, Rebel fight songs, Yankee drinking songs and some that should never reach a lady's ears."

"Well then, we should get a reader of fine books or poetry like the cigar makers do," added a farm wife while scissoring a scrap of old cowhide. "Problem is, there's scarcely a man around here who's even read a book."

Amelia played two more hymns then let the music die out, but the idea began to mulch in her mind. *Reader of fine books? None more so than Felix DuBois. And wouldn't he be a curiosity in this white citadel? A black scholar orating in a French accent. Singing? Maybe a sailor's jig from Jimmy. Maybe a quartet of patients. Yes, two from each floor – another way to break down the walls that isolate them. Who? Well, start listening, start asking! Next Wednesday's topic will be knitting. Ladies will be moved at the sight of thread-bare young men. More socks and mittens for winter. Mittens to keep away frostbite in flimsy POW tents. Stop. Don't go there.*

It was nearly four o'clock when the shoemakers packed their kit bags and drifted away. Amelia, leaving the church with a bulky carpet bag, decided to go looking for DuBois before her new ideas evaporated. She found him in his tidy small office, making entries in the hospital ledger, which he had pre-empted from the U.S. Treasury Department. He was also counting coins as he placed them in a metal box on the desk. The managing director had also assumed the role of straw boss in assigning patients to various repair jobs, rewarding them with The King's Grog and lesser emoluments. Jimmy, every-one's sailor-nurse, had named the volunteers "The Hurricane Handymen."

DuBois looked up as he heard Amelia's footsteps in front of him and asked, "What is in that sack?"

"And what ees een your leevrah," she countered in her Savannah drawl.

He rolled his eyes in mock horror as he always did when she maimed the French language. "I am putting two dollars and twenty cents into our treasury, representing a day's work by two men at the farm of a Madame Mason. This brings us to just over seventeen dollars, which should get us about seventeen miles towards Baltimore when they learn we have no more money and throw us overboard.

"But that is not all," he declared with a flourish, pointing to a cake box on the shelf. "We have a fruit cake from a grateful Madame Mason. Too small to be divided among the patients here, so what shall we do with it?"

"Donate it to the needy hospital staff for tonight's dessert," Amelia answered without hesitating.

"Like Pontius Pilate, I shall wash my hands of any such decision," he said, rising to hand her the cake box. "And the purpose of your visit?"

"You'll be surprised." Amelia began embroidering a flower on a swatch of truth. "The ladies were mending shoes at the church today," she said. "Everything had become rather quiet when one of them spoke up, saying it would be lovely if someone knowledgeable in literature could read poetry or passages from books to us just like the cigar makers do. Everyone thought it would be a wonderful idea, but I didn't have the nerve to ask what this has to do with cigar makers."

"Ah, Miss Beach, that is *facile*," he said. "It all began years ago in a Havana cigar factory, where the men rolling tobacco became just as bored with dull work as your ladies. So they had one of their older men sit on a tall stool in the corner and read great books aloud to them. It has since become a hallowed tradition in most cigar factories."

"So, will you be the one to do it?"

"Sit on a stool in the corner?"

"Not necessarily," she said. "Anything you wish. You certainly look the part."

"What part?"

"The part of a distinguished man of letters. And your French accent makes you seem a man of charm and mystery."

"But I *am* a man of charm and mystery," he said with feigned solemnity.

"Then you'll do it!" she exclaimed.

"Well, my repertoire is quite limited," he replied. "My library consists of the contents of one trunk. But it does include some poems by Byron and Robert Browning."

"Something French would be even better."

"Really?"

"Yes. They might not be able to understand everything, but they just love to hear about anything French."

DuBois agreed to his debut at the following Wednesday's knitting circle, which had Amelia changing the subject before he could reconsider. "Now for the Sunday potluck suppers," she rolled on. "We need some entertainment to liven things up and draw more people, so the ladies today suggested that we cast about the hospital and find a quartet of patients who could sing songs that go beyond the same old church hymns. I would like to try to recruit two Rebs from upstairs and two Yankees from the first floor. If we could find decent singers, we could convey that we have harmony in the hospital. Perhaps it would spread throughout..."

"You need to change one thing," DuBois interrupted. "Start with four men from upstairs or four from downstairs."

"How is that supposed to breed harmony?" she said with a trace of pique.

"It will not at first," he said, "but if you promise four men from one floor a special ration of King's Grog, the ones on the other floor will become jealous and combative. They will want to supply four of their own men, which now gives you two singing groups or an octet."

At that point Amelia lifted her heavy carpetbag and pulled out four pairs of newly-repaired leather shoes. "You are brilliant, monsieur and I have learned from you," she said triumphantly. "These shoes should be reward enough for the first group and drive the rest of them wild with envy."

"And they in turn will inspire your ladies to make more shoes," said DuBois with a tutorial air.

Just then they heard a rap on the door and looked up to see Mrs. Conley, their first volunteer and the first to donate old clothes. "I am fortunate to have found you here together," she said with a nervous tremor.

"I was just leaving for the day and wanted to offer a proposal."

She seemed so solemn that the other two could only say "Yes?" in unison.

"I can no longer abide by those two out there in that tent with winter coming on," she said in the same quivering voice. They knew she was referring to the two young Union soldiers with suspected contagious fevers. Captain Hawkes had ordered them to remain outside in one of the army field tents until he returned. Since he hadn't stipulated where the tent should be located, DuBois had agreed to have it placed just behind the hospital building, sheltered from the bracing ocean winds.

"It's not humane," declared Mrs. Conley. "I propose to care for them at my home. I have a loft and a spare bedroom."

"I can't contravene military orders," said DuBois.

"Closing your eyes is not the same as 'contravening' orders," she replied firmly. "I can take them now and they can re-appear in their military tent the day that man from Fort Macon visits again."

"Billy, the tall one, has diarrhea," said Amelia.

"I know. Maybe there's something here causing it."

"We have no diagnosis yet," said the Matron of Hospital. "Both still have fevers and the eruptions on their faces and backs could be smallpox or typhoid fever. They could also be signs of syphilis, which requires regular inspection of private parts."

"I know." Mrs. Conley wasn't flinching.

Amelia bore in. "We have very few medicines here, as you already know. Any one of these diseases could spread to you and your life would be shattered."

The tall woman in the plain gray dress tossed her head back and returned a rueful look. "It already has been," she said. "My husband is dead and my son is in a prison camp somewhere. I need a reason to keep on living."

Amelia looked to DuBois for guidance. "I see nothing," he said. "My eyes are already closed."

A week later, after the knitting session had already begun, Felix DuBois appeared in the doorway, a volume in one hand, eyes searching for Amelia. Soon all heads had turned towards him and the needlework chitchat had been replaced by a low hum. It was a rare Carolina woman who hadn't seen a Negro preacher in a suit and tie, but this man was different: polished black shoes, striped trousers, frock coat – the full Royal Victoria regalia except that the church ladies saw him as a foreign diplomat with regal bearing.

Amelia introduced him as a graduate of the Sorbonne in Paris who had "served with distinction throughout the French Caribbean." *If lies are like whole notes, these are only eighth notes.*

DuBois stepped upon the small wooden platform that sufficed as a stage, opened his book on the podium, and looked out on the upturned faces. "I thought I would read to you a book about travel – not by me, but by a French nobleman who visited Russia in 1839," he began. "The writer was Marquis Astolphe de Custine. His father had become very wealthy because he owned a large porcelain factory, and perhaps some of its fine dishware and vases have made their way into your homes."

"Mine are made of tin," one voice called out. "The Yankees got all of mine," said another to a chorus of cackles.

"In any event," continued DuBois, his dignity unruffled, "the young marquis had no need to work for a living, so he traveled between his country estate and his home in Paris, mingling with literary people and diplomats. In fact, I knew him slightly myself.

"Now then, all was not quite so lovely in his life. As part of the aristocracy, his father had met the guillotine during the French Revolution and most of the nobles were still in disarray, some even living outside the country for fear of more repression. De Custine felt this himself one night when he was spotted coming out of a bistro by a group of drunken sailors. They followed him onto a side street and beat him severely. During his long recovery, he pondered what to do with the rest of his life."

DuBois took a pause and noticed that Reverend Hiram, Charles Timmons and Saint Matthew were all standing just inside the rear door. These were already more words than they were accustomed to hearing from this enigmatic man. "Well," he continued, "de Custine decided to become a travel writer. By being out of the country, he perhaps believed he would be safer from harm. Also, this was the year when the most popular book in France was a travel book entitled *Democracy in America*, by another Frenchman named Alexis de Tocqueville. You have heard of him?"

Several hands went up, some holding knitting needles.

"Well, I must tell you first that the Marquis de Custine went to Russia with the intention of admiring its aristocracy and sharing its virtues with his readers. He had hoped to reassure the many nobles in Europe who feared that the Russian masses would be next to foment their own French Revolution. But, instead de Custine was shocked and disgusted at the cruel behavior of Czar Nicholas and the Russian Orthodox Church."

DuBois then picked up his book and began translating passages from a writer who saw a country with "terrifying uniformity" …with "a regularity so contrary to the natural inclination of mankind that it cannot have been achieved and could not survive without violence" …where people "were like trained bears who made you long for the wild ones" …where "everyone disguises what is bad and shows what is good before the master's eyes."

After a half-hour of hearing the marquis' impressions of Moscow, St. Petersburg, Boyars and babushkas, DuBois looked up from his book and found that the knitting had stopped. Some were no doubt transfixed with the refined personage and melodious accent – all while their subconscious tried to imagine one of their black field hands delivering polished prose in formalwear. But far more had quickly realized that they were the Carolina bumpkins and that this scholar from abroad was treating them as equals. And they thirsted to learn anything that went beyond the suffocating strictures of a windswept island and its imprisonment in a mindless war.

"Encore, encore," they called out, perhaps exhausting their reserve of French.

"Well, I think I have read enough from the book for now," said DuBois, "but de Custine was also a poet, and I thought you might like to hear just one of his poems." He unfolded a single sheet of paper, cleared his throat and read:

> Through cell bars I see the Truth to set me free
> So near, as an eagle perched upon a tree.
> Hark! An angel of mercy proffers a key!
> But 'twill not unlock the prison that holds me.

Alas, my fortress is three prisons in one,
The first wall built by those who wished me undone,
The next, by those I allowed to define me.
The third I built with my fear to contest thee.

This night I will lie down and rue my sorrow,
And pray for new courage to face the morrow,
So, when Truth again perches within my sight
I'll burst out and chase it with all of my might.

THE BEACH BEACON

Nov. 21, Mon.

The first shoots are peeking out in the churchyard garden. Onions and radishes in a race to be picked first. Dug up a potato, but it asked to be buried again. "Ready by Christmas dinner," it said.

Spent last Wednesday planting winter herbs, thanks to tips from Mrs. Stonecroft. She saws an old barrel in two and fills each half with soil. She keeps them out on sunny days but drags them inside when the weather gets too cold. Others now using old tobacco crates, tomato boxes and the like. Some growing just rosemary or garlic or sage with the intention of having a "winter herb festival" where they trade their specialties back and forth.

Our second Knitting Club session will be Wednesday. Felix to read again. This time from Balzac's "Human Comedy." Will he skirt around the racy parts?

Charles again preoccupied with drying and boiling brine, this time with a real kettle found underneath Mrs. Sawyer's porch. Unlike the other volunteers, I think Charles intends to sell salt and keep proceeds towards his passage to England. Is this proper?

Oh, the singing! My (our) crowning achievement! After two contentious practices, with more shouting at each other than singing, our quartets debuted at the Sunday potluck with a decent performance. Yes, we have two quartets, thanks to Felix. He said it would be a contest, with the winning quartet each getting shoes. Well, we had shoes for both all along, but neglecting to mention it made for competition at practices. More like a schoolyard tug-of-war contest. Lots of taunting and growling, but now it seems to be more good-natured than murderous. Rebs sang "Dixie" and "Oh Susannah." Yankees sang "John Brown's Body" and "When Johnny Comes Marching Home." They managed some harmony and I saw tears in some ladies' eyes. Heard calls to have a full chorus sing next time. That may be too much to ask, but the eight will be back in one form or another. Dare I bring the contrabands, too?

Dec. 6, Tues.

Church attendance good. Never under a hundred. It may be the Lord's work, but I think it's more to do with the potlucks, garden, etc. Forgive me for boasting.

Still no big frost and garden is sprouting cabbage, onion, garlic, kale, etc. If we can make it through winter, we should eat more grandly. Farmers here have been used to planting cash crops like tobacco and corn. Not familiar with large field crops for food, but now they understand because both Abe Lincoln and Jeff Davis are writing editorials urging them to do so. One of Ocracoke women brought a newspaper clipping where Jeff Davis wrote an editorial suggesting that people eat rats. Says that in Vicksburg they hang by their tails in butcher shops and fetch $2 per rat. Taste like squirrels, he says. Well, I'm glad Saint Matthew can't read.

Forgot to explain that they now have a "ferry boat" in Ocracoke that brings us four or five volunteers a week, thanks to Rachel and the preacher's wife at the Methodist church there.

At first, they just seemed curious to see what things looked like over here. One of them is Molly O'Malley, a widow who operates the lighthouse. I think she just came scouting for a husband who could to climb all those stairs, but she has come back every week like the others. More women than actually needed in the hospital, so they spend hours at the church knitting, sewing winter clothes for patients. Among all this cheerful chatter I feel a cloud of foreboding hanging over me. I know Hawkes is coming back for sure in December and one week has already gone by. I find myself scanning the ocean horizon. I also picture him as a grim reaper with me as his accomplice because I am fattening calves for slaughter. But I also know that none of them, myself included, can stay here forever.

Charles has a new "business." He has declared that the yaupon shrub makes the best tea substitute. He now offers jars of crushed yaupon berries, twigs and roots in the church and calls it "English tea." A bit cheeky. We shall see about the tea.

Amelia and Bessie had known – observed – each other from a distance ever since Amelia and her shipwreck survivors had first glimpsed the large woman and her six contrabands loitering outside the linen shed. Amelia had convinced herself that she really didn't want to get close enough to look inside the linen shed and see how seven people existed in so confined a space. Besides, the shed and the people therein were really "the responsibility of" Felix and Antoine. Nearer the truth was that Amelia Beach lived in a household of "upper class" servants and was uneasy trying to converse with field hands who might not even understand her.

And Bessie had felt the same way for the same reasons in reverse.

But Amelia had certainly noted how Bessie took to her new title of linen "captain" and how she had waded out into the watery field after the hurricane to retrieve windblown sheets and pillowcases – and how the women sang and swayed their hips as the Georgia slaves did when picking cotton.

Often, as Amelia would walk up the well-worn footpath towards the hospital, she could hear singing and feel the tune's rhythm even though the words seemed to collapse into a low hum, she passed by the linen shed.

But on this clear, cold morning in December, Amelia heard another song ahead on the footpath and decided that she had never taken time to listen. This time she paused a few yards away and recognized the slave song, *Go Down Moses*. A single female voice would sing the melody in perfect pitch while a chorus of baleful basses followed her with a syncopated rhythm that neither Reb nor Union quartet could ever be taught.

As Amelia continued the routine that taken her dozens of times past the shed, she let impulse take over. "Captain Bessie," she said, extending her hand, "I'm Amelia Beach."

Bessie, a ragged black sweater covering a tattered gray dress, took the hand limply and with undisguised suspicion. "Yes'm," she answered, barely audible. Two other women poked their heads out of the shed, where they'd been folding laundry.

"Bessie, was that *Go Down, Moses* you were singing?

"Yes'm."

"Bessie, you have a magnificent voice – better than any of the men who performed down at the Methodist church. You've heard them practicing up at the hospital?"

"Yes'm." She smiled faintly and Amelia read her mind.

"You're smiling because you know your group can sing better."

"Could be," Bessie ventured. Without another word, and without any pitch pipe, she stood and launched into *When Israel was in Egypt Land*, and the three men, seated on upturned crates around her, followed flawlessly with

> *Let my people go.*
> *Oppressed so hard they could not stand.*
> *Let my people go.*
> *So, the God sayeth, Go down Moses,*
> *Way down in Egypt land*
> *Tell all Pharaohs to*
> *Let my people go!*

"Would you sing another for me?" Amelia asked when they had finished. They responded with Bessie singing with an air of desperation,

> *Wade in de water.*
> *Wade in de water, chilluns,*
> *Wade in de water,*
> *God's gonna trouble de water.*

"What does 'wade in the water' mean?" Amelia asked when they finished. Bessie gave her an impassive stare, but the man closest to her smiled and looked up from his stool. "Well Missy," he said, "dat's a song about some darkies escapin' de massa. De bloodhounds is trailin' 'em and dey comes to a river. De woman tells her chilluns to wade on across because de dawgs will lose the smell."

Before Amelia continued on with her walk, Bessie and her troupe had agreed to perform with the patients at the next potluck supper. Would the white patient quartets stand for what would surely be an upstaging? Would Rev. Hiram allow this ragtag, sometimes surly quartet of contrabands in his church? Amelia decided to simply "plow on through" rather than ask.

On Wednesday, December 14, the church social hall was crowded, with some forty Portsmouth Island ladies and four more from Ocracoke, all hunched over knitting or sewing projects. Charles also was there, going from table to table with bags of salt and tea for sale. So was Jimmy, who was seated sideways on a bench, his hands spread while holding a card of wool for a plump red-haired woman. Had Jimmy been ensnared by the lighthouse widow?

Amelia introduced the two quartets after coaxing the leader of each to show off shoes, socks and other winter items that had been made by the assembled ladies. The Union group sang *Just Before the Battle, Mother* to tearful applause. The Rebel group followed with the mournful *Rebel Soldier*, which evoked an equal display of sorrow.

"We have one more singing group – a surprise for you," Amelia announced from the podium, "but they may not have arrived yet." She excused herself and opened the back door to look out towards the hospital. Instead, she found Bessie and her three basses standing outside as if too timid to open the door. Amelia quickly led them in and bounded up the platform to announce that the "special treat" had arrived before anyone might demand that the treat be evicted.

With no accompaniment, the men began a drum-like beat before Bessie entered with a protracted *Go Down Moses.*

Biblical and safe from white objections, Amelia thought to her satisfaction. Then, with only a scant pause, the men began in a babble of guttural moans and wails that coalesced into a rhythmic beat. Two octaves above them, Bessie began a haunting lament:

> *Nobody knows the trouble I seen,*
> *Nobody knows my sorrow*
> *Nobody knows the trouble I seen*
> *Glory, Hallelujah.*

> *Nobody knows the trouble I seen,*
> *Nobody knows but Jesus.*
> *Nobody knows the trouble I seen,*
> *Glory, Hallelujah....*

All the women in the room had known hardship and four years of wartime suffering. All knew the old hymn, but when Bessie had run an arpeggio of her emotions through six verses, all felt a slave's sorrow to their bones and none had a dry eye when she finished.

The silence ended when Rachel walked up to the podium holding a heavy knitted shawl. She stared up at the woman who was twice her size. "This here I was makin' for a Christmas present for my daughter," she said, "but I want ye to have it. I can make another by Christmas."

Then Amelia was at the podium. "The best way to conclude a performance like this," she said, "would be to have all three groups become one chorus and sing the same song. But there isn't a song yet that unites everyone. Perhaps we can pray together that one day…"

"Oy knows such a song," the Cockney voice cried out. She could see Jimmy lay down his yarn at a back table and hop up on the stage. *I hope this isn't going to be "What Do We Do with a Drunken Sailor?"* Instead Jimmy looked out and said, "The song Oy'm thinkin' of was first sung over on my side of the ocean, but it's something we've all heard. From the laddies – and lady," he said with a nod to Amelia, "it says that we thank ye for your many favors to all of us at the hospital and that we will remember ye always."

And this is Jimmy, the hornpiping balladeer? Just then he broke into a perfectly-*pitched tenor:*

Should auld acquaintance be forgot
And never brought to mind,
Should auld acquaintance be forgot
And days of auld lang syne.

And there's a hand, my trusty friend
And give a hand to thine,
We'll take a cup of kindness yet
For auld lang syne.
For auld lang syne, my dear
For auld lang syne
We'll take a cup of kindness yet
For auld lang syne.

Before Jimmy had finished, he was joined by all.

Chapter Eighteen

Redemption, December 1864

On December 15, the skies were cloudy and windy, with choppy waves hurling themselves onto Portsmouth Island beach with no cadence. As afternoon approached, Amelia had seen a schooner in the distance but assumed that it must have been headed north for Hatteras or Norfolk.

About an hour later Matthew rushed into Felix DuBois' office saying he'd gone to the town dock to fish just in time to see a schooner with seven Union soldiers tying up. The big fellow Hawkes was pointing and shouting. When his men began to unload piles of canvas, Matthew slipped down the path to deliver the news.

Now DuBois, Amelia and a dozen Union patients were standing on the hospital portico looking down on Captain Benjamin Hawkes, who followed a supply cart pushed by two soldiers. Instead of transporting food as usual, it was now piled high with gray canvas. Since it was too cold and blustery for their customary rendezvous on the porch, Hawkes made the most perfunctory of greetings and asked to meet in DuBois' office.

There, Hawkes took a chair opposite the only desk, stretched his long legs and began rubbing hands that were red and raw. When Amelia began to ask a question, he held up a hand and said with a finger to his lips.

"First, the usual complete secrecy and low voices. Second, a man who has just been bounced about a cold and cruel sea could use a little medicine to bring up his body temperature – preferably some warmth from the whiskey that I so kindly brought you last month."

"You mean six weeks ago," said Amelia as DuBois rose and headed toward the locked commissary cabinet. They waited until DuBois returned with a canister and tin cup and watched Hawkes sigh and smile as he took his first sip.

"As I've told you, the movement of men and materials isn't all that precise in war," he replied. "But I can say now with certainty that a transport will arrive for your men tomorrow or the next day, depending on the weather.

The army has contracted for a private supply ship and I saw it lading on the wharf as we left Fort Macon."

"I haven't seen any provisions – only piles of canvas," Amelia observed.

"Those are army field tents," said Hawkes, "I can't say that they will be used, but the army issued them because it doesn't know how many Rebel casualties the battle will produce. The tender will bring both food and medicines – more than you've seen so far, because it is now part of an official army battle plan. Not like before when we had to beg and borrow to supply this place."

It was only beginning to dawn on Amelia that this army officer actually meant that all the people in the hospital and all those who had cared for them would suddenly disappear from Portsmouth Island in a day or two. The church would be a lonely place again, the organ stiff and cold, the social hall dark and lifeless, patients scattered to the winds, roaches scratching out new nests under the floorboards.

Amelia found herself dark and lifeless as well, unable even to imagine living elsewhere. She asked a question without much aforethought. "The last time you were here you had four men. Now I counted seven, and when they walked up the path they had rifles on their backs with bayonets sticking out. Why is that?"

"You must understand that this is now a military operation," Hawkes answered. "There are those who could attempt to escape."

"Who would want to escape?" DuBois asked.

"For one thing, all of the Rebels on the second floor," he shot back. "Remember the 'Buffaloes' I told you about? For another thing, there could be any number of Union men who don't look forward to going back into battle. For those reasons, we will position a sentry at each entrance to the hospital around the clock – six four-hour watches."

Hawkes poured another splash in his tin cup and declared himself "fit again." He asked for the number of men they expected to be ready for travel.

DuBois returned fire. "I don't think we can give you an exact number at this point," he said. "Wait until they respond to your call and then we will help you assess the remainder."

"What about the two we isolated for observation? the captain asked.

Tell him the truth and dare him to do something about it.

Amelia: "The only way we could isolate them was to take them out to a private home where the owner could look after them. We have no definitive diagnosis as yet."

"Then the army will want them isolated aboard ship."

"Or perhaps not." *My intuition again.* "The owner, an army widow, wishes to adopt them as her sons," she said. "Then they will have no reason to roam, will they."

"One never knows," he replied. "This is one reason why I will be remaining here until the battle is over and we know the effects it will have on this place. And until we have a surgeon in charge."

"Then you will be managing director?" DuBois asked.

"After you leave, I hope I will be managing director of an empty building. But no one knows, of course."

"The tender will take our party to Baltimore?" asked DuBois.

"That is my expectation. The Rebels will be taken to Point Lookout on the Chesapeake and the Union boys and contrabands will go on to Washington. But making a detour to Baltimore for your party must still be negotiated."

"You're taking the contrabands?"

Hawkes drew a sheet of paper from his breast pocket and unfolded it. "My orders are to transport all 'inmates of the maritime hospital off Portsmouth Island,'" he said as if reading good news. "As I reckon it, these people are living in a part of the hospital – the linen shed – and shall require no sentries, I am sure. They will be delighted to know that they are headed for the land of Lincoln and the carefree lives they believe him to guarantee."

"One more thing," Hawkes said, rising from his chair. "At seventeen hundred hours, my men and I will be explaining to the hospital patients the nature of this transfer and what they must do to follow orders properly. I trust you will convey the same to your own people."

He reached inside his breast pocket again. "Amelia," he said, "I am pleased to deliver this letter to you, which came to Fort Macon by way of some sort of military clearinghouse in Virginia. I had not forgotten it. I merely wished to have your attention while we discussed our evacuation orders."

Amelia scurried down the footpath, giving only a quick wave to her new friends in the linen shed. She found herself in the church social hall, seated at the same table she had sat at during the preceding day's "concert." The only other person in the room was Matthew at the kitchen sink, preoccupied with cutting vegetables and potatoes.

Savannah, October 27, 1864

My Dearest Amelia,

I forgive you for everything and pray to God for deliverance from your plight. We miss you greatly but worry about you with all those rambunctious young men in the hospital. We don't want you to fall prey to the temptations that overcame your sister Lucy. Are you keeping warm as winter sets in?

Life here is one of want and need. Our home has become headquarters for General CENSORED, General CENSORED and his CENSORED. We do our best to be gracious hosts, but men come and go every day and leave mud from the street all over the rugs and spill ashes everywhere. My dining room table is ruined with burn marks from cigars and our silverware seems to be regarded as souvenirs. We do have a corporal who has included us in the "mess" he cooks for his superiors, but it is plain fare indeed.

Despite the burdens I have described above, none has drained my energy more than Lucy and baby Joseph. Because of the officers quartered here, Lucy and baby must make do in her bedroom. He seems to cry all night and by day Lucy is so spent that she sleeps the day away while I am left to change diapers and entertain Little Joe.

What about Mandy, you may wonder. Well, Mandy grew intolerably sassy, and the reason, I learned, is that she was planning all along to go off to her sister's in Atlanta. And not a word of thanks for all the years we fed and clothed her. I think she stole some silver on the way out along with the gold broach my daddy gave me. Leastways I can't find it.

Meanwhile, I seem to be a servant in the eyes of my Yankee "guests." My weak ankles have gotten worse and I have developed artheritis, which I daresay is from carrying little Joe around when I walk about the house. Lucy, who never had any reserves of flesh to sustain her in lean times, seems exhausted all the time and even has fainting spells that make me all the more anxious. With Lucy and child requiring so much supervision, I can scarcely leave the house to buy necessities, which are in scant supply and require great patience. I hope your Portsmouth Island has more than we do.

Your father sends his love as I write this, but I can tell you here that he needs the cheering up that the sight of your face can bring. He sits alone here in his office much of the time, a CENSORED in his own house, as his warehouse has been transformed by the Yankee army into a CENSORED.

Again, I say, you are needed at home acutely. Please consider that caring for one's family will be much easier on your constitution than keeping track of all those patients in a big hospital. Please do write and give us the good news as to when you expect to rejoin your loving family. We miss you and hope you do not get sick from something in that hospital.

Your forgiving mother.

Amelia looked out the social hall window, her eyes following the path to the hospital. A sentry had taken up a position outside the main entrance. She knew that Hawkes would soon be inside, telling dazed and morose patients that their stay on Portsmouth Island would end on the morrow, that their new quarters would be quite to their satisfaction and that the war would probably be over very soon anyway.

Amelia decided to return and offer the inmates moral support, but when she reached the sentry he barred her from entering on "captain's orders." She realized then how much she had seen it as *her* hospital, and her sudden loss of control – no, *belonging* to a worthwhile cause – left her empty and confused.

It was getting dark now and Amelia walked back down the path, aimlessly, slowly, stopping to gaze out at the broad beach that she had always seemed too busy to admire. The moon was nearly full, casting a yellow shimmer across the waves. As she approached the linen shed, she saw Bessie and one of the men shooing the others inside so they could confront their new friend.

"Miss 'Melia," said Bessie, "dat tall soldier man said we goin' to Washington City. Is dat right?"

Amelia nodded. "Tomorrow, it looks like. A boat is coming to take everybody."

"Lord Almighty! Hallelujah!" the two chorused.

"Do you have some clothes to take?"

"Nuthin' mo' than what we got on," said Bessie, her new shawl stretched atop her tattered dress and threadbare sweater. "But don't worry. We can make it. Don't need no new clothes in de Promised Land!"

The man beside her slapped his knees and Amelia managed a smile as she moved on. "Maybe you'll sing for Mister Lincoln," she called back. *No doubt they'll travel to the Promised Land crammed in the ship's hold, the same way their grandparents were.*

The shipwrecked six were soon assembled in the social hall. Matthew's chopped potatoes and vegetables had become a fish stew that looked much like the one they devoured greedily on their first night on Portsmouth Island.

They ate in silent unease. A few minutes later, DuBois broke the tension. "I just calculated that we've been here a little more than a hundred days," he said. "I would like to think we have done some good."

"Hear, hear," chimed in Jimmy. "This ain't the Last Supper, ye know. Take this here fish stew in remembrance of Saint Matthew."

"He's right," said Charles. "This should be a happy occasion." They poked fun at Antoine for the time when he scared Rachel's cow into toppling the old latrine. They laughed at Jimmy's description of Matthew, water up to his hips in the cistern, trying to grab frogs as they scooted along the surface. Even Felix DuBois tried his hand at levity when he described how Amelia had jumped back, "just like the cow," when first peering inside the death house and seeing the coffin.

Then they sunk into a collective reverie again, as if all were trying to re-kindle hopes and dreams that the past hundred days had left in a closet.

A tap on the door and Hawkes was before them, looking more military than usual with tall boots, full blue uniform and captain's bars on his shoulders. He declined Matthew's offer of fish stew, saying "I just want to make sure that all here have been properly informed about tomorrow's plans. I assume all of you are leaving on the tender?"

Hearing no sound, Hawkes was about to turn and leave when Jimmy cleared his throat and raised his hand. "Well, Oy suppose Oy better tell ye now," he said sheepishly. "This sailor will not be sailing tomorrow."

"Why?" they all seemed to ask at once.

"Oy concluded that Oy have sailed one ocean too many. Even if Oy goes back to me hallowed shores, the queen's navy would probably throw me back into the sea. Too old, methinks."

Amelia interrupted: "Does this have anything to do with that Maggie O'Malley?"

Jimmy tried to hide his flushed face in his shirt. "Aye, she's a bit of it," he said, still flourishing a blush. "Oy never thought Oy'd consort with the Oyrish, but climbin' a lighthouse with me spyglass is a lot like climbin' the riggin.' Oy'll still have the sea all around. Oy just won't be seein' it from a wobbly deck."

The first to declare. What a surprise!

But no surprise in the case of Charles. "Captain," he said to Hawkes, "I presume you do understand that I must go to Baltimore, and the others here as well. Were I to be put ashore in Washington I would be placed in custody of the British embassy and held until they sort out my status with the Royal Navy by transatlantic correspondence. Rather than grow old in Washington, I would rather plead my case to the navy in my own country."

Hawkes nodded. "Other comments?"

Amelia spoke up. "I agree with Charles. If I go to Washington, I could be arrested as a Confederate spy."

Hawkes gave a start. "What?"

"She is not a spy, I assure you." It was Felix DuBois. "The American consul in Nassau had amorous designs on Miss Beach, and when she refused his advances, he threatened to have her arrested as a Confederate spy. You have my word that she is innocent."

"Well, then," said Charles. "Can we be assured this ship will go to Baltimore long enough to let us off?"

Hawkes: "Legally speaking, the captain is a civilian contractor and can command his own ship if, say, it were endangered and incapable of putting into Baltimore. Otherwise, he is under military orders and can be expected to follow them."

Timmons: "What if he demands a special fee for going out of his way?"

"If so, I will deal with it," answered the captain. "And now I would like Mister DuBois and Miss Beach to visit the hospital before the patients bed down and tell me how many are in condition to travel tomorrow."

As the two strode up the path, perhaps for the last time, Amelia again felt the same wave of betrayal that had first seized her the moment Hawkes had revealed his orders. "I suggest we serve The King's Grog as a parting gesture," she said.

"It might incite more rebellion than peace," he replied.

The sentry waved them through and they were soon in the commissary alcove. "Well, do you want the first floor or second?" she asked.

"Neither," he said. "You see, I am in charge of soap and sheets and cleaning latrines. You are in charge of patients."

"Well, The King's Grog is the price for *my* not rebelling," she answered with a haughty head shake. And so, Amelia began mixing the popular brew, adding two cups of brandy more than she should. DuBois went outside, where two soldiers were shivering in front of their newly-erected field tent and offered each a cup of grog if they would bring in more firewood for each of the hearths.

Mess had been served earlier by Rachel and two volunteers. As Amelia began her rounds on the top floor, she found the Rebel patients all healthy, but sullen and snarly at the idea of giving up their private rooms and fireplaces for another island packed with fifty thousand men subsisting in field tents on icy ground. But their other choices were equally repugnant: try to escape the hospital and be shot by Hawkes' sentries or run off into the coastal scrub and be tracked down by men and dogs from Fort Macon.

As soon as the Union boys on the first floor heard the sound of Amelia's pushcart begin to rattle in the hall, they crowded inside the first room. A cacophony of questions filled the air as she ladled grog into mess cups. Nearly all the queries doubtless had been answered by Hawkes, and Amelia guessed that the soldiers were mainly seeking reassurance. Namely, where was this great battle to take place? When? Just how would it shorten the war?

"If I told you exactly when and where I could be hung for treason," she said. "But I will tell you this: Captain Hawkes is very honest, reliable and well-informed. He says the war will be over in four or five months. Once you arrive in Washington, I don't think they will even bother to re-assign you. So, think of it as taking another step closer to your families."

Before anyone could plead for a second cup of grog, Amelia said she had something of her own to say. "If you ran in here to see me and to have a nip of grog, then you are able to travel tomorrow. But now I want to know: who isn't here in this room and why?"

In a few minutes Amelia had narrowed the critical cases to four – one in acute pain from advanced tetanus and three with chronic dysentery that rendered them too weak to walk or use their own bedpans. The latter three were crowded into a single room at the end of the building. The stench was so overpowering that the volunteer ladies tended to scurry in and out quickly as possible.

All three men had seemed to be asleep when Amelia sat gingerly at the foot of one bed to consider what heroic effort she might make to save them – or at least keep them alive until Hawkes brought in a physician. When the bed creaked, Peter, a teenaged private from Maryland, raised his head a few inches and whispered hoarsely, "Where's ever'body going?"

"Why they're being shipped up the Chesapeake to a place in Maryland – maybe even near your home. Would you like to come along?" she asked in a half-teasing manner.

Peter dropped his head back on his stained mattress and peered up at her with one eye. "Don't think I can make it out the door," he muttered feebly. "You gonna stay 'til I get better?"

Amelia realized it was the first time she'd been asked to remain on Portsmouth Island.

"If I don't, you needn't worry," she said. "I'll tell you a secret. I'm not really a nurse. Captain Hawkes is going to bring in a real doctor, probably some nurses, too, plus food and real medicines."

"Don't know if I'll last that long," he said in a voice muffled into the mattress. The bed began quivering. Amelia leaned over to see if she could mop Peter's brow and realized he was weeping convulsively.

"I'll come tomorrow morning to clean you up," she said.

After promising to say farewells the next day, Amelia found Felix DuBois waiting for her in his office. "How many do you have for the ship tomorrow?" he asked.

"Looks like forty-two," she said. "All sixteen Rebs and twenty-six Yankees. I'm going to insist we hold back the three with dysentery and the poor tetanus patient."

"What about the two smallpox cases you took over to Mrs. Conley's?"

"I did forget," she said. "I was there two days ago and there's just no convincing diagnosis that I can figure. Just blotchy skin."

"Well, in that case you can't put two contagious cases on a crowded ship, can you?"

"If only I could be sure," she mused.

DuBois looked up from his desk with his sardonic smile. "You can be sure because you are the Matron of Hospital. Hawkes is only a soldier. I think I just heard you say they have smallpox."

Amelia smiled back. "Yes, I did say they have smallpox! No question about it. In any case, I'm sure Mrs. Conley will adopt them."

———

Even the contrabands were bedded down in their cozy shed as Amelia walked in the moonlight towards her back room in the farmhouse. As she passed the church she saw a dim glow in the rear window. This time she knew what to expect.

She went in anyway. "I've been invited to unfurl my bedroll on a church pew," Benjamin Hawkes announced, also unsurprised by his visitor. It was as if he hadn't changed positions from that night six weeks before, his long legs and black boots stretched over two chairs. Again on the table was a half-empty bottle of whiskey, a half-full glass and a pad of paper. "The only thing missing from this scene is that you again join me in a small drink," he said raising his glass.

"Just two fingers," she said.

"Same as before."

"Is this an everyday scene – you and the bottle – no matter where you are?" she asked in a schoolmarmish tone.

"Decidedly not," he replied. "Only when I have something important to plan for the next day or some report to write up from this one. Oh no. At home I would be roosting with the chickens because I have to rise with the sun. School starts early, rain or shine, and it's a mile walk."

"I suppose you have many details to take care of tomorrow," she answered.

"After all, if the ship sails away and you forgot to send something, it's not returning to fetch it."

She peered over his shoulder and saw several jottings on the note pad.

"Well, now," he said with a serious look, "the next thing I need to know is whether or not to put you on the passenger list. It appears that the others are all going, except for that English sailor."

"I'm expected to go as well," she said.

An awkward silence. "Yes, so I've been told," Hawkes said, "but *will* you?"

"It all depends," she answered after a second sip of her whiskey. "What about *you?*"

"My intention is to remain here until this war is over," he answered. *Diversion accomplished.* "There is no plan for artillery activity at Fort Macon. In fact, one of our gunboats pulled in the other day and made off with half our ordnance for the battle at Wilmington. Even if they hadn't, I don't want to kill any more people. Might look good on my military record, but not up *there*," he said with a finger pointed heavenward. "Maybe I can even save a few lives here and balance the ledger sheet a bit."

As Hawkes finished, Amelia rose, drained the rest of her glass in unlady-like fashion, and strode towards the back door.

"But I asked, what about *you?*" he called out as she swung open the door.

"As I said, it all depends..."

Amelia sank down on the edge of her small bed, barely three feet from the door. *Well, it DOES depend, doesn't it? Supposed to depend on Charles, but not a word, not an overture since Nassau. Back there he talked of our marrying in England. Nothing since. Man is supposed to ask woman. Did I miss a romantic overture up here the other night? Or was it a clumsy lunge like men do in bordellos? Must get sleep. Tomorrow will tell.*

During dinner Hawkes had ordered everyone to pack the same evening in case the ship were waiting at sea in early daylight. Amelia muffled a laugh as she surveyed her "wardrobe." In her only kit bag she stuffed a pair of high-fashion shoes, *circa* Nassau, brush and comb, hand mirror, and one of Rachel's gray cotton farmwife dresses, wrinkles and all. Folded and stacked in the dresser were the skirts, tops and dresses that belonged to Rachel's daughter. Hanging on a hook and ready for another voyage was the same man's plantation garb she had worn from Savannah to Nassau,

Nassau almost to Wilmington and to Ocracoke by lifeboat. The medical books she would leave at the hospital for a real nurse who could properly understand them.

The last thing she did was reach under the mattress and remove from its velvet pouch the heavy gold chain and locket that her father had given her by way of Captain John Wilkes. She layered it around her neck and ordered herself to fall asleep.

Guilt! Amelia knew that Portsmouth Island had begun the day without her when she opened an eye and, out the window, saw Rachel disappear into the milking shed. That told her it was seven, because if she had heard Eliza bellowing for attention it would be seven thirty.

Amelia packed her bag, scooped up her medical books and took a last look around a room she had come to love more for its pure simplicity than her elegant bedroom in Savannah, with its porcelain figurines and embroidered pillowcases.

No one was at the church, and she quickly realized why. Strung out on the footpath to the hospital she saw the backs of hospital folk as they stood gawking out to sea. "It's come," said Felix DuBois to her while keeping his eyes transfixed towards the rising sun. In the distance before them was a squat, beamy schooner, sails furled, wallowing in two-foot waves as it attempted to maneuver sideways into water just deep enough to anchor. Large dories hung from both sides.

"Those lifeboats will be here soon enough," Hawkes said to the shipwreck crew. "You'd better try to get some breakfast."

Inside the social hall, Matthew and Rachel had planned something special. Eggs! Two per plate, accompanied by hoecakes generously topped with peach preserves. There'd never been enough eggs for all at any sitting, but the chickens from Ocracoke had been happy in their new henhouse. And the hoecakes prompted laughter because in September they had barely been tolerated. By now they had become Saint Matthew's most popular fare, with diners vying to invent names like "Crabapple Croissants" (hoecakes with crushed preserves) and "Dumpling Delight" (hoecakes topped with sorghum and jam).

Amelia was the last to throw her kit bag alongside the other belongings that were piled atop a table that, just days before, had been used for shoemaking. As she took a place at the breakfast table, Charles appeared and seated himself next to her as he had the previous night. He was attired again in the southern planter's blouse and broad-brimmed hat that English sea captains seemed to don when they wished to slip incognito through Union blockades.

Well, Charles? The ship is out there. What now?

He smiled as he turned and looked her over. "You seem ready for another sea voyage," he said.

"Yes, just two southern farmers, aren't we?" she said absently.

Is that all, Charles Timmons? Sand is rushing through the hourglass.

As plates were cleaned and people got up, Charles cleared his throat and said, "Amelia, I know you've recently had a letter from your parents. Correct?"

"Correct."

"Well, I know you'll be sending a reply, and I wonder if you would be kind enough to include this." He removed a folded sheet from his pocket, adding that "It certainly would shorten the delivery time if it were mailed from here."

"May I?" she said, already unfolding it.

"If you must."

"I think I must." She began to read to herself.

December 15, 1864

My Dear Mr. Beach,

I trust you are well and will look favorably upon the following.

Since my first delivery of cargo to Savannah and Wilmington I have received no further compensation for my services as Captain of the Sea Breeze, Accordingly, I am owed, in pounds sterling:

3,000 for the trip Wilmington-Bermuda.

1,000 for the trip from Bermuda to Nassau to pick up your daughter, Amelia, and cargo.

3,000 for the second trip to Wilmington.

470 for expenses in the above ports of call, the last one being Portsmouth Island, North Carolina.

I entreat you to send a bank draft in my name to the Bank of Liverpool with instructions that it be held there for my arrival.

I regret the loss of The Sea Breeze, which was beyond my control. However, I am gratified to have delivered your daughter Amelia safely from Nassau to Portsmouth Island, N.C.

Your obedient servant,

Charles Timmons,
Captain

So, there it is plainly. I am an item in a bill of lading. Amelia gave Charles a piercing look. His eyes turned away.

Any conflagration between the two was aborted when Hawkes bent over Amelia's shoulder and said, "I believe you are wanted up at the hospital."

"Yes, I have some *other* farewells to say," she said, eyes still fixed on Charles. As she left the church and walked toward the hospital for perhaps the last time, she could see that the tender had wallowed its way to within a few hundred yards of the beach. It had anchored and was already lowering the first dory. Bessie and her contrabands had rushed onto the beach, as if not believing they would be boarded unless they squirmed onto the first lifeboat.

As Amelia walked up to the portico, Hawke's soldiers were beginning to put up large field tents along the hospital perimeter, giving the grounds the look of a military encampment. Ahead of her was Rachel standing on the porch, perhaps waiting to ask her a question about a patient.

"Good morning!" the little woman exclaimed more brightly than usual. Before Amelia could respond, Rachel pushed open the main door and a chorus of male voices shouted, "GOOD MORNING, MISS BEACH." She entered the vestibule to see two rows of soldiers standing at attention in the corridor. On the left were the Union boys, head-to-foot in their blues, some wearing black military shoes, some conspicuous in new cowhide uppers and wooden soles. On the right were the Rebels in patches and tatters, but with enough blue and red to resemble a military unit. Her eyes swept to the end of the hall, where in the middle stood Jimmy the sailor with his hands raised. When he brought them down the men began a gusty, discordant rendition of *Auld Lang Syne* that left Amelia in tears.

When she had finished going down the line and hearing their words of thanks, the last two men held gifts in their hands. From the Union soldiers: a large handkerchief upon which each man had signed his name and home-town in India ink. For the others, it was a Rebel private's cap with fifteen names scrawled inside.

With that, one of the sentries yelled "muster out" and the men dissolved into their rooms to retrieve their gear. In the midst of the hubbub, Amelia walked to the bedsides of the four immobilized Yankees, bent over each one and whispered something in his ear.

As the two longboats were making their way to shore, Hawkes gathered the five remaining shipwreck survivors and asked how much they could of-fer the captain for the extra leg to Baltimore. The total was thirty-two U.S. dollars. "That may not be enough," said Hawkes. He reached for the billfold in his back pocket and drew out three tens, the first Abe Lincolns Amelia had seen since the "doctor" had given her six of them to "manage" the hos-pital before he disappeared.

Hawkes took his ever-present notepad from his coat pocket, scrawled a message, and tore off the page. The first longboat was about to land, and when it was loaded with contrabands and soldiers, he handed it to one of the rowers and asked for an answer from the captain.

When the lifeboat returned for its next load, the bosun motioned Hawkes aside and said something that clearly left him grim and tight-lipped.

"Wait here a moment," Hawkes told him. He approached the five would-be travelers to Baltimore, who were clustered on the beach. "The man says the captain won't do it for less than a hundred," he said. "We need to go out there and talk to him," he said, climbing over the gunwale. Charles was quick to follow. As Amelia swung a leg over the gunwale, she looked back to see the others remaining motionless on shore.

"Mister DuBois, Antoine, Matthew…" she began to call out.

"Not yet," DuBois shouted back. "I prefer not to be rocking at sea any longer than necessary. There will be another lifeboat."

The "water taxi," as the bosun had nicknamed his craft, took only ten minutes to reach the port side of the tender. The sea was not angry, mere-ly its usual restive self, but the jarring spray from the rising oars brought memories of the harrowing night in a lifeboat a hundred or so days ago. As the landing craft bounced against the rusting sides of the tender, the men were quick climb the jute netting that had been thrown over the side. When Amelia struggled to follow, a half-dozen men rushed to propel her upward by her arms and shoulders.

As soldiers went about finding their bunks and hammocks, Hawkes, Charles and Amelia were left standing on deck wondering where the captain was. "This is not the courtesy one captain expects from another," Hawkes complained. "Two captains, in fact."

They headed for the wheelhouse.

Could it be?

Standing inside the glassed-in pilot house was the lanky, black-clad form of Doctor Samuel Drummond. "I didn't expect *this*," Hawkes whispered.

"You survived New Bern, I see," said Hawkes to Drummond when they were inside.

The tender captain was clearly just as ill at ease, and Amelia quickly surmised that Drummond might have put the fare to Baltimore out of their reach so as not to be embarrassed by their company.

"Yes, God called me to save that stricken city," he declared to Hawkes while ignoring the others. "For well-nigh on to six months this boat and its dedicated crew have labored unceasingly to deliver quinine and other desperately needed supplies from the Union capital to the suffering people of New Bern."

"And Fort Mason and Beaufort and Ocracoke," interjected Hawkes.

"Ah, yes, all of whom reached out to us for help," he replied, seemingly oblivious to Hawkes' bitter tone. "We felt the Savior's call to provide for one and all, even knowing that we scarcely could spend an hour in our own rest."

"Aren't you anxious to see your hospital patients in such a healthy state?" Amelia asked.

"I haven't had the opportunity to greet them yet," he said. "But I am not surprised because I had already told you that proper food and a little rest was all they needed."

Interrupted Hawkes: "We know you don't want to spend all morning rocking about in the ocean, so let me be direct. We have offered you sixty-two dollars to take five persons to Baltimore after you drop the Rebel prisoners at Point Lookout."

"It has to be a hunnert," Drummond said, straightening up and crossing his arms.

"My good fellow, a hundred is what it costs for a transatlantic trip between New York and London."

"Well, that's what it has to be," he said while appearing to be preoccupied with some papers on his chart table. "It's outside my military contract. It causes delays in other deliveries. Besides, I got to feed extra people for three, four days. Fair's fair."

Drummond had them over a barrel, just like the nasty storekeeper's wife in Ocracoke. "Perhaps we need to step outside and have a private meeting," Amelia said.

"You do that," said Drummond, still not addressing her directly.

When they had gathered aft of the wheelhouse, Hawkes began to reach for his billfold again. "I suppose I can dig out more," he said. "Don't know if the army will reimburse me."

An image of the *Sea Breeze* lifeboat, tethered at the town dock, flashed before Amelia. An orphan boat with an uncertain future. Drummond would no doubt trade it in a heartbeat for the rest of his hundred, but all she could feel was raw anger.

"No! Do not!" she seethed. "This man of God is nothing but an evil, conniving snake. No, *serpent* – just like in the Bible. Enough is enough." She proceeded to recount all she knew of Drummond since their arrival: the sparsely-equipped hospital, the neglected patients, the "management contract" that was soon forgotten, siphoning off hospital supplies, the bullying of an entire church, her visit to his home and amply-provisioned storehouse.

Hawkes took it all in silently. "Tell me everything you can about that storehouse," he said.

When she did – hams, nails, barrels of grain and all – he said, "All I ask is that you leave this matter to me."

They filed inside the wheelhouse again. Drummond was moving some markers on his chart table and seemed not to notice three persons unlatching the steel door and clanking their heels on the floor. Amelia gave the door a loud slam for good measure and Drummond casually glanced over his shoulder.

"All right, Drummond, God's merciful messenger," Hawkes announced in a loud voice. "I am now addressing you as a Union army captain who has the power to put you in irons!"

Drummond turned his head condescendingly from his chart table. Hawkes continued: "On July 28 of this year the provost marshals of Fort Macon and New Bern attempted to put an end to hoarding and excessive inflation when they issued an order requiring that all wholesale transactions be conducted at the wharf in Fort Macon and not to exceed the prices on a list published by the army. Even though posters have since been displayed on every dock piling at both places, you have regularly ignored these orders or skirted around them with impunity."

"Oh?" Drummond said with a defiant look.

"We have visited your home and discovered a barrel of large nails that you sequestered at a time when people needed them and stores had none to offer," said Hawkes, in his military provost voice. "You hoarded quinine when the patients at your own hospital needed it. You took what the army had already paid for and fattened your profits by selling it elsewhere. You have so many barrels of grain that some were found rotting at a time when hospital patients were on the verge of starving."

Drummond's mind was clearly churning to select the best of many excuses he had stored up for such an occasion. "You army people don't understand commerce," he said with scorn. "You order a hundred bushels of wheat when only ten are needed, then you send a dozen shoes when your men need ten dozen. Most of the money I made from those sales went to buy things the people around here really needed.

"And you know what?" He pointed a finger in Hawkes' chest. "I seen you struttin' around Fort Macon orderin' around all those men when you was probably a chicken farmer back where you come from."

"Enough!" Hawkes pushed Drummond's finger down hard as if he were about to jam it into the chart table. "Here is a decision for you to make. You are going to take these people to Baltimore for sixty-two dollars or I will see that you never supply Fort Macon or New Bern again. And if you do show up at our dock, I will have you arrested and tried by a military court. Not some Carolina jury that you can bribe, but a military court with one judge."

Drummond was quiet while his mind explored other alleys of egress.

"All right, you give me no choice," he said at last. Then the finger pointed out again. "But 'vengeance is mine!' sayeth the Lord."

The three left the wheelhouse. Amelia motioned silently with her eyes for Charles to walk with her down the deck. She looked into his eyes and said in a low tone, "Tell me now. Are you expecting me to go with you to England?"

"Well, I didn't know," he answered with a shrug. "You never expressed your intentions to me."

"Nor you to me," she answered. "I guess we really have no such intentions, do we? All I know is what you wrote my father. You carried his daughter safely to Portsmouth Island in North Carolina like Doctor Drummond over there, and now you present him with a bill of lading for transporting the goods undamaged." She continued looking into his eyes, searching. His wavered from hers and returned, but her look remained transfixed. "Charles, I feel I have much to regret about the sinking of the *Sea Breeze* and all that caused us to wash up on Portsmouth Island. But there is one thing I can apologize for right now and set you free with a clear conscience. I apologize if I was too clinging, too amorous, too intent on making a husband of you. And I further apologize if all that compromised your naval career. I want you to go to England as soon as possible and resume it. So, I am giving you this."

With that she reached into her blouse and freed the long, Spanish chain that she had wound around her neck, the one that had always given her assurance that there would be a safe passage, somehow, back to Savannah. "This will buy you passage home, I'm certain. Just don't show it to the jackal Drummond.

"Goodbye, Charles," she said, walking towards Hawkes, who waited to help her descend to the bobbing lifeboat below.

Captain Charles Timmons stood speechless, the gold chain dangling from his palm.

The last 'water taxi" to the beach carried only Hawkes and Amelia. He stood over her, saying nothing, but looking down on her with the most pleasing smile she had ever seen. His only words before they landed were, "I'm not sure what just took place, Amelia, but I'm glad you're in this boat and not *that* one. The people here need you, and I am among them."

As the oarsmen leapt ashore, the only remaining travelers awaiting the lifeboat were Felix DuBois, Antoine, and Matthew, all with perplexed expressions. Rachel and Jimmy stood in the background. Hawkes boosted himself on to the sand and Amelia took his hand to follow. "You are not leaving?" DuBois asked her.

"No. Too much work to do here," said Amelia with a broad smile. "I can't abandon these sick men, even if there are only four. You know, when you have fifty patients, four desperately sick ones don't seem like a great number. But when there are only four, the number is great indeed."

"Well, then, neither will we. Oui?" DuBois turned to the others. "Oui," they chorused.

They stood on the beach silently watching four rowers pilot the empty lifeboat to the ship. One crewman stood ready to place the hooks that would winch up the longboat. Another crew appeared near the bow, ready to weigh the anchor. Charles was nowhere to be seen – perhaps facing the sea and already trying to forget Portsmouth Island.

"I didn't give you much time to change your minds, did I," said Amelia at last.

"*Au contraire*," responded Felix. "We decided what we wanted to do just after you left."

Amelia looked at all three, shaking her head. "But Matthew," she said, "you could go back to your life in Nassau."

Matthew shrugged and smiled. "Sponging is hard," he answered. "So is cooking. But no one ever said thanks to me for giving them a sponge. Besides, who will take care of my chickens?"

"And you?" she addressed the man who had done the most to guide her through so many travails.

"Many, many reasons," said DuBois simply. "Perhaps I will tell you one day."

DuBois and Antoine headed back to the hospital, presumably to the quarters they had just been expected to vacate. Amelia decided she needed a respite from the icy ride to the tender and the tension aboard it. She sat alone at the same table she had just occupied with Charles, her hands wrapped around his only legacy to her, a steaming mug of yaupon tea.

The only other person she could see in the room was Matthew, who was humming contentedly as he scrubbed some pots and pans. She took a first sip and was beginning to wonder why she felt so wonderfully at peace when she heard a shuffle and sniffle. She spun around to see Jimmy standing behind her, looking the part of a nervous supplicant. He held something behind his back.

"Jimmy," she said, "I suppose you feel bad about being separated from the captain you had sailed with for all those years."

"No, Oy don't exactly, milady," he answered. "And Oy hopes you don't feel bad either. Oy surely don't want to hurt your feelings none, but sometimes knowin' the truth is better than livin' without it."

He pulled one hand from behind his back, revealing a slender packet of wrinkled envelopes. "The cap'n left this under the mattress in our room," he said sheepishly. "Methinks if you just let yerself read any one of 'em you'll get what Oy'm tryin' to tell you."

Amelia pulled one of the envelopes from the middle and removed a thin letter as Jimmy continued. "Oy be so sorry. Oy knew this from the beginning. Used to pick up his mail, even. But he's the cap'n, y'know and Oy be a lowly deck hand."

"I understand," said Amelia. She unfolded the delicate paper, written in a woman's hand, dated May 7, 1864 from Potter's Lane, Lymington, England.

My dear Charlie, who sails the ocean blue in search of our fortune. The children and I loved your description of the Bahamas, with dolphins racing your ship and manta rays swimming below like birds in the air. I hope we will all see it together one day soon.

I try to keep such pleasant thoughts in my mind right now because it has been raining here for two days. Mother came to spend the day and help with chores, but Mother demands a lot of time herself, and so it is only now that I have had time to sit down and answer your letter (received on the 1st instant). I am sorry to report that whatever it is that drives the pump to the kitchen sink has given out. I had to send Catherine to the public square with a water pail. Little Charlie insisted on helping her carry it home and when they arrived it was only half full and they were fighting over who made it spill. I would say both because each was splashed about the knees and....

Amelia let the letter drop in her lap. She sat quietly until Jimmy could bear it no more.

"Oy, Oy 'jes don't want you to feel bad," he stammered, biting his lip.

"He told me he was from Cornwall," she said absently. 'Is Lymington in Cornwall?"

"No ma'm. Hampshire, Oy thinks."

"So even the part about gazing at the sea from the cliffs of Cornwall was a fantasy, just like my expectations."

She looked up with a crooked smile. "Well, at least he'll be with his family soon enough. But he'll have to explain to Mrs. Timmons why she isn't going to get her fortune."

She stood up and turned to Jimmy with an air of bravado. "Well, you have your lighthouse. I have my hospital. We can wave at each other across the inlet."

"Aye, but it don't need to be forever," said Jimmy. "If you'll please sit down again," he said, "Oy wants to give you something else."

He went to the other side of the table, reached into his trousers and took out a fistful of something gold that seeped through his fingers. He opened the fist and spread on the table a heavy gold chain with the familiar locket.

Amelia nearly recoiled with shock. "What?" she exclaimed reflexively. "Did Captain Timmons give this to you? No, he couldn't have. I saw his ship leave!"

"No, no, ma'am, Oy had it all along," said Jimmy. "Always carried it wherever Oy was because it was me own Lloyds of London insurance policy. No matter if me ship got sunk or Oy got stranded, Oy always knew Oy had the means to get back to Liverpool.

"Now Oy won't need to go to Liverpool because Oy'm stayin' here with the widow O'Malley. So Oy'm givin' this here rosary chain to you as your passage back home whenever you want – war or no war."

Amelia stared down at the chain as she tried to collect her wits. "But Jimmy," she exclaimed, "this chain is exactly like one my father gave me. You must tell me how you got it. And where."

Jimmy's eyes rolled heavenward and she knew one of his sea stories would soon follow. "Ah, milady, it were the Duke of Gloucester. His young son tipped over in a rowboat just as Oy was passin' by in me own dinghy. Oy dove over, rescued the little feller, and the duke was so beside hisself with gratitude that he gave me this valerble airloom. Seized from a Spanish vice-er-roy in the Battle of Cadiz."

"No he didn't," Amelia retorted. "My father had two just like these and now you have a third, unless there's someone inside the locket besides the Virgin Mary."

"No, she's in there awright," he said with eyes lowered.

"Did you know my father somewhere along the way?"

Jimmy sat quietly, seemingly deciding between the truth and another fable. "Well, Oy did too many years ago," he said at last. "Almost too many to remember. He was a lad on that island off Beaufort. We passed it in the life-boat. Shackleford Banks, Oy now recall." He described how he had encountered seventeen-year-old Will Gaskins and how they relieved Blackbeard of his heavy burden during three days of diving.

"Thing is, we didn't exactly depart on the best o' terms," continued Jimmy. "Oy had just jumped ship. Oy thought it best to make up a new name for meself, so he knew me only as Horatio. Oy was a wild 'un. It took me just over a year to lose me share of the gold on gamblin' and ladies of indecent repute. But yer father was already a practical feller, even at seventeen, and Oy knew he would make somethin' of his share.

"When we split up, Oy never heard from him again until, what, all these years later Oy come over with Timmons from Nassau and we was loading up at the wharf in Savannah. Oy was loungin' on top of some cotton bales. Oy looks down and Oy sees a carriage pull up. Out steps this older man in fancy dress and another bloke dressed like a farmer. Only Oy look agin and this farmer is really a young lady and she's climbing up our gangway. Well, Oy double takes at the man down there and surely enough he looks like this Will Gaston, only mebbe his father. Oy asked about and they said his name was Beach. But somehow Oy knew."

"Why didn't you introduce yourself again?" asked Amelia.

"Well, Oy didn't know fer sure it was him, and Oy wasn't sure Oy wanted him to see me like that, what with him bein' a rich tycoon and me in this lowly state because o' me many sins. By the time Oy decided to do it, he was away in his carriage, so Oy just left it alone."

"Well, you have since become a man of great character and worth," said Amelia.

"Only by workin' alongside you," he answered. "Oy think it's been a way to make up for some things Oy done to others. Like the Reverend Hiram says, 'Forgive us our trespasses as we forgives them what trespass against us.'

"So, you'll keep the chain then?"

"I don't want you to feel bad," she answered, "so I'll hold it in trust until one of us has a need for it."

Then she tried a little Savannah cockney. "Oy made some promises to them blokes with the shits," she said, "so let's me and thee go over there and see if we can plug them bungholes."

In December, with only two fireplaces lit, the marine hospital at Portsmouth Island seemed like a large, drafty version of the ominous death house outside. As Jimmy and Amelia changed their four remaining patients' linens and cheered them with a banter of jokes, the emptiness of their surroundings revealed a heap of preparation needed if the place were to serve the survivors of a major battle: stains on folded blankets, shelves showing dust that had been hidden by clothes, the half-cleaned bedpan, the rag cast in a corner. Amelia had been making her own mental list when she passed DuBois in his office. When she peered inside, he was writing in the U.S. Treasury ledger he had come to call his "Bible."

They had discussed linens and bedpans for a few minutes when she suddenly veered off course. "Well, you said you would tell me 'one day' of your 'many reasons' for staying here," she said, knowing she had him trapped between his desk and the door. "This is that day."

"Oh *mon Dieu*, no," he said. "I have not had time to arrange my thoughts."

"But as you can imagine, I am most anxious to know why you stayed when you could have gone anywhere else in the world."

DuBois took a deep breath. "Because, wherever I went, there I would be," he replied, straightening his cravat. "If one cannot free himself from the prison in his mind, then it matters not where he physically resides."

"But why this 'prison', as you call it. You have me confused."

DuBois assumed a pensive pose, both elbows on his desk, chin resting in cupped hands, exposing the silver links in his French cuffs. "It seems I have been just an actor in a costume, running from theater to theater, always playing a role written by another."

"But again," she pursued, "why this running, playing roles written by others?"

"How far back should I go?" he said. "French Guinea? We cannot go back there because there never was a French Guinea in my life."

"I've known that," she interrupted.

"How so?

"Beatrice Peters, of course, who doubtless learned it from Ambrose the governor. You ran a sugar plantation in Martinique, then burned it down as part of a slave revolt and fled to The Bahamas as a fugitive."

DuBois shook his head and held up a hand. "You could say I did burn it down, but not as part of a slave revolt," he answered. "Slavery had been abolished in the French colonies years before, but it is what came afterward that proved even more strangulating. The same owners who had once bought and sold these people now had a second source of income besides their sugar crops. You see, the slaves continued to live on the plantations as so-called employees, but whereas their food and clothing had been provided for them in the past, now the goods had to be paid for. They could only be obtained at the plantation store and the owners – including my father in Paris – saw to it that the workers always owed more than their wages could cover.

"So now, you see, Amelia, the people were deep in debt with no hope of escaping. As my father's son, the overseer, I could see the respect for my authority dwindling and the prospect of a rebellion coming. So instead of seeing the whole place burned down by an enraged crowd – and with it all the treasures of civilized life my family had accumulated – I elected to depart with the money we had on hand, my books, my clothing and a few of the workers who expressed interest in starting a new life. At that point, I faced the decision of burning everything down. I realized that if I did not, another owner would arrive in time and imprison the people again. All of us decided to wipe the whole place off the island. Those who didn't escape with me would scatter to their various villages. They would return to a simpler life knowing that at least they were now safe and free of debt."

"And this led you to The Bahamas and Ambrose Fairchild?" said Amelia.

"Yes. I had departed with enough sugar money to invest in the Royal Victoria – not that much, but enough to gain the governor's attention. I was attracted, I admit, to his charm and the fact that he recognized the culture and manners that I had absorbed during my school years at the Sorbonne.

I appreciated his civility and the sense of order that the British were able to impose even on the remotest reaches of their empire. But, as ever, I was to find it a gauzy veneer."

"Governor Fairchild, another cruel slave owner?" said Amelia in mock horror.

"You jest, but in a way, yes," said DuBois. "It seems to be a trait prevalent throughout human history. The Mongol invaders must crush the Tatars of Russia beneath their hoofs and the Tatars must inflict their own cruelty upon their indigenous Slavs. Why? Because to do otherwise would be inconsistent with what is expected of rulers. And so, we saw the English imposing their iron will upon the American colonies and Ambrose expecting to do the same to The Bahamas."

"And how did he do that?" asked Amelia.

"He knew his mission was to extract wealth – tribute – from his subjects. I was the perfect one because I was a fugitive in his domain illegally. I could manage his hotel for less remuneration than he had to pay anyone else, and the band of uneducated fugitives I brought with me were ideal for running his little side business dealing coal."

DuBois leaned back and paused for effect. "But you see, Amelia, it was exactly the same. He was both the plantation owner and the plantation store. We were as imprisoned as ever. Your ship seemed to be another way of escape, and so I took it."

He paused and Amelia expected to leave, but DuBois was only gathering more thoughts.

"There is still more," he said solemnly. "I am not proud of it because it shows me succumbing to the very avarice I have just attributed to Ambrose Fairchild and others. But I must reveal it to you and beg your forgiveness. The very day you and the *Sea Breeze* were to depart Nassau, Captain Charles came calling on me at the Royal Victoria, looking quite distraught. He said he must have an entire shipload – one hundred twenty tons – of anthracite coal. I knew I had the leverage because the Union captains also wanted it and were willing to pay fifteen a ton U.S. cash. Captain Timmons said he lacked the money, but perhaps he could offer me a greater incentive.

"This is when he mentioned a sizeable shipment of gold aboard. I had already heard a rumor about the gold from the governor, but then when others told me about my hotel guest being involved in a bank robbery, I saw reason to believe him."

He looked up at Amelia and found her staring straight ahead. "Go on," was all she said. *I am a priest hearing confession from a man almost my father's age.*

"I remember feeling that the governor might be angry at me for selling our entire supply of anthracite to a Confederate ship, so my first thought was to see if Timmons would accept half the amount, which appeared to me to be sufficient to get him to Wilmington. No, he said. He needed everything in anthracite because he was going to attempt Wilmington but be prepared to go on to Bermuda if the entrance was too dangerous."

Charles again.

"I could sympathize with his plight," said DuBois, "but I owed him no special obligation. I was prepared to walk away and do the expedient thing of accepting Union cash, but that is when Captain Timmons startled me with an unprecedented offer. I personally would receive a tenth share in the gold upon arrival in Wilmington, or one-fifth if the ship were diverted to Bermuda. He said he had heard it described as worth two hundred fifty thousand U.S. by the Confederate captain Wilkes. Well, either share translated to more wealth than I had known before. It would afford an opportunity to buy a charming inn somewhere in Europe. It would sever the relationship with Ambrose Fairchild like the blade of the guillotine. He would keep the money I invested in the Royal Victoria. I, in turn, would relieve him of a month's supply of anthracite."

"Why the difference in shares between Wilmington and Bermuda?" asked Amelia.

"Timmons kept looking at his watch, so I knew he wanted my decision without much delay, so he did not explain fully. I can only surmise it was something as follows. A tenth share in Wilmington could be explained as a necessary risk under unusual circumstances. The one-fifth share to be paid in Bermuda was because the gold represented your father's investment in the ship and that the builder in Liverpool wanted to retrieve it as soon as possible at a time when Confederacy's fortunes were waning."

"None of this was ever confided to me," said Amelia. "Perhaps Charles was working more for the shipbuilder in Liverpool than for my father. And it would follow that he intended to go to Bermuda all along. Would you agree?"

"It was never said directly, but yes," replied DuBois. "I was pledged to secrecy regarding my shares. And in all candor, I did not know you well then. I assumed you were a typical young lady, more interested in dances and carriage rides and quite above the sordid business that men conduct."

"It might have been true to begin with," she said, "but not today."

"Oh no, indeed," he affirmed. Then it was his turn for a detour. "Thus far I have explained why I left Martinique and Nassau, but not why I have remained here on Portsmouth Island. The truth is that, despite the fact that you have been describing me to these people as a French diplomat, I have never been one and have no papers whatsoever. I am an escaped fugitive, who until recently was sheltered by Ambrose Fairchild at a dear price. Equally important, Antoine has no such papers and no protective armor of manners and education to charm and trick his way through strange lands."

"Yes, I have seen that Antoine is dear to you," Amelia said.

"You may have perceived him first as a cane cutter from Martinique or a coal yard worker, but he is much more to me. As a child in Martinique, there were no sons of white planters who would play with a mulatto like me. So my friends became the boys from the sugar fields. Antoine and I became very close at an early age. He was always the strongest and best athlete, and often he would protect me from bullies who would see me sitting under a tree and reading a book, something they associated only with girls. Today his strength gives me the will to be intellectually bold, to take command of a situation, knowing that my decisions will not be challenged by physical harm. Together we are a whole man, and I will not abandon him for the sake of gold or anything else."

Then you and Antoine are a male couple? But Amelia could not utter the question and DuBois saved her from it.

"I said there were many reasons for remaining, and now I give you the last one," he said with a smile and perhaps relieved that he had just shed his heaviest burden. "I will begin by saying that I did not leave without funds, oh no. One cannot travel without proper papers and with an inconvenient skin color unless one has sufficient cash to apply the international language of commerce."

"And what is that?" Amelia asked.

"The language of persuading ship captains and customs officials to look the other way. I had pounds sterling, of course, and when Yankee captains came to dine and dance at the Royal Victoria, I would see that their U.S. dollars came my way," he said. "I probably could have found a way to get Antoine and myself off this island at any time, but I became absorbed at watching what you might call the blossoming of a flower."

"A flower?"

"Oui, mademoiselle. *You.* When we arrived here, you were a portrait of despondency. But from that chasm of despair I watched you rise up and lead the people in a righteous cause that made me think of *Jeanne d'Arc.* I was so involved in being a part of it – so fascinated with your ingenuity, your *joie de vivre*, that soon I had forgotten about finding a way to leave the island. Yes, I could have bought supplies for everyone, but it would have destroyed the *renaissance* that was happening within so many people."

DuBois straightened in his chair, leaned on his elbows and clasped his hands. As a few seconds passed, Amelia could see that he was struggling to overcome a trembling lip. "You see, Miss Beach," he said at last, "despite what I have told you about my failures, more than anything I value the fulfillment that comes with honest achievement. I admire someone who strives toward that goal with good cheer and with no conniving or manipulation of others. I always sought to find such a person in some learned male philosopher or literary giant, made wiser to me by having died centuries ago.

"But I found it right here in a young woman."

Felix DuBois leaned back in his chair, spent but smiling for the first time. Now it was Amelia searching her mind for proper words, still uneasy at hearing "confession" from an older man. "Strange," she said at last, "but I'm thinking of that poem you recited the other day by the French marquis about his many prisons."

"Yes," he answered. "The poem was not by de Custine. I wrote it about myself. But even then, you see, I was masquerading, hiding under another's coattails.

"No more."

Felix DuBois' words still swirled in Amelia's head as she walked alone in the dark, past the empty linen house, past the faint yellow glow from inside the army tents that illuminated the black forms of two soldiers, huddled in the cold as if actors in a shadow play. Soon she was empty, cold and alone again, torturing herself for not detecting the many signs of disengagement thrown up by Charles Timmons.

Absorbed in her thoughts, Amelia had already passed the church on the way to her farmhouse room when something made her look back. *Ah! The door to the social hall.* Someone – Rachel? Matthew? – had nailed up a pine bough with holly berries and radishes skitter-scattered about. She smiled, then caught herself in a chuckle because it compared so pathetically to the verdant, red-ribboned greenery that had hung on the iron gate to her Savannah home on the night of the Christmas season social the year before. Then she found herself recalling her first night as a "nurse," clutching her caduceus pin for confidence in the Marine Hospital of Portsmouth Island. And she remembered the young soldier, devastated upon receiving a rejection letter from his supposed sweetheart, only to rebound the next day with a burst of joy at realizing that he had avoided marrying "such a trifling girl" who "never would have made me a good and faithful wife."

Amelia turned around and opened the door, careful not to brush against the delicate holly bough. Inside was the familiar flicker of the oil lamp, with the equally familiar form of Benjamin Hawkes in the act of pouring from a whiskey bottle.

"Just having a wee nip of nightcap before I face my freezing tent," he said. "The usual?"

"Just two fingers."

The oil lamp cast only a dim glow, but in that moment she felt as if she had been warmed by the sun.

A week later, after all had retired for the night, Amelia sat alone in the social hall composing a letter on a blank page she had snatched from the back of the *U. S. Treasury Ledger.*

December 24, 1864

Dear Daddy, Mother, Lucy, and my nephew "Little Joe,"

This is in response to your last letter, dated October 27. I know that much has transpired at home since then, but I can only assume that you are still "occupied."

Earlier today I realized that this is an anniversary of sorts. It was just about one year ago that we hosted the wonderful, glittering Christmas reception for our Rebel boys and their families. I know we spent much of the day fussing over the details, with Lucy and I taunting one another as to who was the most fetching, but as I look back, what I remember the most was the grandeur of the decorations and the amplitude of the table. How fortunate we were!

Tonight, on Portsmouth Island, we had a Christmas Eve dinner in the social hall of the Methodist church, whose grounds adjoin that of the hospital. The patients, except for six too sick to move, were recently transported by ship to other locations as we prepare the hospital to take on new wounded from the battle of Fort Fisher, near Wilmington, which is supposed to be launched on Christmas Day. A hospital ship stands ready to treat Union soldiers, and our mission here is to treat any Rebel defenders of Fort Fisher who are wounded and captured. We will, of course, treat all who are sent our way, as we have long ceased to think of a sick soldier as "Yankee" or "Rebel."

Our modest meal seemed grand enough, considering that Matthew, our cook, had to scrape together what he could from the sea and various sacks of cornmeal, peas, beans and the like, but the people here were in a festive mood because we had just finished cleaning and stocking the hospital and decided that we could do no more but sleep late on Christmas Day and await the outcome of a battle that is beyond our control.

What a strange group we are to get along so well! Around the tables in the church hall were Jimmy the sailor from England, his wife-to-be Molly from Ireland, Matthew from The Bahamas, Felix DuBois and his dear friend Antoine from French Martinique, Captain Benjamin Hawkes, a schoolteacher from Long Island, New York, six Union soldiers from various parts north and our indispensable hosts, the Rev. Hiram and Rachel Staley, lately of New Hampshire.

You may have noticed my failure to mention Captain Charles Timmons. A Union supply ship came by the other day and Timmons seized the opportunity to board it as a first leg on a journey back to England (and his naval career, I presume). Before he left, Captain Timmons gave me a letter – a bill of lading I suppose you could call it – which I herewith enclose. I suggest Daddy withhold any payment until I have had a chance to write a separate letter. I have had a cup or two of what we call "The King's Grog" tonight and want to be sure to report all details of his conduct accurately.

And now a special surprise for my Daddy Beach! The man I have been describing as "Sailor Jimmy" is none other than your old gold diving partner that you knew then as "Horatio." As I'm sure you predicted, he soon squandered his fortune on lascivious and licentious living and spent the rest of his life bouncing upon the seas as a common sailor. He recognized you when I boarded the Sea Breeze in Savannah but was too ashamed of his prior life to reveal himself. All I can say now is that he has more than redeemed himself in a thousand ways by working at my side in the hospital.

I know I have not addressed Mother's various complaints about life under the "occupation," but I can only speak for myself. I, too, am tempted to react personally to various insults and afflictions. When I hold a patient's head who is vomiting, I imagine that my stomach will soon be rebelling in similar fashion. When I treat a patient with dysentery I imagine that I, too, will soon be "riding the steel horse," as we call a bedpan. Right now, I have a rash of sorts on my forehead that shouts "smallpox" at me when I look in the mirror. But this, too, will no doubt pass if I just stay busy and don't think about it.

The key to surmounting all human trials and tribulations, I think, is to be useful and happy being so. The first day I was here I met my friend Rachel, a little scrawny chicken of a parson's wife, who seemed at the time to be carrying the whole hospital on her shoulders. When I asked how she did it all, she said, "Well, when the cock crows, I swing my feet over the side of the bed and say, it's time to get on with it."

I try my best to do the same. And I hope that whenever it is that I am able to return home, you will find me a better person than when I left.

Merry Christmas, from your loving daughter.

Afterword

THE DATES, PLACES AND MAJOR EVENTS OF THIS BOOK ARE FACTUAL. AMONG THEM:

• The carcass of Blackbeard's galleon, *Queen Anne's Revenge,* discovered in 1996 in twenty feet of water just outside Beaufort Inlet, North Carolina.

• The unique Civil War role of the Royal Victoria Hotel in Nassau, since torn down and reduced to its foundation of coral rock underlying a large parking lot in the Bahamian capital's busy downtown. The silk cotton tree still broods over it.

• Graycliff, still elegant as Nassau's oldest hotel, and the venerable Fort Charlotte, facing the beach just below it.

• John Tyler Wilkes and his gunboat. Yes, a fictitious character, but one based on the very real persona of John Taylor Wood, a nephew of Jefferson Davis, a daring gunboat captain and a central figure in trying to rescue what remained of the Confederacy's shrinking gold reserves.

• The ghost-like village of houses and churches on Portsmouth Island, North Carolina, now a National Park Service visitor site. The marine hospital, which morphed into a community social center, hotel and apartment house before burning down in 1894, is marked today only by its durable cistern.

• The life of the French Marquis Astolphe de Custine and its effect on Felix DuBois. When DuBois told his audience of church ladies how Custine had been beaten severely by some drunken sailors outside a Paris bistro, one is left to assume that it was because he was one of the much-despised nobility. Left unsaid was that Custine was one of the first Parisian men to openly declare himself, in his words, "a proud homosexual."

• The horrific yellow fever pandemic that struck New Bern, North Carolina in the summer of 1864. The descriptions of suffering in this book are taken from journals and correspondence of those gruesome days.

• The battle of Fort Fisher, the largest of many fortifications guarding the Cape Fear River and Wilmington, North Carolina. It began on Christmas Eve, 1864 with a deafening bombardment from more than sixty Union gunboats. A month later, over twenty thousand shells had been fired into what was called "The Gibraltar of the South," only to make marginal penetration because the fort's exterior consisted mainly of thick dune sand. The desperate Union then launched a bloody land invasion that finally succeeded in overrunning the fort. Soon after its capture came the closing of Wilmington harbor, cutting off the railroad that supplied the battered defenses of General Robert E. Lee in Richmond, Virginia. Just three months later, the Confederacy capitulated at Appomattox.

The main characters in this book are all fictitious. But one can still wonder what could have become of Amelia Beach. Perhaps she married a certain Yankee officer and moved to his home on Long Island, New York. Perhaps she remained caring for patients on Portsmouth Island until succumbing during a smallpox epidemic and being buried beneath a plain marker somewhere out behind the Death House.

All I know for sure is that Amelia never became anyone's spinster nanny.

– JDS –

About the Author

Award-winning author James D. Snyder was raised in Evanston, Illinois and graduated from Northwestern University's Medill School of Journalism and The George Washington University graduate school of political science. He spent many years in Washington, DC as a magazine editor and publisher before moving to South Florida and becoming an author.

Snyder lives in Tequesta on the Loxahatchee River and is active in several organizations devoted to preserving its history and environment.

Other Books by James D. Snyder

All God's Children: *How the First Christians Challenged the Roman World and Shaped the Next 2000 Years.* An historical novel. 2000, 680 pp.

Black Gold and Silver Sands: *A Pictorial History of Agriculture in Palm Beach County.* 2004, 224 pp, 205 photos. Sponsored by the Historical Society of Palm Beach County.

The Cross and the Mask: *How the Spanish 'Discovered' Florida, and a Proud Native Nation.* 2013, 390 pp. Winner of the Florida Historical Society's Patrick Smith Award for best book on Florida historical fiction. Florida Authors and Publishers Association Silver Award winner for best fiction book, 2013.

The Faith and the Power. A chronological history of the early Christians in the turbulent forty years after the crucifixion and how they confronted the Roman Empire in the darkest days of its debauchery. Winner of the Benjamin Franklin Silver Award for the best book on religion, 2002.

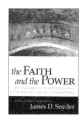

Five Thousand Years on the Loxahatchee, *A Pictorial History of Jupiter-Tequesta, FL.* 224 pp. Over 200 photos and maps. Sponsored by the Jupiter Inlet Lighthouse and Museum. Newly-revised and released in 2019.

Life and Death on the Loxahatchee. The story of Trapper Nelson, a real-life Tarzan who fascinated a generation in South Florida. 156 pp. Silver medal award for the best book on Florida history, Florida Authors and Publishers Association, 2002.

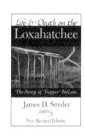

A Light in the Wilderness: *The Story of Jupiter Inlet Lighthouse and the Southeast Florida Frontier.* How it grew from 600 settlers in 1850, aided by a lighthouse, some steamboats and a very short-line railroad. 2006, 288 pp.

A Trip Down the Loxahatchee. The history and beauty of the Wild and Scenic Florida river as seen through the eyes of 52 leading painters and photographers. 2015, 160 pages, 162 images.

The above books are also available in eBook format from
Amazon Kindle, Barnes and Noble's *Nook,*
iBooks, Goodreads and nearly all other
eBook providers worldwide.